DARKNESS
BRUTAL

DARKNESS BRUTAL

BOOK ONE OF THE DARK CYCLE

RACHEL A. MARKS

SKYSCAPE

SKYSCAPE

Published by Skyscape, New York

www.apub.com

Amazon, the Amazon logo, and Skyscape are trademarks of Amazon.com, Inc., or its affiliates.

ISBN-13: 9781477830796
ISBN-10: 1477830790

Book design by Cliff Nielsen

Printed in the United States of America

For my daddy, who taught me how to see.

Blood from bone, skin from earth
it walks,
feet to stone.

Darkness brutal, darkness fair
it waits,
eyes to soul.

Words intoned, fire in hand
it drinks,
marrow from bone.

At its feet, I lay
sprawled crooked, broken doll
it licks,
I stare.
Red teeth-marks, pattern porcelain skin
laid bare.

Darkness brutal, darkness fair
at last
payment for my sin.

~ scrawled on a napkin stuffed into Mom's grimoire ~

ONE

The demon is crouched in the corner, between the Cheetos and the onion dip. It's a small one, only about four feet tall: a low-level creeper. I flick my gaze over the spot like I don't see it and open the cooler door to get a Coke.

I watch the cashier behind me in the security mirror as he finishes ringing up a customer. He notices me—eyes my ratty hoodie, grungy backpack, scruffy jaw, tattooed fist gripping the cooler handle—and reaches one hand under the counter, probably to grab the butt of a shotgun or a bat he's got hidden there. He's totally oblivious to the real danger that's hanging out in the junk food aisle.

The bell on the door rings as the customer leaves.

I walk past the demon, hoping it doesn't sense my awareness. It's not here for me, though; its bulbous black eyes are trained on the cashier. Its scarred and misshapen wings twitch and knock at the shelf as its leg muscles tense, like it's ready to pounce. Clawed feet dig into the linoleum floor, surrounded by traces of black ash and sulfur that seep from its skin.

I set the can of Coke down on the counter and toss a Snickers up there too—dinner of champions.

"Hey," I say to the cashier. The chill of being too close to the demon crawls over me, but I clench my jaw and ignore it.

The cashier nods back, ringing up the soda. "Two fifty." He glances at my tattooed hand again—probably looking for a gang symbol, which he won't find. Then he studies my face, like he's trying to memorize it for the cops, just in case: *about seventeen years old, olive-skinned male, dark brown hair, hazel eyes, five foot eight, looks like a homeless junkie.*

He'd be right about everything but the junkie part. I am homeless these days. Everything I own is in the backpack I'm wearing.

I pull change from my pocket. It clangs onto the counter, along with an old stick of gum, some lint, a rubber band. And a Star of David.

Damn. Forgot I had that in there.

I slip the gold star into my pocket again, but not quick enough. The chill of the demon stings the back of my legs as it comes alert to my presence.

"You know, forget it. I'm good," I say to the cashier. The medallion was blessed by a rabbi a few weeks ago—it's supposed to keep me from seeing *things*. It doesn't work, obviously. Instead, it has the opposite effect. I'd meant to ditch it, but . . . well, I have a lame inability to ditch anything.

I head for the exit, leaving my meal and change. It's my fault, really. I should've known better than to roam around on the night of the full moon without taking precautions. I almost make it to the exit before the smell of sulfur fills my nostrils. The demon's right behind me.

"I wouldn't follow me if I were you," I say. I really don't want to deal with this shit tonight.

"What'd you say?" the cashier asks. "Don't want no trouble here."

I ignore the guy and turn to face the demon, scanning the shelves for salt or rye, but there's not much rye in a Circle K. My stomach rises, the scent of sulfur bringing back old memories.

My sister, Ava, screaming in her crib, the demon's claw digging into her tiny shoulder, marking her. Mom on the floor, eyes wide to another world, the blood spreading beneath her like a growing shadow . . .

I start to whisper a prayer for protection under my breath: *"The light of Elohim surrounds me; the love of Elohim enfolds me. Wherever I am, Elohim is . . ."* The demon hisses at me, backing away a little. "I'm telling you. Just leave me be," I say.

Saliva drips from its teeth, and it makes a garbled noise in its throat, like words, but all backward and upside down. It can't hurt me, not physically, since it's not corporeal. Right now, it's like the demon's behind glass, on the other side of the Veil that separates the human world from the spirit world. It's only able to influence people, to whisper into their minds, telling them to do dark things. It feeds off their negative emotions. And it'll likely cause bad shit to happen if it follows me.

"You want this?" I ask, pulling the Star of David from my pocket again and dangling it in front of the demon's hole of a nose. It seems more interested in the tattoo on my hand, though, and hesitates at the sight of it.

"Get the hell out!" the cashier yells. "I'm callin' the cops!"

"I've had a rough night," I say to the demon. "And you can see I'm not scared of your sick mug, so you know this game isn't new to me. Just do your job and leave me alone." I wave to the spot it was crouching in before, and it follows my motion, head bobbing up and down like a cat following a string.

Then it lunges and sinks its teeth into my tattooed hand.

Fire shoots up my arm and into my head. I fall back, banging into the glass door, shock and pain sparking in my gut.

I scream and kick the thing, but it doesn't do any good. Its jaw only locks tighter.

This can't be happening. It can't. The thing's not manifested! It's not even *here*. Still, the teeth sink deeper, stinging like a swarm of bees on my hand. I breathe through the burn and fumble in my jacket pocket. I've got a pouch of sacred dirt somewhere. Old habits die hard. But it's been so long since I've been this stupid, letting one know that I can see it. And now I'm suddenly lunch.

My fingers find the pouch, and I pull it out, shoving the earth into the demon's eye socket. The creature's flesh sizzles and pops. It lets go of my hand, stumbling back and screeching so loud I'm sure my ears are about to start bleeding.

I snatch up the Star of David again and begin reciting Zachariah 3:2 in stuttered Latin and English: "*Increpet Dominus in te Satan. The Lord rebuke you, O Accuser—*"

Then I'm hit in the back of the shoulder, the wind knocked from my lungs.

"Out!" the cashier screams. "Get out, crazy bastard!" He swings at me again with a bat.

I try to shield myself from the blow, but he hits my arm with a painful thud, rocking my bones. Now I'm pissed, and I catch the bat tight in my fist on the next swing.

The guy pulls back, but I grip harder and yank it out of his hands.

"Enough!" I toss the bat across the store. "You're in danger, moron. You need to leave, now!"

The demon is still sizzling on the floor, its skin getting paler, almost blending into the linoleum. It'll be gone any second, heading back home to tell its big brothers about the guy in the Circle K who could see it. With my blood, like a fingerprint, on its teeth.

Can't let that happen.

"Go home!" I scream in the cashier's face, hoping I'm scaring the shit out of him. He should be scared. This demon was waiting here because something was about to go down—a robbery, or a shooting. The guy's days are probably numbered.

He stumbles back and fumbles for his cell phone. Then drops it.

I grab the closest thing I see—a can of bean dip—and hit him square in the jaw, knocking him to the floor next to his phone, out cold.

The can slips from my hand, and I realize I'm bleeding pretty bad. Blood's dripping onto the linoleum. The smell permeates the air like raw meat.

I drag the cashier's limp body into the alley behind the store and go over the Rite in my head, trying to remember everything. It's been too long since I've done this. I start reciting Zachariah 3:2 again, this time in Hebrew, as I go back into the store and find the salt on the shelf.

I pop the top off the shaker and start making a circle of white around the demon. It takes another three saltshakers before I've completed the prison walls. The creature's twisted body flickers for a second, disappearing into the linoleum, before it comes back, full-bodied and louder than ever, green smoke rising from it. The thing squeals and screeches like I'm stabbing it with a hot poker.

I finish reciting the verse for the third time and stand over my little prisoner. "I warned you. Now you're gonna be stuck in this altar to the carb gods for the rest of eternity. Hope you're happy."

I don't have a spirit bowl or a hex box to lock it up, so I have to do the best I can with what I've got and hope it holds. I go behind the counter and find a Sharpie.

The bell rings on the door, announcing a new customer. An older woman.

"We're closed!" I bark, and she doesn't even question, just turns and goes back out. Hopefully she won't call the cops. Better hurry, just in case.

I focus back on my task and kneel at the edge of the salt circle. I scribble the words on the floor, just on the outside of the prison, following the same line, starting with Zachariah 3:2 and ending with a bit of Psalm 91—both in Hebrew so they'll hold their meaning firmly. I write big so the symbols wrap around the circle from right to left, two and a half times. Should be plenty. But I need to be sure. I can't have this little bastard getting free now that it knows I can see it. Mom was always clear about that: "Don't let them know you *see*. Don't let anyone know." I'll have to burn the verses in.

I find the lighter fluid and start in the center of the circle, squirting it over the squirming demon, then out and over the letters, then farther out until I've covered eighty percent of the store and the smell is making me light-headed. The wall of booze will take care of the rest. I hope the owner's got insurance.

I go behind the counter and grab the video recorder, yanking its wires free and tucking it under my arm. Then I pick up a lighter.

I move to the back door, wave good-bye to my new friend, and spark a flame to life. I hold it to the floor where there's a little pool of fluid.

It catches with a whoosh, pushing into the room, consuming Cheerios, Milky Ways, and Little Debbies like a hungry monster. I watch for a second to make sure it burns the symbols into the floor, trapping the demon for good. The flames lick up the drops of my blood, leaving no evidence behind. I back into the alley and stare down at the cashier, who's still out cold. I should wake him up and tell him he needs to get his shit together—get right with his Maker—before something really bad happens to him. But I know the words'll just fall on deaf ears. They always do.

I drop my Star of David by his head and step over his body, finding my path into the shadows as the sounds of approaching sirens fill the night air.

TWO

There's a line all the way down the block at SubZero when I get there. The club pulses blue neon light, giving the lemmings waiting for their turn at depravity an alien hue. Music beats at the air, and the smell of liquor spills out into the street. Some people crane their necks to watch the limos that pull up every few minutes; some just stand and talk on their cell phones like it's totally normal to see Kesha or Timbaland a few feet away.

You've got to love LA.

I'm standing across the street calling my sister, Ava, to check on her.

I listen to the line ring and flex my chewed-on hand.

What the hell *was* that? Demons can't just bite humans. No way. If I wasn't looking right at the bite on my own hand, I wouldn't even believe the memory.

It's a full moon tonight, so everything is bound to be a little off kilter. But that doesn't mean demons can randomly get through the Veil. And bite you. There's an order, rules to the spiritual realm. And they never change. I've had them ingrained in my brain ever since I can remember. It's knowledge I was born with—one of the many things Mom always said I had to hide from people. Just as much as I have to hide it from the demons or ghosts that know I shouldn't be able to look them in the eye.

Keep it hidden, keep it safe. That's what my mother always said. And she was right. People can't handle the truth about what's around them. So I don't mention my "abilities" to anyone. Ever. I let them stay blissfully unaware of the hidden orders that make up the spiritual world that intersects with this one.

And my ability to see ghosts, demons, and angels, and my innate knowledge about their world—that's not all I have to hide from people. It's just the tip of the iceberg. After all, how would people react if they knew I can smell emotions or tell if someone's lying? Or that I speak and understand ancient languages as if they were my own? Or that I have this endless codex of sacred texts in my head?

I'm used to it; it's all a part of me, like the dark color of my hair. But that doesn't mean I don't have to hide it.

My sister is "different" too, but Ava is nothing like me.

The line rings and rings in my ear, but no one answers. I hang up at the sound of her voice mail message and try again.

I look down at my mangled hand again. This demon bite means something. Maybe not something to do with Ava, but still, I can't be too careful when it comes to her. Especially because it's that time of year again: her birthday month. I've been outside her foster home every few nights, checking on her. It's the best I can do for now, since I can't take care of her on my own.

She still doesn't answer her phone. Panic starts crawling to the surface, but I force it down. She's eleven, almost twelve. It's not like she's at the most responsible age.

But she's not a normal girl. She knows what's at stake.

I start to turn away from the club, heading to the bus stop, when my phone vibrates in my hand. "Are you okay?" I answer without saying hello.

"Fine, silly," she says. "Calm down, or you'll get an ulcer. I was practicing for the Summer Solstice Festival." She plays the violin. First chair.

I make myself settle for a second. "Okay. I just want to be sure you're good. Something happened and I—"

"Tell me, tell me!" she bursts out, sounding more excited than frightened.

"Nothing good," I say. "But if you're okay, I'll come by in the morning. I have to clean this up right now." I study my hand again.

"You never tell me anything."

"I tell you what you need to know."

"Neanderthal."

I smile. "You're too smart for your own good, you know that?"

"I'll just ask Mom, then."

My smile disappears. I wait a second to respond so I don't growl at her over the phone. "We have two weeks until your birthday, Ava. Just two weeks. Can you please keep yourself in check until after that?"

She sighs. "Whatever."

"I'll see you tomorrow."

"I have music academy."

"I'll come early."

"Great." But she doesn't sound thrilled.

It's silent for a second, and I don't like the tension. It's been growing between us for a few months now, like a spring coiling tighter. "Love you, Peep," I say.

"'Night, demon dork."

Even as I hang up I feel like it's not enough. I hate it when things are imbalanced. And I know a lot of this new tension is my own fault. I'm having trouble figuring out her moods lately and what all the emotions mean for her growing abilities. And I admit I can be an ass sometimes. But I love the girl to death. She's all I have left.

And I made a promise to my mom before she died. To protect Ava. With everything in me. There's no way I'm going to let myself fail.

I take a deep breath and walk across the street toward the club, deciding I need to focus on one thing at a time. Demon bite, then sister drama.

I move through the crowd outside, putting up my internal walls against the press of emotions as I pass, and make it into the alley and down the stairs to the back entrance without sensing anything too horrible. One of the bouncers—Frank or Biff, they all look alike—stops me.

"I need to talk to Eric," I say.

He notices my wounded hand and makes a face of disgust.

"I'm on the list," I add. "Aidan O'Linn."

He glances at his clipboard, finds my name, and opens the door, waving me past.

In the darkness of the club the black walls glow purple from the lights on the floor, and the beat of the music throbs in my chest. There's a scattering of people standing in line for the bathroom. I keep my eyes on the floor, seeing only shoes as I head down a side hall and up a staircase to the office door.

I knock and try to ignore the growing pain in my hand. It burns like hell. The flames spread through my body with my pulse. Must be the damn demon spit. I swallow the sting, wondering what'll happen next.

Another bouncer opens the office door. His wide shoulders fill the doorway.

Behind him, Hanna stands in front of a wall of glass, looking down at the mass of bodies writhing on the dance floor. She turns to me and frowns. "Aidan, what happened?"

"I was stupid." I walk past the large guard and collapse onto the couch facing the window. My stomach growls.

"Get Eric," she tells the bouncer, then goes to her desk, pulling an apple from the drawer. She holds it out to me, and I only hesitate from pride for a second before taking it.

I make myself eat it slow, even though I want to scarf it down in three bites. She sits and lets me chew in silence, which I'm thankful for.

Hanna's sort of mom-ish. Her eyes are kind, and she seems strong, like life doesn't affect her the same way it affects others. She's seen too much of it, maybe. She's in her midthirties and has smooth skin the color of rich soil. Her features are model perfect and never seem to age. I'm sure men want her, but by the way she looks at Eric, I think she's already taken. She helps him run the club so he can do his side work without too much notice.

Side work. More like an obsession. He trades in ancient artifacts and is an expert in demon lore and all things biblical and Bronze Age. His collection of spirit bowls and amulets, not to mention his many yellowed scrolls, puts the Smithsonian to shame.

"Eric got more phones for the staff. Do you need a new one yet?" she asks.

"No, this one's good." A perk of working for Eric. Homeless boy gets a cell.

"I've got something for you," she says, bringing a small stone box across the desk toward her. "We found it at an estate sale. Eric wanted me to give it to you." She lifts the lid off and pulls a thin chain from inside. A small charm dangles on the end.

I hold out my hand, and she places it on my palm. The charm on the necklace is a *hamsa*, an amulet in the shape of a hand—silver inlaid with colored glass. It's a ward against the evil eye and sometimes an object of luck. It creates a sort of bubble around the keeper, muffling any negative activity around them. Mom gave me one for my sixth birthday, but it got lost in all the moving around we did back then. It feels good to have one against my skin again. I'd like to pass it on to Ava. She needs it more than me right now.

"I can't pay for this," I say. They're worth a good seventy bucks brand new.

"Eric said if you want to trade for it, you can, but he insisted you need it."

"I don't have anything to trade," I say, rolling the charm in my palm. Unless you count a Stephen King paperback as collateral.

"Then you can do something for me instead." She hands me a piece of paper. "Call this guy. Eric won't have work for you until the next shipment of relics comes in, and this guy can help find you work."

"I don't need charity." I study the paper. There's a phone number on it.

"I know, but this guy . . . he works in odd stuff, like Eric. He helps kids like you. With similar . . . gifts. Kind of like a mentor."

I hand the paper back to her. "No thanks." This isn't the first time she's tried to push me at some mission, or church, or do-gooder cause. It always ends up the same—with me tossed into the system.

She shakes her head, refusing to take it. "Call him; his name's Sid. And he can get you steady work—the kind you're best at. You owe me, remember."

"I won't go on the grid, Hanna, you know that. It'll be foster care before I can even finish reading this guy's pamphlet. I won't do that again. I can't." Foster care means crowded, filthy houses with drugs and gangs and heavy air, being at the mercy of pissed off men with big fists or women with weird fetishes, and trying to keep my abilities hidden from the demons lurking in every corner. When I'm under the thumb of strangers, I have no way to keep the *other* stuff out of my space without looking like an OCD freak. I'm *not* going back to that.

Hanna folds her graceful arms across her chest. "You're being stubborn, Aidan. This man can get you what you need. No grid. No social services. And he can help you with your gifts."

I pause and look at the phone number again, wondering if I'm pushing away a miracle. No one can help me with my "gifts," or whatever they are, but Hanna doesn't understand that. Still, with more steady money, maybe I could take care of Ava for real, get myself off the street.

"I'll think about it," I say and slip the piece of paper and my newly acquired *hamsa* into my pocket.

"He's helped a few boys like you get back on their feet. I think he could use someone with your talents." She smiles. "You'll fit right in there. You'll see."

Eric comes in the office. He's dressed in his usual five-thousand-dollar Italian suit and five-hundred-dollar shoes. His golden hair is slicked back, and dark-rimmed glasses frame his cool hazel eyes. No one would guess by looking at him that he spends his days poring over crumbling manuscripts and digging through piles of ancient bones. But Eric likes to fool people, pretend he's all about the green. It helps him fit right in—this is LA, after all. It also helps him find the really rare stuff no one in brainy circles even knows about. Black market is where the meat is, he always says. If it's legal, it's probably not worth his time. I've helped him sniff out some of these goodies, detecting the energy they carry—or letting him know when something's authentic. It's why he lets me come around without trouble. Why he helps me sometimes.

I met him outside my last foster house. He came by a garage sale my foster mom, Theresa, was having. Eric came up and asked if we had any old vases or urns available. I thought it was such an odd question. And he was so shiny and slick looking; he really didn't fit in with the neighborhood at all. I told him Theresa didn't own anything made before 1980, and he laughed and then asked if I wanted to work for him.

I wasn't quick to say yes, but once I realized I wouldn't be selling my body or my soul, I jumped into Eric's world with both feet, running away from foster care and living wherever I could find a place to set up wards—protections against darkness—and crash. The money isn't great, but the freedom is heaven. And Eric seems to get it. He knows I'm different and accepts it without question. The first and only guy I've met like that.

He listens as I tell him what happened tonight, then goes to a cupboard and gets out some first aid stuff, setting it on the table beside the couch.

"A demon bite. That's a first, Mr. O'Linn." He seems confused as he studies my face, looking for something, but I don't have any answers. I assumed he'd be more freaked out. He's calm as always, though.

"Clean it well," he says to Hanna. "I need to get something out of the safe. I'll be back."

I unwrap the mess of my left hand, and Hanna helps me clean the wound with alcohol. Needlelike teeth holes pepper my wrist and hand, the bright red welts warping my tattoo. Or birthmark. Whatever. I'm not sure what the design on my hand is. I don't recall getting the mark—I could've been born with it for all I know, though that feels impossible.

Who am I kidding? I live impossible.

The mark is a kind of knot made of letters all woven together, not that I know what it says. It reaches from the base of my middle finger across the back of my hand and then curves around the outside of my left wrist. It's dark brown in color, a few shades darker than my skin, like faded henna.

I'm fairly tan, unlike my pale mom and sister. Maybe my dad was from India.

Or maybe he was from Mars.

I'll probably never know. It's not like I'll ever be able to ask my mom.

Eric comes back with some herbs and an amulet. He lights the cluster of herbs—called a smudge—and sets the amulet on the back of my hand where the wounds are deepest. It's made of pure gold, a cleansing metal. Engraved on the piece is what looks like a leaf and a sword, and Greek lettering around the edge that reads *earth* or, more accurately, *soil*.

"Now, it says to clean a spiritual wound, you're supposed to say Psalm 91." He waves the smudge over my hand, letting the smoke billow over my skin in grey puffs, then he offers me a slip of paper with the verse on it.

But I don't need it. I hear it in my head: *He who dwells in the secret place of Elyon shall abide under the shadow of the Almighty. I will say of HaShem . . .*

I start reciting the scripture from memory. "*Yoshëv B'sëter el'yôn B'tzël shaDay yit'lônän. Omar l'Adonai—*"

Hanna stops me. "What's that?"

"The verse. In Hebrew," I say, and continue the recitation. Hanna glances at Eric with a strange look on her face. I forgot she's still more clueless about me than Eric.

Eric just listens, his features still. When I'm done, he takes the amulet and wraps my hand in some clean bandages. "How did you learn Hebrew?" he asks.

I shrug. "I don't remember. Maybe I'm secretly Jewish." Despite my last name, I've had a lot of people assume I'm Jewish—Israeli, that is, or Middle Eastern of some kind—from my coloring. But hell if I know.

"You also know Latin," he says. "I've heard you speak that. You even translated that Anglo-Saxon engraving I picked up in Paris last July." By the tone of his voice he seems to be trying to make a point. It's not as if he doesn't know these things about me.

"So what?"

"For a seventeen-year-old who knows so many languages, you could be doing much more than helping a club owner make money on the side. You could be using your talents for something truly amazing and profitable. Why don't you?" When I don't answer, he adds, "Do you want to tell us any other languages rolling around in that mysterious head of yours?"

He's thrown me off guard by asking such direct questions, which makes me open my mouth and nearly reveal to him that I speak Ancient Greek and something else that I think might be Assyrian—plus maybe two or three more languages—but I catch myself and shake my head instead.

Mom made me say it over and over: *Keep it hidden, keep it safe.* If anyone truly knew everything, it would freak them out in a large way. It freaks the shit out of me too, so I get it. I have no clue how I know this stuff, I just do. Like how I know the orders of angels and demons, or can tell on sight if an apparition is a ghost or a time slip, or if someone's a virgin, or if they've ever killed anyone.

Why can't I just know how to play Xbox or baseball?

It's like I fell from the fucking sky.

THREE

I let the pulse of the music coat me and mute my surroundings. A mass of people crowd the dance floor of the club, and I sit on an abandoned couch in the corner. The lights beat at the air in blues and greens, and bodies twist and merge to the thunder. I lean back, close my eyes, and try to get lost in it, the smells and sounds of people and their collective high.

Something moves next to me. I look over to find a girl sprawled on the seat beside me, trying to catch her breath. She's not dressed in the usual club gear, more like a girl who got lost on her way to a beach party: Hurley T-shirt, jean skirt, and red Converse. Her cheeks are flushed pink. Her throat and forehead glitter with sweat. She glances at me like she didn't know I was there. She licks her upper lip, her eyes not leaving mine. Then she says something I can't hear.

I point to my ear and shake my head.

She smiles and laughs, lighting up the space around her. She rests her hand on my arm, like we're friends and I just told her the most hilarious joke, and then she gets up and disappears into the mass of bodies again.

My arm tingles, my body reacting to the moment of contact in a sudden and disconcerting way. I think I've had my fill of watching people indulge their baser instincts. I need to get out of here.

The beat of the music speeds up, vibrating faster as I move through the crowd. I try not to touch anyone, which is nearly impossible. All the emotions and appetites are overwhelming, as if the rising rhythm of the music makes their yearnings rise, too. Lust buzzes in the air. A hunger stirs in me, a gaping hole, needing to be filled. With touch.

The touch of female fingers. A hand on my arm, taking my wrist, pulling me into the fray, into the pressing bodies. And I don't try to escape. I let her take me.

Because I'm tired.

Because I'm a dumbass.

A girl moves in front of me—not the Hurley girl, not the one I was hoping for. She presses closer, so close I can almost taste the salty perspiration on her skin. She has thin, birdlike shoulders, a swan neck, a heart-shaped face, and black hair, long and tangled, turning blue and green with the light. Her hands slide up my chest. She wraps her arms around my neck and tilts her head to look up at me.

Her lips are full and painted dark purple. There's a dimple in her left cheek that gets deeper with her growing smile. And her eyes . . .

Fog fills my head for a second, interrupting my thoughts.

"Hi," she mouths, calling attention to her lips again.

And then she's rising up on her toes, pulling me down to her, twisting her fingers in my hair, her lips smashing against mine.

My body buzzes from her touch, and my hands react, drawing her into me. I drink her in. She tastes like the air around me, hunger and urgency, and—

Green apple Jolly Ranchers?

I grip her sides, her ribs so delicate beneath my fingers. The sweet tang of her teases me, the hunger becoming a monster deep inside. I have to press her closer, tighter, try to feed it, as I feel the fire of her need link with mine.

She pulls back a little and looks at me with wide eyes, like she's shocked. That's when I see the mark, a glowing, blue-inked line of what looks like Chinese symbols, trailing down the nape of her neck to her shoulder blade. Symbols that I'm suddenly sure mean *touch this girl at your own risk.*

It's the only thing I see for a second: *Beware. Beware.*

Until her energy reaches for me, wispy tendrils of blue light wrapping their way around my wrists and snaking up my chest.

I jerk away, into the guy behind me, stepping on his girlfriend's toes. I get shoved—thankfully farther from the hypnotic girl— through a space in the crowd, saying a hundred excuse-me's even though I know no one can hear them. I find my way out of the press of bodies to the edge of the room again where it's safe.

It's time to leave. I should've left an hour ago.

I grab my backpack from behind the bar on the way out. In the hall I stop to use the bathroom, splash handfuls of cold water on my face, then make my way out the back door.

The bouncer nods goodnight, but I can't do much more than grunt as I head past him, up the alley stairs. My hands are shaky. I feel like I got dosed with some sort of paranoia drug. As I move toward the back of the building, I try to get control of the shivering. No taking the bus tonight. I need to walk this mess off. It's a nice night, and the abandoned building I've been crashing in lately is only a mile or two away. Less human contact that way, too.

I start making my way through a small parking lot that's reserved for club workers. When I pass the last car, air tingles at the base of my neck. My pulse speeds up, the paranoia growing. Something—

A crash and a laugh. Something bangs against a Dumpster to my left, about ten yards away.

I move behind the car, trying to see through the darkness.

There's three of them. Young men surrounding a body on the ground.

A small demon about the size of a cat crouches in the shadows nearby, watching with beady white eyes. It's got a bulbous head and a curved spine and is wearing a necklace made of tiny skulls and what look like baby bones. Its claws clench and unclench as it whispers something into the night air, words slow and feather soft.

You've got to be shitting me. I know it's the full moon, but dammit—could this night get any screwier?

One of the guys says, "Prop her up against the Dumpster."

"Dude, we shouldn't be doing this here. It's nasty-ass sick."

"We could take her to the car."

"It's a Porsche, genius."

"Then you go first. Let's see you get it up in this place."

"Whatever. You two pansies can go back into the club. Me and Miss Malibu here will figure it out."

The ringleader props the girl's limp body against the Dumpster. Then he pulls up her skirt.

My insides catch fire, and I nearly lose it completely, fighting back the urge to run full tilt at the guy and pound him bloody. But I swallow my rage and make myself think through the tangle in my head. I move slow, slipping closer and closer, silent as a ghost, until I'm right behind them and can see the color of their designer clothes, the sheen of their glossy hair.

"Hey, assholes."

They spin, the ringleader letting go of the girl so she slides back to the asphalt. Fear pours off them in sticky waves. The cat-demon turns and tips its rotund head at me in curiosity, crawls a little farther away, and then focuses back on the three boys.

Now that I have their attention, I'm not so sure this is a good idea. I've done three against one before—defending my space or my stuff—but it usually ends with me in more pain than I like. Up close, I can see they're just bored rich boys, thin in the soul and thick in the head.

The one on the end backs away a step, then takes off running down the alley.

One down. Two to go.

"Can't get a date the normal way?" I ask.

"She said she needed to puke," the taller one says—the ringleader. He's got the mark of murder on his soul; small fissures grow out from around his left eye like his soul's been cracked. He smirks, his fear fading as he looks me over. "We were just holding her hair." A red spark lights his iris for a second, revealing the lie.

The other guy nods his head, mute.

"Aw, how nice of you." I smile at the ringleader, trying to steady my breathing. "A regular philanthropist." I move my hand to my back pocket where my knife is—slowly, so they won't notice—and pull it free, keeping it behind my back. It's never good to show your hand too soon. If this guy's killed before, he's less likely to back down easy.

Ringleader steps into me, testing my resolve. "Don't butt in, rat boy. Go back to the hole you crawled out of. This is men's business."

The mess of his rotten energy comes at me like dark, sticky tar. I grit my teeth, gripping the hilt of the knife harder. "Leave her alone, or I'm gonna get blood all over those nice designer jeans when I cut your balls off."

The other guy pulls on Ringleader's shirt. "Come on, man," he says. "It's not worth it."

Ringleader stares at me, his jaw working, the cracks in his soul becoming a little more obvious, like he's considering killing me, too. "I should kick your ass."

I stare back, daring him to try.

Logic wins out, and the two of them move away, heading for the street. The demon lingers, though, slinking into the shadows, like it plans on seeing what happens to the girl next. I move my gaze so it can't tell I'm watching it and put my knife away. I give my insides time to settle for a second and make sure the demon keeps to the shadows rather than coming out to mess with either of us before I turn back to check on the girl.

I kneel next to her, looking her over, checking for a bump on her head, even though I'm pretty sure she just drank too much. Hopefully she wasn't roofied. Her hair is soft against my palm, her skin milky in the moonlight. And then I realize she's familiar. This is the beach girl I saw inside. She's wearing red Converse sneakers and a Hurley T-shirt.

I feel a new wave of rage wash over me, recalling her smile and knowing what these bastards were planning on doing to her—in a parking lot, next to a Dumpster. That light inside her would've been snuffed right out.

My hands shake trying to fix her jean skirt, to pull her shirt down. I tap her cheek a little. "Wake up," I say, hoping, praying they didn't drug her. She looks so pale. Her head lolls.

I have two choices here: call 911 and open myself up to scrutiny from the cops, or drag her somewhere and leave her so someone else will call—which feels kind of chickenshit.

She moans and pushes away my hand.

"Can you hear me? Open your eyes."

She shakes her head and frowns like she's about to say, *It's not time for school, Mom.*

Seeing she's somewhat lucid opens up a third option: find her ID.

With apologies, I reach into her pockets.

Bingo! A license.

Rebecca Emery Willow McLane. That's a mouthful.

5'5".

130 lbs.

DOB: 05/16/1995.

That makes her sixteen. How the hell did she get into the club? Eric won't be happy.

Her address is in the hills, near Universal.

Near Ava.

The back of my neck prickles, but I shake it off. I'm being too suspicious. I have to force myself not to glance back at the shadows to see if the demon is still there, watching.

I pull my cell out and call Hanna to ask her if I can borrow the car service to get somewhere, and she agrees without question, telling me a car will meet me out back. I hang up and gather Rebecca in my arms. She's waking up more, but I can tell she doesn't know where she is. Maybe she does need a doctor.

After about five minutes, a black car pulls out from the garage behind the club. It stops beside us, and the driver rolls down the window. "Looks like she had a bit too many," he says with a laugh, then motions for us to hurry. Since she's more awake, I'm able to help her into the cab. I close us in, recite the address to the driver, and we're on our way—no strange looks, no questions.

I'm not sure if I should be relieved or worried by his lack of concern for the girl.

It's about a thirty-minute drive with traffic. Rebecca stirs a few times, sighing and mumbling about someone named Charlie. She doesn't seem drugged, not really. Just really drunk. She turns and rests her head on my chest, nestling into me like a cat as her slim fingers clutch my ratty hoodie. Her hair smells like citrus and mango. And her breath smells like Jack and Coke.

I hope I'm doing the right thing.

We pull up in front of a house that's set back off the road. A low stone wall encircles the property. The lawn is perfectly trimmed, accented with bushes, and some flowers run along a winding stone path. The windows are dark, and the long driveway's empty. Ritzy people keep their cars in the garage, though, right?

I check the license again to make sure it's the right place.

Rebecca stirs and starts to open her eyes, but then she hisses through her teeth and grabs her head, like she's trying to keep it from exploding.

"You okay?" I ask.

She shrinks from my voice and moans in pain.

"We're here, Rebecca. I'll help you to the door, but you'll have to do the rest." I get out of the car with her in my arms and tell the driver not to wait. I'll find my own way back.

Rebecca mumbles something as I half lead, half carry her up the walk, whispering to her, "It's okay, you're home now." She whimpers a protest against my chest.

I study the shadows as we come up to the door, putting my feelers out, looking for the demon from the alley, but it doesn't seem to have followed us. A little luck, at last.

"Do you have a key?" I ask.

She waves her hand at a potted plant next to the door, then moans again and throws up into the bushes.

I step back as she leans on the wall. She heaves some more and slinks down to the ground.

I find the key in the planter—these people must not care about their crap—and unlock the door. I pick her up and put her arm over my shoulder, ushering her into the dark house. I have to hunch so I'm not dragging her; she's not helping with the walking much.

Our breathing echoes in the large entryway, her Converse squeak on the marble floor, and no parents come running. But I'm tense, ready for flight any second.

I take in the surroundings, trying to feel for spirits or demons or residual echoes. There's a slight hum in the air, like maybe there was an argument recently, but otherwise it just smells like Lysol and new paint. There's the comforting ticktock of a grandfather clock. I look around for a couch to set her down on, but she starts heading to the stairs, so I follow, slowly, up the large staircase, past double doors to what I assume is her room.

Her bed is huge, with thick puffy violet blankets that make a *poof* sound when I set her down. She falls back onto the mattress and rolls onto her side, curling into a ball.

"Okay, so, you're good. I'll just—"

She grabs my wrist, stopping the words in my throat. "Stay."

What? This girl doesn't know me from Adam. "I don't think your parents will approve."

She frowns and shakes her head, then says into the pillow, "Not home. Paris."

I sigh and look around the room, trying to decide what the hell I'm supposed to do. She's home. Safe. That's enough. She'll wake up in the morning and forget all this, thinking one of her clever rich buddies brought her home—the same ones that nearly raped her in an alley.

Her naïveté makes my chest tight.

She starts to sit up and moans, covering her mouth. "Oh, God, I'm gonna hurl," she says through her fingers. Then she stumbles from the bed before I can help her and starts crawling to a doorway on my left—probably a bathroom.

I grab her and lead her to the toilet, barely making it before she explodes again.

Lovely.

I hold her hair, vaguely noticing its strawberry strands twisted around my fingers. I rub her back and curse myself for caring about her at all. She wouldn't be so eager to hang with me if she was in her right mind.

We sit there for what feels like hours, her body trying to rid itself of poison. I'm not sure if it's the alcohol or drugs those bastards might've slipped in her drink, but she's going to regret it in the morning either way.

After a while, the convulsions subside and her breathing evens out. She's falling asleep with her head on the toilet. I nudge her a little and help her wipe her mouth with some toilet paper.

"Thanks, Charlie," she slurs, calling me that for the second time tonight. Then she goes totally limp in my arms.

I immediately check her pulse and her breathing; both seem normal. She's just passed out. Hopefully.

I wait a second to see if she'll wake up and barf again, but it seems she's done for now, so I carry her back to the bed. I lay her down and then just stare at her: her pale brow, beaded with sweat, her fluttering eyelids, purple-lined lips.

I can't leave her alone like this.

Shit.

I go downstairs to find the kitchen and get her a glass of water for when she wakes up. The hum in the air grows a little when I walk into the large room. The family must've had the argument in here over bowls of tofu and grapefruit.

By the hum, it feels like the argument was at least a few days ago. Makes me wonder how long she's been alone.

I shake off the questions and get the glass of water, then head back upstairs. I set the glass on the bedside table, suddenly feeling completely out of my element.

I haven't been in a home for so long, I almost forgot what it's like. I've been in houses, but not *homes*. I lived in houses—too many—with roofs and walls and anger and darkness and bruises. But I haven't been in a home for . . . well, since Ava lived with the Marshalls. After they adopted her, I got to visit a few times.

Then they were dead. And there was only a nine-year-old, blood-splattered Ava left behind, her eyes so big and blue that night, looking like they held all the pain of the world in them. Her tiny hands and arms were coated in crimson to the elbow from the spell she'd done to protect herself.

Now she lives with a foster family—her third one in three years. She gets to be passed around from house to house, like I did all those years. No more *home*.

Supposedly my mom, Fiona O'Linn, had family in the city a long time ago—grandparents, I think. But if they're alive, they haven't done anything to help me and Ava. And I'm not sure I'd even want Ava to have anything to do with the people who raised my mom. Fiona was broken inside, and they did nothing to save her.

I run my fingers over Rebecca's desk. It's covered in notebooks and colored pencils, smears of paint and ink. There's a collage of photos above it on the wall. A boy with dimples and freckles and sun-bleached red hair is in several of them. In the most prominent picture, he has a surfboard under one arm and a girl who looks like a younger version of Rebecca under the other; she's looking up at him like he's made of gold. There are photos of other people, too— normal high school kids, raising red plastic cups or making funny faces. Everyone's hugging, laughing, living life in bright colors.

I look over the rest of the room. There's an empty easel in the corner. A few posters on the walls of singers like Adele and Florence and the Machine, and movies like *The Notebook* and *Twilight*.

Then I notice something on the floor. In the far corner beside the easel are bits of paper scattered everywhere. I go over and pick up one of the larger scraps. It's a fragment of artwork—part of a wing. Yellows and blues rage in the background. I stare for a second at the other pieces by my feet. Drawings of some kind, all torn up. The sight makes me feel uneasy, but I'm not sure why.

I put the scrap of paper back on the floor with the rest of the pile. Then I go to the small bookshelf and look at the titles. My eyes glaze over the teen romances and vampire novels, until they find something more palatable: *Les Misérables*. I sit on the floor and lean my back against the side of the bed, telling myself not to get too comfortable.

———

Mom's sitting in her pentagram on the floor, black candles resting on each point of the star. The shifting flames make the light look like it's dancing on the walls in deep oranges and reds as she whispers in Latin, a benediction.

My insides go cold, but I stand and watch, shivering in the doorway as the darkness comes alive. I'm only six. And it's my mom. She knows my secrets, my terrors. She wouldn't do anything wrong . . .

FOUR

Something pokes my cheek.

I blink and squint at the sunlight beaming into the room. Did I fall asleep?

Something pokes again. "Hey!"

I look up and see the girl, Rebecca, holding a pencil with one of those frizzy-haired trolls on the end. Her own hair is in a nest of red tangles, her green eyes are rimmed red from last night's drama, and she's got glittery lip gloss smeared down her chin. She's frowning at me, body tense. She looks pissed.

"Who the hell are you?" There's a phone in her other hand, held like a weapon.

I scramble up and back away. "Did you call the cops?" My legs get ready to bolt.

She looks down at the phone like she forgot she's holding it, then back at me. "Maybe."

I relax a little, seeing the red spark of the lie in her eyes. "Maybe not," I say, raising my brow at her.

She chews on her bottom lip. "You brought me home? That was *you* last night?"

"Yeah," I say. "Do you remember anything?"

"Some," she says. "Thanks . . ."

"I live to serve." I give her a mocking bow and start to leave the room, ready to get back to where I know the rules.

"Wait."

I pause in the doorway. She's pinching the bridge of her nose like she's trying to hold back pain.

"Don't go," she says.

"Excuse me?"

"Just hold on." She groans and falls back down on the bed. "God, my head is pounding."

"Drink some water, it'll help."

She squints at me, so I point at the glass I'd set beside her bed. She looks at it for so long that I start to worry. Then—God, help me—a tear slips from her eye.

All I can do is stand there, shifting my feet, unsure how to react. After a few seconds of silence I say, "Listen, I'm sorry if I scared you. I meant to be gone before you woke up. I just wanted to be sure you were okay."

She wipes the tear away and sits up, taking the glass in her hand. It trembles in her grip as she lifts it to her mouth. When the water's gone she sets the glass back on the side table and then stares at the floor.

I can't stand the awkward anymore, so I motion to the door and say, "I'll just—"

"No. Please." She looks up at me. "I can't be alone."

Seriously? This girl needs a lecture about being too familiar with strangers. Maybe I should sing her that "Stranger Danger" song you're supposed to learn in kindergarten.

"I don't bite, I swear," she adds.

"How're you so sure that I don't?"

She lays back on the bed again and stares at the ceiling. "I don't care."

Something is very wrong here. I try to feel for spirits or old emotions again, something to point at why she looks so lost, why she doesn't care about herself, but there's just that distant hum in the air.

"I can't stay," I say. I need to check on Ava this morning before she goes to the academy.

Rebecca doesn't move.

"You don't know anything about me," I add. "You should be more careful, Rebecca."

She startles at the sound of her name and sits up. "How . . . ?"

"Your license. The same way I knew where you lived. Like I said, you need to be more careful."

She seems to settle. "My name's not Rebecca. Well, it is, but everyone calls me Emery."

I look her over. "Rebecca suits you better."

Her eyes go glassy again, and another tear slips down her cheek.

"Or not."

"You could take a shower," she says, like she's looking for a different subject. She motions to her bathroom. "You can shave, or whatever. I might be able to find some clothes that'll fit you."

She stands, only leaning a little, and goes into the bathroom and through another door on the other side. After a second she comes back with some jeans, a T-shirt, and another hoodie (a really thick one, with a fur-lined hood). She sets the guy's clothes on the foot of the bed. I guess she must have a brother.

"There are towels in the bathroom cupboard." She's motioning with her hands as she talks, looking distracted. "And there's a razor in the medicine cabinet you can use. Should be some shaving cream in there, too."

I want to jump at this chance to get clean, but it's all so freaking weird. "What's going on? Why are you doing this?"

She frowns at me like she doesn't understand the question. "It's no big deal. If memory serves, you had a hell of a night last night. Kinda my fault. You should shower, relax . . . eat some of my dad's food. He's not here to care."

Ah, I see. Daddy issues. "Last night you said your parents are in Paris."

"Just my dad. With his new girlfriend. Mom escaped him long ago." She scoffs, "He told me the trip was for work, but he packed *way* too many T-shirts. And the girlfriend was all giddy when she came over for the good-bye dinner. Bitch." She frowns at the wall, then turns back to me. "So do whatever you want. My dad's house is your house."

I glance at the nice clothes, then at her, trying to decide. I have a good hour and a half before Ava leaves for practice.

"I'm gonna go shower in the master bedroom," she says. "For, like, an hour." She sighs and pulls clothes from the closet, then leaves without another word.

I stand in the middle of the room for a second—but just a second—before I slip my shoes off, my hoodie, my shirt and pants, leaving them in the middle of the floor. Then I go look for the shaving supplies.

I'm not sure how long I'm in the shower—the hot water feels so damn good. I wash my hair three times with the mango shampoo and scrub my skin until it turns red. I'm going to need new bandaging for my hand, but I don't care.

When the temperature of the water finally turns lukewarm, I step out of the glass enclosure, reveling in the billows of steam around me. I grab a towel and bury my face in the cotton, captivated by the spring smell. It's like drying myself with a cloud.

The teeth marks on my hand are almost completely healed now. Apparently demon bites aren't like regular bites, because I know I don't have any super healing powers.

And then I notice something else. My mark. It's different. The part that winds up past my wrist is halfway to my elbow now; it's grown thinner vines and more shapes and curves.

I stand there staring at it, completely stumped. Could the demon bite have done something to it?

Damn. More questions. Wonderful.

I decide for now to stick it all in the dusty file called "My Screwed-up Life." There are plenty of more pressing things to worry about at this point—like Ava approaching her twelfth birthday.

I wrap the towel around my waist and open the bathroom door, heading for my new clothes. My feet stop. So does my heart.

Rebecca's lying on the bed, on her side, looking at a magazine. In her underwear.

Her fucking underwear.

She looks up and smiles. "You must've been really dirty." Her eyes travel over my torso, and she bites her bottom lip as the heat of her intention fills the space between us.

I make myself study the floor, but it's too late. The image of her is burned in my brain: hair falling in damp strands around her face like amber seaweed, black lace panties against milky white skin, a smooth belly with a monarch butterfly tattoo on her ribs, just below her breast.

And . . . God. Oh, God.

She's a virgin.

This girl is offering herself to a stranger, and she's a virgin.

Someone who's had sex carries soul marks on their neck, chest, or shoulders—a palm print for each partner, like a brand.

Rebecca's skin is white as snow.

I grab the clothes off the bed and go back into the bathroom, shutting the door behind me.

Shit shit shit.

It takes a million deep breaths to get control of myself. I lean on the counter and think about demons and guts and blood. I can't get dressed until the horrors overwhelm the burning—which takes way too long for my own comfort.

When I come back out, Rebecca's fully clothed.

I'm *sort of* relieved.

She won't look at me, though. She's pissed again.

"Thanks for the shower," I say.

She runs a brush through her hair in jerky strokes. "Are you gay or something?"

I bark out a laugh. I can't help it. "No."

Her shoulders tense. I see in her eyes that there's only one other reason I'd reject her offer—she's not pretty enough.

I let myself step a little closer. "Screwing me won't help you feel any better."

She sits on the edge of the bed and stares at the floor. "I just can't pretend anymore. I don't want to be alone. I feel like doing something insane."

I try to convince my body it's best to walk away. This girl is bad news—a ledge I'm heading straight for. The free fall would be amazing—the landing, not so much. It would be so easy to sit beside her, comfort her, kiss her, touch her until I can barely breathe. Until I can't stop.

So I say what I know will jerk us both awake. "You were almost gang-raped last night."

She flinches. "What?"

"I found you with three guys hovering over you in an alley behind the club. They were talking about who would get you first."

She shivers, and her eyes search the room, like she's looking for something to prove I'm lying.

"You're running straight into hell's arms, Rebecca." I gather my old clothes as she sits there hugging herself. I tuck the old rags under my arm, grab my backpack, and move to the doorway of her room. "Thanks again for the shower and the clothes." I start to walk away, but hesitate for a second. I turn back and say, "Be careful," before I leave her life for good.

I head for the stairs and start down, feeling frustrated and confused. I'm walking away, but I don't want to. If God loves me, he better let me get laid eventually.

I'm lost in thought, landing on the last step, when a new smell hits me like a wall in the face.

Sulfur.

My heart starts to gallop, beating at my ribs so hard I'm pretty sure it's leaving bruises. I scan the entry hall, and then I see it. Only a few feet from the base of the stairs: burn marks on the marble floor—three crossing lines, each ending in a symbol of power. A sigil.

A demon was here.

A large one.

There's no way this is related to the smaller one from the alley last night. This sigil is from some serious demon mojo. I close my eyes and breathe in the air, feeling for the creeper that might've left it, trying to tell if it's still close and how long it stood here, but I don't sense anything. Just the leftover buzz of lust between me and Rebecca from a few minutes ago.

Whatever was here, it's gone now.

FIVE

I used to have a bike, but it got stolen. I miss it. Now it's all skateboarding, buses, or my own two feet. No way I'm taking that monster they pretend is a subway, in earthquake central. From Rebecca's, it takes me more than a half hour to get to Ava's neighborhood by bus—worst possible way to travel. The thing stops every eight feet even on a good day, not to mention all the traffic heading through downtown. It's not like Ava's place is that far. Probably would've been faster to walk.

I'm in a pissy mood all around. Leaving Rebecca like that makes me feel like a bastard, and the idea of a demon that close to her turns my stomach inside out. It wasn't even an underling staking territory. By the smell and the look of the marks, the thing was at least midlevel, if not higher. Maybe even a body-hopper.

My skin goes cold. How the hell didn't I feel it when it was there? How the *hell* could I leave her open and vulnerable like that?

I can't save the whole world, I know this. But the realization never stops the ache. What else is this curse good for if I don't use it to help people?

Ava's newest foster house is the nicest one she's ever lived in. It's breathtaking, actually. Like a museum. She calls it the Taj Mahal. But it's more like a Spanish-style hotel, if you ask me. It's a sprawling single-story home, with cream stucco walls and a red tile roof, wrapped in pink and yellow climbing roses and night jasmine.

I sneak around to the back and find our tree—an old willow at the far corner of the property, down a little ravine, out of view from the house. Demons and monsters don't like trees. They like metal and jagged edges and death. So Ava and I stick to the grass and the trees as much as we can when we meet. The longer it's been in the ground, the better—fifty-year-old trees work perfectly. Not always easy to find in LA.

I close my eyes and picture Ava, her strange, knowing smile, her liquid blue eyes. Then I picture where I am and push out, *I'm here*. We recently figured out we can do this, connect to each other without words, but it only seems to work if we're close enough, maybe a block or two away.

The morning sun is warming the air, so I pull off my newly acquired hoodie. Maybe I should ditch it. It reminds me of Rebecca, of the way her hair felt against my palm. And I can't let people in, I can't let myself care. I have to stay focused.

As I start to toss the thing over a nearby branch, something catches my eye—a name along the inside of the neck.

CHARLIE M.

In bold block letters.

I run my finger over the name and get a flash of the woman who wrote it: Hispanic, wearing a maid's uniform. She smiles and folds the jacket up, putting it back in the drawer. There's someone sitting on the bed behind her, a young man. He says something, joking, and she smiles, rattling off words in Spanish to him. I recognize him from the snapshots in Rebecca's room.

Charlie, I hear Rebecca say again, just like she did when she snuggled into my chest on the ride to her house.

Charlie with his arm around her while she looks up at him in admiration.

Charlie, her brother.

But something happened. And Rebecca's alone. Something—

Ava appears in a small cluster of orange trees that rim the west side of the yard, stopping my thoughts. She pauses and plucks one of the oranges from a branch and puts it to her nose. "You can smell the sunshine," she says.

I shake off the revelation of Rebecca's *Charlie* and give my sister a smile. "Oh, yeah? How's it taste?" There's nothing I can do to fix whatever happened to the boy now.

Ava tosses me the fruit, then sits at my feet, looking up at me with her wide grey-blue eyes. "You look tired."

"I am."

Her shoulders sag. "Me too." The eagerness she had in her voice last night is gone.

A weight settles in my chest. "I'm working on a solution. I swear," I say, sitting beside her on the ground.

"It's getting harder again. To stop stuff."

My pulse speeds up with her worried tone. "Did something happen last night, after we talked?"

She shrugs. "I just don't want to mess up again, you know . . ." Her voice catches a little and fades to silence.

"The Marshalls' deaths weren't your fault, Ava." *They were mine.* I wasn't watching her. It was too easy to ignore stuff back then—to feel like I deserved a normal life.

The night *it* happened I was making out with Lindsey Sawyer from chem lab on that leopard-print beanbag, trying to decide which of my foster brothers to ask for a condom. I was so sure that I'd finally found my chance to join the World of Real Men, when the Man of the House banged on the bedroom door.

I had a phone call.

It was Ava, babbling that she'd had a vision. She'd seen blood on the picture of us with the Marshalls and thought I might be in trouble. But it wasn't my blood she saw.

By the time I got there, it was too late. Ava was in the middle of the room with her adopted parents' dismembered bodies around her, their blood in her hair and on her cheeks.

"I sent them away," she said, her voice sounding far off.

I looked over the carnage in horror. For a split second, I thought the darkness had gotten her. I thought Ava, my baby sister, had done it. Cut her loved ones to ribbons. Then she whispered, "The dogs were so big, Aidan. They came with a man who had black eyes."

Hellhounds. *Thank God.* Relief flooded me. It hadn't been her. I hadn't lost her yet. The beasts must've come with the killer. I still don't know how she got rid of the hellhounds before I showed up. But I know she protected herself with a circle of the Marshalls' blood.

I look at her now as she stares into the orange trees, the slim line of her neck and shoulders, her pale skin, so unlike mine. My half sister. Her hair is white fire in the afternoon sunlight. She looks so much like our mom, Fiona. So not like me.

"Ava, don't listen to that darkness," I say. "You know the truth."

She takes the orange back from me and tears into the skin, spraying the sweet juice on her legs. "The truth. Even *you* can't say what that is for sure when it comes to me." She rips more skin off in a huge chunk and then tosses the orange into the dirt, like it's upset her. "Before it happened, I was trying to see how long I could levitate my pencil instead of doing my homework. Then I saw the blood on the picture . . ."

My muscles tense, but I try to stay calm on the outside.

"You shouldn't use your . . . talents," I say. "But we don't know if that's the reason they found you." We're still not sure how the demons find her. Maybe it's her energy, maybe it's something else—something our mom did. But I want to be careful. I need *her* to be more careful.

The year the Marshalls died, Ava had more visions and *incidents* than ever. She burned up a rosebush after its thorns tore her favorite sweater. She found her rabbit dead in its cage and shattered all the windows in her room with her grief. Her powers were never as out of control as they were that week, before her ninth birthday. I should've known something was coming.

I scoot toward her, taking her fingers in mine. "I love you, Peep." I kiss her hand and pull her closer, until she's snuggled against my chest. "I'll protect you. I will."

"I don't like hiding from what I can do. It feels wrong."

Helplessness presses in. "I know." Ava's never run from her abilities like I have. She sees them as a part of her, like her nose or her fingers. She just doesn't seem to believe as strongly as me that using them might put her in danger—or bring her to the same end as our mom.

"Things are happening again," she says. "And it's a million times stronger."

"What things?"

"Two days ago I broke the TV in social studies because a girl was making fun of my shoes." She wiggles the oxfords on her feet, looking for all the world like she's telling me about how she skinned her knee. "I have control now, more than last time, but it's like I don't *want* to control it."

"You should've called me. You know what this means." There's no more time. If she's manifesting like that, unwilling to control herself, then things are going south again. I have to hide her. But *how*?

She nods and picks at a fingernail. "I know. I just wish I knew why the demons want me so bad."

So do I. Mom told me again and again that I'd eventually need to protect my sister, but she never said why.

On Ava's third birthday, the demons came for her. But it was my mother who was taken from us instead, her heart clawed from her chest. I watched her blood pool underneath her dead body in the shape of the demon's sigil. And as the wolflike demon hunched in the circle, like it was waiting for something, a mark appeared on Fiona's forehead.

Sacrifice, it said. *One for another.* My mother's life for Ava's.

Three years later, on her sixth birthday, Ava told me that a man stood beside her bed while the dark of the moon passed. If I had to guess, I'd say he was an angel, protecting her; no one close to her died that night.

On her ninth birthday, no angel came, and the Marshalls got ripped to bits in front of her.

This is year twelve, and the dark of the moon falls on her birthday again. I can't count on an angel showing up to guard her. I see more and more demons every day in the shadows, but I haven't seen an angel in years. Ava's going to have to depend on me this time.

And I'm useless right now. A clueless idiot who gets mixed up with strange girls and knows nothing about the source of his own abilities, let alone how to help his little sister with hers.

"I had a dream last night about Mom," Ava says, knocking me back to the present. She wipes her hands on her academy uniform skirt.

My skin turns cold, and I want to say, *so did I*—and the night before, and the night before, and the night before—but instead I say, "Oh." I've never told her that I dream of Mom, too. I only dream memories. Ava dreams new moments with her, like she's making memories even after death.

She sounds defensive when she adds, "I know you don't like it, but I had to ask her about what happened to you last night. And she answered me. Sort of. I think." In addition to being able to move things with her mind, Ava also has Mom's gifts—she has visions and *sees* things. Things to come, things in the past. Especially about our mom.

I don't say anything, I don't scold her, so she continues, "She was on the beach this time. A really lovely beach with white flowers. And there was this cave. She kept looking back at it like she belonged there or something. But it made her sad."

The scene sounds like one of Fiona's drawings.

"She told me you'd take me with you now," Ava says. "That last night was a warning, and it's time to stop hiding."

That's new. "She did?"

"She also said . . ." Ava scrunches up her face.

"What?"

"It was strange. She said—" She pulls away and studies me. "Well, I think part of it was about your dad."

I go still, and everything slows around me.

Ava squeezes my hand, urgency filling her voice. "Do you think she was good, Aidan?"

I don't know what she means. I'm stuck on the word *dad*.

"If our mom was evil, maybe we shouldn't listen to her," she says.

"What'd she say about my dad, Ava?" If I've learned anything in this life, it's this: listen to Ava's dreams.

She looks at our clasped hands.

"Her exact words were: *Your brother is growing in his gift of the in-between, but he doesn't know which way to walk the line. The Light he found will lead him; its wings sit beneath the heart. But he must touch the violets and lilies to find surrender, to find his hidden blood.*"

Damn riddles. "What about my dad?" I ask.

"That's the hidden blood, I think, because next she said: *The father's place is another time, the son is becoming Fire Bringer.* I guess that's you. Fire Bringer—whatever that means. And your gift is something called the in-between? I dunno." She shrugs, looking as lost as I feel.

I rub her shoulder in comfort, resisting the urge to shake sense from her. She's just a kid. Only the messenger. She doesn't understand it any more than I do.

Ava and I are different. She has Fiona's gifts. I don't. Not even one.

Which makes me assume that my own shit—knowing all those weird languages, seeing people's souls on their skin, seeing demons and angels and ghosts, the ability to feel certain energies—must come from my dad.

I want to know who my dad is—or *was*?—but I'm terrified at the same time. What if he was something wicked? Something *wrong*? The truth might be worse than not knowing anything at all.

"I wish this stuff came with instructions like that TiVo thing that Mr. Marshall bought me," Ava says.

"Yeah."

We sit in silence for a few minutes, until she leans into me and says, "You'll find him, Aidan. I know you will."

That's exactly what I'm worried about.

SIX

I've been trying to deny it. I told myself we'd have time, that maybe nothing would happen this year, or maybe the angel would come, but deep inside I know. Someone else will die. The demons will get their claws into her one way or another. Unless I do something.

As I leave Ava's neighborhood, I finger the paper in my pocket, the one with the number that Hanna gave me. I could check it out. Some steady cash, maybe? Just enough to get us on our feet before the bomb drops.

I have to try.

The area code is in LA. I punch the number into my phone, and the line rings once, then a voice mail picks up. A female voice comes through the speaker: "You've reached the Los Angeles Paranormal Investigative Agency. Are your troubles falling into the 'strange' or 'unexplained' category? Don't be afraid to reach out. We can help. Please leave your name and number and a short summary of your case. We'll get back to you as soon as we can. Peace be with you."

Paranormal investigating? *What?* I punch the number in again and listen to the message a second time. That's what it says. And it doesn't *sound* like a joke by the tone.

It has to be a front for some con or something.

But I'm sort of out of options at this point. I need help, and Hanna seems to trust this guy, Sid. He must be the head of the . . . ghostbusters, or whatever. I could leave a message on the voice mail and hope I get a call back. But I'm not sure I have time for formalities. Plus, I won't know if I can trust the guy unless I get a look at him, a feel for his energy.

I do a reverse search on the cell number and get a recent address. I catch the bus into downtown, passing under the 101, where these old buildings from the forties and fifties are nestled farther back. I get off at a stop on Hollywood Boulevard near Prospect and start my walk farther into the neighborhood. The buildings come in all shapes and sizes—apartments, old hotels, restaurants, and some houses. There's a library and a place that looks like an art gallery. After several more blocks I come to the address I'm looking for, on the corner of two tree-lined streets.

It has a white picket fence—that's the first thing I notice. A thin house with two stories and what looks like an attic room for a third floor. The style is Victorian, and it's recently been fixed up with new windows and new paint: canary-yellow for the siding, white for the trim, and red for the door. The small grassy area out front is actually green, even in a drought, growing in emerald patches on either side of a new brick pathway that winds up to the wraparound porch. The whole look is topped off with a white bench swing, creaking in the early Santa Ana winds, beside a pot of pink geraniums.

It's like I'm looking at an old TV set from a fifties show or something. It's so normal. Too normal.

I'm torn for a second, thinking I must have the wrong place. I glance up and down the street. Weeds are growing in the cracks on the patchwork sidewalk, a rusty tricycle is tipped over in the gutter. Not exactly high-end living. But whoever this guy is, he must take care of his stuff. And I don't hear gunshots, so that's a bonus.

I pull the *hamsa* Hanna gave me out of the old jeans in my backpack and slip the chain over my head, feeling a little better when the charm settles against my chest. I watch the house for a few more minutes and then decide to take my shot and see what I can get out of this.

A job. Money. A place for Ava and me to stay. Together. That's what I need to focus on.

I hover on the porch for a second, feeling around for spirits, but it's all just emotions on the wind. So I knock.

The door swings open, and a black guy about the same age as me is there in the doorway.

"What?" he asks, looking me up and down. I do the same to him. He's got to be about sixteen, wearing skinny jeans that exaggerate his height and lankiness, with well-trimmed hair, thick-rimmed glasses, and spiked gauges in his ears. A young Lenny Kravitz without the dreads.

Before I can say anything, he's shoved out of the way.

"What kind of way is that to answer the door?" A second kid is standing in the doorway now. He can't be more than fourteen, dark hair, wide chocolate eyes—Indian, maybe—and feet too big for his short body. He gives me a wide grin. "How might we help you?"

The first boy snorts and peeks back around the door. "You've really gotta stop reading all that Charles Dick crap, Lester. You sound like a freak show."

Lester's smile vanishes, and he turns to the older boy. "Just 'cause you can't read anything but *Playboy*—"

"Which is very educational, by the way. You could learn a thing or two from me about life, Lester the lezzy-boy, who can't get a girl to save his—"

The taller boy is silenced with a sock to the gut by Lester. The two collide, shoving, stumbling back with *umphs* and grunts and a little laughter on the taller boy's part.

"Seriously," a girl's voice says from the shadows. "Grow up." A small hand shoos the two tussling boys back into the shadows of the house.

Her full form appears in the doorway.

I step back in reaction, a sudden jolt of recognition coursing through me. But then it fades as quick as it came. If I do feel something familiar, I can't place it.

Her hair is long, dark, and wild. Her large eyes are rimmed in black eyeliner; there's no other makeup on her heart-shaped face. She's small, only five three maybe. A thin reed of a thing. Not exactly goth, but not really punk either, with tall boots over tight black jeans and a Nirvana tank top.

"Hey." She looks me over, her light eyes curious. But I feel an undercurrent, a buzzing around her, like she's anxious about me, the same as I seem to be about her. "Sid isn't home. But you can come in, or whatever."

"What in God's name is going on down there?" Another female voice comes from inside the house. "It sounds like Bonkey Kong in stereo. I'm trying to study!"

Boots Girl rolls her eyes and calls, "Earbuds, Holly. Remember?" Then she turns back to me. "You comin' in or what?"

I hesitate. I don't sense anything horrid.

Actually, I don't sense much of anything at all—which in itself is weird. I usually sense *something*. Even if it's just a memory or an emotion. And this place certainly looks like it's not lacking in either of those things. But it's almost like the air is muffled or fogged up here. Not sure if that's a good or bad thing.

I decide to throw caution to the wind. I nod at Boots Girl and step into the house.

"I'm Kara," she says as I follow her into the main room. She waves at the back hall where the two boys went. "That was Lester and Jax. They'll say hi later."

We pass a couch, and she points at a mound on the end. "Finger doesn't talk much, but there he is." Not a mound. A very round boy, hunched over an Xbox remote. His eyes are trained on the flat-screen TV on the other side of the room. A tangle of greasy brown hair tops his head. His focused features are badly pockmarked. A bag of Funyuns is spilling out onto the floor next to him.

Kara adds, "That's not his usual space. He camps out in the basement, but lately Sid wants him socializing more with the rest of the house, so . . . well, that's Finger socializing." She shrugs and heads up the stairs.

"Listen," I say. It suddenly feels like she's giving me a tour. "I'm not sure who you think I am, but—"

"That's Holly's room," she says, ignoring me and pointing at a closed door across from the head of the stairs. "She's high strung and very weird about her hair products, so it's best if you just steer clear of any bottles in the bathroom. Mark your soap and keep it in your own room. Which is . . ." She pauses, scanning the doors. "That one." She nods at the door at the far end of the hall. "You're next to me." She chews on her lip, looking nervous, and then she turns to head toward the door of *my room*.

I touch her shoulder, stopping her. "I just want to talk to Sid."

She blinks up at me. "I know." Her voice shakes a little, and a slight current runs up my arm from where my fingers grazed her skin.

I pull away, and we just stand there looking at each other.

She felt it, too.

"Do I know you?" I finally ask.

She licks her lips, and a dimple sinks into her cheek.

My memory flashes again, this time with details: lights and music and heat.

"You don't remember me?" she whispers. Her head tilts a little, and she's suddenly closer. "I'm hurt." Her energy is thick in the air around me now, like she's spread herself out, a cloud of energy and static, prickling against my skin. "I could remind you."

And then I smell it: green apple Jolly Ranchers.

The club. The girl. The kiss.

I jerk back so hard I nearly fall down the stairs.

She raises her brow. "Curiouser and curiouser."

The urge to run away vibrates through me . . . along with the urge to press her into the wall, kiss her, touch her, dive into her . . . or dive down the stairs headfirst to escape.

"What the hell *are* you?" she asks.

The exact same question is on my tongue.

Then she lets out a forced laugh and holds her hands up. "I should be insulted, but I'm more impressed than anything." She waves for me to follow and heads down the hall. "I mean, the other boys, I have to pretty much threaten to cut their balls off if they touch me. I can see you won't be a problem." She laughs again.

She's terrifying. I *cannot* live here with this girl. *What is she?* I'm suddenly sure she's not a regular human.

"All in time, sweetie. All in time," she says, like she can read my mind.

"I'm just here for Sid," I say again.

I should go. Forget this. I'll get help another way.

She leans on the doorjamb of *my room.* "You don't need to bolt. Really. I promise to never kiss you again." She waves her hand and adds, "Or whatever."

And the air settles, like she flipped off a switch.

I shift my feet, unsure of the right move.

Her face grows serious. "I'm sorry if I freaked you out. I really didn't mean to. It was just, well, you feel it, too; I know you do. And come on. Even you have to admit that kiss last night was pretty damn well off the charts."

Something surfaces in my head, a knowledge about her: she doesn't smile much. She doesn't feel comfortable being happy.

She smiled last night, though. I remember it now. That grin that made her blue eyes lighten. And she had a thin blue energy and a glowing tattoo on the back of her neck. But I don't see that now.

I let myself look at her, really look at her. Her hair's dyed black, with a violet tint in the light. It's in low, messy pigtails, resting in layers on her chest. She's got earbuds hanging around her neck, and there's an ever-so-faint beat coming out of them. She looks casual, bored at first glance, but there's a tension under the surface; her jaw is clenched just a little too much.

And then I see the markings, not on her flesh, but on her soul. Her skin is covered. But not in Chinese symbols. In handprints. The darkest one is almost turning her skin red, firm around her throat.

My own throat goes tight with the knowledge of what that means.

Rape.

Then there are scars. Real ones. Lots of them. Thick scars up the inside of her arms, wrist to elbow.

I've seen so many souls like hers in the street, wide eyes glazed, looking over their shoulders as they slip into a stranger's car or down an alley. Demons cling to them, feeding on their sorrow and desperation, as if it's ripe fruit ready to pluck.

"Kara," I say, like saying her name might heal something. My fear of her has evaporated in an instant. Whatever she is, she didn't choose it.

The sound of her name seems to affect her, or maybe it's the look of knowledge on my face. She clears her throat, sticks an earbud in. "Sid'll be home soon. You can wait downstairs." Then she slips away into the next room, closing herself in.

I watch her shadow move under the door. I watch it pace back and forth for several seconds.

Then I go downstairs to wait for Sid.

SEVEN

I sit on the couch beside Finger and his Funyuns.

Across the hall and through an archway, I can see Lester and Jax playing a game at the kitchen table. They keep smacking down cards and yelling out numbers and calling each other "fart nugget" and "pencil dick." I wonder if it's ever quiet here.

Just as I start to think the answer is probably no, a somber-looking guy comes into the house through the back door. He's tall and broad, maybe eighteen, with dusty-blond hair, cut neat over his ears, and a serious tan. The skin on his nose is peeling—obviously a surfer.

"We got the job," he says, walking into the kitchen. "Time to get to work, boys."

"Yes! I knew it!" Lester shouts.

"You didn't know anything," Jax says.

"The peek stone showed the outcome looking positive," Lester says, a smug grin on his face. "And it got us the freaking Benson job." He folds his arms across his chest.

Jax snorts. "You mean the *fucked-up* Benson job. You're just lucky that ghost had a thing for peppermint schnapps or you wouldn't have gotten her Depression-era ass outta that sticky skin of yours, and you'd have been one weird Italian-Indian lady—"

The older blond boy spots me then. He hits Jax on the arm. "Shut it. We've got a spec hovering."

All eyes fall on me. Jax leans back in his chair, giving me a harder look than he did before. "He's waiting to see Sid. Kara let him in. She thinks he's a keeper, Connor." He makes a crude gesture with his hands to the older boy. "Kara likes 'em fresh and dumb."

"Then why'd I shoot you down, Jax?" Kara asks, coming down the stairs. She doesn't look at me, just walks by the living room and enters the kitchen. She asks the Connor guy, "Where's Sid?"

Lester grins. "This new job's a shoo-in, Kara. The peek stone said—"

"Shut up!" Connor snaps. "We wait till Sid is here, then have a vote for a go or not, like always." He looks at Kara and adds, "Sid's right behind me. He just stopped to do something in the shed." Then he looks at me. "Ten more minutes, Kara, and if Sid isn't inside, this spec needs to be gone."

Kara follows his gaze. "He's harmless, Connor. Guy doesn't know what the hell's going on."

Very true.

———

Sid reminds me a little of a young used car salesman. Not just because of his suit—though it's really nice, well fitted, and stylish. He's got a pin-striped vest on, a thin silk tie loose at the neck, and his shirtsleeves are rolled up to just below the elbow, revealing heavily tattooed forearms. He grips a black walking stick with long and delicate fingers, tapping it on the floor as he paces in a semicircle in front of me.

He could definitely be a used car salesman, but I get the feeling I'm not a customer. I'm the car he's trying to figure out how to sell.

He looks like he's in his early twenties, not much older than the blond kid, Connor. He's medium height, with dark eyebrows and sun-kissed skin, bald as a billiard and clean shaven. His features are almost feminine, graceful. But there's a sharp line to his hazel eyes. They cut into me, peeling back layers of my defenses until I wonder if he's seeing me for real. Like through my skin. How I see people.

It's a bit terrifying to imagine how I might look from that angle.

By his face, I'd say it doesn't look good. That frown could strip paint.

The other inhabitants of this madhouse clutter the opposite side of the room, facing the couch where I'm still sitting beside Finger. They watch Sid watch me like they're not expecting much. This must not be the first time they've considered another recruit to this . . . whatever this is.

It's definitely not a church-charity group home thing, obviously. And I don't get a drug house vibe or a sex thing—if I did, I'd be out the door faster than Finger's fingers tap on that Xbox controller. If this ghost hunter thing is a front for something else, it's a really good one.

"Stand up, boy." Sid waves his walking stick, pointing at a spot in the middle of the living room floor.

I rise from the couch and move to where he motioned. "Listen, Mr., um, Sid. I just—"

"No talking," he grumbles, tapping my leg once with his stick.

It's just a small tap, but I jerk back and glare at him. I don't like people touching me, not ever. And I've had too many people think I'm a punching bag. If he does that one more time, I'll take that stick from him and shove it up his—

"Yes! Fire! There, I see it now." He smiles, changing his entire face. He glances behind him at the audience. "You were right, Kara."

When I look over at her, her eyes move away to the window.

"Listen," I say. "I just wanted to talk."

"You need help," Sid says.

I open my mouth to deny it, but then let out a sigh and just nod. What's the point in pretending?

"Who sent you?" he asks.

"Hanna from SubZero. She gave me your number last night."

He looks me over again. His eyes pause at my wounded hand. "What happened?"

I just stare back at him. Silent.

"Let me see it." He waves me forward.

I don't move. I can't let him be in control, not before I know his angle. "I have a few questions first."

He leans back on the arm of the couch beside Finger and nods for me to continue. A few members of the audience look impressed at my stubbornness, especially Lester and Holly, a young Hispanic girl—the one who's high strung, according to Kara, and apparently obsessed with hair products. Her tight pink T-shirt says, *I see stupid people.* She kind of looks like an eighties throwback with rainbow knee-highs, pink Reebok high-tops, hair tied up with bright ribbons, and a headband with Hello Kitty on it.

"First I need to know exactly what it is you people do around here," I say.

"Would you like to take that one, Kara?" Sid asks.

"We're like fumigators," she says to me. "We kill bugs. Otherworldly bugs. Kill 'em, lock 'em up, or cast 'em out. Whatever suits at the time. And we get paid pretty good to do it, too."

"Otherworldly bugs?" I ask, feeling the blood leave my head. "Like what, exactly?"

Sid responds, "Don't play dumb, boy. You already know what kind of bugs she means. The same kind that helped you get that wound." He nods at my hand.

This is unbelievable. "Demons?"

I realize too late that he tricked that piece of information out of me. First he opens his mouth in shock, then his lips shift to a slight, knowing smile. "The rare demon, here and there, but mostly ghosts and poltergeists." No red spark. He's not lying—or doesn't think he is, anyway.

Lester pipes in, "We killed a vampire once!" He sticks his chest out a little, like he's the one that made the kill. Which is ridiculous.

"Vampires?" Okay, they're full of shit.

"It wasn't a *vampire* vampire," Kara says, glaring at Lester. "It was a spirit that liked blood energy. We just didn't know what else to call it. This old man had to put a fresh bowl of pig's blood out every night, or the thing would rattle his windows and turn off his TV. So we helped him get rid of it."

A million questions are spinning around in my head. They know about this stuff. But how? I look at Kara. "You can see them."

"Not exactly," she says. And I'm surprised by the disappointment that filters into my gut. For a moment I'd thought she might be like me. "I feel them. Sometimes hear them. But I can't see them."

"Kara is invaluable," Sid says, giving her a fatherly look that seems a little . . . off.

She glances away, back to the window again.

I glare at Sid. "And what is it *you* do?"

He moves closer, right in front of me. "I can help you." He points the handle of his walking stick at me. It's tipped by a clear ball with what looks like a pentagram inside. "Eric told me about you. Said you have several unique gifts. But I'm guessing these gifts feel more like curses, don't they?"

My hands are shaking.

He motions to the audience. "Each of the souls you see here was living in hell until I found them. I pulled them from gutters and padded cells and foster homes and helped them learn to use their gifts. To accept who they are. And now they're lights in the dark places, keeping us connected to the spiritual world like bea-cons, and earning a living helping others."

Connor clears his throat. "It's true."

Sid moves over to Connor's side and pats him on the shoulder in a way that looks like he truly admires the young man. "Connor was once on the streets," Sid says quietly, "selling drugs and living in a very dark place. Now he's able to use his gift to help others, to help himself out of the dark. Just by seeing the places an object has been. Very useful. He's already reunited a family with their lost child since he's been with us. He's a hero now."

Jax pipes in, pointing to the Hispanic girl, "Holly dreams about dead people. Like that kid in *The Sixth Sense*."

Holly spins her head, her ponytail whacking against her cheek, and glares a hole through Jax's head, obviously not happy about the revelation of her gift. "And all you can do is tell if it's gonna rain, dumbass."

Sid holds out a hand to Jax as if trying to calm the waters. "Every gift is important in its own right. From Kara's sensory skills to Lester's very useful ability to channel spirits, or Connor's object reading, Jax's sky predictions, and Holly's budding dreams."

I glance at Finger. He's the only one who hasn't been men-tioned. Maybe his gift is focusing, because the kid hasn't looked away from the TV since we all gathered in his domain.

Sid taps his cane again and points it at me. "And now you've come to me. I'll ask again: Do you need help?"

I take a deep breath, then plunge. "I need a job. I need a place to stay. Not just for me, for my little sister, too. Someplace safe."

Sid frowns at that. "Your sister." Eric must not have mentioned Ava. Of course, I barely ever say anything about her. Maybe he forgot I have a sister.

"She's with a foster family right now, but they don't take good care of her, and she's getting scared. I can't leave her with them." Can't tell him too much, or there's no way I'll get what I need from these people. No one wants a girl living under their roof who's the target of demons.

Sid takes in a deep breath and lets it out slowly, then says, "No, I suppose not. But you and your sister must each bring something to the table if you're going to earn your way. Food and shelter aren't free."

"My sister's just a kid."

"So are you. What can she contribute?"

I sigh. There's no way I can tell them the truth about that. "She can't do anything."

"His sister's just a blank," Connor says. "Can we really afford the dead weight right now?"

Sid eyes me, ignoring Connor's comment. "Well, what can *you* do with us to provide for her?"

I consider my options. Hanna seemed to think I could trust this guy. I can at least tell him what Eric knows, since Eric probably already spilled the beans on that score. "I can see things. Ghosts and demons and shit."

Jax whistles low. "Nice."

The others gape. Except Kara. She's got a terrified expression on her face.

Sid frowns. "You *see* them?"

"That's what I said, isn't it?" I don't know why, but I'm suddenly getting irritated. Why is Kara looking at me like that? Her hands clench into fists.

Sid has his car salesman face on again. "What else?"

"What, that's not enough?" I laugh. Then I realize Eric probably told him about my talent with languages. "I know Latin and Hebrew. And a little Ancient Greek." I shrug. *And Aramaic and Anglo-Saxon and a bunch of others I have no clue what they are.*

He's frowning at my hand again. "You can see them. With your human eyes . . ." He hesitates then asks quickly, "Are they a blur? Shadows?"

I shake my head. "Living color."

He stares at me with such intensity that my pulse begins to race.

"Do you know what that means?" he asks.

The growing excitement in his voice sets a warning off in my gut.

I swallow and say no. And I'm pretty sure from that giddy look on his face I don't want to know.

He takes my hand, turns it over in his, studies my markings, the bite. "I'm assuming the demon that did this was corporeal?"

I snatch it back. "What? No."

His head jerks back. "No? Are you saying the creature was still on the other side of the Veil and yet it somehow *bit* you?"

My teeth clench at the memory and at the realization that I didn't want that piece of information known yet.

"Did you fight it off? You did, didn't you?"

"What the hell difference does it make?" It's suddenly getting harder to breathe. Because I know it makes a difference. A huge difference.

Sid shakes his head, looking almost awed. "You made physical contact with the other side." And then he says, almost as if to himself, "How else could you have done that unless you exist on both planes?"

My chest constricts in fear.

The bodies in the room stir.

Sid's voice grows a little stronger. "That's why you can *see* them. Unlike Kara, you must have one foot on the other side of the Veil. A part of your soul is on this side, and a part is on the other. You're *between*." He smiles suddenly, brilliantly, as if he just discovered the next big Internet craze that'll make him millions. "That's a lot of power, boy. A lot. You may have talents you haven't realized yet."

In-between. Like Ava said this morning. "You're insane." I say it because I want it to be true, but I know he's right. I just wish I knew what it meant.

"Did you give yourself that mark?" he asks, pointing to my hand.

"No. I've always had it. I don't even know what it is." *And it's growing now, apparently.*

"You should move in as soon as possible!" he shouts, making me jump. "Don't hesitate!" Then he says under his breath, "This house is protected and hidden from anything that would want to harm you from the spirit world. I have done my due diligence in keeping it covered in wards. You will have no worries anywhere you stand on this property. Stay! And bring your sister as well. Today."

"Today?" A second ago I was figuring I'd have to bargain for a chance to prove myself.

The others look surprised, too.

"We need to make sure you remain in one piece. If the demons find you out, you'll be in bits before sunset." Sid points at Kara. "She'll take you to gather your things and your sister. I'll let Connor or Jax fill you in on the house rules." He leaves the room, whistling as he goes out the back door.

The others stare at me. I can only stare back, trying to get my head together.

I'm moving in. With Ava. My sister will be safe, and with me.

That's all I can focus on right now. Everything else feels too overwhelming. It wasn't something about the demon that made it able to bite me, it was something about *me*. So it won't just be *that* demon. It could be any demon. That could bite me. Claw me.

Kill me.

"We should get going," Kara says, snapping me back.

I look over at her and realize the others have wandered off. It's just her and me and Finger in the room. He's still hypnotized by his game.

"I'm fine," I mumble. "I don't need you to come." I head for the front door.

She follows after me. "Sid says I go, so I go." Even though she says it, she doesn't seem too sure. There's a skittishness in her wide-open gaze as she looks at me now, and she's not getting too close.

I stop before opening the door. "Really, you don't have to be around me. I can see you're freaked."

And she doesn't even know it all.

Imagine how she'd look at me if she knew I could smell her fear in the air, a slight burnt tinge, or see the evidence of every sex partner she's ever had on her skin. She'd run screaming in the other direction.

"I'm not freaked," she says, swallowing. A red spark reflects in her eye.

I raise my brow at her.

"Okay, I'm a little freaked." She grunts. "I'll get over it."

I shake my head. "Fine, come if you want. But know that I can tell when you're lying."

She gapes at me again, but follows. If she thinks *I'm* scary, it'll be interesting to see her reaction when she meets Ava.

EIGHT

It turns out that when Sid said Kara should go with me, he meant she'd drive me. She waves for me to follow her through the kitchen, out the back door, across a long yard. We walk on a dirt pathway through tall weeds—obviously Sid is more concerned with the way the house looks from the front than from the back. A few cans of paint are stacked up beside an old bed frame that rests against a shed.

Earlier, Connor said something about Sid going out to "the shed" to do something. My feet slow a little as I study the small structure. Three heavy padlocks latch it tight, and there's a small circular symbol of power in red paint at the center of the white-washed door. It's a symbol I don't recognize, but I know instantly that it's a lock all its own—an anchor, keeping everything inside the structure tied to this plane. *Grounded.* What the hell would that be needed for?

My mouth goes dry as realization settles in. Casting. Casting magic is performed in that crooked shack. I can't tell from here what type of power is being used, but my stomach feels uneasy anyway.

Kara shouts from the end of the yard, "We need to get this done."

I turn away from the questions I don't want to ask about my new benefactor and follow Kara into the garage.

It takes several seconds for my eyes to adjust to the dark. When they do, my jaw drops at the two gorgeous, shiny cars and the motorcycle.

Kara walks beside the closest vehicle, a sleek black Camaro— probably a '67 or '68.

I can't help smiling as I take it in. "This is *your* car?"

"I wish." She pets the hood, her fingers sliding along the new paint job.

Once we get in, it's obvious the whole thing's been refurbished, from the leather bucket seats to the eight-track player holding a blue tape that says *The Carpenters* on one side.

My smile grows as we back out of the garage, the engine rumbling around us. I don't have to walk, or skate, or ride the heinous bus. It's perfection. I call Ava, but she doesn't answer. My guess is that she's still at her music lessons. I hang up without leaving a message and text her a zero. She'll know that means I'm on my way to find her: time's up.

"My sister's in the summer arts program at Saint Catharine's Academy," I say. The Carpenters in the tape deck are singing about birds and love. "Is there something else to listen to? Do you maybe have anything from this millennium?"

Kara snorts. "Wow. Bashing the jam. Not cool, sir." She pops the eight-track tape out, silencing the groovy bell-bottom orgy. "For your information, Betsy runs better with The Carpenters in her deck."

"Betsy. The car has a name."

Kara pulls into the traffic and puts an earbud back in. "Every car has a name. You just have to find it."

I laugh. "Really. What's that one's name?" I point at a white van ahead of us.

She shakes her head. "You can't seriously expect me to know a stranger's name. I'd have to hang with the thing, get to know it."

I watch her profile, the way her chin juts as she speaks, like she's defending her gift of naming cars. "I see," I say, deciding to play along. "I'm not a car, but maybe you can guess my name." 'Cause, weirdly enough, I realize it hasn't come up yet, not even during that whole meeting with Sid.

She looks sideways at me, like she didn't realize it either until I mentioned it.

"I know we haven't really hung out yet," I say, "but we have, um . . . connected."

She smirks—almost a smile.

It's quiet for a second. Then I say, "So it's more of a vehicular naming power, then?"

She stays silent, but her smirk is definitely a smile now, and warmth fills my fingers and toes with my accomplishment.

"If you can't do it, it's fine," I say, "but at least admit it."

"I'm leaning toward *Asshat*. Am I close?"

I laugh. "You've got the first letter right."

"Points for me."

I see she's not going to ask, so I say, "It's Aidan. Aidan O'Linn."

"I was feeling a lion, actually," she says. "Well, several of them. For your name. I was gonna say Daniel." She glances sideways at me again. "Like Daniel in the lions' den."

My skin tingles. "Daniel," I repeat under my breath. My mom painted that scene on my bedroom wall when I was little. She painted me in the den, lions surrounding me, Daniel a shadowy figure off in the distance. I always wondered why she drew him like that.

Mom runs her hand over the lion's image, like she's pretending its mane is trailing through her fingers. "The lions won't touch you, Aidan. They can't hurt you. God's closed their mouths."

When Mom drew her dream images, she drew a lot of ocean scenes with caves etched out of the side of a cliff, but the only time she mentioned God in relation to it all was the day she painted those lions on my wall. She was a witch, after all. God didn't really come into the picture much.

The familiar weight of the memory presses down on me. I wonder if she was trying to tell me something, to show me my future as she saw it in her fractured mind: danger always surrounding me. Danger only I seem to see.

"Daniel's okay in the end, though," Kara says, like she's sensing my troubled thoughts.

"What?"

"Daniel, in the story. He doesn't get eaten by the lions." She shrugs. "And the king—Dairy Queen or whoever—was so stoked that Daniel was unmarked by the lions that he made the people start worshiping Daniel's god. I guess you could say Daniel was a rock star."

"Is that right?" I know the story—it's ingrained in my soul with all the other sacred texts—but her version is very entertaining. "And it's Darius, not *Dairy Queen*. King Darius."

"Yeah, sure. But did you know that Daniel was the head magician? Who knew they had Harry Potter people in the *Bible*?"

"He was a prophet," I say, correcting her again.

"Whatever you call it, he kicked ass. The guy went into the palace a slave and ended up a Babylonian bigwig. Very inspiring."

It's odd hearing the prophet Daniel talked about like he was some Middle East version of Steve Jobs. "Bigwig, huh?"

"Yep."

"Inspiring?"

"Something like that."

She goes quiet as we merge onto the 101 freeway. I let my mind wander through the ancient worlds and legends in my head as I watch the scenery of the city, the buildings, the funny mismatched moods of art and culture everywhere. Life meets death in the paintings that adorn the concrete walls on either side of the freeway—the artwork of famous people, long dead; some images colorful and new; some overlaid with chaotic graffiti; the names of gang members as big as buses, painted alongside images of children jumping rope.

"So, Aidan O'Linn," Kara says as we pull off the freeway, "what's your sister's name?"

I rest my head on the back of the seat. "Ava."

"And she doesn't have your *talents*?"

"Ava's nothing like me."

Kara seems to know where the school is without me telling her, and after a few more lights we're pulling into the busy parking lot.

"Which side?" she asks. The campus is large, at least two city blocks of buildings and grassy areas.

I scan the faces in the crowd, try to get a feeling for the emotions and energy I'm about to dive into, and point at the back corner of the lot where there aren't as many cars. "Just park back there, under the trees."

"Are we about to kidnap this girl?"

"She's my sister."

"Maybe I should leave the motor running." She parks the car and turns off the engine.

We get out, but I don't move far. Kara's right, this is a little sketchy. And once I take Ava, we'll have to hide—her foster parents will call the police when they realize she's disappeared, and it's not like we can get in touch with them and explain what's going on. Ava's never had to hide, not like me. She's always had a bed, food, and running water. She's never had to depend on me like she's about to.

Kara waits in silence, maybe sensing my nerves.

"She's got music classes. Over there." I point across the parking lot to a building on the west side of campus. "I don't think her foster parents send the car until three thirty because she stays for extra practice hours. So we'll have a good hour to cover our tracks."

"And how are we supposed to do that?"

I chew on my lip, trying to decide if I should tell Kara what I'm about to do. She's going to figure out about Ava eventually. But I really don't want that guy Sid to know anything, or he'll be looking at Ava the way he looked at me: like merchandise. "Just trust me. And don't ask questions."

I bend down, pretending to tie my shoe to buy me a second. I focus my thoughts on Ava, pushing an image of myself out there, into the air, hoping she hears me: *I'm coming.* Then I stand and start toward the west buildings. Kara follows. We move through a line of BMWs and Mercedes-Benzes, and I ignore the stuff around me as much as I can. There's a sleek wraith of a demon to my left following a young girl in a blue blazer who's getting into the back of a black Lincoln; there's a wash of envy and desperation coming from a tall brunette, about sixteen, who's waiting for her ride as she stares down a bouncy blond walking by hand in hand with a guy with floppy hair.

I try to focus on Ava, on where she might be. I can't let her music tutor see me pick her up, so I need her to meet us halfway, maybe near the bathrooms. I picture the hall and the door to the bathrooms as I remember them, and then I push the image out to her as hard as I can.

"You all right?" Kara says.

"Fine." I unclench my fists and try to relax, hoping my messages were received.

"You look like you're about to flip out. I'm not really in the mood to get arrested, so just be aware that I'll deny knowing you if this goes bad."

"Calm down," I mumble, trying to convince myself I'm not freaking out, that the ghost of a young girl in the window to my right isn't making my flesh crawl. That I'm not worried I'll screw this up and the system will swallow both of us again.

Kara looks at me sideways. "Wise words."

We cross a grassy area and walk through an arched walkway with climbing roses. The mood in the air changes with the shift in our surroundings, and the lacy sunlight softens the jagged edges of my nerves.

I glance at Kara; her eyes are half closed, like she can feel the calming energy from this place, too. "Thanks for the ride," I say.

She gives me a questioning look.

"I mean I'm just glad I'm not doing this alone."

She considers me for a second and then says, "It's gonna be fine, kid. Really."

I wish she hadn't said that. Statements like that perk the ears of mischief-makers.

We leave the peaceful archway and go through the double doors, into the wide hall.

Where I collide with a gaggle of chattering girls.

Books fall, squeals erupt, and I lurch away, trying to avoid stepping on any toes, only to lose my balance and land firmly on my ass. Of course.

Kara's quickly distanced herself—she's already down the hall, by the lockers. No one would guess she was with the klutz that just barreled in. The guy trying not to be noticed.

"Ohmygod, you okay?" one of the girls asks.

"You almost broke my phone, you freak!" another one screeches as she tightens her shiny lips and messes with her iPhone.

The third one in the group starts picking up some books. She reaches down with ink-stained fingers to grab the one by my hand—the one that I'm now gaping at: *Art and the Psychic Mind*.

My mom had that book.

A shiver runs over my skin.

The third girl gasps, her hand gripping the spine of the massive tome. "It's you!"

I look up at her, and my lungs stop working.

Rebecca.

Holy shit. I might have said it out loud. I'm not sure.

I'm frozen for a second. And then I'm all movement, scrambling up, grabbing the last few books off the floor, handing them back to her as I babble out an apology. My brain screams at me to get the fuck out of here, and I tense my legs to bolt. But before I can move away, she's suddenly closer, whispering, "How did you find me?" her emerald eyes wide with amazement.

She thinks I'm here for her.

Her copper hair is almost gold in the thin beams of light coming through the doorway behind us now, her skin is milky white, porcelain, and little freckles dot her nose. My heart begins to race as the familiar smell of mango shampoo fills the air.

"You know this freak?" iPhone Girl asks, looking me over like I'm a pile of trash.

The other girl blinks at me and then gives me a crooked grin. "Emery, introduce us," she says, using the middle name from Rebecca's ID—the name she said everyone calls her.

Another girl seems to come from nowhere. "Oh, hey, he's cute. Who's this?"

iPhone Girl smirks. "The asshole who owes me a new phone."

Rebecca just stares at me. "I . . ." She's probably realizing she doesn't know my name.

I'm not about to give it, since I came here for a kidnapping.

"I . . . I met him at a club," Rebecca finally gets out, questions surfacing in her eyes. "SubZero."

iPhone Girl looks doubtful. "Seriously. This guy?"

The other girls just keep smiling. One bites her bottom lip, the second licks a lollypop suggestively, like a bad cliché.

Something seems to dawn on Girl #2, because her eyes get huge. "Oh, God! Is this one of the guys you met the other night? From USC?"

iPhone Girl rolls her eyes. "Does he look like frat meat, Samantha?" She scrunches up her nose like she's smelling garbage again. "More like Reseda Community College."

I turn to Rebecca at the mention of the other guys she met at the club—those guys in the alley. "You knew them," I say without thinking. College boys. How the hell did she get mixed up with a bunch of USC frat boys? Fresh anger rises at my memory of them, at the way they manhandled her, that guy with the mark of murder on his soul . . .

But wait—I don't even really know this girl. I take a breath and push the anger back down.

I need to get Ava.

I point down the hall and start to say, "I've gotta—"

Girl #2 (Samantha, I guess) cuts me off, squealing: "Invite him to the party on Friday, Emery!"

"Oh, yes!" the other girl adds. "We need more boys!"

"Never enough boys," another girl who I hadn't noticed before says as she nods.

Rebecca looks reluctant, but she says, "Sure. I mean, yeah, you should come."

"Oh, please," iPhone Girl groans. "Charity invites will only cause problems with the group, Emery—"

I interrupt, "I can't—I mean, I'm supposed to be . . ." *Shit.* My brain's completely blank as they all surround me. I search the hall for Kara, but she's nowhere in sight.

Samantha grabs the waist of my pants and slides a card in my back pocket. "Text me, and I'll have all the deets, yeah? It'll be epic, I swear." She tucks a piece of dark hair behind her ear, then licks her lollypop again.

iPhone Girl rolls her eyes. "Ohpleasegod, can we go now? I'm supposed to be at Lenox for my appointment at four. It took me six months to get it, and I won't be late because you're all mooning over a ratty Valley reject." She flips her perfectly straight blond hair and walks off.

Her entourage appears to not know what to do.

"We'd better go," one of them says, looking at Rebecca.

"You go ahead," she says.

The rest of the girls whisper and smile at each other, hugging their books to their chests as they walk away. Samantha looks over her shoulder at me as they slip outside and gives me a wink.

I look around the hall for a hole to climb in. "I really have to go," I nearly whine as I start to walk toward the music room. I don't see Kara anywhere.

"Wait." Rebecca steps in front of me.

I try not to notice how touchable she looks in that fuzzy pink sweater.

"How will I find you again?"

"You won't." I force the words, wishing I didn't care about this girl, wishing the smell of her loneliness wasn't making me feel like a shmuck for abandoning her again.

She blinks once. Twice. "Oh."

I want to say, *I'm sorry about your brother*, or ask, *Why was there a demon in your doorway?* but there's nothing more important now than keeping Ava safe.

I can't save everyone.

"Good-bye, Rebecca," I say for the second time.

As her shoulders slump and she turns from me, I see *it*— or, more accurately, its silhouette—through the double doors, standing at the entrance, its horns nearly scraping the wooden beams over its head: a seven-foot demon.

I'm frozen in terror watching Rebecca walk away from me toward the dark beast, unaware. I open my mouth to yell for her to stop, but Kara appears and grabs my arm, freezing the words in my throat.

"Be still," she hisses.

Rebecca walks past the demon.

The beast nods to me in recognition and turns to follow her as crystal fissures of ice spread through my chest.

The demon knows. It knows I can see it.

NINE

"You're freaking me out, Aidan. Snap out of it!" Kara pulls on my arm, trying to get me to move.

"I have to stop her!" I say.

She grips my bicep tighter. "No way. I felt that—whatever that was. And there's no way I'm letting you run after it."

I jerk free, my body in a panic, my feet desperate to chase after Rebecca, to warn her. "But I—"

"We're not here for this," Kara hisses into my ear.

There are footsteps behind us, and we go still as a man passes, looking at us with a frown. He stares more than long enough to get a vivid image for the cops. "There's no fraternizing allowed on campus," he says, studying Kara more closely. "Are you in the art or music program?"

She lets go of my arm and mouths at me, like a secret, *don't move.* Then she turns to the teacher, and, with a slinky smile, she starts to move a little closer. Not much, but enough that a nervous twitch by the man's nose reveals discomfort. She's got an intense look in her eyes that I'm pretty sure isn't good. The air around him begins to shimmer.

What the hell's she doing? She shouldn't be confronting him. Then he'll definitely remember us.

The teacher clears his throat and messes with his collar, like he's looking for a tie to loosen.

"Oh, I'm sorry," she says. "Is this the art building?"

The teacher nods. "If you—"

"I love your shirt. Is it new?" She moves closer.

He makes a slight choking sound, and my skin jolts with his reaction to her. It's not a proper teacher reaction. The air around me feels sticky and wrong. "Kara, what the *hell*?" I say, backing away.

She ignores me, focusing all her energy on him. He doesn't seem to hear me either now. His gaze is fixed firmly on Kara. On her eyes. Like he's hypnotized.

And then I recall the way she made me feel so strange back at Sid's house, and how, when I danced with her in the club, I felt drawn to her and that strange icy-blue energy curling around me.

The mark on her neck—I see it there, pulsing against her skin. And I realize: Kara has a very unhealthy soul talent that she apparently doesn't mind using for her own devices.

"You're a bad man, Mr. Teacher," she whispers. "A very bad man."

He nods, never letting his eyes leave hers. Her intent is pulsing from her in slowly vibrating waves that I can feel the effects of now.

It's suddenly very hard to breathe. Dark urges circle around us. Urges best left under rugs and kept in closets.

I'm about to grab Kara and drag her ass around the corner like a possessive older brother when she leans into the man, touching his chin with her fingertip. "You're going to do what I say, yes?"

He nods again.

"It's time to go home to your wife now. No more lingering in the halls and drooling over English lit girls or touching their sleeves hoping to get a glimpse down their shirts. Got that?"

Again he nods, slow, the dark urges shifting, morphing into a heavy weight. A crease appears in his brow, as if he's remorseful.

"Good," Kara says, moving a little away. "'Cause if you don't, something even worse than me is going to come after your ass."

He swallows, believing her, and the air begins to lift a little.

"One more thing." She points at the room around us. "This hall is empty right now. You never saw a boy here. Okay?"

He shakes his head this time. "Never saw a boy . . ."

"Perfect. Time to head home, Bob." She waves him off.

He blinks and wavers for a second, then walks away, looking a little lost as he heads through the double doors.

"Let's go," Kara says to me, her voice trembling, "before someone else shows up."

"What in God's name did you just do to that guy?" My feet don't want to follow this girl anywhere.

She won't look at me. "Not now, Aidan. Not here." Her skin is sallow. The smell of guilt and sour embarrassment curls into the space between us.

"Are you okay?" I ask.

She blinks up at me, her eyes glassy.

I shift my feet, uncomfortable with the way she's staring at me—like I just handed her something she's never seen before. She starts to speak, but then shuts her mouth tight. I realize that she's warring with herself, too.

After a few seconds she says, "I'll explain. I will. Just not now."

I decide that's the most I'll get from her at the moment and accept what my instincts are telling me: Kara's messed up, but she's not evil.

"Okay," I say. I'm not so sure she'll really tell me, but I'm sure I'll find out the truth eventually—it always has a way of clawing to the surface. And I have secrets of my own, so I get it.

We walk to the end of the wide hall and turn the corner. A door that says *Janitor's Closet* opens.

Ava peeks her head out, and a tiny smile fills her eyes when she spots us. She looks down the hall and then comes out, shutting the door behind her. She slips her hand in mine, and we make our way back to the car as quick as we can without running full throttle.

As Kara pulls out of the parking lot, she keeps looking in the rearview mirror, studying Ava, who's sitting in the center of the backseat, black-and-white oxford shoes bopping up and down, hair in messy white-blond braids, smiling like she just snuck a piece of Halloween candy.

Ava hasn't said anything, but she keeps smiling at me with knowing eyes. Seeing her happy, having her safe with me—all of it makes my chest lighter.

"How old is she?" Kara asks me out of the corner of her mouth as we pull back onto the main street. She's barely watching the road.

"Twelve in a little less than two weeks." Something about Ava is clearly freaking Kara out.

"She doesn't look anything like you," Kara says, sounding annoyed.

"She can hear you, you know."

Kara rolls her eyes.

"She's my half sister."

"So you don't share fathers?" she asks, like it means something.

"No." I frown. "Why?"

Kara shakes her head. "No reason."

But there is a reason—I can tell. "Sure," I say, not really caring. I want to enjoy the relief of having Ava with me as long as I can. "Maybe you can tell me when you explain what happened in that hall with that teacher?"

Her jaw clenches.

That's what I thought.

Ava starts humming "A-Hunting We Will Go," still bopping her oxfords, as we head into our new life.

When we get back to the house, it's nearly sunset. Ava and I close ourselves into the room Kara pointed out for us. The door beside ours shuts as Kara darts inside, obviously not yet recovered from her uneasiness about Ava.

"She seems nice," Ava says. Then she giggles. "Skittish, though."

I shake my head and toss my backpack on the bed closest to the window. "Just be nice to her, okay?" I dig into the bag, pull out a mezuzah, and rest it on the windowsill. I'll place it in the doorway later; for now, it can guard this opening. I rest my hand over the Hebrew symbol for Shaddai and then bring my fingers to my lips.

Ava sets her violin case gently onto the opposite bed. "Do you have a crush on her or something?"

"No way." I lie down on my new bed and study the ceiling. It looks like yellow cottage cheese. But it's safe cottage cheese.

Ava is quiet. I glance across the room at her, not liking the way her silence feels like disapproval.

"Do you want me to have a crush on her?" I ask.

"No way!" she says in an overly forceful tone. She flips her shoes off and curls her legs under her. There's a hole in her white stockings at the knee and a little scab on her skin there, like she fell. Or was pushed. "I wouldn't want you anywhere near that girl if I could help it."

"Wow," I say. "Don't hold back. Tell me how you really feel."

She sighs and leans against the wall. "Never mind. Just be careful."

"She's fine. Not a great first-impressionist, but she's harmless."

"Hardly. You can't trust her, Aidan." She frowns as she picks a wool string from the hem of her skirt. "She could hurt you real bad."

Here we go. "Thanks, but I can take care of myself, Peep. It's not your job to protect me."

"Yes, it is." She starts wrapping the red string round and round the tip of her finger.

I take in a deep breath and let it out slow.

Ava pulls another string from her skirt and begins the process of winding it onto another finger. Then another. I find myself closing my eyes and drifting off. Suddenly she asks, "Can we paint the room purple?"

I roll over to stare out the window. I look down into the yard next door and watch a small dog play with a stuffed toy on the neighbor's porch. I try not to think about how hiding Ava's abilities might become impossible very soon, and I wonder what Kara will tell Sid about my strange sister. She obviously had some issue with her.

Not to mention that the demon haunting Rebecca knows I can see it.

I shove all that down and tell myself not to worry about it right now. We're safe. It's such a rare feeling—however short-lived it'll be. I let myself revel in it for a few breaths.

I close my eyes, realizing there's dangerous hope in feeling safe, like I'm almost a normal boy. Lies. Such lovely lies.

Rebecca's soft features rise into my thoughts again, and I don't stop them. I drink in the dream of her, the simple idea of boy meets girl. If she was here—if I was normal—I'd talk to her about the books she's read, what she wants to study in college. I'd lose myself in the sound of her voice and ask if I could hold her hand.

And with that dream in my head, I drift off to sleep.

———

Mom's kneeling in the sand, her skirt damp from the tide pools, her grimoire tucked under her arm. She's always kept the tattered book close by since the day she told me I'd be a big brother. Everything is vibrant around us, colors bright and full of life: the blue of the sky, the green of the sea, the alabaster foam chasing up the shore.

Mom lifts a small starfish to show to me, the shadow of a smile on her lips. "She got lost. Can you put her back on the rocks over there?" She points to the black giants emerging from the tide behind us.

I stand and take the creature from her, feeling the bumpy surface against my fingers as the moist suckers tickle my palm. I watch the waves crash against the rocks. They sound like they're trying to beat them back into the sea. The impact vibrates the soft ground under my feet. How can that be safer?

"Don't worry, Aidan," she says, sounding sad. "That's where she belongs."

TEN

There's banging. I sit up with a jolt, disoriented.

"Get up, farkwad!" someone yells though the door. Sounds like that Jax guy. "Morning family meeting. Assholes and elbows!"

I run a hand over my eyes, trying to wipe the fog of sleep away. It's late morning. I can tell from the high sunlight streaming in through the window. Damn, I haven't slept that sound for a whole night in forever. For the last few months I've been crashing in an abandoned warehouse where my hourly alarm clock was a family of rats that liked poking around what little shit I had with me.

Ava's sitting on her bed, her back against the wall. She's squinting at a book that's open on her lap, reading intently. "They're going on a job," she says.

"What?"

"That rude boy." She puts her finger on the page to hold her place and looks up at me. "He says there's a meeting. They're going to talk about one of their jobs."

My pulse picks up. I'm not ready to work with these people—whatever it is that they actually do. I still don't have a good grip on what goes on around here exactly, who I can trust, and what'll be expected of me. My guard will be up way too high to be any help to anyone.

"Shouldn't you go down?" she asks.

"You stay here."

"I know."

I stand and slip my shoes on. "What're you reading?"

"You don't wanna know."

Unease fills me. "I don't?"

She shuts the book and holds it up. At first glance it looks like any other leather journal, a little worn at the edges, its binding stretched to near breaking from all the pieces of paper and dried leaves and stems glued inside. Then I see the faded marking on the cover: the sixth pentacle of Jupiter from the *Key of Solomon*, for protection against all earthly elements. The key has been burned into the brown leather. "*Thus shalt thou never perish*" is written in Latin around the circle.

Mom's grimoire.

Her blood is in that book. Her tears. Her rage. Her terror. All left behind. *Never to perish.* Protected from anything this earth could do to it.

"How could you bring that here?" I ask, turning cold with fear and fury. "You were supposed to get rid of it!"

I told Ava to bury it after the Marshalls died. She said she would, and I trusted her. I'd have buried it myself, but every time I touch it, my skin starts crackling like it's about to catch fire. It would take dark magic to break the key. And I don't go there. Not ever.

Ava sighs, as if I'm the small child and don't understand adult things yet. "I did, Aidan. I swear. I buried it. Three times."

"So why's it in my face right now?" I look at her closely, but she's the only person I can't read when it comes to lies.

"Every time I buried it I woke up the next morning covered in dirt, the grimoire back in my hand. I think I was digging it up in my sleep. After it happened the third time, I didn't see the point in burying it anymore."

"Why didn't you tell me?"

She shoves the book back into her bag. "It's between me and Mom."

"Mom's dead, Ava."

Her lips thin. "Maybe. But pieces of her are still here. That's why I've been reading it. I need to know if she's evil. If I should be listening to her or not."

I want to tell her—*Mom nearly got you killed with her magic; she's the reason we're running*! But I can see it all happening again, repeating in my sister. The darkness is gaining a foothold in her. Or maybe my fears are right, maybe it's been there the whole time, slumbering in her skin since the moment that demon scratched her, my mom's heart still in its other claw.

"Please don't read it again," I say, "until I can figure some things out. Until we get settled and we know we're safe." I try not to listen to the voice in my head that reminds me it's pointless to stop her reading it now—she probably has the whole thing memorized already.

She rubs her nose and releases a sigh. "If that's what you want." She sets the book to the side and picks up her violin. "I'll wait for now." Then she sits up straight and slides the bow across the strings, beginning to draw out a quick, frantic tune that seems to match exactly with my insides.

———

They're all downstairs in the kitchen. Jax and Lester are sitting at the table, Holly's buttering a piece of very nutty toast and tapping the toe of her red shoes to a silent rhythm, her ribbon-braided hair swinging across her back. Connor is standing beside Kara, who's perched on the counter. A faint pump of music comes from her, and I notice she's got her earbuds back in.

She doesn't look up when I enter. Connor does, though. He leans in closer to her, looking protective. The action makes me instantly like the guy—which is good, 'cause my readings are muddy as hell in this house. Probably because of the protections against demons and ghosts that Sid mentioned. But it's going to make getting a bead on these souls that live here a lot tougher. I'll need to be that much more cautious.

It occurs to me that that's probably the reason I didn't realize Mom's grimoire was nearby.

But I don't want to think about that anymore.

Jax brightens at the sight of me. "Ah, the Chosen One has returned!" he says in a very dramatic voice. "The One who shall be the most powerful!"

I give him a look that I hope says: *Shut the fuck up, ass face.*

"Can you really see 'em?" Lester asks, biting on his lip, like he's nervous. "Like *see* 'em, see 'em? With your eyes?"

Jax laughs. "No, he sees them with his butt—what the hell's wrong with you?"

Holly takes a bite of her sandpaper toast with a loud crunch, watching us all like she's solving a puzzle.

"Well, Sid sure is thrilled," Lester says, ignoring Jax. "You'd think we found the pot a' gold at the end of a rainbow."

Someone snorts, and I notice Finger in the corner by the refrigerator, watching the exchange.

Connor leans close to me and asks under his breath, "Is what you said true?"

I study him for a second. This guy has seen his own set of horrors, I'm fairly certain. On the outside he looks like your typical California dude, but there's not a lazy bone in him. He's all business, this one.

I wonder what happened for him to find his way off the street and into this clan of misfits. It's hard to picture him as the drug dealer Sid said he was.

I nod, looking him right in the eye, so he sees that I get how serious this all is, too. I want to ask him about his gift—or *curse*. How he reads the past of an object, what it's used for. But I figure I'll find out soon enough.

Sid comes in, and the room falls into nervous silence. Sid looks us all over like he's proud of what he's collected. "I'd like to wrap up the Reese job tonight, boys." He glances at Kara and Holly. "And ladies." Kara pulls the earbuds out and hunches her shoulders. Again I feel annoyance toward my new benefactor without knowing why. Then I catch Connor glaring at him and realize I'm not the only one.

Sid has a suit on again—a different one, but the same style: no jacket, rolled-up sleeves, silk pin-striped vest. He holds his walking stick loosely in his left hand. A bolo hat tops his bald head to round out the look.

He starts talking again. "Day two of filming's tonight, and we have several things still to get in the can. Remember the details: a haunting—could be psychosomatic, keep that in mind."

He directs his next words at me. "The subject of the haunting is a boy, about nine or ten. Marcus. His parent is a single mother, and he's the only child. No male in residence. There are several key components we see a lot in this type of case. One: a recent trauma—in this case, job loss. Two: only the child in the house is encountering the manifestations. And three: the land is a frequent kill site. There've been several reported murders over the decades on the land where the apartment complex is located. Might even be a place of sacrifice."

My pulse picks up speed, realizing by that one statement that this guy really knows his spirit rules—rules I've known as long as I can remember, like they're ingrained in my DNA. I've never actually met anyone that understands these things like I do—but then, maybe I just don't get out enough.

Sid continues, "I told the client we'd be there after seven. Connor, you text me when you're on-site ready to go."

Connor nods.

"The camera crew will meet you about forty-five minutes after eight, so we can get shots of the internals, and I can do the mother's interview. Plus, a few shots of the dead circle."

I speak up before I realize I shouldn't. "Camera crew? What the hell's that mean?"

Jax winks at me. "It means you're gonna be a star, Pretty Boy."

"Jax," Sid says with a warning in his voice. Then he turns to me. "We always film our cases, Aidan. It's nothing to worry about. We have a budding YouTube channel—you may have heard of it: *Paranormal Truth*. Our *Queen Mary* case has more than three hundred thousand hits."

"The sitch we filmed at the Hollywood sign was my fave," Holly says. She takes her last bite of toast and adds, "Mostly 'cause Jax practically peed his pants when the EVP said his name afterwards. That was some fan-friggin-tastic television."

"No, that was fucking scary shit," Jax says, like he's trying to defend his fear.

"Language." Sid scowls at him then nods to Connor, who turns and pulls a jar off the counter. He holds it out to Jax.

Jax rolls his eyes and reaches into the jar, pulling out a small white paper.

"Read it aloud," Sid orders.

"Ten lines of Hamlet," Jax says, sounding annoyed. He tosses the paper back into the jar.

"By tomorrow," Sid says. "Written and oral." Then he turns to me to explain. "Foul language will earn you a recitation that will grow your vocabulary. Positive reinforcement. Got the idea from this supernanny; she's a genius." He gives me a quick smile. "But as to the filming, if you don't want to be a part of it, that's fine. We also have a possible deal in the works with a production company, but we can always leave your part of it on the cutting room floor." He leans in and gives me a look, like he senses why I'd be worried about it—even though I'm not sure why myself. "I don't leave trails to follow either," he says.

My gut churns.

"But don't just observe," he adds. "Feel free to speak up about what you see or feel on this one. Let's see your stuff, Aidan." He knocks me on the arm with his cane, the crystal ball at the tip thudding into my muscle. I bite my tongue as he walks out of the kitchen.

Once Sid clears hearing distance, Jax says under his breath, "Yeah, let's see what you can do, newb." And then he swings back to punch me on the shoulder.

I grab his wrist before his fist catches my arm.

The room goes still, all eyes on me.

Surprise, then alarm, fills Jax's features when I don't release him right away.

"I'm just playing, man." He fake laughs. "Shit!"

I let go and back up. I'm used to other boys trying to kick my ass; I'm used to having to defend myself, and I'm good at it. But I see in Jax's eyes that he's telling the truth—just a joke, no harm intended. I say what comes to the tip of my tongue anyway. "Touch me again and I break your fingers."

Lester releases a low whistle.

Jax chuckles nervously. "Wow, Kara, I think we finally found your soul mate."

And then they all laugh—even Finger's shoulders shake. Not Kara and Connor, though. Those two just keep looking at me, Connor with curiosity and Kara with growing anger.

Holly starts to sing, "Kara and Aidan sitting in a tree, K-I-S-S-I-N-G . . ." as she dances from the room in a blur of colorful clothes.

Lester follows, giggling. Jax walks past smiling and flipping the bird in my direction.

Finger disappears like magic. For such a large guy, he's silent as a ghost.

Connor comes up to me, looks me over, and then says, "We meet at the van, in the back. Six thirty. A minute late, and you stay home." He stares at me for a tick longer than is normal—like an alpha dog—and then turns and walks away.

Kara's the only one left. She doesn't move off her perch on the counter, looking down at her boots. There's a skull painted in what looks like Wite-Out on the toe of the left shoe.

"Hey," I begin, hoping I don't regret trying to explain this, but knowing I need to get it out of the way, "I could tell Ava kind of freaked you out. She can be—"

Kara hops down off the counter, stopping the words in my throat with her sharp glare. "Just stay away from me," she says. "Both of you." There's no trace of fear in her words or on her face, but I feel it, like a razor against my skin. It's the only thing I've felt in this house since I got here yesterday.

She walks past me, putting the earbuds back in, and a strange foreboding fills me as I watch her go.

Not a good way to start my new life.

ELEVEN

It's nearly seven thirty at night by the time we get to the apartment. I leave Ava at the house with Holly—reluctantly. There's no way she could have come with me. I know I can't watch her every second, but I feel like I need to. Ava pushed me out the bedroom door, saying I was being ridiculous, that I'd only be gone for a few hours and she'd be fine.

But I'm not sure I trust that house yet. I'm not sure if I trust Sid's protective measures. And I've only just gotten her back.

When I talked to Holly about keeping a close eye on things, she frowned at me and asked, "Isn't your sister, like, eleven?"

"She's almost twelve."

Holly laughed and shrugged. "Sure. I'll watch out for her," and then she walked away mumbling, "Hyperprotective much?"

But I didn't feel any bad vibes from her, so I decided to loosen my grip a bit and trust Sid that the house was protected. Plus, it won't be until Ava's actual birthday that the demons come.

We reach the apartment complex off Balboa. The van pulls into the alley, parking in the rear garage. I try to make myself stop worrying—I need to focus on getting this right. Don't let them see too much, but let them see enough to win their favor. Sid seems to have pretty high expectations from the sound of it.

The boys all start piling out and unloading the equipment, obviously having done this hundreds of times. Connor and Kara disappear through the gate, entering the building's poorly lit courtyard.

The apartment complex is small, old. Most likely built in the sixties, but obviously rebuilt, probably after the Northridge quake in '94. It's surrounded by wrought iron and fir trees.

"Hey!" Connor yells from the van. "Make yourself useful." He tosses me an orange extension cord and points for me to follow Lester, who's walking next to Jax through the back iron gate.

I trail behind and follow directions as the boys set up video and audio in the courtyard. I don't ask any questions as the lights are positioned and a small area is cleared for a table and computers. I just do what I'm told and keep my mouth shut.

Connor talks to the camera crew when they get there, three guys who look more like hipster coffeehouse rejects than a serious crew, but what do I know about Hollywood? After he gives them some instructions on how small the apartment is, a timeline for the night, and descriptions of what kind of "frames" and "moods" he's looking for, he waves for me to follow him.

Kara's standing in a tiny alcove patio, which is really just a slab of concrete decorated with a cracked pot spilling over with wilted pansies. She's got her back to me, facing a blond woman, and they're passing a cigarette back and forth like they've bonded already. The orange tip glows in the dark.

The blond woman looks like she's in her midthirties, but as I get closer, something tells me she's more like midtwenties. Her hair is dull and brittle, her skin is leathery, and her shadowed eyes are full of confusion, like she's not sure how she got here.

Kara spots Connor and me. She takes one last drag from the cigarette and grinds it into the pot of drooping pansies.

Connor and Kara trade looks, and I can see the silent conversation in their faces:

Seriously, Kara?

Lay off, Connor.

Connor nods to the blond woman. "Miss Reese, thank you for being so flexible with the schedule. We'll try to make this session simpler than when we did the day shoot. We just need to get a few more questions on film and do our dead circle so Kara can be sure about her reading before giving it to you. Mr. Siddhapati will be here in the next ten minutes or so, and he can finish off the interview with you as soon as you're ready." He motions to me. "This is our new trainee. Is it okay if he follows Kara on her walk-through?"

Miss Reese barely looks at me. "Sure, whatever. Will it cost me more?" She gives a weak—but still somehow flirtatious—smile to the crew behind me.

"No," Connor says. "The price Mr. Siddhapati quoted you is what it'll be. Not a penny more."

She nods and pulls out another cigarette with shaky fingers. "I need sleep."

Connor gives her an understanding look. "We'll try to finish this up tonight and get you the peace you need, Miss Reese."

"Or your money back," comes from behind us. Sid's voice. He waves to the camera crew, and they scramble across the now perfectly lit courtyard to obey. They place the cameras firmly on their shoulders, and one guy follows Sid with a boom mic raised high overhead.

"Ah, Miranda," Sid says, "you poor thing. You didn't get any sleep again last night?" He takes Miss Reese's fingers in his, and her face loses its tension immediately. "I'm so sorry," he says as he pats her hand. "We'll fix this mess up by the morning, I promise."

Tears fill her eyes, and she nods again.

He pulls her in for a fatherly hug. "You'll be fine." Then he motions at the camera crew, and they lower their aim.

Watching him is fascinating. His words and actions feel so close to the truth that I almost buy his sincerity. Stunning.

I try and get a better bead on him, his soul, away from the muted fog of the house, but Connor taps my arm and motions for me to follow Kara as she slips away.

So I turn from my curiosity and comply, figuring there'll be plenty of time for reading Sid. I follow Kara to the door of the downstairs apartment on the end. The smell of dryer sheets fills the air; it mingles with stale cigarette smoke and mildew as she reaches for the doorknob.

A buzz of lingering violence reaches my skin. I really don't want to feel this. I hate knowing people's business, especially the dark kind—which is all I ever seem to see lately.

Kara stops before she opens the door. She glances behind me, maybe checking to see if we're alone, and then she says, "Just so we're clear: I don't like you."

There's a fierce look in her eyes.

"I mean I *really* don't like you."

"You mentioned that."

"But we have to work together. So I'll suck it up. But you should know where you stand."

Her hostility is taking me off guard. I'm fairly certain she's not the kind of girl you want on your bad side.

I raise my hands in surrender. "I'm reading you. Loud and clear. For some mysterious reason, you now hate me." Even though I'm pretty sure it has something to do with Ava. Kara's barely said two words to me since meeting my sister.

She looks to the side like she's searching for something and chews at the corner of her lip.

"Shouldn't we start the torment of working together now?" I ask.

"What's your deal?"

"You're the one with the deal, Kara. You've given me the ice treatment since I moved in. Apparently the kiss at the club the other night was a mistake. I get it. Apparently you're freaked out about my sister. Whatever. Can we just move on?"

She opens her mouth to speak and then closes it. After a second she says, "Fine. We have to work together, so we'll call a truce. Just keep yourself out of my space."

I have no idea how those two things are mutually possible, but I nod in response anyway. "Sure. Got it."

"And if this is gonna work, you need to tell me everything you see. Everything."

"Sure." *Not*. I study her, trying to figure out how to balance this, trying to find something trustworthy about her that I can connect with. "I'll tell you what I see," I say more gently, shoving away my frustration. She revealed parts of herself at the school to save me, so maybe I can peel back a layer or two of my own for her in return—an olive branch of sorts.

She nods, looking more lost than nervous now. "We need to focus—I need to focus." She turns and opens the door.

I let my internal walls down reluctantly, step into the apartment after her, and hold my breath, waiting for the first blow.

A wave of nausea hits me, then there's prickling against my skin, like something pulling on my arm hairs.

"It's Kara, Marcus," she calls into the apartment. "Are you here?" She whispers to me, "Marcus is the kid. He's the one stuff keeps happening to, his mom says. Nightmares, night terrors, shadows. Typical stuff."

"What do you think it is?" I whisper back.

She shrugs. "Negative energy for sure."

All I can do is pray it's not a demon. I don't have anything but some salt and sacred dirt in my pocket, the *hamsa* I got from Hanna—which isn't much good in a fight—and my old Star of David amulet that my mom gave me. The last thing I need is another demon figuring out I can see it and trying to make me its lunch.

Looking at the Other realm, opening myself up wide in front of strangers, isn't on the top of my to-do list. It's like being naked in a pit of snakes. But it's too late to turn back now.

I look around, collecting my thoughts. There's a maroon vinyl couch with cigarette burns on its left arm. The walls and ceiling are yellow from smoke. The carpet is shag—green and ratty. A weak light shines in the corner, and the muted TV plays Nick at Nite. A crucifix hangs over the doorway to the hall, and there's a dent in the drywall to my right that looks suspiciously like a fist. Echoes of past anger tinge the air.

My own memories of bruises and punctured drywall swirl through my head.

Mom grabs the man's arm. "Stop, Frank, please. Leave Aidan be."

The man turns, like a spring being released, his fist colliding with her delicate features in a meaty thud. "Shut up, bitch!"

I shake it off and bury the memories as far down as they can go, not wanting to attract whatever's in this place.

Kara pauses as we come to the hall and says, "Marcus, I have a friend with me. Can we come in?"

I wait behind Kara, watching the dark hallway.

"You shouldn't have come back," someone says from the other side of the farthest door, a little boy.

My heart stutters at the sound of the small voice, at the fear in it.

The door opens and a brown-haired head peeks out. "I think it's angry from the last time. When you guys left the other night it got real bad."

Kara ignores the comment. "Marcus, so good to see you. Can you come chat with us on the couch, buddy?"

Marcus steps out farther. There's a Superman comic book gripped in his fist. "Yeah, sure." He sighs and pauses to glance up at me through thick-lensed glasses. "Who's that?" He's wide open as can be, his colorful energy reaching out in curiosity—no trepidation, no fear, just innocent vulnerability. He's got no walls at all.

No wonder the stuff is touching him. It sees his soul like an invitation to connect. It might even be using his energy to manifest.

"This is Aidan," Kara says.

We move to the couch, and Marcus and Kara sit down. I turn off the TV and settle in a chair across from them.

Marcus studies me for a second before turning to Kara. "Isn't the camera stuff done yet?"

"Sorry, bud, just one more run-through. We shouldn't be long. And you already did your talking with Sid, so we're good. In a few days you can tell the camera if we did our job or not, okay?"

He kicks at the shag carpet with his shoe. "Yeah. Okay. But I'm not sure the ghost is gonna leave now." He starts chewing on his bottom lip and rolling the comic book tighter.

"What'd it do?" I ask quietly.

Kara gives me a look; obviously she wasn't expecting me to talk.

"It was throwing stuff around. My mom's mirror broke."

"Does it scare you?" I ask. He doesn't seem terrified like most kids would be. Mostly just annoyed at Kara and everyone being here again.

"Why do you think it got mad?" Kara asks, which is what I was wondering.

Marcus shrugs, looking evasive. "It's just that you're not helping none. And it makes my mom real mad when stuff happens. She yells at me and makes me sleep in her room on the floor."

Kara frowns at his words. "Why didn't you tell us last time how your mom reacts?"

"'Cause she wasn't too bad off," he whispers. "And . . . well . . ." He shrugs again.

Kara and I share a look.

"Does she hurt you, Marcus?" Kara asks, sounding a little like a social worker.

The kid looks at her like he's thinking the same thing, his energy closing off some. "She just gets mad is all. Like always."

Kara takes the hint and asks him about his comic book. He lights up immediately at that and begins telling her a million things in rapid succession about how the villain gave Superman red kryptonite. I motion to Kara that I'm going to walk around, and she nods, then goes back to listening to Marcus's story of red kryptonite and fast cars as Superman goes rogue.

I slip into the first room across the hall. There's an ocean of laundry on the floor. The bed is nearly stripped, only a sheet and a pillow on it. Surfaces are mostly bare, and things are scattered on the floor—lotions, cheap jewelry, candles, nail polish—like they got swept off the dresser.

I take a deep breath and place my hand on the wall as I try to look deeper.

A flash of red and a scream. I stumble back a little but hold firm to the feeling coming at me, pull on it a little to maybe see more.

A kitchen knife falling to the carpet, covered in blood.

Screaming, screaming, screaming her throat raw.

I close my eyes tight and try to get a better, clearer image, but all I can see is the red flashing over and over and the knife, the woman's screams. It doesn't feel recent. It must be something from another resident. Not this boy, not this woman. But whatever happened has left its mark. It's still echoing. The red energy of death.

Sid did say it was a kill site. That usually means there's been more than one murder in the same spot over the years—again and again—caused by some dark energy that attached itself to the area a long time ago.

Energy that attracts all kinds of things.

I walk out and into Marcus's room, slowly. The emotions hit me like a kick to the center of my chest, and I see the hint of a shape on the other side of the bed, sheer white energy swirling over the spot.

The air's sucked from my lungs; I have to grip the wall to hold myself up.

The thing's not happy to see me. A female spirit, young when she died. She tried so hard to please everyone, but Robert was never happy, not even after she quit her job. And then the night came when she let her guard down and burnt the dinner. Frank didn't like the smell. He bared his teeth and called her vile names. Then he took hold of the steak knife and stabbed her with it. Fifteen times. Right in front of their son.

It all comes at me as an onslaught of knowledge and anger, like watching a movie play out in a flickering rush.

I don't look at the spirit, not straight on. But I think she senses my awareness anyway, because her energy crackles at the air around me. She doesn't like all the commotion that's been going on. She doesn't like what it's doing to the boy.

Of course.

She's protecting the boy.

"We won't let anything happen to him," I whisper, and the crackling subsides a little.

"Who are you talking to?"

I turn to see Sid standing in the shadows of the hall, watching me.

My pulse speeds up. I'm not used to people being aware of what I can do.

Apparently I need to get over that now.

I walk out of the room into the hall, thinking if Sid goes in there the female spirit will become agitated again.

"I'm doing what you wanted me to," I say under my breath. I can't seem to keep the nerves from my voice, though. I feel myself shivering even as I look down at the carpet.

"Don't let it overwhelm you," he says gently. Almost fatherly.

I glance up at him, surprised.

He leans closer. "You're letting it in. Stay outside of it, Aidan. There's a difference between seeing it and being in it."

I pause, thinking about what he just said. "How am I supposed to see it if I don't open myself up?"

"It's all about balance. We'll work on that later. I promise. But for now, just take a few deep breaths and focus your energy on relaxing. You keep so many guards up, always so tense. There's a lot of energy expended on living that way. It's easier to see things when you're centered and calm." He looks me over like he's studying my clothes, but I have the feeling he's seeing past that, straight into me. "You're not balanced at all, kid. We need to work on that."

Before I can ask him what he means, the camera crew comes in the front door to the apartment, and my nerves are back on edge.

"Deep breaths," Sid mumbles as he turns to greet them.

After that it's a bit chaotic. Most of my energy is spent feeling protective of the boy, Marcus. I sit with him on the couch as the cameras and lights are set up.

"So how long have you lived here?" I ask him.

He scratches his nose and shrugs. "Not long."

I consider what it is that I need to know, then ask, "When did you first see her?"

He blinks up at me, maybe realizing I understand. "Mom's last boyfriend gave me a BB gun, and he used to take me out to shoot soda cans back in the hills; it made Mom real mad." He lowers his voice and leans closer. "She threw a glass at his head one time and the cops came. Millie—the white lady—she came after that. I don't think she likes my mom."

Understanding filters in. "How do you feel about her?"

"My mom? She's fine." He scratches his nose again then starts picking at a string coming from a tear in his jeans. "I just wish she was happy, like other moms."

The sting of his pain suddenly feels very personal. I clear my throat, not wanting to show it. "What about the spirit? Are you sometimes scared of her?"

"No, I like her. She makes me feel better about stuff." Then he bows his head as weighty guilt spills from his shoulders.

"I'm sorry, Marcus," I say. "My mom was real sad, too."

He sniffs and nods again. Then he leans into me, pressing his side against mine, like he's looking for comfort.

I release a sigh to let go of some of the tension that's winding itself into a ball in my chest. When I look up, Sid is watching Marcus and me intently, and I realize that I'm boxed in. How can I let them get rid of the spirit if it's protecting the boy from his mom? But if I botch this job then I might be out on the street again with a dependent sister who has demons coming after her in a few days. I can't let that happen, obviously.

So Marcus will be left to his fate.

TWELVE

After a while I feel Marcus grow limp beside me. His head rests on my arm, and soon his comic book slips from his fingers to the floor. Kara motions for me to move, and we situate him so he's curled against the other side of the couch, resting soundly.

She whispers to me, "Come talk for a sec," and I follow her past a camera and into the tiny hall. She leans close. "What did you see?"

I'm still not sure what her thoughts are about it all, so I ask, "What do you think I saw?"

"Is this a game show? Tell me what the hell you saw so we can get this dead circle done right and get the hell out of here with the cash."

"What is this dead circle thing everybody keeps talking about?"

She rolls her eyes. "It's where we do a spell to get rid of whatever *thing* we're casting out. We use infrared cameras and everything; it's all very dramatic. Now tell me what you saw."

Magic? "Messing in spells only makes things worse," I say. "Trust me."

She frowns, looking like she's taken off guard by my words, but then she says, "It's like tricks, Aidan. That's all. We draw symbols and chant, and the people get a show. Usually it's a simple thing that pushes the ghost, or whatever, out. Trust me, Sid can tell us how to get rid of whatever's here. He may not be able to read much spiritually anymore, but he can sure file away info."

"Sid tells you how to cast it out?"

"Sid knows all. He's got so much stuff in that bald head of his it's a wonder he can balance the thing on that short body." She gives a quick, stiff smile then demands, "Now what in God's name did you see?"

"A ghost."

"No shit, Sherlock. Like I don't know that."

I sigh and glance around to be sure no one's listening in. Sid is still interviewing the mother on camera, and Connor's taking notes on a little tablet. So I lean closer and whisper in Kara's ear, "I think the mom is abusing the kid. The spirit seems to be protecting him by tormenting the mother."

When I move back, her hair brushes my cheek and fills my head with the smell of vanilla and coconut. I hesitate, thrown off by the rush of emotions that follow—emotions coming from her: fear, curiosity, and need.

I clear my throat and try to pretend like I didn't just feel her insides, but I can't look her in the face when I add, "The ghost died here about thirty years ago. Stabbed by her husband. She had a child around the same age as Marcus."

Kara glances over to the activity in the other room. "So that's why Marcus isn't afraid of the ghost. The mom kept saying she wasn't getting any sleep 'cause Marcus was having nightmares and his bed was shaking. But then when I talked to him, he said it never bothered him. I thought maybe Marcus was trying to be macho or something."

"No, he's telling the truth."

She sighs and looks toward Marcus's room.

"We should go in there now," I say. "Before the others. I can tell you what I see, and hopefully we can figure out what to do."

She frowns at me. "What do you mean? We do the job. End of story."

I study her. Maybe she's been burned too much to let herself care. "If the ghost goes, Marcus'll be vulnerable."

A thread of anxiety and then anger weaves through the air between us. "This isn't a game," Kara says. "We do the job."

———

"Okay, Kara, what have you got?" Sid asks. He, Connor, Kara, and I sit at the table where the mom was being interviewed.

"Simple ghost, no cementing, no problems. It's got an attachment to the boy, but I don't see anything we can't get rid of."

I glare at her from across the table, wondering why she's lying to him.

Sid turns to me. "What about you, Aidan?"

"Yeah." I take a deep breath, still trying to decide what to do. "It's a ghost. And it's attached to the boy."

"So you and Kara agree?" This seems to make him almost giddy. "Wonderful."

I clear my throat and add, "Except . . ." Kara is giving me an impassive look, but I can feel her fear, and it makes me pause. What's she afraid of? Me or Sid? "Well, I also think there might be something the mother needs help with."

"What's that?" Sid asks.

Kara's fear grows thicker, and I'm second-guessing saying anything at all.

"Apparently she has a bad temper," Kara finishes for me.

Sid laughs. "We're not social workers. We're here to fumigate. That's it."

Kara gives me a *see, I told you so* look, but the air around her is shivering.

Sid nods, looking satisfied that we're back on track. "So this is a basic job, guys. A simple block is all we need, or if we're feeling generous, we can send the thing into the afterlife. For the cameras, the dead circle will include a few chants and some dramatic questioning to the spirit. I'll have Kara do the smudge for this shoot. She's always so much more graceful at it than you, Connor, no offense."

A smile tugs at the corner of Connor's mouth. "None taken."

Sid turns to me. "Your job, Aidan, is to make sure it's working. The dead circle will be in here, so you'll sit in the other room and make sure the spirit is done away with. Do you think you can manage that?"

I nod, my heart sinking. I could probably help the boy by protecting the woman's spirit. I could lie, saying it's done. Except that Sid'll hear about it from the Reese lady, and it would hurt the ghost-hunting business—which apparently pays all the bills. I won't be on Sid's good side anymore after that, that's for sure.

I need to focus on the goal—my *one* goal—to keep Ava safe. Nothing else. And I need Sid to help me with that for now.

"Wonderful!" He smiles and pats my shoulder. "Kara, you get the boys in here. Aidan, you and Jax can make a space for the circle. And I'll collect the supplies from the van. Let's get this done."

Connor shows the camera guys where the angles should be while the rest of us follow directions. Sid goes outside with a small vial of something clutched in his hand. I watch for a while as the cameras begin recording. The others hold hands and chant things that sound vaguely like a section of the Apocrypha in really bad Latin, something about the levels of the heavens—it's obvious they have no clue what they're saying. Kara stands in the center of the three boys, lighting the smudge and waving the herbs before each of them, and then she walks the circle to mark it with the smoke.

There's a small shift in the air after that, and I catch Sid from the corner of my eye pressing what looks like an oil-coated finger to the jamb of the glass slider, his lips moving.

He pauses and glances at me then shoos me away, into the boy's bedroom.

When I enter, the white energy is thinner, greyer. There's less fight in the spirit now. She's weak, searching for her little boy.

I close my eyes and sink to the floor, my back against the dresser. "I'm sorry," I whisper. "I'm sorry for what happened to you."

Anguish washes over me like a thick black wave, and I'm not sure if it's hers or mine. It tugs me down, pulling me toward something, like a precipice, and I realize I'm feeling her leaving, sinking away to the place beyond, where the dead belong.

"You'll be free there," I say, even though I'm not completely sure of that.

And then she's gone, slipping away into the mystery that is death. And I'm not sure how to feel. Because now Marcus is next in line to become a victim of this cursed place.

THIRTEEN

When it's done, I keep my mouth shut and follow orders as we clean up. No one asks me if I felt like the chanting worked. Sid's talking to the mother and son outside, telling them someone will be back in a day or two for the afternoon shoot where they do the "post interview" about how it feels since LA Paranormal Investigative came and saved them from the wicked ghost.

My stomach hurts—I can't look at the boy. I avoid his eyes whenever he glances my way.

When everything's put back into place, Sid waves me over. "You'll ride home with me."

And so while all the others are piling into the van with Connor, I follow Sid to a bright orange Mustang convertible, black top up, with a white pinstripe along the side and white-rimmed tires. This wasn't one of the cars in the garage. I can't help being impressed.

"Wow."

"You like old cars?" Sid asks, smiling at me over the hood.

I nod and open the door, slipping inside. It smells like new leather and Armor All.

"I just got it back from the shop," he says. "I hardly ever drive because it makes me terribly anxious, but this gem of a machine can't just sit in a shop forever. I had the interior completely restored." He points at the black dashboard. "Except for the instruments. Got a Bose stereo system and Gizmo-Nav. All digital gauges."

"Wow," I say again. It's completely beautiful. All the green lights and dials and perfectly placed instruments. "It's really nice." And expensive. I look over at him as he starts the engine. "So this YouTube gig pays well, I guess."

For a second I worry that I overstepped, but Sid just smiles like a kid at Christmas and says, "LA Paranormal is the top paranormal investigation agency in Southern California, soon to be the best in the whole country."

I nod, unsure what to say in response. It's odd being connected to something that's so public, and a little nerve racking. I'm so used to hiding—living in the shadows, not letting anyone know anything about me.

"But unlike this car, old things aren't always worth much in this world," he says. "Most times old things are left, forgotten. Ancient is not a positive term in this time." His words are simple, just an observation, but the tone in his voice makes it seem like he's mourning something. He's not readable at all right now, almost as muddy as inside the house, but I can see in his body posture, in the set of his jaw, that he's feeling a sort of anxious longing, and it puzzles me.

"I like old things," I say, unsure why I feel the need to add anything.

"Yes, I've heard," he says. "Eric mentioned you were quite handy with all things ancient."

I glance out the window, not sure if I want to delve into this stuff if it means talking about me and my *talents*. "I just sense when something old is important from the energy."

"You know, Eric's found me several things I've requested. When I asked him how, he mentioned you because he thought that I might be able to help you. He thought you seemed . . . lost."

My pulse speeds up.

"Are you lost, Aidan?"

It's suddenly harder to breathe.

He clears his throat and says in a very important voice: "*For whatsoever from one place doth fall, is with the tide unto another brought: For there is nothing lost, that may be found, if sought.*" He smiles wide. "Edmund Spenser knew his truth." He turns to me, intent. "Why do *you* think you can do these strange things?"

I pick at a fingernail, unsettled. I don't trust people. Ever. Why do I feel this need so strong—the desire to trust this strange man—especially when everything in me rings with warning at the same time?

"Any thoughts?" he asks, insistent.

I've held secrets for so long, I'm not even sure how—*if*—I should let go.

"Maybe you're a part of it all—did you ever think of that?" His voice is soft now, inviting.

Something clicks in my gut, but I'm not sure what it is. We've stopped at a light, and when I look up, he's studying me intently again.

"Time is like water, like a stone, or anything else in nature," he says, his eyes nearly glowing now from excitement. "It has form; it has rules. Time is a part of the energy you feel more than anything else. Like the frame of a house, it holds things in their rightful place." He pauses and then adds, "You're a part of this order, Aidan. More than you realize."

I swallow and stare at him, my eyes stinging. A faint memory of Ava's dream comes back to me, what Mom said about time: *The father's place is another time* . . . But I have no idea what the hell it means.

I do understand what Sid means about time, though. Like everything is held together by it.

A flame sparks to life in my chest, something coming to the surface, and I realize . . . everything I see, everything I sense, is linked to what Sid just said. Somehow. And my mom's dark spells . . . maybe that's why they felt wrong and twisted. Why the grimoire won't let me read its pages. Those things are a crack in the boundaries of nature, a fissure in the order. And I'm a part of that order.

Sid drives on, and we sit in silence for a time, like he's letting everything sink in.

We reach the house and pull into the garage, and I'm not sure I can get out of the car yet. I'm still working through it all in my head, still wrestling with the idea of being connected to something larger than myself. It's the truth, though. I feel it in my gut.

And my gut rarely lies.

Before I can open the door to get out, Sid says, "I'm glad you're here with us now, Aidan. You fit right in. The light of kids like you is vital to keep humanity connected to the spirit world, and now you'll be one of them. A beacon to reveal truth."

I can only nod. I'm still not sure I want to give in to this whole thing—being part of a team. I just want to keep Ava safe. What he's saying is all very "Kumbaya."

Then he adds, "I could tell you weren't on board a hundred percent with the results of the job. I know things were unclear for you. Soon you'll begin to understand what our role is."

I drop my hand from the door handle and decide to just say it. "The boy needs help, and we ignored it. Because of the money."

Sid smiles, surprising me. "So clear. Such conviction. That's good." He sits back and studies me. "But it's also shortsighted."

"How's that?" It's shortsighted to give a shit?

"Each of us is here for a purpose, Aidan. Your role, mine, the role of LA Paranormal, is to create balance, nothing more. Having a gift doesn't give you the right to mess in the affairs of the heart—in that realm you'll lose and likely drag others off the cliff with you."

He must see I'm not buying it, because he asks, "If we'd helped the boy, where do you think it would have ended? We could have dug deeper, discovered all the darkness there in that place, and called someone to help. But then what? Marcus would go into the system and be passed around. Just like you."

My chest tightens.

"You, of all people, would never wish that on a kid. We all have a role to play. And when we stray from that, we get others in trouble."

FOURTEEN

The next day I wake to the commotion of the morning routine taking over the house. Out in the hallway, everyone's arguing about turns in the bathroom. Holly's pissed because someone used her lotion—she's yelling at Lester in Spanish about how she hopes it rots his toes off.

I lie there and listen to it all, to Ava's breathing, thinking about the things Sid said in the car last night. I fell asleep with everything roiling in my head, trying to piece it together. Am I really a part of a larger order? Could my abilities be that important? It feels unreal to even think about it like that.

I look over at Ava and study her sleeping form curled around her violin. There's sheets of music on the floor, ones she wrote by hand. Her talent is obvious in the complexity of the notes, but I don't really understand any of it. She's a genius, always has been. In music, in mind, and in her ancient soul. And she needs me to save her.

But I am no genius. I don't even go to school. I don't know about anything except demonology, really. What I need is cleverness. Like Sid has.

And we only have days left before her birthday . . . before the demons come.

Maybe if I knew more about myself, understood more about my abilities. Maybe I could help her then. Actually save her. We might be safe in these warded walls for now, but I know if the darkness wants her it'll find a way in. Past whatever protections that Sid or I set up.

Ava's book bag is hanging on a hook by the closet, my mom's grimoire taunting me from inside.

Yes, the darkness is already finding a way in.

A knock sounds on the door. "Hey, newb! You're on phones, so get your ass up!" Jax again.

I roll out of bed, run a hand through my hair, and pull on my pants. Ava groans and curls tighter around her violin. She's going to break it if she isn't careful. And it's not like I can afford to buy her a new one.

There's a velvet ear sticking out of her book bag: Mr. Ribbons, the stuffed rabbit that Mr. Marshall got her for her fourth birthday. I pull it out and trade it for the violin, setting the instrument safely back in its case. Ava only rolls over and mumbles something into the cheek of Mr. Ribbons, who's now wrapped in her arms.

I wish it was as simple as that to trade danger for safety in real life.

Jax is waiting on the stairs. He waves me over, pointing down to the first floor. "In the den. You've got work to do."

I follow him to the bottom of the stairs and to the back corner of the house, into a small den beside the family room. Lester is the only one in there, wearing large headphones on his head and sitting in front of a row of five different computer screens, looking like a digital spy.

It's a dark, bare space. The windows are covered with what looks like a black sheet pinned to the wall. The light from the five screens is the only illumination in the room. Two large tables line the far wall with several rolling chairs to sit on. "Wires" seems to be the decorative theme of the room, with thick bundles of black and yellow and red and orange cords running along the walls, duct-taped across the floor, or curled like sleeping snakes under the tables.

"The phone and the machine are there." Jax points to the corner on our right where a small table and chair rest. The table is covered in stacks of paper with a postage stamp of space available for actual use. "Holly was going to be filing today, but since she has summer classes and you're here and have nothing better to do, it's your privilege. So pull up your pantyhose and get to work." He pats me on the back, shoves me toward the corner, and then leaves the room without a single word of further instruction.

I sit myself in the wooden chair and stare at the stacks of paper. There's a red blinking light on what looks like an old answering machine from the nineties.

Lester spins his chair, taking off his headphones, and rolls himself closer. "Jax starts out as a dick, but once you get used to him, he becomes only a minor jackass."

I nod.

"Sid asked us to toss you in the mix right away," he adds, like he's apologizing. "Just let me know if you have any questions."

"And where is our illustrious leader this morning?" I ask.

"His shed. He'll be out around noon."

My brow goes up in question, but Lester just acts like the idea of a guy sleeping all night and half the day away in a rusty old shed is perfectly normal. Makes me wonder even more about that grounding lock he's painted on the door of the place.

"And what're you doing?" I motion to the many computer screens, all of them showing what looks like security footage. "Spying on LA? Is this place a front for the NSA?"

He grins. "I'm watching footage for our next case. The couple's been a bit of a neurotic mess, thinking their house is being broken into every night. They say there's proof of what they're calling a banshee on the footage, but I'm not findin' it. Just looks like two hundred hours of two guys who live together and who like to get kinky when they clean."

"A banshee, huh?" No such thing, but I don't want to sound like a know-it-all. "And there's no clues?"

"Well, technically, there's no such thing as banshees—"

Hmm.

"—but Sid was thinking maybe they were experiencing what he called a time slip, told me to look for outlines of white light figures or orbs. I still have about a hundred hours to go. We'll see what I find."

A time slip. I know all of zero people who are aware of that— the echo of an event crossing over through time. Kind of like an instant replay in a place where a scar was left from old trauma. Happens a lot in a place where a building was burned down or if there was a battlefield nearby. We see a piece of it, like a replay of history crossing over. Most people get it mixed up with ghosts.

If Sid really understands his shit about this stuff, maybe living here and working with these people for a little while will actually be interesting. "All that footage and you haven't seen anything?" I ask.

He shakes his head. "Nada. So I better get back to work." He rolls away again toward the desk.

"I can help," I say, more interested in looking for a real paranormal event on video than answering phones or filing papers.

"Not a good idea. Sid wants you grunting it for now. You're supposed to earn your keep. Be thankful it's summer, though. If school was in session, we'd have to work around Sid's idea of homeschool where he teaches us about embalming and how plastic was invented. A real snooze-fest. Holly's the only one allowed to go to real school since she's a freaking genius."

"Lovely," I say, kind of glad I won't be here long enough to see the lessons on embalming. As soon as we get through Ava's birthday, we won't need to be tied down anymore.

"All you have to do for now is take that pad of paper and make a detailed note for each message on the machine. Easy as samurai pie."

I find the paper and start searching for a pen in the chaos of the small table. "How long have you been with Sid?"

He doesn't answer right away, and after several seconds go by, I decide he's not going to. But as I find a pen and open my mouth to say "Bingo!" I hear his quiet voice. "Since my brother died."

"I'm sorry," I say. "I shouldn't butt in."

"No, it's fine. I get it. You're just curious about us all. I was never on the street like Connor or Jax, like you were, but I figure it must be lonely. I always had my brother. He was more like a dad, maybe. He brought me here from India when I was three and he was seventeen. Then he died last year. And Sid found me really quick after that."

"I'm so sorry, man."

"It was a demon, I think. Or my brother just went nuts or something. He'd been having nightmares for weeks, and he started sleeping in my room with me. He kept talking about a huge snake waking him up, biting him in the arms and legs. Pretty soon after that he shot himself in the head."

"My God." Suicide. Sounds like a demon was trying to possess him. Maybe he thought a bullet was the only way to stop it.

Lester swipes at his cheek like he's wiping away a tear, but I can't tell in the dark. Then he rubs his nose and sniffs. "Yeah, it was bad. But I know Jax had it worse. And Connor. That guy saw some pretty crazy stuff."

"My mom was killed by this shit, too," I say, wanting him to realize he's not alone. "There's nothing about death that isn't horrifying and wrong. You don't have to make excuses to me, man. I get it."

He nods and wipes his nose again. Then he puts his headphones back on and returns to the light of the screens. I slide the pad of paper in front of me and press "Play" on the prehistoric answering machine. Seems like this is a house full of horror stories. Time to figure out how and *if* I fit in here.

———

A few hours later, I walk back up the stairs to the bedroom to check on Ava. I've heard the sounds of her violin trailing through the house over the morning hours, but that stopped a while ago, and she still hasn't come down. When I walk through the door she shoves something into her shoulder bag like she's trying to hide it. My body freezes.

I know it's Mom's grimoire. My gut clenches at the thought, but I decide to let it go. I've had enough drama and tension the last few days to last me a lifetime.

"You okay up here?" I ask, not mentioning what we both know she's hiding. "I think it's past time for lunch. Holly made sandwiches. They have jelly happy faces on them."

"No thanks, I'm not hungry." Her voice shakes, and I know instantly something's gone wrong. She stands up from the bed and comes at me, hugging me tight.

"I was just downstairs, Ava, not in Kuwait."

But she squeezes me tighter, shivering.

I lean back to see her face. "Are you okay? What happened?"

I can feel her panic in my skin, and her mind is spinning with frantic thoughts that press into mine in a tangle I can't sort through to see clear. Her light hair is a silver halo around her face as I wait for her to say something, anything.

"Something's changed, Aidan. Something big."

I ask as gently as I can through the panic beginning to rise, "What did you see?"

"I don't know . . . I was playing the Brahms concerto, and in the middle of the second movement I saw . . ." There's confusion and fear in her voice. "It's coming for you. The dark shadow."

"Dark shadow? What do you mean—?"

"It tried to take you, to swallow you up. It made you disappear. You were gone. Just gone. And I was all alone." She shivers against me. "The evil dogs came back, like when the Marshalls . . . There were so many of them. They got me. They—" She chokes on her words, then starts moving her palm over her shoulder, like she's trying to rub away the feeling of the teeth sinking into her flesh. "Something's changed, Aidan. It found you."

My pulse accelerates. What found me?

"My visions always come true," she says in a hushed voice.

"No, Ava." I kiss her head. "I'll never leave you. Not ever."

But I have no idea how to keep that promise when her birthday arrives and we have to face what may be coming for her.

———

The rest of the day is tough. Ava seems to be almost in a trance. Only once does she make sense: when she's telling me that she's sorry, confessing that she had to look in Mom's grimoire for answers. That she has to talk to Fiona; she has to know the truth. I'm not sure what truth she means, exactly. I'm beginning to think I should just tell her what I know and stop believing I'm protecting her from anything with my silence. It's not as if her lack of knowledge about how Fiona was the cause of all this is keeping her heart safe.

But I'm not sure I even know what really happened that night. It's as if those last days are all condensed into that one horrifying moment when the ground shifted and everything changed forever.

Now I'm the one, the only one standing between Ava and the demon who marked her. And worse than that, I don't know how to stop this shadow growing inside of her, this obsession that took our mom captive and is now trying to claim her, too. That terrifies me more than any demon.

I stay upstairs with her for a while before going back down to make excuses about not coming to dinner. I say she's not feeling good and that I'll be hanging out with her in the room if they need me. No one seems to care. Holly looks more worried about germs. All Jax says is that I better not get the pukes because we've got three investigations in the wings from those phone messages I took and there's no time for being sick.

By the time I get back to the room, Ava is shivering again. She climbs onto my bed beside me with Mr. Ribbons held tight to her like she's two instead of twelve.

"I've missed you so much these last few years, Aidan, and now we're finally together again. I can't let anything happen to you," she says, gripping my arm and snuggling into my side.

"Nothing is going to happen. I found a place where we can be safe for a while." I brush the hair from her face. "Why don't you just try to sleep for a bit. I'll sleep, too. We won't think about the darkness anymore." A tear slips down her cheek, but she closes her eyes, so I say, "Remember when the Marshalls were alive and we'd go to the beach and make tunnels in the sand? You'd catch crabs and we'd give them all names. There must've been hundreds of them. You told me you were a mermaid and that they were your cousins and that you were all having a family reunion." Her breathing is even now, settled, like she's finally drifting off. "You were happy, remember?"

I lie beside her and get lost in the memories, all the colors and light of those years. Ava was a child for a little while. The memories lull me to sleep, too, my limbs getting heavy. My eyes close, and just as I'm floating off, my head close to Ava's, a scene rises through her mind to the surface of my own.

I stand on a familiar beach, facing away from the churning waves behind me, staring at a cliff wall. The wind stings my cheeks, cold and salty. The ground seems to rumble, like when the tide crashes against the rocks, but then a dark shadow surges forward. It billows out of the cliff wall, becoming a cave opening, growing wider and wider, inviting me inside. The dark hole tugs at my clothes, pulling me closer, into it. And then I realize I'm not alone. A man stands beside me, his hand resting on my shoulder, firm, comforting. But I can't see his face.

On the other side of me stands another figure, tall and inhuman, with red eyes and twisted horns growing from its skull. A demon. The same demon that was following Rebecca.

It turns to grin down at me, like it's satisfied. At last.

And I step forward, letting the darkness take me.

———

I emerge into the waking world, to air made of ice and sharp edges. I open my eyes slowly, carefully, afraid of the chill on my skin.

Because that is the chill of a monster.

A red glow pulses, back and forth, ticktocking under my bedroom door. Joined by the sound of a crackle far off.

Fire.

I grip my blanket and bring it to my chin, teeth chattering from the cold, from terror. I listen and wait, eyes locked on the flickering light.

Mother called it again. She called the monster back to us, even when she promised me yesterday that it was going to be over. Why would she lie to me? Why would she do that when she knows . . .

The crackle grows louder, and something crashes against the floor. My muscles jump in my skin, and Ava's scream fills the walls.

Ava. The idea of her small form in her playpen, there, beside the casting circle, shakes me from my terror enough to move. It lifts me to my feet and propels me to the bedroom door. And as I enter the hall, the glow brightens, casting blood-colored light over the wall opposite my mother's room. I know I'm going to see the monster. I'm going to feel its darkness. But I'm going to save Ava.

I step into the casting light, into the open doorway, the sound of fire hissing around me. The red and silver flames dancing around the room should be warm, but instead of sparks, they send ice crystals into the air. They run along the circle she painted in blood; they lick and crack the prison walls, like they too are alive, making the barrier peel away.

When I see past the moving fire my insides turn to ash.

My mother's feet dangle over the floor. A massive claw grips her neck, lifting her higher and higher as her body remains still, allowing the creature to claim her.

The beast is massive; a man, but a wolf, too. Its snout is long, dripping with long strings of saliva. The teeth glisten sliver in the flickering flames.

It doesn't feel me there. It doesn't know my eyes watch as it shakes my mother, turns her into a doll made of rags, jerking her head, shouting a garbled word that I don't understand.

I am a statue of horror and confusion. My nightmare is taking her. It wants her, and I can't stop it, even as it sneers, lip rising like it wants to tell a funny joke. Its tongue emerges, long and thin, catching a line of blood sliding down Mom's shoulder.

Then it punches its claw through her rib cage.

A gasp of air and shock puffs from my mother's lips, from mine. My whole body screams, but I have no voice. She's tossed to the floor, a broken doll now. And the demon is left holding her dripping heart in its claws.

The monster waits. Until its sigil, its signature, appears in the growing pool of blood. Until a mark surfaces on my mother's still forehead, claiming her as a sacrifice.

Then the monster turns to my weeping sister, reaches out to her shaking form, its talon pointed at her tear-stained face. Before it slices through her soft baby shoulder with a prick, releasing a drop of blood.

Ava goes silent, the flames sink away, and it's as if all the sound is sucked from the room. She stares wide-eyed at the wolf monster, fascination filling her tiny face.

It grins down at her, pats her white hair with a blood-coated palm . . .

pat

pat

pat

. . . before it disappears in a suck of wind and ash with my mother's heart still clutched in its fist. And I stand in the doorway, useless, having done nothing to stop any of it.

FIFTEEN

I wake with a start. Everything's foggy in my mind, like I've lost something, like I've misplaced the one thing I was supposed to take care of, the most precious thing I've ever been entrusted with.

"Ava?" I squint in the sunshine-filled room. She's not sleeping beside me, and her bed's empty.

I sit up, heart racing. I dreamed . . . something. I can't remember. But something's wrong.

My head throbs, but I ignore it and leap from the bed, bursting into the hall. "Ava?!" I yell—but it comes out muffled, coated in the remnants of sleep.

I stand there listening, holding my breath. One second ticks by, two seconds . . .

Everything in me shakes, panic becoming full-blown terror. She couldn't have run off, could she? She can't be gone. She just can't.

The bathroom door opens with a squeak, and I spot white-gold hair and hear her humming "Alouette," the French song Mom used to sing when she cooked. I don't stop to think. I rush forward and scoop her up, hugging her tiny form to me.

"Ugh," she grunts. "Aidan, you're gonna break my ribs."

I release her after another second. "You scared the shit out of me."

"I had to pee." She pats my arm and walks past me back to the bedroom.

I stand for a second trying to catch my breath. Why did I react like that? Way over the top. All Ava's anxiety from yesterday must've gotten to me. I'm losing it.

My head stops spinning, and I turn back to the room. Before I make it inside, Kara barrels through her door, head down, earbuds in, and runs smack into me. I grab her arm, pulling her into me to steady us. She tenses, becoming aware of her surroundings. Her eyes look straight at my torso and then trail up my neck to my face.

She pulls an earbud slowly from her ear and blinks.

"Uh . . ." She stares for a second. Then she glances down at my hand on her arm. She blinks and jolts back, stumbling into the wall as if I zapped her. "Why're you walking around like that?" She gapes at me.

I look down at myself, my bare chest, my boxers, not sure what the huge deal is. It's not like I'm naked.

"Sorry." I shrug.

"Have some common decency," she says, pushing off the wall. "And watch where you're going," she adds, trying to act as if the last six seconds didn't happen.

Fine by me.

She walks past, heading to the stairs. I open the door to my room, pretending I'm not paying attention. But I hear her footsteps pause at the top step, and when I look behind me, she's taking one more peek before heading downstairs out of view.

———

Ava doesn't mention the vision of that dark hole swallowing me again. I certainly don't want to say that I saw part of what she had seen, too—that cave.

And I definitely don't want to tell her I saw a demon standing beside me.

But it's clear now that I can't ignore the demon following Rebecca and the fact that it's aware of my ability to see. That vision Ava got was a warning. I can't leave a loose end out there at a time like this. I need to do something, get a firm grip on what I'm dealing with. That demon was major, no simpleminded foot soldier. None of them can know I see, especially one that strong, especially now. If that demon or others come looking for me, they'll find Ava.

I grab my phone and dig into my pocket for the card that Rebecca's friend Samantha slipped in there the other day. I could ask her for Rebecca's phone number, ask Rebecca if she could meet me somewhere, like her house. But that feels too close, too personal. It needs to be in a crowd, a place I can keep things strictly superficial, so to speak.

I type a text: *This is the guy from the hall—Emery's friend. You invited me to the party. When and where?*

I press "Send" and set the phone down, but it vibrates almost immediately.

The white answer bubble reads: *OMG! Totally come! Tomorrow night off PCH 2492 Malibu Rd ;)*

That was easy. Now I just have to figure out how to get there.

I go downstairs and find Kara sitting on the couch next to Finger. The two of them are playing some sort of zombie war game.

I walk into the living room, pausing in the archway to watch them.

Kara spots me, and her thumbs go still on the controller. If the house wasn't muffling all the emotion, I'm guessing I'd be feeling irritation.

I lean on the wall. "So you're part of the gamer crowd?"

"Is there someone else you can annoy?" Screams come from the TV, and she growls. "Great. Now I'm dead."

"I need to find out how to borrow a car," I say.

She sets down her controller. "Excuse me?"

"I need a car tomorrow night."

"Um, no."

"Where's Sid?" I ask.

"He'll be in soon," she says.

Oh yeah, the shed. "Why does he sleep in that tiny shack?"

"Why're you so nosy?" She stands up from the couch and walks past me into the kitchen.

I follow her, but I remind myself to stay focused. I need the car. Sid's odd sleeping arrangements aren't my business. "So about the car."

Jax comes into the kitchen behind me. "Where do you think you're going?"

I glance at him. "Not exactly your concern."

"But it's an easy question," Kara says, pulling a basket of strawberries from the fridge. "Where *are* you going?"

I shrug like it's nothing. "A party."

She squints, and then something dawns on her. A grin spreads across her cheeks like the Cheshire cat. "You little slut! You're gonna go to that prep school sex party, aren't you?" And she laughs like it's the funniest thing she's heard in a long time.

"Whoa, you're not going to a sex party without me," Jax says. "With that face you'll definitely need a wingman. I'll do the honors." He pats me on the shoulder like he's trying to be buddy-buddy.

Kara snorts and bites into a strawberry. "You just wanna check out that red-headed girl with the boobs," she says to me.

"Ooh, nice," Jax says. "I wanna meet her."

"Never mind," I say. "Forget it. I don't need a car." I'll ride the damn bus. It'll take all day, but at least I won't have to deal with these two.

"Aw, the boy's feelings are hurt," Kara says.

"Tragic," Jax adds, opening the fridge and searching the insides.

"Want a strawberry?" Kara holds out a plump red fruit to me like she's presenting a peace offering.

I take it, popping the whole thing in my mouth.

She laughs again, but this time the sound is pleasant, and I can't help feeling pleased with her good mood. At least she's not hating me right now.

"I'll take you," she says, setting the basket of strawberries on the table.

"Sucker," Jax says, giving up on searching the fridge contents and moving to the pantry.

I shake my head. "Don't worry about it." The last thing I need is to try and check out a demon and keep it all off her radar while she—this girl who supposedly hates me—follows me around the party.

"Tomorrow night?" she asks.

I sigh and plop down in a kitchen chair.

Kara smiles in triumph and leaves the kitchen, saying over her shoulder, "Be ready at eleven."

"I'm ready now," Jax says.

———

The day goes by fast. Sid's not around for most of the morning, but at noon he comes in carrying about twenty shopping bags. "I would've taken you with me," Sid says from the hallway outside our room, "but I thought it would be more fun to surprise you. It'll count as your first paycheck."

Ava shoves her bags into the closet without even looking in them, but she seems pleased. She probably knows what he bought her without looking. I love the stuff he got me—shoes and jeans and tons more. It's been so freaking long since I've had anything new. The crisp smell of each item is striking and unfamiliar.

After Sid goes back downstairs, I start to settle in. Ava and I pick drawers in the dresser, and I put away my new clothes. Next I pick up the mezuzah from its resting spot on the windowsill and hold it to the outer doorpost. I find some nails in one of the kitchen drawers and a paperweight on the mail table by the door, which'll work as a hammer. Once I get the mezuzah hung correctly—right side, upper section, within three inches of the opening—I press my fingers to the Shaddai and whisper the Hebrew blessing: "*Barukh atah Adonai Eloheinu melekh ha'olam, asher kideshanu bemitzvotav vetzivanu likboa' mezuzah.*" Then I bring my fingers to my lips before going back into the room.

I dig in my backpack and find the tiny vial of myrrh oil inside a folded-up ad for the mystical bookstore where Eric sent me to pick it up. I put some on my finger and run the slick liquid over the sill of the window and across the floor of the room's entrance. Myrrh stays stronger longer than salt or rye. Plus, it doesn't blow away.

Last thing I do is take my pocketknife out and carve into the windowsill in Latin: *Deus meus protectio*—God is my protection.

Now that I'm done with all that, the air feels light. Maybe the energy following Ava and me can balance itself out better. I have a sudden feeling of rightness, like everything's actually going to be okay.

SIXTEEN

The house where the party is supposed to be is huge, set against the bluff of a small cliff overlooking the ocean. As we get out of the car, the salt and brine cling instantly to my skin. I breathe deep, taking it in, feeling lighter now that I'm away from the city, away from the smog and the sin.

A cypress tree hangs over the main entrance, darkening the shadows. The lights along the path are bluish green, and they give Kara's skin a haunted look as she walks beside me. Music spills out into the night as we head up the walkway. I didn't tell her that the reason I'm here is a demon. I probably should've. But then she wouldn't have brought me.

"You can wait in the car, you know," I say.

"And miss this?" She slips her keys into her back pocket. "Anyway, I need a drink."

"No drinks." I reach out and open the front door.

Kara sighs. "Sure, Dad."

We walk into the pulsing air, pausing in the barely lit entry. The smells of sex and drugs and alcohol hit me like a rolling wave, pungent and thick. I push it back the best I can as we move past bodies dancing in the center of the living room, a mass of sweat and urgency. Couples twist together, pressed against the walls, tangled limbs on the couch, in sync with the music, like some strange, erotic symphony.

I turn away. There's no demon in there.

"Wow," Kara yells over the music. "Rebecca's quite the girl to invite you to a party like this."

I steel myself and follow her deeper into the house through an archway into the kitchen. The marble counter is covered in spilled bags of chips and M&M's, red cups tipped over next to pools of liquid. There's a large glass bowl filled with pills in all shapes and colors—rich kids collecting their parents' prescription drugs from the bathroom cabinets and pooling them together for a form of LA roulette. The sight of the bowl makes me tense up more, wondering if Rebecca's taken any yet.

Kara sticks her hand in an open bag of chips and then pops one in her mouth. "What now?"

"I need to find Rebecca."

She eyes me. "Now that we're here, you don't sound like you want to."

I lean on the counter and stare at my new shoes. I'm here for the demon, not for Rebecca. But thinking about her makes my insides twist. What if she's with someone? I really don't want to see that. I don't even want to think of her that way—I shouldn't. There's a list of a hundred reasons why it's a bad idea.

Those damn *if only* thoughts roll through my head like thorny tumbleweeds, and I have to bite the inside of my cheek to hold them back.

"It's not my business what she does," I say, mostly to myself.

"Or who." Kara pops another chip in her mouth and winks at me.

"Don't be a bitch, Kara."

A spark of pain comes from her skin, and I realize I may have said the wrong thing. I shouldn't have called her that.

She moves within an inch of me. I can smell the salt on her lips and that candy-sweet taste of her soul. "But, honey, I'm so damn good at it." She gives me a forced smile. "You know what else I'm good at?"

I shiver a little, feeling her energy bite at my skin.

"Parties," she says. "I'm really, really good at parties." She moves back and unzips her hoodie, then slips it off her shoulders and tosses it aside. "I think I'm feeling a little smothered." She pulls her rocker T-shirt over her head and drops it, too. "I need some air."

I swallow and stare at her bare stomach, her purple bra, not sure what to say.

She smirks and pulls the keys from her jeans pocket, dangling them in my face. Then she shoves them at my chest. They stab through my T-shirt.

"You just won yourself designated driver, jackass. Congrats."

My mouth opens to tell her to get dressed, that I'm sorry, to calm down, but none of it shapes into actual words. All I seem to be able to do is reach up to catch the keys.

"Have fun finding your virgin earth angel." She reaches over and snatches up a full red cup. Then she sticks her fingers into the bowl of pills, grabbing a handful. "Better hope she's not wrapped around a chunk of frat meat." She slides past me.

I catch her by the arm, her skin buzzing against my palm on contact. This has gone way too far. She's off the rails.

She turns and glares at me. "Let. Go."

"Kara, don't be stupid."

Her nostrils flare.

I reach for the fist of pills, but she tosses them in my face. "You're not my father, asshole, even if you are just as big a dick as he was."

I let go of her arm, stung. "I'm sorry," I practically yell. I obviously hit a nerve.

"You're worse than all of them, you know that?" she says through gritted teeth. "You pretend to be so pure and kind, but I can see right through you. You're a shit. A faux hero. I can't believe I almost fell for the show."

She turns away, leaving me behind before I can try to talk her down—even though I'm not sure what I'd say. I'm not exactly sure what just happened. I do know I didn't handle it very well, though.

I follow her into the mass of bodies, but the energy slams against me, clouding my head with muck. My feet stop and my stomach rises. I knew I should've come alone. I spot Kara across the room; she's climbing the stairs. Her bare back moves through the crowd, a flower tattoo I never noticed before winding up her side. She grabs some guy's hand—a slick-looking boy in a pink polo shirt—and leads him up the steps to the bedrooms.

I consider pushing my way through the crowd to go pound the pink bastard's face in and drag her ass back home. How is sleeping with some dickhead going to make her feel better? I stare and seethe and wonder why I even give a damn.

Someone grips my arm and I spin, every muscle in my body full of tension.

"You came!" It's Samantha—the one who slipped me the card. "Ohmygod! I was so excited when you texted me!" She pulls me toward the back of the house.

We come to a glass sliding door and she pauses. "You have to save her. She's being all gloomy and needs a pep-me-up. Can I count on you?"

I have no idea what to say.

She slides open the door, and I glance back at the stairs inside, thinking of Kara.

But she made her choice.

"She's there, on the shore." Samantha points.

I look away from the party and follow her finger and the sound of the waves to a white figure standing beside the moving darkness of the ocean.

My pulse picks up.

Rebecca.

I can't sense anything from this far away, but I don't see the demon anywhere. That doesn't mean it isn't close, though. It seems to have a way of sneaking up on me.

I walk out onto the deck, heading toward the shore. The wind hits me, erasing the sticky energy of the party. I let it clear my head as I walk past a couple making out on a lounge chair. It's about thirty yards to the water's edge where Rebecca's standing. The walk finishes cleaning my insides, and I'm surrounded by the salt smell and the soothing rhythm of the tide. She doesn't turn as I come closer. She hugs herself, staring out at the dark ocean, allowing its reaching white fingers to touch her bare toes.

I pause, watching her.

Wrapped in a white sweater and white lacy shorts, she's almost a ghost against the colors of the night. She turns a little and spots me, her hand going to her throat.

I open my mouth to speak, but nothing comes out.

She steps closer, and a tiny shiver fills the space between us: anticipation. "You came . . ." Her hair moves with the breeze, covering her lips and chin, shadowing her curious eyes. I clench my fingers into a fist to keep from touching her. She tucks the copper strands of her hair behind her ear, saving me.

"I need to talk to you," I say, glancing around. There's no sign of the demon—not that I can feel in the air, not that I can see. All I smell is the brine of the ocean.

"I don't even know who you are, your name . . ."

"My name's Aidan. Aidan O'Linn." I study her face, wondering how to begin, wondering whether to say anything at all.

"Aidan," she says, like she's testing the feel of it.

"I need to ask you something."

She looks at me curiously.

"I'm sorry, so sorry I have to ask this . . . but . . . what happened to your brother?"

Her eyes turn glassy. She shakes her head, terror growing on her face.

"Don't be scared," I say.

"Why are you asking me that?"

I need to find out what kind of demon I'm dealing with here. I shore up my courage and ask, "How did your brother die?"

She lets out a small whimper and shakes her head again. "He . . . he drowned." A tear slips down her cheek. "Went out surfing at night."

My chest tightens. "I'm sorry," I say, but it's so quiet I'm not sure she hears.

The fact that her brother drowned means the demon managed to kill him and make it look like an accident. A high-ranking soldier for sure, but likely not a body-hopper—that would've been messier, and a possessed Charlie would've taken others with him.

I think of the low-level creeper in the alley that was encouraging the guys to rape Rebecca. Probably the higher-ranking demon that killed Charlie is working on her now, sending minions to do its dirty work. But why go to so much trouble for just one family?

She moves a little closer. "I should have stopped him, but I wasn't thinking." Her eyes are pleading, like she's asking me to take away the pain.

"I'm so sorry, Rebecca. It's not your fault."

She looks away, back out at the water. "I was thinking just now of walking into the waves. Maybe I'd find him again out there." Her sorrow spills out, feeling like a tide all its own.

"I know it hurts. I know . . . but . . . your brother would want you to live." The words feel useless as they leave my mouth. But I need to pull her back somehow. Despair thickens the air; it's obvious the demon is winning this battle.

"I thought you were him," she says. "That night you brought me home, I thought you were Charlie. You were so gentle, so kind. I thought he'd come back to me." Our eyes lock. "Maybe he sent you." She reaches out and takes my fingers in hers. "To watch over me."

My skin burns where we touch. My lungs freeze up. It's almost unreal how quick my body reacts to something so small, as if she's right and it's all falling into place. But it's not, and I know that. It's chemical, physical. Hormones. Not a good reason to give in to the feeling.

She's close enough now that I can smell dryer sheets on her clothes, mingling with her sorrow . . . woven with a slight thread of hope?

Her fingers grip me tighter, like I'm a lifeline. She moves even closer, and her chest presses against mine.

I know she wants me to kiss her, to comfort her. My skin aches with the urgency to give in, but I—

She licks her bottom lip.

God, help me.

The tide comes in fast, drenching my shoes, an instant jolt back to reality.

I pull away, just a little, but I don't let go of her hand. I don't want to hurt her any more than I have to. And I really don't want to stop touching her.

"Rebecca." I swallow, trying to form words. "It's important that you—you need to realize how important it is that you live." A demon would only be working overtime on her and her family if she was important. Vital in some way for the endgame. A threat to the darkness.

"What do you mean?"

"You're important. You need to be strong."

Her eyes fill and spill over, tears streaking her cheeks.

I start to pull back, but she grips my hand tighter and won't let go. "Please. Tell me I'll see you again."

I stare at her, not sure what to say. Then I reach up to my chest and touch the *hamsa* charm I got from Hanna. Pulling it over my head, I realize I'm not supposed to save it for my sister like I thought. Rebecca needs the protection more than Ava right now.

I press it into Rebecca's palm as I slip my other hand from hers. "Take this. Wear it. And don't let go. Please . . ."

She studies the gift, rolling it with her fingers. After a second or two she nods, agreeing to live. At least for one more day.

Relief washes through me, a rush of hope, and before I can stop myself, I pull her close and kiss her forehead. But I release her in almost the same breath, stepping back, allowing space between us.

"Good," I say. "I'll be around." I'm not sure it's true, but I want it to be. God, help me. I want to be a part of her redemption.

I turn and walk away before I can say it out loud.

SEVENTEEN

I don't look behind me as I return to the house to find Kara. Rebecca will be okay for tonight. I tell myself I've done what I could. All I could.

But I'm full of shit. I could have told her the truth. I could've warned her about the demon, about what it's trying to do to her. Maybe she would've listened . . .

No. No, she wouldn't have. The news would've gone over like a ton of bricks.

Keep it hidden, keep it safe.

It's time to go back to reality. I need to find Kara and get her home before she does anything too stupid because of my big mouth.

I step onto the deck, which is abandoned now; the couple that was making out on the lounge chair is gone. I'm about to grab the door handle when something moves in the corner of my vision.

The scent of sulfur hits me, forcing a cough as I choke on the sudden strength of it. It's here. My pulse races. I grip the door handle, staring at the glass, trying to decide if I should face it. My reflection stares back at me, jaw clenched, fear in my eyes.

Why bother pretending I'm not aware of its presence? It knows I see. I know it knows.

There's a scratching at the deck. I look down. A cat-sized demon with a warped spine emerges from the house *through* the glass door. It glances up at me, pointed ears perking in my direction. A necklace of tiny bones clinks around its neck—it's the demon from the alley, from the night Rebecca was almost raped. It hisses through dagger teeth that drip with saliva, back hair bristling.

My muscles tense, ready to act, but the demon turns and crawls over to the other side of the deck, resting at the hooves of a ten-foot creature three yards away.

Holy shit.

The larger demon stares at me with red eyes—stares through me, as if trying to burn me to a crisp by mere will.

All I can do is gape back. Thick horns sprout from its head, at least a foot and a half high, and its feet are cloven like a goat's. Muscles wrap each limb, strong as iron. The body is a man's, except for the places where bone juts through the black skin and takes the shape of thorns and prongs.

"Seer," it growls in a low rumble that shakes the air.

My insides turn liquid. This thing could crush me into nothing.

I slide my hand into my pocket, gripping a pouch of sacred dirt, and recite Psalm 91 in my head: *With His feathers He will cover you, and under His wings you will trust; His truth is an encompassing shield . . .*

The small demon climbs up the larger demon's leg and up its side to perch on its shoulder. It tips its oversized head at me curiously.

I take a step back. The chill of the large demon surrounds me, forcing my breath out in quick white puffs. "Stay back."

"How are you here?" the large demon asks, and I wonder why its words don't sound garbled. I can understand it.

Still, I have no idea what it means. *How am I here?* What?

"The father," it says. "It is the father's magic. The others claim you are not possible. You should not exist, Seer. You have no father in this world—I have searched."

My mind spins. What the hell's it talking about? How does it know these things about me? And what does it mean that it *searched* and found no father?

I lean on the sliding door to keep myself up.

"Don't say it," I plead. But I don't even know what I'm talking about. Don't say what? The truth? I've both wanted and feared the answers for so long.

In a flash, the beast is close enough to touch me, a breath away.

I press into the glass at my back, positive it's about to crack from the pressure.

The monster hovers over me, its sulfur breath stinging my lungs. "I will be watching you, Seer," it says. "Your flesh is mine if you meddle in my task. Hordes of my kind will chase after you, tormenting you until you break. They will strip the flesh from your bones and tear the heart from your chest." It licks its cracked lips, tongue slick grey. "I will make sure of it. It should not be so difficult to destroy a boy who should not exist."

Then it backs away a little. "But your presence will not be known to the dark prince of these lands if you stay away."

All I feel is the thunder in my chest.

The beast turns to the smaller demon on its shoulder. "How is the seer's companion?"

The small demon rises up and whispers in its lord's ear. The large demon's sneer grows, and it looks over at me, face turning smug. It takes a deep breath, filling its lungs. "Yes, I smell it now. She bleeds."

And I know who they mean.

Kara.

"What have you done?" I ask.

The smaller demon hisses, baring its teeth.

The large one laughs with a low rumble. "Merely a little insurance for your cooperation, Seer-boy. I'll find you again. Soon."

With a suck of air, both of them are gone, leaving only the reek of death behind.

I fumble for the door handle, rattling the glass in my urgency.

Images of blood and bits and horror flash through my head . . . the sound of my voice calling her a bitch . . . me caught up with Rebecca while Kara was in trouble.

I crash into the crowd, pushing back at the thick, dark energy, reaching out, searching, *searching*. The scent of copper and pain fills my chest.

Breathe, just breathe. That's not the smell of blood. It's not.

But it is . . .

I scramble up the stairs, stepping on a passed-out body, nearly tripping on a bong, sending it crashing into the wall with a crack. I grab the first doorknob I come to—burst in on two couples tangled together—move on to the next, and the next. By the third I'm nearly coming out of my skin.

The knob won't budge. My fist pounds on the wood. "Let me in!" I growl. "Let me the fuck in!"

I hear a moan.

"Kara? Is that you?"

Another moan. Not of pleasure but of pain.

My skin catches fire, and I kick, cracking the doorjamb. One more kick and the door swings open.

I take in the shape of a couch on the far wall, a TV on the other. An end table knocked over, a lamp on the floor. A bloody handprint near the window.

My throat clenches tight. "Kara . . ."

Another moan comes from somewhere in the room, and there's movement behind the door. An arm. A bloody-knuckled hand. The smell of dagger-sharp fear.

I rush over, pulling her from the shadows, lifting her up. "I'm so sorry," I say, gathering her into my arms.

Please be okay. God, please let her be okay.

I look her over, her arms, her legs. Nothing looks broken. Her face is swollen and bloody, one eye already purple, a cheek puffed up and split.

"Hey, that's mine," comes a slurred voice behind me.

I turn to see Pink Polo Boy. He's swaying a little.

I set Kara back down gently. "What'd you do to her, you little shit?"

"Nothing yet." He sounds pissed. "The bitch's playing Fort Knox." He waves at his face, pointing out something I hadn't noticed before. Scratches. And his jaw looks a little swollen, like she hit him. "You can have at her if you want." He smiles, all twisted and wrong, like he'd be thrilled to watch me use her.

My vision turns red, and I lunge, pummeling him before he can move. A left to the gut, bending him to knee him in the face. Then I lift him back up, his nose gushing blood, and thud him in the side of the head with my fist.

He falls over in a heap.

I go back to Kara, lifting her into my arms. She moans, curling into my chest. "I'll kick his ass," she mumbles.

I release a small laugh, relieved to hear her voice. "Yeah," I say. "He'll be down for the count any second now."

I carry her from the room. A small group of onlookers stands outside the door now. I pass them and walk down the stairs. They follow, whispering to each other, craning their necks to see the damage done. Rebecca's one of the faces, her mouth open in shock as she watches me pass by with Kara in my arms.

When I'm back in the night air at the front of the house, I have to gasp to breathe. My head is fogged with all my lingering rage, the mess of what just happened, and what it might mean.

Pink Polo Boy was so drunk he won't remember me or Kara. But the demon made itself very clear: it's planning on keeping tabs now.

I never should have come.

EIGHTEEN

Kara's quiet the whole way as I drive us back home. She stares out the car window, watching the sleeping city blur past.

I want to plead her forgiveness, knowing it's my fault she was knocked around. But in order to explain that, I'd have to explain everything else, and I'm not sure how.

"Are you okay?" I ask—maybe six times.

She doesn't answer.

When we pull into the driveway, she stays quiet, looking out the window. I turn off the car and get out, but she still doesn't move, so I go around to her door and open it. Without a word she scoots out, grabbing my arm for support.

She leans on me all the way to the house, stumbling a few times.

My feet stop the second time she loses footing, and my heart speeds up. Maybe I should call a doctor, put her back in the car, and take her to the ER. "Please, Kara, this is killing me. Tell me you're okay."

She looks up, her eye swollen a little, her cheek cut. "Not my first time at this rodeo, cowboy. I'll be fine."

"I could take you to the doctor."

"Calm down. The prick didn't get in any body shots, just a knuckle to the face and a penny loafer to the thigh. Maybe two. I'm good." She motions to the back door. "Now put your big boy pants on and take me upstairs so I can sleep this mess off."

I get her to her room, set her on the bed, and tiptoe down the hall to my own room to check on Ava. She's sleeping soundly. I slip off my shoes, toss my hoodie onto the bed, and head downstairs to the freezer and then the bathroom, grabbing a wet washcloth for Kara's face. I enter her room again with a bag of frozen peas and the rag.

She takes them, muttering a thank you. As I settle myself beside her, she gives me an odd sideways look. "What's wrong? Don't you have your own room?" She puts the bag of peas over her left eye.

"Just making sure you're okay."

"Always gotta save the girl." She moves the peas and studies me. "Why is that? Isn't it exhausting?"

I laugh, but it has a bitter edge. I'm glad she's warming up to me, but I say, "I'm no savior." *I'm the reason you're sitting here with frozen peas on your face.*

As we both fall silent, I look around the room, realizing we're surrounded by a collage of newspaper clippings and images, scribbled words and drawings. There's a strange theme of life and love. Every inch of the walls is covered. It's a work of art, really. There's a sunscreen advertisement with children playing in a pool, a flyer for an unwed mother's home with a teen cradling her round belly, and a drawing of an older woman gazing out a window with longing in her eyes.

The largest image is a tattered movie poster of *Gone With The Wind*. The stars embrace in frantic desperation against a backdrop of images from the Civil War.

None of it is what I expected from this sad, dark girl.

Kara breaks through my thoughts. "I'm sorry I freaked out at you in the kitchen. You're not a total ass."

"Actually, I *am* an ass." I take the rag from her and pick up her hand, wiping her bloody knuckles with the wet washcloth. "This shouldn't have happened."

She stares at my attempt to clean her wounds for a second like she's frozen, but then she pulls her fingers back and shivers. "You need to go to your room."

I study her face, her white-blue eyes. The memory of kissing her at the club surfaces, and I realize that she's still only wearing her bra.

I try to swallow. "Okay."

I stand and head for the door, feeling off kilter. This is Kara. I don't even like her. What am I thinking?

"There was something there," she says, stopping my movement. "In the room when he attacked me."

I turn back. "What do you mean?"

She shakes her head. "I told the guy that I just wanted to sit for a second, and he flipped out. A complete one-eighty—too quick for me to stop him. And there was a faint rotten egg smell. I didn't even connect the dots until he started hitting me."

I shift my feet. "What do you think it was?"

She looks right at me. "As if you can't guess."

"Kara, please believe I—"

She raises her hand, waving off my words. "Yeah, yeah, I know. You didn't know." She touches her cheek absently, feeling for the bruise, and flinches when her fingers find the wound. "So how was the Angelic One?"

My heart sinks. "She was fine." I move closer to the bed, wondering what to do, what to say. It's obvious she's hurt by what happened, but it's more than the violence. She almost seems . . . jealous.

Why would she be jealous of Rebecca?

She puts the bag of peas back to her cheek. "Well, good. Did you get the information you needed?"

"Yeah, I think so." I study her, wishing the house didn't muffle her emotions so I could know what she's really feeling. "Your arm's bruised."

She moves her arm, looks at the emerging violet splotch, and then says, "My hip, too." She puts the peas down and stands, peeling back the waist of her pants a little, showing me another bruise. "Kinda looks like a turtle."

I can't help smiling at her silly observation. And then something beside the odd-shaped bruise catches my eye. Her tattoo. I hadn't gotten the chance to see it close-up until now. It's made up of woven green vines and a cluster of small violet flowers. There's a pink lily off to the side, and the vines continue to climb from her hip, reaching up to her rib cage.

Violets and lilies. Ava's words. She said something about violets and lilies from the dream about our mom the other day. But what was it?

. . . he must touch the violets and lilies to find surrender, to find his hidden blood . . .

Without thinking, I step a little closer, reaching out slowly to slide a fingertip over the largest petal of the lily. Instantly a vibration moves up my arm, and I swear the mark on my hand burns against my skin.

I clench my fingers into a fist, but I don't step away.

"Did you feel that?" she asks.

I shake my head. "I don't know." I feel so much, always so much.

She takes my hand and brings it to her side again, resting it on the violets. I look at the purple flowers between my fingers and feel the heat of her skin, the way it slides beneath my palm, soft as silk. And that vibration moves through my arm again.

Her breath quickens.

I find myself moving closer as her blue eyes go wide with wonder. My heart stutters and my chest aches with some unknown need.

"Are you doing this?" I ask. *Are you making me want this?*

"No," she breathes. The smell of her turns to spice, sharp and warm, and I know I'm sensing her now, even through the block in the house.

We stand like that for an eternity, still as statues on the outside, but inside I'm running, running toward a place I've never been. I should be terrified. But all I feel is strength. Rightness.

And then Kara moves, her hands skimming up my chest, testing the boundaries. Her palms slide to my shoulders, her fingers tracing the line of the muscles in my arms, down to my waist. She grips my shirt, stretching it a little, waiting for me to tell her to stop. But I watch her lift it, let her pull it up, raising my arms, and I even take the last of it off myself, dropping it to the floor.

We breathe, staring at each other.

The vibrations move between us. My left arm buzzes with them. I think she's doing it. Whatever's happening, it's her.

I reach up and brush my marked knuckles across her cheek, amazed at the feel of her, the way her eyes seem to see everything, the way she pulls me into her. I can't seem to remember why I shouldn't kiss her. And kiss her. And . . .

I kiss her, taking her face in both hands, skimming my thumb over her jaw as she leans into the touch, reaching out to curl her fingers around the back of my neck. I have to remind myself to breathe. I need more of her. The emotions roll over me in a rush, a tangle of sensation and movement, heat and sugar and heady aromas.

I grip her tighter.

Her nails dig into my shoulders. My hands slide down her spine. The kiss deepens, goes on forever, until I can barely see sense. I explore her shape, the feel of her ribs, the textures and taste of her skin on my tongue as I kiss her neck, her shoulders, her chest. As I draw trembling gasps from her lips, she grips me so hard it hurts.

Our bodies mesh. Our breath mingles in frenzied desperation. Nothing else exists except her. Her warmth. Her spice. Her.

I whisper her name into her neck, pressing her against the wall.

She rocks against me in answer, and the poster behind her rips at the edge, falling to the floor. I kiss her harder and fumble for the waist of her jeans, not sure what I'm doing. My fingers tremble against the denim.

I need everything. Everything.

But as I pop the button of her pants and the sound of the zipper scratches the air, she goes still, whimpering. Her body shivers against mine like a frightened animal, and everything turns cold. Guilt rears its head as our lips part.

Disoriented, I stare at her pain-filled features, and my palm slides down her arm, trying to reassure her, reassure myself she's real and what I think just happened actually did.

She bows her head, forehead resting against my chest, breath coming in stops and starts.

Then realization falls over me in a rush, and I'm aware that I wasn't acting fully on my own a moment ago. I didn't see her ice-blue energy tangle around me this time, like I did at the club, but I could feel it. And there's no way that was natural. There's no way I could lose it so completely with someone I'm not even sure I like.

I wonder when everything changed. I wonder when she took control. And I wonder why the fact that she used her strange power on me doesn't bother me. Not even a little.

It all was so real, so urgent, so much like my own feelings.

A small sound comes from her, another whimper, like she's in pain. At first I think I hurt her. But then her shoulders shake, and she presses harder into my chest and begins to weep. And weep.

I hold her against me while the bitter tang of it all swirls around us. Dark sorrow in her bones and her skin, years and years of pain and hurt. She pours it over me in salty tears and waves of energy.

"I'm sorry," she whispers. "I wasn't . . . I didn't . . ."

"Shhh." I run my hand over her hair, attempting to comfort her as my body comes back to earth in a crash and I try to figure out where it all went wrong.

She cries until her tears are used up, until the connection between us becomes something else, a soothing link I don't think I've ever felt before: peace and stillness. After a while she goes limp, leaning into me more, falling asleep standing up.

I take her to the bed.

She's unsure at first, ashamed, looking at her hands rather than at me, so I lie down and pull her to my side. She settles after that, nestling her head into the crook of my arm, her hand on my chest, over my heart. We breathe and feel the rhythm of each other's pulse through skin and bone. And soon we both drift off into sleep.

———

I drop my backpack onto the floor and head for the fridge, pulling out the carton of milk before I hear the crash—the sound of glass shattering and a deep thud.

My body goes still as chills fall over me in a rush.

A cry comes from the walls. Mom's room.

Muffled words and another crash.

I drop the milk. It spills onto the yellowed tile to the rhythm of the thud . . . thud . . . thud *in the walls.*

Everything goes still. My cheeks are wet with tears. My heart is the only sound left on earth as it crashes like thunder against my chest.

Mom's bedroom door opens, and one of her boyfriends stands there. The smells of violence and terror and wrongness *spill out from* behind him. He adjusts his belt, his knuckles stained with blood. Then he sniffs and wipes his nose with his shirt.

"What're you looking at, you little prick?"

I can only shiver and stare past him at Mom's fetal form in the bed.

He growls, grabs his jacket off the back of the couch, and heads for the door. "See you next week," he sneers as he walks out.

When the latch clicks, I run to her side. I stare down at her on the bed, not sure if I can touch her. There's so much pain coming off her. It weighs me down, presses at me.

She wraps her hand over mine, and I see pink scratches, a smudge of blood. "I'm okay, Aidan. Don't worry. Mommy's okay. Just a disagreement is all."

A whimper escapes my throat as a million questions circle in my head. "I'm sorry."

A tear slips down her bruised cheek.

All the men that come here seem to hurt her and make her cry. Why does she let them?

"Why did my daddy go away?" I ask without thinking. "Didn't he want to protect you?" I wish I was bigger so I could punch the men away myself.

Her brow creases in pain, and I'm suddenly sorry I brought it up. I should know better.

Her voice shakes as she says, "He tried, but he couldn't stay."

"Where did he go?" Maybe I can go find him.

She shakes her head, biting her lips together.

And something comes to me, something a girl said to me yesterday at school. She kissed me on the cheek and said she loved me because I told Mark to stop pulling her hair. So I ask, "Did you love him?"

She goes so still I feel like even the people outside are frozen. And then she stops crying. She sits up and moves to kneel in front of me, biting back the pain.

"I loved your father like a fire, Aidan. He was a part of me, and I was a part of him. It will always be that way. He would protect me if he could. I promise." She kisses my cheek with her swelling lip. "And he gave me you. You're just like your father. Brave and good. Never forget that."

She stands on shaky legs and wipes the tears from her face. "And those men won't be coming anymore. Mommy's going to have another baby."

I stand back and gape at her thin tummy where I know babies usually grow. "Really?"

She nods and begins pulling the rugs off the wood floor and tossing them in the corner. Then she goes into the closet and pulls a large box from the darkness with a symbol on the curved top.

Hidden is what my insides tell me it means.

Out of the box she takes candles and chalk. A bowl and some bottles and a fist of dried plants. Then she moves to the center of the room and begins to draw on the floor. A wide circle, large enough to hold two of me lying down. Then she goes back to the box and takes out a tattered book.

Placing it open on the floor beside her, she begins to write inside the circle, copying the book's secrets onto the wood.

"Things will be different now," she says, "I promise. Mommy's going to protect us all."

NINETEEN

I open my eyes as voices from the hall filter into my consciousness. Kara's still curled up against me, her hand resting over my heart. Her dark hair spills over my bare chest in a tangled mass. I want to get a look at her bruised face, but she's turned away from me.

Someone knocks on the door. My body tenses as I think of who it might be and what they'll see if they come in. I lift my arm from her back and glance at my shirt on the floor and then at her, her form still as death. If I'm quiet, maybe whoever it is will go away.

No such luck; the door opens.

Connor peeks in. "Kara, time to—" He stops, and his eyes go wide.

I'm frozen, caught, and he stands there, looking at Kara's face, her bruised skin, her half-naked form. His shock shifts to anger, then rage. His lips tighten and his nostrils flare.

And he charges.

I barely have time to move Kara off me before I'm being swung at.

He misses as I duck my head and roll off the bed, but I'm unbalanced and he's pissed. His knee catches me in the gut as I try to slip out of the way.

Kara grips her head and starts to sit up, holding onto the wall. "Connor, stop," she says.

But he lunges again, pushing me into the dresser. "What the fuck did you do to her?" He swings.

I dodge, and half the stuff on the dresser gets knocked to the floor by Connor's arm. Something shatters, and Kara groans.

I shove back while Connor's unguarded from the swing and yell, "Calm down! Let me explain."

But his rage bubbles like thick oil. He comes at me again, and I punch at an opening, hitting him square on the side of the face, sending jarring pain through my hand and up my arm, reminding me of where my knuckles have been.

He stumbles back, stunned.

"What the hell, Connor?" Kara rises from the bed on shaky legs to shut the door and almost trips on my discarded shirt. I reach out, catching her as I shake the impact of the hit from my hand. That kid's got a steel skull.

I kick the door shut as Connor growls, "Get your hands off her or I'll slit your fucking throat." His eyes are full of crazy, and I totally believe him. He'd happily slice me in half to protect Kara.

"It's all right, Connor," she says, moving away from me as much as she can without letting go of my arm for balance. "It wasn't Aidan that kicked my ass; he just brought me home."

Connor sneers. "Sure he did."

"What the hell?" I say, exasperation spilling over. "I get it. I do. But I just brought her home and that's all." *Sort of.*

We glare, daring each other to make the next move. I can see he's not buying any of it.

His jaw jerks after a few seconds, and he folds his arms over his chest, looking resolved. "She gets hurt on your watch, that's on you. Doesn't matter if it was your fists that did the pounding. Your ass is mine."

"Just go, Connor," Kara says, grabbing his arm and pulling his large form closer to the door.

"I don't trust this asshole, Kara," he says through his teeth.

"No kidding," she says, giving him another shove.

He points at me as he opens the door and then walks out, slamming it behind him like an exclamation point.

"He didn't mean it," she says, moving back to the bed. "He's just pissed."

I release a tight laugh. "Really. I barely noticed." I rub my stomach where his knee met my gut. "Look, I'm sorry. You two obviously have something going on."

She shakes her head. "No, it's not like that."

"Then what is it like?" I ask, as if I have a vested interest. Which I don't. But I can't keep my stupid mouth shut when it comes to this girl.

She sits down on the bed. "He just . . . I . . ." She covers her face with her hands and grumbles through her fingers, "I don't know. It's a long story."

I pick up my shirt and pull it over my head. "I get it. It's complicated. Friends with benefits, or whatever."

She laughs. "Hardly. No, Connor and I . . . we never . . ." She motions, like I know the rest. And I do. "We're really just friends. He's like a brother to me."

"A very protective brother."

She looks up at me. Her left eye is rimmed in purple, her cheek swollen and pink. Looking at it makes my chest ache. I kicked a guy's ass to protect her last night, so I can't really blame Connor— he's known Kara a lot longer than me.

"Can you hand me that tank top?" she asks, pointing to the pile of dark grey on the floor.

I pick it up and hand it to her. As she slips it over her head, I can see that she's obviously stiff and uncomfortable. "Thanks." She looks at me through her hair, subdued and embarrassed. I'm not sure why since we slept all night with nothing but skin between us.

"How's your face feel?" I ask.

She touches her cheek gingerly. "This isn't anything new. I'll be fine."

"You keep saying that. I don't get it. Why would you let guys do that to you?" My words come out a little too forcefully, childhood memories sharpening my feelings. "You seem stronger than that."

"I'm anything but strong. More like cursed."

"I seriously doubt that . . ." But the words fade from my tongue as I notice the mark on her neck through her hair. The mark on her soul.

"Trust me. I'm cursed—thanks to the man who spawned me."

Chills work over me. I know about parents and curses. "What happened?"

"Dad wasn't much of a nurturer. He figured out I was more useful to him as a tool than a daughter. So he sold me off."

My God. "He . . . sold you?"

"Not at first. At first I was a good piece of his game—it was always about what was good for the con. For a while, I was tiny and cute and made him seem sympathetic—a single father and all, just trying to get by." She laughs bitterly. "But after a while it got thicker and darker, and soon he was in it too deep. I was just a good girl who thought it was a fun game—until my eleventh birthday when he took me to a medicine room in Chinatown and asked the man there to *bless* me with the spirit of attraction.

"It burned. I've never felt anything like it. With all the smoke and chanting—you haven't heard a spell till you've heard it in Chinese—very creepy. And after that, nothing was ever the same. Men would offer hundreds of dollars just to pet my head for a minute. I was a gold mine. And eventually the world became his as I was passed from rich man to rich man."

My stomach rises, and I have to lean on the dresser. "Kara . . ." But there's nothing to say; no words can fill that darkness.

She acts like I didn't speak, her chin high, determination set in her shoulders. "For three years, there were so many faces. So many nameless, soulless faces. But Daddy wasn't very good with keeping money. It slipped through his fingers like sand. The man had no self-control at all.

"And the *blessing* that medicine man put on me had a bit of a side effect. Attraction is a funny thing, apparently. I didn't just draw in men. I could feel energy. In everything. Pulsing. Pushing at me." She shivers and hugs herself.

Then she glances at me, a pleading look in her eyes. "You know, don't you? That smothering feeling from so much coming at you?"

I nod. Boy, do I ever.

"One night when I was fourteen," she continues, "my dad was especially down on his luck. I think he owed some bookie fifty grand—or maybe that was just the first payment. They were threatening to cut a few pounds of flesh from his oversized midsection as a down payment if he didn't pony up.

"So when a man came into the club and offered him six hundred grand for me outright—no questions, no names, no strings attached—he jumped at it. He didn't care that he'd never see me again."

She laughs, sounding a little off kilter.

"I should've been relieved, I guess. I mean Dad treated me like shit. But it crushed me when he passed me off like that, because I couldn't even pretend that he cared anymore."

I move to her side, wanting to touch her, to comfort her, but I decide against it.

"I was handed over to a bald guy who looked like a carnival worker from the twenties—Sid. I was terrified of him at first, but in the end he was my savior. He brought me here with Connor. And soon we had Jax and Holly, then Lester and Finger. And now you." She gives me a sad smile. "It's been three years, and no one unwanted has touched me since. I'm safe."

"So the thing you do . . . like with that man in the school . . ." *And me.* "That's part of your curse?"

"Actually, it's not. When Sid brought me here, he reversed the curse." She lifts her shirt a little and motions to the tattoo on her side. "He did a spell and flipped the curse on its head. The next morning this tattoo appeared."

My stomach rises again. "That thing just showed up after a spell?" That means it's magic, and for some reason it affects me. Could my own mark be from a spell, too? In Ava's dream, Mom said I should touch the violets and lilies to find my hidden blood. And the violets and lilies are there on Kara because of magic.

"It was faded at first," she says, interrupting the questions rolling around in my head, "but with each session Sid did to bind the curse, it got brighter and brighter. He said it was some sort of lock to keep the curse held down but also to harness my own energy and turn the curse power on its head. So I'd never be used by any man ever again. I use them instead."

"This is dangerous stuff, Kara," I say.

"I know. I feel it. But it's worth it. I'm free."

I release a long breath. "I assume after the tattoo appeared your ability to feel things got stronger, too."

"Not really *stronger* but clearer. More focused."

"Oh," I say, wondering what to think. "Can I see it again?"

Nervous vibrations muffle the air between us. "What? The tattoo?"

I nod.

After a second she turns her back to me and pulls up her shirt.

I follow the green vine and flower pattern down to her waist, where it disappears into her pants. I focus my energy, trying to really *see* what the tattoo is, not just what it looks like, trying to get a vision of it on her soul.

A pattern emerges, faint but there, in the curls of the vines, in the shape of the flowers coming together.

Three circular symbols.

The first I know means *Intimacy.* Or *Knowing.* Below it, the symbol for *Power* is overlaid with the symbol for *Awaken.*

Awaken the Power.

The third symbol dips past her pants.

I swallow. "Can I see all of it?"

She gives me a pained look, like she's almost embarrassed. I clarify by saying, "I see something, but I need to see all of it to be sure."

She bites the corner of her lip and unbuttons her jeans, pulling them down past her hip.

The third symbol is one I've seen before, but I'm not sure where. It's a double circle, overlapping. Inside one circle it says *Demon,* and inside the other it says *Seer,* and where they intersect the space is filled with the marks for the three types of death—*Mind, Body, Spirit.*

Demon. Seer. Complete Death.

And I suddenly realize where I've seen it.

I lift my marked hand and look at Kara's mark. Then I look at mine. A section of my own mark rises from the rest, almost as if it's calling out to me. Or showing itself for the very first time . . .

Demon. Seer. Complete Death.

It's exactly the same.

TWENTY

Ava's downstairs at the kitchen table. She's eating Froot Loops and laughing at something Lester is saying. Jax sits beside Lester and flicks rainbow-colored Os into the sink one at a time. Holly's frying eggs on the stove top and talking a mile a minute even though no one's listening. There's no sign of Connor.

I watch from the stairs, trying to gather my thoughts. I left Kara in her room. She said she needed to take a shower, get dressed, that we'd talk later. But I think she just wanted to be alone. After she zipped her pants back up she practically shoved me out the bedroom door.

I thought things were awkward *before* last night.

She didn't ask why I was comparing our marks, so I didn't mention that something hidden on her tattoo matched mine. Things are weird enough between us as it is, and she probably only sees flowers when she looks at hers.

Until I know what it means, I don't want to let my imagination run rampant.

As I walk into the kitchen, everyone goes silent.

Jax grins wide. "How was she? Does she bite?"

My vision narrows. "Wipe that smirk off your face before I cut it off for you."

"Ohhh . . . tough guy," Lester says in a singsong voice.

"Calm down, man," Jax says, holding up his hands. "Just admiring your work with getting the ungettable. That girl's as frigid as Antarctica."

"And there's been others standing in the NTL, naked-time line, for years," Holly pipes in, not turning around, still frying her eggs. "You show up and *poof!*" Her spatula waves in the air, sending a bit of egg flying. "It's suddenly Kara-Aidan Fest 2015. Or Kaidan Fest, if you will."

Ava's watching the whole thing, her gaze moving from person to person, a look of open curiosity on her face.

Jax flicks another Froot Loop toward the sink. It bounces off the counter, joining a rainbow pile on the floor. "Connor looked like he was gonna cut you to ribbons. Is there about to be a little WWF shit?"

"Nothing happened, so he can calm down," I say. "You all can."

Ava frowns. "Did you have sex with Kara?" She doesn't look mad, not exactly. Maybe irritated. "What about Rebecca?"

Lester grins. "Ooh . . . who's Rebecca?"

Ava knows about Rebecca? Great.

"The boy's a slut," Holly says with a giggle. "Want some eggs, lover boyo?" She holds out a pan of overcooked yellow mush.

I can't help scrunching up my nose. At both her words and offer.

Finger comes in, stealthy enough that I didn't feel him behind me. He holds out a plate, and Holly fills it with eggs. Then he slips away again, heading into a doorway under the staircase.

"There's bagels, too." Holly says, pointing to the top of the fridge. "You must be hungry after a night in the bouncy house with our resident emo chick—"

I stop listening and say to Ava, "Can I talk to you?" I motion to the entryway, and she gets up and follows me out of the kitchen as Holly continues entertaining herself with the soap opera in her head.

Ava stops at the base of the stairs and turns to me. "This is about Kara." She frowns again, obviously not a fan.

"That dream you told me about the other day, the one where Mom talked to you about me. What was it she said again about violets and lilies?" I fold my arms across my chest, feeling jittery just talking about it.

Ava steps back. "No way."

"What did she say, Ava?"

"It's not right. Something isn't right." I give her a look, and she continues with a sigh. "Fine. What she said was: *He doesn't know which way to walk along the line. The Light he found will lead him. Its wings sit beneath the heart. But he must touch the violets and lilies to find surrender, to find his hidden blood.*" She watches me absorb the words for a second and then adds, "Now tell me what happened."

I shake my head, not keen on talking to my little sister about my love life. But her words—my mom's words—mean something. Kara has a tattoo with the same flowers in the dream, and for some reason it affects me. Could she be the "Light" who'll lead me? Sid did call the kids in this house lights and beacons. Maybe that's what it means.

But where does Rebecca fit—if she even fits at all?

"How did you know about Rebecca? I never mentioned her." I'm used to Ava *knowing* things out of the blue. But there's usually a reason.

She blinks at me and then walks past, heading up the stairs.

"Ava . . ." I turn and follow her.

"You'll get angry," she says as she slips into our room, trying to shut the door in my face.

I push into the room, shutting the door behind me. "Tell me. Now."

"I'll say if you tell me what happened with Kara. It's only fair."

"Seriously?" As much as she seems to have an ancient soul, in reality she's just an eleven-year-old little girl. And by *little* I mean annoying. I breathe through my nose. "I promise not to get mad."

If she thinks I won't like it, then I know what this is about: she must've used her powers.

She squints at me, trying to see if I'm lying.

I raise my hands. "Swear."

She chews on her lip for a few seconds, and then she says, "I may have done one of . . . of Mom's spells."

My jaw goes tight.

"I told you," she says in a tiny voice. "You're mad now."

I try to reason past the red blocking my vision. "A spell." I can't even express how terrifying and inevitable this all feels. "From *her* grimoire. Why in the hell would you do that?"

"I wanted to see if I could."

"Of course you can!" I wave my arms, exasperated. "You know what kind of shit you can do!"

Her chin goes up in defiance. "You swore you wouldn't get mad."

I cover my face with my hands and try to calm down. Getting pissed isn't going to help. The shit's already hitting the fan. No stopping it now. And Ava doesn't remember the darkness Mom brought into our world with her casting. She doesn't remember that horror.

Maybe it's time to tell her what I know. I just have to say it: *Your mother's spells cursed you and got her killed.* Easy.

But the words won't emerge. Instead I say, "I'm sorry." My head aches from it all. It feels like I'll never stop any of it. "You can tell me. What spell, Ava?"

She digs into the back of the closet, pulling out her bag and the grimoire.

I step back as she opens it and points to a drawing of swirls.

No, not a drawing, it's a series of words written in a swirl shape.

"I wanted to do a small one, just see what it felt like," she says, "to see if I could do it. So I did a protective-link spell." She glances up from the page. "On you."

I'm fairly sure my eyes are about to pop out of my head and roll across the floor. "Me? You did a spell on *me*?"

She shakes her head violently. "No, no! I did a spell *about* you. It's different. It's a looking spell, a spell that unveils hidden things. I just wanted to see a little of your future, that's all."

"Damn it, Ava. You shouldn't have done that."

"I know."

"How did you do it, anyway? Don't you need innocent blood and something from the subject for a spell like that?" I remember far too much of Mom's casting habits.

She pulls a puff of fuzz from the folds of the grimoire and holds it out as an offering. It's splotched with something brown and crusty. "I cut some of the fur stuff from inside your hoodie and used bird blood for the conduit."

I take the blood-caked fuzz from her and sit on the bed. The weight on my shoulders just gained about a hundred pounds. "When was this?"

My little sister did one of my mom's spells.

My little sister killed a bird.

"I did it after you left me the other day, in the orange trees," she says. "I felt something was different when you showed up. You were distracted, and there was this thing in your eyes."

"What *thing*?"

"A connection thing. Like you were suddenly worried, but not about me. I wanted to know who it was."

"So you did something horrible that'll only make me worry more?"

She fidgets with the edge of the grimoire, looking urgent. "Aidan, when I did the spell, I saw her. Rebecca. She was really strong in the object I was using. I saw her really clear."

"That's 'cause it was her brother's hoodie you stole that fuzz from. And she loved her brother, but he drowned."

Her eyes grow like something's suddenly coming clear. "So she loved the boy who wore that hoodie?"

I nod.

"But now she loves you."

"She doesn't even know me, Ava. She can't love me."

"But what I saw was very real. And there was a bond between you guys. It totally felt like love."

My ears perk up at that. And even though I shouldn't be pushing, even though my curiosity will only encourage her, I ask anyway. "You saw *both* our futures? And we were together?"

"She wanted to stay by your side. No matter what. It was like she was somehow linked to you in a spirit way."

"But there's no way that can happen," I say, more to myself than to Ava.

"Why?"

"It just can't. I won't be seeing her again. It's not safe. For you or the others."

"But you have to!" she whines, sounding as if her favorite TV couple just broke up. "You can't let that Kara girl get in your head!"

"Kara is *not* in my head."

She gives me a disbelieving look. "You kissed her, didn't you?"

Twice. "It was just a moment. We were both tired." And somehow fell into each other's arms? I sound like an idiot.

She rolls her eyes. "Whatever you do, just be careful. I don't like her."

"Why do you keep saying that? There must be a reason. Did you see a bad thing in a vision about her or something? An image of darkness maybe?" I really would like to know this. I have complicated feelings about Kara myself, but mostly that's because she seems so unhinged. So unpredictable. All I see with my own sight is wounds. Loads and loads of wounds.

"She's broken."

"So am I, Ava."

She shakes her head. "No. She's nothing like you, Aidan. Nothing." She hugs the grimoire tighter.

I wish she would tell me what's going on. I wish she hadn't done that spell. And it's probably not the first time she's done one from that grimoire by the sound of it.

I shiver, thinking about it all, seeing the look on her face, the frantic widening of her eyes, like she's reliving Mom's descent . . . If this gets much worse, there's no doubt in my mind that it's going to kill her. I have to find a way to change the outcome—to find out if I even *can* change it. Maybe if I knew more about my own abilities . . .

But my abilities will lead to my dad. They'll lead to the part of me I've been trying my whole life to bury. Maybe it's time now to start facing it, though, to start seeing how far it goes. And if it does bring me to my dad, then I'll face that too, when the time comes. But I have to use everything in me to save Ava. Even if it means confronting what I'm always running from.

TWENTY-ONE

After a while, I wander downstairs and sit on the couch next to Finger. His thumbs are flying on the controller as he attempts to kill a dragon with a sword. It looks like some kind of medieval game.

"What's the score?" I ask.

He shrugs. He smells like Funyuns.

"Looks exciting," I say, even though I don't really give a crap.

He shrugs again.

"Man, life sucks."

Finger snorts.

We sit there in silence for a while as he kills the dragon and then a horde of trolls. After an hour or so I begin to feel like I can breathe again.

As if he felt me relaxing, Connor comes into the archway. "Garage, now. Sid wants you on a job."

I stand to follow him, but before I leave the room, I turn and say to Finger, "Thanks for the chat, man. It really helped." And strangely enough, it did.

Finger smiles, but he doesn't look away from the TV.

On my way to the garage, I work up my nerve to ask Sid for help. I'm not sure what to say to him or how, but I need more information than what I've got. I need a clearer understanding of my abilities and how they link to my mom. I need more of the story of how she started down her dark path.

Whatever I request from Sid, though, needs to be simple and not point back to Ava. I'm not ready to trust him with her yet—or anyone, for that matter.

In the garage, Sid is sitting in the passenger seat of a Jeep, walking stick in hand. He's always holding that thing, and he doesn't even have a limp. He frowns at me as I open the door to get in the backseat. "You look horrid, son."

Gee, I wonder why.

"Connor mentioned there was an altercation," he adds, nodding to Connor, who's entering the garage behind me.

"Just a misunderstanding," I say, watching Connor as he gets into the driver's seat. "Nothing major."

Connor doesn't say anything; he just starts the engine and backs out of the garage. Sid makes a sound of agreement, and I wonder if he actually believes me or if he's just going along with it to keep the peace.

As we drive down Hollywood Boulevard, heading for the freeway, my pulse races. I can't shake my nervousness about asking for Sid's help. But I need to do it as soon as possible. I need to do it now.

"So how are you and your sister settling in?" Sid asks, looking over his shoulder at me.

"Fine," I say. "Thanks."

"Your sister is very talented," he adds. "Hearing her music fill the house is lovely."

"Yeah, she's been playing one instrument or another since she was five." The music helps her channel her abilities better, she says. It definitely feels otherworldly when she plays.

"Does musical talent run in the family?" he asks.

"Um, no. I can't tell one note from another to save my life."

Sid laughs. Connor hasn't reacted to our exchange at all. He just focuses on the road ahead. There's a slight tinge of purple on the side of his jaw where I hit him. I'm thinking he won't be laughing at anything I say for a while.

I decide to take the segue. "Speaking of family, I'm wondering if you could help me with something."

Sid turns a little in his seat to face me. "I'll help with whatever you need." No red spark lights his eye. He's being truthful. Whatever I need.

"I want to try and find some of my mom's family. Her mother or her grandparents maybe."

He nods slow, considering.

"I'm not sure I want to talk to them," I add, "or let them know Ava and I are around. I just have a lot of questions."

"Understandable," Sid says. "You have questions about your mother. What about your father?" His voice is careful as he asks the question. Measured. As if he knows my fears.

I look out the window. "I'm not sure about that yet. But he's also the reason I want to contact my mom's family. They may know who he was."

Sid nods again. "Answers are important." He turns back around and adds, more to himself, "We all need to know where we come from if we're going to fulfill our destiny."

It's silent after that. My nerves settle knowing that Sid's willing to help me, knowing I might actually be one step closer to answers.

We head to what I think might be Brea or Anaheim. The neighborhood we end up in is nice, with each house a perfect stucco replica of the next. Lots of peach and tan. Not a word has been spoken about the job we're here for or why Sid wanted me to come.

We park in front of one of the clone lots, and Sid pulls out a folder from a file organizer at his feet.

He hands the folder to Connor. "Lester said you saw the footage and read the summary, so I'll let you take this one. All we need to do for now is get them to sign the papers and hand over the check."

"Why me?" Connor asks, looking perturbed. "You're the paperwork genie."

"Actually," Sid says, glancing at me, "Holly is the paperwork genie. I'm just the closer." Then he looks back to Connor. "You need to start doing more of the front work. I won't be here forever, and you'll need to forward the mission."

What does he mean by *that*? Sid's only in his twenties.

"Also," he adds with a sly grin, "these clients are more into pretty blonds."

Connor rolls his eyes and gets out of the Jeep.

I follow them, catching up to Sid on the walkway. "And what am I doing here, exactly?"

"Just observe. I'll be asking for your thoughts after we're done." He knocks on the front door. "It won't take long."

"Just pretend you're not here," Connor says to me.

"No problem."

A thin guy in a suit and tie opens the door. My first thought is that it's a bit formal for around the house, when another man— short, rounder, and a bit more . . . flamboyant—comes up behind him, clasping a hand to his chest. "Oh, thank God. I'm not crazy. You've found something."

"We have," Connor says.

The man in the Hawaiian shirt brightens up as if Connor were Justin Bieber. "Oh my, aren't you cute as button."

Connor just glances at Sid, looking tired.

"Come in," the man in the suit says. "I have about an hour before I need to be back at the office."

"I've got all day," the other man says, waving Connor and Sid in. "When you work in the industry, it's feast or famine, you know."

I follow Sid and Connor in, keeping my walls up against any energy as I walk over the threshold. I still feel a bit of a shiver in the air, but it's not uncomfortable. It almost feels like a restless child. It seems to be coming mostly from the brighter man.

The two clients give me curious looks, as if I'm a stray cat who followed them all home.

"This is Connor," Sid says, motioning. "He's going to take point on this case. And this is Aidan. He's new and will just be observing."

The two men shake hands with Connor and introduce themselves. The taller guy in the suit is John, and the other one is Simon. They turn to me, but they don't offer their hands. Simon just gives me an awkward wave, and John gives me an odd look, like he's not sure about me.

We all sit at the dining room table. I listen with half an ear as I study the house and its simple decor. I think most would describe it as tasteful. I don't see any religious symbols or occult items, or feel any energy emanating from one that might be hidden.

And then I recognize a picture hanging on the wall. It's a watercolor painting of a boy standing and looking out at the ocean. And the couch is familiar, too. I've seen it all before. In the footage Lester was watching the other day.

Is this the banshee house?

Connor points at the top page of a stack of papers he's placed in front of the clients. "This is the release for filming both your property and your person, and in the next section"—he flips up to the third page and points at the bottom—"it says that you agree to the services we're offering and that there's no guarantee for the process. It may work, it may not."

John looks over the papers and nods.

Simon pats his arm. "See, honey, they speak your legalese."

"And the payment?" John asks.

Connor flips to the back page. "That's here. And all moneys have to be exchanged up front."

John, reading intently, nods again.

Simon smiles at me. "He said *moneys*," he says and laughs. "Sounds like monkeys. Are we exchanging monkeys?"

Connor and John barely seem to notice Simon's goofiness. But Sid grins back and says, "No monkey business." And they both laugh like they're at a party.

Once John and Simon are done signing, and a few more goofy jokes pass between Sid and Simon, the conversation turns to the case. Connor explains what they found in the video while showing pictures that were in the folder and pointing out things I can't see from where I'm sitting.

From Simon's descriptions—John hasn't experienced any weirdness—it sounds like a definite time slip: a tear in the circle of time's fabric that lets a small moment slip through to another, parallel time. Just a quick moment—in this case, a woman wearing a dress from the 1920s standing in Simon and John's kitchen. A ghost would cause more of a ruckus and would be more obvious on film. But there's no ghost or anything here—not that I feel.

However, Connor is saying right now to the clients that it *is* a ghost. And he sounds very sure about it, bringing out news clippings and old photos. He's explaining that a woman was murdered and her body was found in a nearby ravine. He's saying that *we*, LA Paranormal Investigative Agency, believe it's the spirit of this murdered woman who's roaming their kitchen. Looking for her lost love or something.

It's all total bullshit. Red is sparking in Connor's eyes like it's Christmas.

He's making it sound very convincing, though.

And John and Simon are buying it hook, line, and sinker. They shake their heads in sadness for the poor dead woman in their kitchen, and Simon even tears up a little. Then John writes a check and hands it to Connor, while Sid and Simon discuss where a guy can get a decent manicure.

I sit in shocked, revolted silence. It's a complete con?

TWENTY-TWO

When we're back in the Jeep, I can't stay silent. "You were totally lying to those poor guys."

Connor starts the engine and drives away before responding. "It's not as if we're not going to help them."

"There's nothing you can do about a time slip," I say. "Except move. You're not going to help them, you're going to con them."

Sid turns around and looks at me with open surprise. "You could tell it was a time slip?"

I raise my brow at him.

"Amazing," he says, pulling out a small piece of paper from his front vest pocket and writing something down on it with a tiny yellow pencil.

"Are you seriously taking notes on me?" I ask, leaning forward to see what he's writing.

He holds it to his chest to hide it. "I need to know what assets all my soldiers have."

"Does Connor have 'dreamy blue eyes' on his list of assets?"

Connor rewards me with a small laugh.

Sid holds out the paper. "Don't be ridiculous."

At the top of the paper it says *Aidan*, and under that: *Speaks/reads Latin, Greek, and Hebrew.* He's just added: *Time slip knowledge.*

"No sinister intent; I'm just not as quick in the head as I was when I was young."

"You're only . . . what, twenty-five?" I say.

"Twenty-four, actually," he corrects.

Connor smiles like that's funny to him.

"Let's get back to the fact that you both should be in jail," I say. "Why are you conning those guys?"

"We're not conning them," Connor says. "Not exactly."

"There is a way to be rid of a time slip," Sid adds. "But explaining all the magical facts and physics of how time works to those men wouldn't have helped business much. So we put it in a story form they could understand."

"You lied," I say. "Now they think there's a ghost in their house."

"No," Sid says, "now they can have peace. And soon as we do the sight-blocking spell, the image of the woman in the past won't be seen by them anymore. Then I plan on doing an added blessing for their home as a bonus. It's a win-win, you see."

But before I can start asking more questions about this spell he's talking about and why they didn't just lay out the truth for the two guys—who looked perfectly capable of understanding the subject—before they took their money, my phone rings.

I pull it out of my pocket, but I don't recognize the number, so I slip it back in my jeans.

"You don't plan on answering that?" Sid says.

"Nope."

It stops ringing and then starts again a second later.

I pull the thing out of my pocket and answer, "What?"

No response. I look at the number—it's the same one. I put the phone back to my ear. "Hello? Anyone? You obviously want to talk to me, so speak or I'm hanging up."

"Aidan?"

I go perfectly still. "Rebecca?"

She stutters a bit, then says, "I'm sorry, I shouldn't have—"

"No! It's okay. Are *you* okay? How'd you get this number?"

"Samantha had it. She said you texted her about the party—that was crazy stuff once you left. We found Will upstairs, out cold. How's the girl you were with? Is she okay?"

"She's fine." *Not really. Nothing's fine.* I ask again, "Are you okay?"

"I . . . I'm . . . I don't know." Her voice cracks, and my pulse speeds up before I can keep myself from caring. "You're gonna think I've totally lost it. God, maybe I have, I don't know . . . I don't even know if I've really seen it, if it's really happened."

"What's happened?" I ask, trying not to sound like I feel: stretched thin.

"Charlie texted me," she says with a sob. "I have his phone in my closet, and no one's touched it. But somehow . . . he texted me. But that's nuts, right? He's *dead*!"

The demon. It must be the demon playing with her.

Now that she's started telling me, she can't seem to stop. "Charlie is gone! I saw him in the coffin. How could it be real? How could he text me—oh, God, what the hell's happening? I don't know what's happening, Aidan. I'm losing it. Samantha says I need medication, that I should see a shrink. No one understands. I don't have anyone, and I'm so lost I can't breathe. I want to just swim all the way to him, even if that means leaving this place. I can't keep feeling this . . . death. The only time I've seen light is . . . is when . . . I see you."

My breath catches at her words, and the feel of it all—her despair, her fear, her need to die—rakes over my skin. "It's okay, Rebecca." But it's not. That demon is about to pounce. And I can't fix any of it without breaking all my rules about letting people in, helping them, and revealing the secrets that I've lived with my

DARKNESS BRUTAL   181

whole life. If I don't let her in a little, though, I'm talking to a dead girl right now, because she's ripe for being pushed off the edge.

Rebecca sobs into the phone, and I can almost see her curled in a corner somewhere clutching it to her ear like a lifeline. "I'm right here," I whisper.

I glance at Sid. He's hanging intently onto every word.

"Listen," I say, "I'm going to give you an address, and you're going to pack a bag of clothes for the night. Then you're going to go there. Are you ready?"

She sniffs. "Uh-huh."

I give her the address for Sid's house, repeating it twice. "You got it?"

"Yeah." She sniffs again. "When can I—"

"Just come. As soon as you can."

"Okay." Her voice is small and far away. It's silent for a second. "Thank you." And then she clicks off the line.

I hang up. *Shit. What did I just do?*

"Why did you give that girl our address?" Connor asks.

"Yes, who is she?" Sid scowls at me.

Neither of them seem happy about what I just did. Well, they can join the club.

TWENTY-THREE

When we pull into the garage, Connor jumps right out, but I stay, still a little in shock at having invited Rebecca here. Sid doesn't seem inclined to leave the car, either. After a few minutes of silence, he can't keep his mouth shut.

"Do I need to say it?" he asks.

"I know, it was dumb."

"This place needs to be kept a secret, Aidan."

I nod.

"Who is this girl?"

"I met her at SubZero."

"A club bunny? You gave our address to a club bunny?"

"It's not like that. There were these guys, and I saved her, and then there was this demon, but I wasn't sure what it meant because the sigil was so monumental, but then I went to the party, and the demon confronted me, and it knows that I can see it, and I have no idea what to do about it, but I know it's not good and that it wants Rebecca dead like her brother and that it'll skin me alive for helping her—"

"Whoa!" Sid says, holding up a hand. "This demon knows that you can *see* it?"

I swallow hard. "I don't think it realized that it could touch me physically, though. I don't think it—hell, I have no idea. Who am I kidding? I'm in so far over my head."

"Do you think it told others?"

"It said it'd keep quiet as long as I stayed out of its way."

This seems to shock him. "It *said*—you understood it?"

"Yes."

He thinks for a second. "I suppose this makes sense, considering."

"Considering what?" Makes *sense*? None of this makes sense.

"You already said that you spoke several languages. Now you say that you understand the language of angels—fallen ones, that is. I could be right: this could be the gift of tongues."

I stare at him, a little stunned. "What do you mean you were right? You knew I had this . . . tongues thing? What does that even mean?"

"It's why I was so interested in the languages you speak. They link to deeper parts of the—"

He stops, maybe sensing how lost I am about what he's saying. Then he starts over. "Look, this gift creates a bridge in your mind—we'll call it *Wisdom*. Some believe that King Solomon had this same gift, an ability to speak in all tongues.

"Legend has it that he also knew many sacred texts by heart and could recite them on command. As his father, King David, said: *Your word I have hidden in my heart . . .*"

My insides go still at the revelation that I'm not the only one who's ever had these odd abilities. Solomon may have lived thousands of years ago, but he lived. And there may be others besides him—besides me—who have gifts like this. My ability to see demons, my knowing . . . it's all pieces of a puzzle.

Sid seems to sense my reaction. "The texts? Is that another one of your gifts?"

I nod.

He blows out a long breath, looking stunned. "Then you definitely have the gift of Wisdom, not just the gift of Sight. Amazing."

That's one word for it. I just want to know why.

"So all that with the demon and the Rebecca girl happened last night?" Sid asks.

I nod again.

"And you brought Kara home after everything and you had *sex* with her?"

"No!"

"You were in her bed this morning. Naked."

I choke out a laugh. Where did this come from? "I had my pants on. She had her pants on."

He doesn't look pissed, which feels weird to me; however, he does seem determined to uncover the truth. "But something did happen."

"We kissed. That's all. And how is this relevant or even any of your business?" I snap.

His eyes hover on my mark and then flick back to my face. "Be careful with her, Aidan. She's . . . delicate."

"Fine," I say, even though she seems like the least *delicate* girl on the planet.

He opens the Jeep door and gets out. I follow, asking, "So maybe you can help me with the demon? And Rebecca?"

"What is it you think I can do for her, exactly?"

"I just . . . I can't do this on my own. I need to somehow trap the thing to keep it from spilling my secret to the rest of the horde."

"Trap a demon." His voice sounds incredulous as he walks out of the garage and down the path across the backyard.

"I do it all the time," I say, trailing behind. "To the smaller ones that discover I can see them. In a spirit bowl or a hex box. Even a simple circle will do it sometimes if you surround it in the right text."

He laughs, throwing his head back. "You, my boy, are perfection."

"Glad you're impressed," I mumble.

"Merely surprised you'd know that kind of trickery. And all on your own. Yet again, amazing." He stops beside the shack and turns to study me for a second. Then asks, "How large is it, this demon?"

"It's a midlevel one, I think."

I can tell by his reaction that he knows exactly what I mean. Somehow I'm not surprised. "And it's assigned to this human, Rebecca?" he asks.

"I think so."

He chews on that and then pats me on the back. "I want to show you something."

He waves with his walking stick for me to follow as he goes to the door of the shed.

I have to force myself to follow him. While I'm insanely curious about what's inside that rickety shack and why he sleeps there, I feel a very strong magic pulsing off the foundation. Like a warning.

"You really sleep in that thing?" I ask.

He stops in front of the door and begins unlocking the many locks. "Sacrifices must be made at times."

I have no idea what he means, but my heart begins hammering in my chest.

One of the chains falls to the side, then another.

"You do magic in there, don't you?" I ask as another lock comes undone.

He glances at me sideways. "You don't approve."

"I'm cautious. Not all magic is good."

He gives me a sad smile. "No. Not all magic is good." And then the shed door is opening. I step back, away from the energy that spills out. It's rich and thick, like molasses or tree sap. It smells like damp earth. And burnt hair. There's fear in there. And urgency. Loss.

What kind of shit is this guy mixed up in? I've never felt anything quite like it. Not casting magic exactly... but what else could it be?

I watch him in the murky shadows as he goes inside and crouches over something. I make myself move closer to get a better look.

He's digging in an old trunk at the foot of a small cot. Next to him, there's a shelf stacked with odd-shaped bottles, chalk markings on the floor, candles, smudge, and an animal's skull on the dresser—the altar. Before I can get a better grip on the good or evil of it all, Sid's found what he was looking for.

I'm dying to ask him a jumble of questions, but before I can choose which one to ask first, he finishes locking the door again and holds out a pouch: blue velvet, drawn with a gold string—like a jewelry bag.

"What's that?" I ask, not sure I want to touch it.

"Don't worry, Aidan, it's safe. In fact, it'll protect you." He moves his hand, urging me to take it.

I can see he's not going to let me get out of accepting, so I pick it up by the golden thread and hold it in front of me, trying to search out the energy inside. But all I feel is . . . nothing.

I open the blue velvet and turn it upside down. Two small coins roll out into my palm. No, not coins. Amulets.

"These are Eric's," I say. They're the same pieces Eric asked me to read a few weeks back. All I could tell him was what the engravings on the amulets said, because the energy was empty—which, by the look on Eric's face, seemed to have told him everything he needed to know.

"Yes." Sid nods. "He was searching them out for me. One belonged to my mentor long ago, and one to King Nebuchadnezzar and King Darius after him."

"You mean, like, the kings of Babylon?"

"Yes."

Wow. I roll them with my fingers. "How did your mentor have one of these? Eric told me he picked them up on his last trip to Iraq."

"A story for another day," Sid says. "For now, all that's important is that Eric found them. And they can be yours."

The conflicting feelings in my gut go a little quieter. "You're *giving* them to me?" I know Eric probably charged Sid a small fortune for the things. "Why?"

"You need them."

"What are they for?"

"I should make you tell me, but since you trusted me, I'll let this be a freebie." He reaches out and touches one of them. "What does that say?"

I don't have to look at it. I remember the symbols. "Cloaked. Or invisible."

"Yes. If you wear this on a chain, over your heart, it will cloak you." When I frown at him he adds, "From demons. Or anything not fully on this plane."

"This will hide me from demons? Seriously?"

"Yes."

I stare at the amulets in my hand in amazement. Two of them. One for me and one for Ava. Could it really be so easy?

"So one's for the girl," he says. "What's her name again?"

I pause, realizing he's not talking about Ava. Obviously he's thinking of Rebecca. He doesn't have a clue of what's going on with Ava. "Rebecca," I say.

He smiles, but it doesn't reach his eyes. "Lovely. Once this is bound to her aura, she'll be safe from that creature following her."

I should've known. "You want to do a spell on her."

"A simple bonding spell. Nothing unnatural."

"I'm not sure I like that idea." I hold out the amulets for him to take back.

He closes my fingers over them and pushes my hand toward my chest. "No rash decisions now. Think on it."

"You can't just cast over someone's soul and not be changing its nature."

"Not all casting is bad, Aidan."

"I know that. I trap demons, I get it. But I've seen what a misuse of messing in the wrong powers can do. It can tear lives apart. It can kill."

His body goes still, and he seems to sense that my struggle is deeper than my words. "You've seen things in your life. I can tell. You have a wise soul in more ways than one, and I admire your caution. Of course, I would never do anything to harm your friend. Or you. There are rules that have to be followed when you walk the fine line of magic. But I can teach you if you'd like."

Do I want to dig deeper into that stuff? The stuff that put me in this place I'm in right now? "I don't know."

"But you will consider what I've said?"

I breathe in through my nose. Breathe out. "I will." Even though I'm not sure what to think. And then something else comes to me. "Was the spell you did on Kara following these safety rules?"

The side of his mouth twitches. "She told you about that? You saw her mark?"

"She told me you bought her for six hundred thousand dollars and locked a curse inside her. But that's just a part of it. Because even I know that when you do something for someone and it's supposedly pure, there's no strings attached. And Kara definitely has strings."

His nostrils flare. "Are you suggesting I've enslaved her?"

"She certainly acts like she's indebted to you."

He comes forward and points his walking stick at the house. "Because I freed her from a horrifying curse. I put the power into her hands."

"Are you sure about that?"

He seethes for a second and then seems to realize something. "You care about her." He sniffs the air. "You smell like her. She's on your skin."

My teeth clench.

A knowing smile grows across his face as he shakes his head. "Oh no—she's not going to be on your list of damsels in distress. She's too important for that. The last thing that girl needs is to be crushed again."

"You don't have to worry about your glass princess. No part of me is in her life." I'm surprised by the sour taste in my mouth. Am I actually bummed about this?

"The Rebecca girl can stay two nights," Sid says, changing the subject. "That's enough time to make sure the amulet works to hide her. But then she'll need to go home. Out of your life for good."

I look at the amulets in my hand and then at him.

"She's not one of us, Aidan. She's not a part of this." He touches my arm in a fatherly way. "I know what you're feeling. I was a boy once, too. But trust me when I say our two worlds don't cross in safety."

I nod my surrender. It is his house.

And I know deep down he's right.

"I'll help you find your family like you asked," he continues. "And I'll help you learn more about how better to use your gifts, if you'll let me. But you'll have to open yourself up to it. And you'll have to let go of your fears." He gives me a tired smile. "As Emerson would say: *always do what you are afraid to do.*"

But I'm beginning to realize my fear is much larger than I thought. I'm afraid of too many things. Of losing Ava, of losing myself.

"Thank you," I say. "Thanks for letting Ava and me stay. And thanks for being patient with me. I want to learn, I do." It may be the only way left to save Ava. "I'm just not sure I want to lie to people, like you did today."

He taps my foot gently with his cane. "Just follow my lead, son. We'll end up on the right side in the end. I promise."

TWENTY-FOUR

To distract myself while I wait for Rebecca, I go back into the office and to my LA Paranormal grunt work. Ava comes in, and I ask her to hang out and help so I can spend some time with her and we can take a break from all the pressure we've been under.

Since the vision of the demon and the cave and our talk about the spell, she's seemed sad, agitated. At the moment she feels more like herself again.

She sits cross-legged on the floor surrounded by files and has fun reading out some of the cases as we alphabetize them by name and color code them by paranormal activity: blue for ghosts, green for poltergeists, or what I would call a lower demon, and yellow for "unidentified creatures." Ava seems to like the yellow category best. She reads me the files out loud for two of them: a house full of "ghost bats" and a place called Scary Dairy where you can hear the screams of the cows being slaughtered.

"Is that real?" she asks. "Sounds ridiculous. I don't think cows can even scream."

I shrug. "Who knows. I have a feeling some of LA Paranormal's cases are a little *embellished*." I pause. "But these guys do seem to know their stuff."

She sets down the folder she's holding and looks up at me. "So you think we're safe here?"

"For a while." I don't want to say what I really think: *I don't know, Ava. I wish I knew, but I don't*. Fate isn't an easy thing to stop.

"I wish I could do something," she says, picking up another folder.

"You just rest and try to focus on holding back your abilities."

She sighs and flips through the folder, looking unhappy. "If that's what you want."

———

I'm starting to worry about what's taking Rebecca so long when Lester hollers "Soup's on!"

Ava skips out of the office, and I follow. I don't bother closing the door of the downstairs bathroom while I wash my hands before eating. But as I'm rinsing, I see in the mirror that Sid is standing behind me, right outside the bathroom. Staring.

"Can I help you?" I ask. Why is he looking at me like that? It's freaking creepy.

He points at my arm. "Have you noticed? Your mark has grown."

The hiss of the running water echoes in my head as I glance down.

My heart stops.

The mark. It's even larger—all the way past my elbow and half-way up my bicep. I've had my hoodie on for most of the day and just took it off a minute ago. So, no, I hadn't noticed.

What the ever-loving . . . ?

"Have you spoken to Kara?" Sid asks through my panic.

"Why?" I can't stop looking at the new lines and twists on my skin.

"She's obviously affected it somehow. You kissed her, didn't you?"

"What? Why would that matter?" Kissing Kara couldn't affect my mark. Could it?

"Maybe you should ask her about it," Sid says and walks away.

"That's insane," I mumble to myself. "It's completely . . ." But the words fade. Because something comes to me: the memory of kissing her in the club. And that next day, after I took my shower, I noticed my mark had changed. I assumed it was the demon bite, but . . .

I stand there, caught in a vortex of what-the-fuck, running over the events of the last several days, trying to piece it all together, as the sound of the faucet hisses in the background.

The demon bit me the day before my mark grew the first time. But I kissed Kara that night, too. And last night my arm buzzed when I touched her.

Plus, there's the stuff that Mom told Ava in the dream about the violets and the lilies, and the symbol in Kara's tattoo, the one that matches mine . . .

Could Kara really be doing this to me? But what is *this*?

. . . *he must touch the violets and lilies to find surrender, to find his hidden blood* . . .

I shut off the sink and go look for Kara in the kitchen.

"Not here," Lester says, doling out some lasagna onto a plate.

"She's probably too scared of Lester's cooking," Jax says. "Smart girl."

As they go back and forth trading insults, I head into the hall and up the stairs. I feel as if I'm being pulled by fate, and I don't like the feeling. I don't like believing I can't change something already set in motion.

I knock on Kara's door—maybe a little harder than I need to—and hear movement on the other side. "Kara, let me in. I need to talk to you."

"Go away," comes her voice, muffled through the wood. "I'm not hungry."

"I'm going to camp out here until you open this door. Eat Lester's lasagna, sleep in boxers, you name it, I'm—"

The door swings open. "You have two seconds."

I push my way past and shut us in her room.

"What the hell?"

"We need to talk."

"No." She shakes her head. "We really don't. In fact, I think it's best if we act like we can't stand each other. This whole thing with you waking up in my bed has become a total mess. Jax is a dick, Holly tried to have a 'girl chat' with me—wanted to braid my hair and paint my nails or some shit." She takes a step closer and points at the door. "You need to get out. Before someone notices."

"You did something to me."

She blinks, frozen, her arm still hovering in the air. The bruise on her forearm is deep purple. "What are you talking about?"

I hold out my arm to show her my mark. "You made this change. It only went halfway up my forearm yesterday morning. Now it's all the way past my elbow. What sort of power are you using on me?"

Her nostrils flare, and she slaps me. Hard. "Get the fuck out of my room."

The left side of my face burns. "Holy shit, woman. What was that for?"

"You prick. What do you think I am?"

I hesitate. Okay, I'm obviously not approaching this right. I hold up my hands. "What am I supposed to think, Kara? We've kissed twice, and both times were . . . weird. Like it wasn't really my choice."

She flinches as if I just struck *her* instead of the other way around.

Damn.

"I've *never* used my powers on you," she says.

"How is that possible?" I say, but I see that she's telling the truth. "But . . . then . . . why did you pull me in at the club?"

"I was dancing, you were there. And I felt something—I never feel anything. So I kissed you."

"You just kissed me? That's it?"

"Yes! And it was like—it felt like *you* were doing something to *me*." She pokes me in the chest. "And then I saw you come up the walk the next day. I was in shock. I couldn't imagine how you found me. But then you didn't even remember me! Do you kiss every girl you dance with at that club?"

I shake my head, still not sure how to digest what's happening. "But in the hall, when I first came here, you were doing something. Your energy was—"

She waves her hand, like she's brushing the notion aside. "I'd opened myself up a little, that's all. I sure as hell didn't use any of my shit on you. Trust me, you'd know."

"And last night . . ."

She glares at me.

Something strange and unnatural definitely happened between us, and I'd assumed it was her curse, her power of attraction. "Then why . . . how come it felt so . . . uncontrolled? And why the hell is my mark growing?"

She shrugs. "You touched the tattoo on my back and something happened."

I try to soften my tone. "What did *you* feel?"

She swallows and backs up more. "That seems like pointless information right now."

"Pointless?" I can't help my exasperation coming through. "My mark is changing, Kara. *Changing*. It's happened twice. And how many times have we kissed? Oh, twice."

"So we don't ever kiss again. Problem solved."

"Kara. You know that's not going to work."

"Why?" There's a pleading edge to her voice now, like she just wants the conversation to be over. "Are you planning on kissing me again or something?"

"Maybe. We should at least see what's going on."

Her eyes grow. She seems frightened. And I can't for the life of me understand why. "What are you scared of?" When she doesn't say anything, I add, "This isn't even affecting you. I'm the one who's changing."

"I told you." Her voice shakes. "It's like you're doing something to me, too."

"What do you think I'm doing to you?"

She shrugs.

"Talk to me, Kara."

Her eyes glisten with tears and her jaw is tight. She shakes her head, like she can't say the words.

The sight of the crack in her wall again—a girl that I know could kick my ass—makes my stomach hurt and reminds me of Sid's warning: *she's delicate*. "*Did* I do something to you?"

She shakes her head again.

"Well, what is it then?" I ask quietly.

"I told you, I'm cursed," she whispers. "You should just stay away from me."

"You're not cursed, Kara."

"Yes. I am."

I step forward to reach out, but she steps back.

"Just go," she says.

I drop my arm to my side, defeated. "Okay." I turn and leave the room.

I stand in the hall for a long time beside her door. There's something going on with her, but she's not willing to talk about it. I could push her, but I'd probably just end up pushing her away. And I'm tired. The closer I get to answers, the more questions rise to the surface. And now another door just slammed in my face.

TWENTY-FIVE

I'm sitting in my room while everyone else eats, staring at the new brown swirls and lines on my forearm, wondering how Kara and I are connecting, wondering why Sid told me to press Kara, and dumbfounded as to why Kara refuses to talk about it. That's when I hear my name being called from downstairs.

I go out and look over the railing. "What?"

Jax yells up to me, "Your other girlfriend is here! The sexy ginger."

If I were close enough, I'd kick him in the balls.

I hurry downstairs and find Rebecca in the entry, an overnight bag on her shoulder. She looks nervous as she studies her surroundings.

"Hey," I say.

She spots me, and a bit of her worry disappears. Before she can say anything, Jax comes up behind me. "Aren't you going to introduce me?" he asks.

"Nope." I move to take Rebecca's bag, saying to her, "Just smack him if he gets in your face."

"Very funny," Jax says.

"Hello!" comes a small voice from beside us.

Ava's standing next to Rebecca, blinking up at her.

Rebecca looks down, a little startled. "Hello."

"You're Rebecca," Ava says, rocking back and forth on her feet, toe to heel.

Rebecca nods.

"This is my sister, Ava," I say, an uneasy churn in my stomach seeing them side by side.

"Nice to meet you, Ava," Rebecca says.

Ava grins at her.

"Okay, well . . ." I give my sister a look, and she giggles, dancing back to plop down next to Finger.

I take Rebecca upstairs, but pause in the hallway, not sure where to go.

"Everything okay?" she asks, her voice a little shaky.

"Yeah." I take her into my room, leaving the door open in case anyone gets the wrong idea again. "Listen, we'll find you a bed, but can you sit here for a second while I figure things out?"

"Okay," she says, setting her bag on the floor. She's even more pale than usual. Her freckles are copper dots across her cheeks and nose, and her hair's pulled back in a haphazard way, half up, half down. She's wearing the *hamsa* charm I gave her—it's hanging from a thin silver chain. She picks it up and fiddles with it.

"You're safe here," I say.

She nods.

"I'll be back in a sec." I head for Holly's room. I knock on the door, and there's quiet for a few seconds until I hear "Enter."

I open the door but stay in the doorway. "Hey, can I ask a favor?"

"I knew it was you." She's at her desk, school books fanned across the surface. "You're the only one who would've knocked like such a gentleman. *Qué pasa?*"

"My friend needs a place to crash for the night, and I don't know where to put her. She can't sleep in my room—"

She slaps her pencil down. "Wait. You brought a girl here?"

"No, she—I mean, she's just staying for one night. Maybe two. Sid said it was okay."

"You sure are a chick magnet, aren't you?" She looks me up and down. "Hmm, I don't know . . . I just don't see it. I mean you have all the usual qualities girls find appealing: thick, wavy hair, glittering eyes, nice muscles, and your butt's not bad." She taps her chin with a finger like she's thinking. "But you don't seem mean or dangerous enough to be such a BFD. Girls are into bad boys. Nice is predictable, ya know."

"Yes, well, thank you for that lovely analysis. Where can my friend sleep?"

"I have a spot free." She points at the stripped bed in the corner by the window.

"Oh, I thought you didn't like people—"

She raises her eyebrows high.

"I mean," I continue, "I was under the impression that you weren't big on sharing—"

She leans back in her chair and folds her arms across her chest.

"I thought you didn't want anyone in your room," I finally finish.

"You're getting more attractive by the second. And you're wrong. I share just fine."

"Then why aren't Kara and you roommates?" Seems a bit sexist for the girls to be the only ones to get their own rooms.

"Well, it might have something to do with her trying to kill me."

"What?" I figure she's exaggerating, but I can tell she's not lying completely. "*Kill*, as in murder?"

Holly sighs, like I'm keeping her from her homework and it's all so annoying. "Well, you're still new to the SWK—the sleeping-with-Kara thing—so let me clue you in. Sharing a room with Kara is like sharing a room with a sleeping shark. She has nightmares sometimes, and they get majorly freaky. One time—the night in question—I woke up to her crying and thrashing, so I went to wake her up. She grabbed my arm, pulled a knife from under her pillow, and put the thing to my throat. NK, not kewl, ya know."

"But she stopped once she saw it was you."

"You'd think so, wouldn't you?" She goes back to studying the book in front of her. "Your friend can sleep in here. Tell her I'll help her make the bed once I finish trig."

"Okay. Thanks."

"No worries, lover boy."

I try to ignore my confusion about Kara as I go back to Rebecca. "Okay, it's all set," I say, walking into my room.

Rebecca's on the bed, reading her phone.

"Everything all right?" I ask, wondering if she's looking at the text her brother sent her—or, I should say, the text the demon sent her.

She nods. "Yeah, I'm just texting Samantha."

"I hope you're not telling her where you are."

"Um, I was going to."

"Don't. This place is off the grid, and it needs to stay that way."

"This place is in the middle of LA. It's nowhere near off the grid."

"I just mean it's supposed to stay hidden."

She shakes her head, obviously thinking I'm ridiculous. "Fine. I'll just tell her I've gone to my aunt's house—even though she'll never believe me."

"Why?"

"'Cause my aunt lives in Florida and I haven't seen the woman in six years."

"Oh." I pick her overnight bag off the floor. "Well, let's get you settled, and then we'll talk."

She stands, slipping her phone into her back pocket, and follows me into Holly's room.

The girls greet each other, and Holly seems pleased to have another female there. She smiles and even closes her book to talk to Rebecca about which bathroom habits of the boys to look out for, using several acronyms that seem more like alphabet soup to me. But she gets Rebecca smiling, so I decide to let them bond.

"Are you okay for a minute?" I ask. "I need to get cleaned up."

Rebecca nods.

Holly goes to help her with some sheets she found. "She'll be fine, LB."

I roll my eyes and head to gather some clothes before taking a shower. I'm guessing Rebecca's about to get grilled by Holly, asked a million and one questions about how we know each other . . . not to mention the earful of gossip she'll get about me since I've been here—and about Kara, too, probably. God, help me.

It's for the best, though. The less Rebecca thinks of me in that way, the better. She's obviously forming an attachment, and that's really not good. If she thinks Kara and I are a thing, then maybe she'll pull back.

I should be relieved by the idea. But I'm not.

———

Someone bangs on the door five times while I'm taking a two-minute shower—probably Jax. I get dressed again, come out of the bathroom with a billow of steam, and yell downstairs, "Whoever's been freaking out can have their turn on the can!"

I turn around. Kara is walking down the hall toward me. I want to talk to her more, but I don't know what to say.

She brushes past me, and I follow. "Kara, I'm sorry if—"

"Shut up." She heads for the stairs. "You are amazingly transparent."

I grab her wrist. "What the hell, Kara? We need to figure this out together."

"Let go of me."

She tries to head down the stairs, but I grip her tighter. "We can't ignore it."

"Let it go, Aidan. Trust me, you don't want to dig any deeper into this."

I should release her, give her time, but I can't. The truth is I can't wait. I have to figure this out now. I can't have anything getting in the way of protecting Ava. I need to know why this is happening to me.

"Kara, you don't understand—"

"Aidan?" Rebecca is standing below us, about halfway up the stairs. She's looking at me, at Kara, at my hand on her. "Is everything . . . ?"

Kara snatches her wrist back and glares at me. "Nice," she says. "Now you can kiss her instead. It's perfect, really." Then she walks down the stairs. "He's all yours," she says as she passes Rebecca. "Enjoy."

———

Rebecca follows me into my room.

I sit on my bed, exhausted and more confused than ever.

"Is everything all right?" She glances back at the door, like Kara might return.

"Fine."

"That's the girl from the party, isn't it? She has a bruise on her cheek."

I sigh. "Yeah, she's okay, though."

"Are you and her—?"

"No!" I say, a little too forcefully. "I have no idea what's going on with her. Or me, for that matter."

"I see . . ." And I wonder if she does. She's studying me like she's trying to figure me out. She crawls onto the bed beside me, curling her legs under her. The tropical smell of her fills my head. "I really appreciate you letting me come here. I hope it won't cause any trouble."

She's close, and I'm way too weak and exhausted right now. I should move over, but I stay perfectly still. The door's open. I won't do anything stupid if the door's open. "It's no trouble."

She tilts her head, and another strand of her copper hair falls to her lightly freckled shoulder. "It's nice not to be alone."

"Yeah," I say absently. My head's warring between how this girl makes me feel and my need to go find Kara and figure out what the hell's really going on.

Rebecca leans on the wall. "I feel safe now. With you. Less sad."

I nod, feeling like I can barely focus on what she's saying.

"Has anyone that you love died?" she asks quietly.

That gets my attention. I hesitate but then just say it. "My mom."

"When?"

"I was nine."

She leans closer. "You were so small. And your sister . . ."

"She was three. It was her birthday."

"How did it happen?"

I look into her eyes, so green they put spring to shame. I've never told anyone what I saw that night; I've never said the words. It's my memory, my secret. Not even Ava knows.

"I don't know. She's just gone."

She nods her head like she's saying a silent *I'm sorry, I understand.* Words don't mean anything when death comes close anyway.

She touches my wrist, her fingers moving slowly over my mark. Then she takes my hand in hers and brings it to her lips. A tear slips down her cheek and runs across my knuckles. She kisses each fingertip and then presses my palm against her cheek.

Everything in me has to focus on not reacting, not pulling her closer.

"Rebecca . . ." I say, my voice rough.

"I know," she whispers, her breath warm on my skin.

She's close enough that I could lean over an inch and kiss her. I'd heal with this girl. I know I would.

"Whoa, nice," comes a voice from the doorway.

Rebecca and I spring apart.

Jax stands there grinning at us. "With the door open and everything. Balls of steel."

———

Waves crash against the rocks as the ocean rages behind us, spraying salty diamonds of water onto our skin.

I want to ask why we came back after lunch—the second time we've stood in this spot today, Mom's birthday. But she's not looking at me. Her gaze is stuck on the cliff wall, on the opening of the cave twenty yards away.

She twists her hair in a spiral around her finger, and a tear slips down her cheek. It could be just the sea on her face, but her eyes are sad. They're always sad when we come here.

She never lets the words emerge, the words of why or how or who or what makes her sadness so big.

I watch her profile and realize she doesn't have to say the words. I can hear it, singing from her with each beat of her heart. The ache of missing my dad is always there, just beneath the surface. But when we come here, the sadness feels like something that might swallow us whole. It moves toward us, crashing against us like the waves beating the rocks.

I take her hand in mine.

We watch the cave opening, waiting for something that we both know will never come.

TWENTY-SIX

The next morning is all work and no play, so I have very little time to think about my stupidity.

Just enough to realize what a jackass I am. I almost kissed Rebecca. I have no right to get mixed up with a girl I'm trying to help, who feels indebted to me. Especially with everything that's going on between Kara and me. Dick move. And it won't be happening again.

Lester and I spend most of the morning in the office. He's got me hooked up to listen to EVPs, or electronic voice phenomena, from some previous jobs. His instructions are to make a note of any moments that sound suspect. I mostly just hear Jax or Kara or Connor asking questions to nobody. "Would you like to talk to us?" or "If you're here, give us a sign." That kind of thing. Then I find one sound file labeled *Roosevelt—rm 928* that has a man's voice on it after Connor asks, "Were you a movie star?" but I can't tell what the man answers. I make a note of the file and the time of the man's response in the notebook Lester gave me.

He rolls his chair over to me. "You got one?"

"Maybe."

"I'll have Jax listen to it later. He's got a great ear."

"So you and Jax get along sometimes?" I ask.

He blows air through his lips. "I guess. He hasn't killed me yet. I think he's just jealous."

"Of your good looks?"

He laughs. "Most definitely." He touches his dark hair dramatically. "No, I think it's 'cause of my *thing*—my ability to channel."

"Is he thinking his *thing* is lame?"

"Maybe. But I'd rather have his *thing* of reading clouds than mine, really. Mine is no picnic."

"Channeling can be dangerous," I say, wanting to tread lightly. I don't think me spouting off on everything I know about the horrors of channeling would sit well, and he's probably very familiar with them. He definitely looks freaked about his gift. How could he not be? Something crawling in your skin and not being sure you can get it out has to feel more like a curse.

"Yeah, you have to be careful, but nothing can get in here without my permission." He taps on his temple. "So I just can't be a dumbass. It's partially why I hang more with the technology than the ghosts."

"You seem pretty good at all this." I motion to the equipment. "How long have you been a part of it?"

He sets his headset down. "Um, a year, maybe."

"And you're cool with Sid? He seems on the up-and-up?"

"Ha. Well, he's good at what he does. And he takes care of us. I can't complain."

I nod, watching him, trying to figure out what he's not saying.

"Look," he adds, leaning closer, "whatever Sid does, he cares. He's not in it for the money. He feeds us and keeps LA Paranormal in the black. He's one of the good guys."

Can I really worry so much about Sid being a little less than truthful with his clients? He's promised to try and help me find out more about my family, more about myself, and I know he didn't lie about that. There's more at stake here than fraud. And if Sid has a spell that can get rid of the time slip, it doesn't matter if they call it a ghost or not, I guess. He's going to give the clients peace, keep their beliefs intact, and that's *something*.

Jax pokes his head around the doorway and points at me. "Time to jam, newb. Another job." And he disappears again.

"He grows on you," Lester says, and he rolls back to his spot, fitting his headphones onto his ears. "Like a fungus."

I make my way to the back door, but as I enter the hallway, I hear Rebecca's voice in the kitchen. I stop just on the other side of the archway, suddenly unsure if I want to see her today. When I peek around the wall, she's got her back to me, standing at the counter beside Holly and Ava. The three of them are laughing about something in the magazine in front of them. Holly is as bright as ever in striped tights and a white polka-dot shirt; Ava is in a long grey sweatshirt that's too big for her.

Rebecca reaches over and touches Ava's hair like a sister would, giving advice on how to wear it. Ava smiles her brightest smile at Rebecca and then says something to Holly, who laughs. I wonder at the way they're all so easy together so quickly. Must be a girl thing.

"Is it the hair?" The quiet voice comes from behind me.

I start and turn to see Kara watching me watch Rebecca.

"Or is it the body?"

I move back, out of sight of the girls in the kitchen. My heart pulses in my skin from being caught. But I'm not sure why I should feel embarrassed. "Shit, you scared me."

"She is pretty. And she has that innocent energy that screams to be protected."

I blink at her, unsure what to say.

She comes closer and leans on the wall beside me. "I bet you're nice to her. You probably say all these pretty things to make her melt in those hands of yours."

"I'm sorry that I hurt you, Kara."

She looks up at me, and I can see it in her eyes: the pain of all the men that have wounded her. Am I now just another name on that list of bastards?

"I really am sorry." I want to reach out and touch her, but I force myself not to. "You deserve a true hero, not a fake one."

Jax pokes his head around the archway. "Quit makin' out. Let's roll."

I follow him through the kitchen to the back door, waving at the girls as I go by. Rebecca gives me a confused smile, her eyes moving from me to Kara, who's standing behind us in the archway, staring at me with the strangest look on her face. As I'm about to close the back door behind me, she's there, grabbing it.

"I'm coming, too," she says.

Jax frowns. "I thought you were gonna help Lester with the prep for that loony bin job. You said you didn't wanna come today."

"I changed my mind."

———

Sid's car is a lot nicer than Connor's Jeep, but it's not exactly meant for five. He's driving and Connor's shotgun. Jax is sitting on the hump between Kara and me. Which I'm not too thrilled about. It's a bit cozy.

As we settle in Jax says to me, "We can snuggle, but I expect you to buy me a drink later."

After a while of driving through traffic, I ask where we're going.

Connor motions to the hills on our left. "Griffith Park. We're just doing a walk-over."

"We walk the property we're considering filming," Sid says, "and then see what we think. Fairly mundane."

"In other words," Jax says, "boring as shit. Or BAS, as Holly would say."

"Language, Jax," Sid scolds.

Jax sighs. "Fine. What's my penance this time? Memorizing the freakin' book of Judah?"

"There is no book of Judah," I say.

Kara laughs.

Connor says, "In that case, Jax, maybe you should memorize the names of the books of the Bible."

"Sounds good to me," Sid says.

Jax growls and leans his head back. "Wonderful."

Eventually we pull onto Crystal Springs Drive and park near the trails. It's a weekday, so the place is pretty vacant. We get out of the car, and Connor starts pulling stuff out of the trunk.

"We walked the trails near the observatory a few weeks ago, but Kara and Connor couldn't feel any entities," Sid says. "We're looking for something to film for our next *Truth Paranormal* special where we focus on somewhere famous."

"Griffith is known to be haunted," Connor says, handing Jax a backpack. "But the stories are all over the place. We've been having trouble pinning anything down."

Jax holds out the backpack to me. "Make the newb carry the shit."

Sid clucks his tongue like a mother hen. "You'll memorize all of the books of the Old Testament in English *and* Hebrew. Properly ordered for each version, both the Western as well as the original Tanakh."

Connor shakes his head, laughing. "Dumbass."

I take the pack from Jax. "So what are the words that'll get me in trouble?" I ask as we walk toward the first trailhead. I always assumed *dumbass* wasn't exactly kosher to the cuss-less crowd.

"You tell him, Jax," Connor says. "Get them out of your system for the rest of the day."

Sid smiles and taps his walking stick on a rock.

"Pretty much my two favorite words are off limits," Jax says, sounding defeated. "Fuck and shit. Fuck, fuck, shit, shit."

"That's it?" I ask.

Connor smiles. "That's plenty for Jax."

"Because he has no self-control," Kara adds.

"Ha. Ha." Jax walks past us up the trail and says over his shoulder, "That's rich coming from you, little newb lover. Too bad the boy's moved on."

Connor's smile fades, and he glances over at me.

Kara looks like she wants to crawl under a rock.

Sid just keeps smiling at the surrounding trees, looking happy as ever, not noticing a thing. "Another few hundred yards or so and we'll start putting out feelers, all right?"

We all follow in silence, crossing onto a narrower trail that leads down a small hill where the trees get more dense, until eventually Sid and Jax stop in a clearing up ahead of us.

Connor waves me over and takes the pack from me. "What was Jax talking about earlier? Is Rebecca your girlfriend or something?"

"No," I say, frustration filling me. "He's just being an ass."

Connor seems to buy that. But then he says, "Just remember, you hurt Kara and I kill you."

"Why is everyone so damn afraid of me breaking Kara?" I ask. "She's stronger than you all think." I glance up the trail where Kara is touching the trees like she's asking them questions.

"You better hope so," Connor says, pulling a camera and a digital voice recorder out of the pack. He hands me the camera. "Take pictures randomly. Try to focus on the shadows. That's where the nasty likes to hide."

Sid shouts over to me from across the clearing. "See what you can feel, Aidan. Don't be afraid to open yourself up nice and wide out here. You need to experience the full force of your abilities when it's safe to."

"Yeah, find us a ghost, man," Jax adds.

I wander the other way, taking my chance to get away from everyone.

Sid wants me to feel the full force of my abilities? That's a terrifying idea. But he's right—I need to figure out what I can do. The more I learn about all this, the more I'll know how to fight the darkness when it comes for Ava. I study the trees through the camera lens and snap a few pictures of shadows, trying to work up my nerve to let my walls down completely.

I spot something covered in pine needles on the ground. As I kneel down to take a picture of what is either a dead rat or an old shoe, something small moves in the corner of my vision to my right. I lower the camera and register two things at the same time: sulfur and a cat. But it's clear when I look right at it that it's no cat.

I have to curl my toes in my Converse to keep from leaping back in reaction.

The demon is clinging to the trunk of the tree two feet away. It bares its fangs, hissing at me.

It's the minion. The one from the party that got Kara beaten up and nearly raped. It almost got Rebecca raped, too.

Its oversized ears lie back. Has it been following me this whole time? Since the party? How haven't I smelled it?

Not good.

My heart speeds up. I scan the trees, looking for its boss. The Big Cheese is going to be pissed when it realizes Rebecca's staying in Sid's house surrounded by all those wards—with me. Unless it already knows.

Why the hell didn't I think before leaving the protection of the house? How could Sid just encourage me to roam around out here?

Luckily there's no sign of the large demon. Maybe I'm okay. Aside from the problem of Mini-Me, that is.

I stand up and back slowly away from the thing.

It turns its head like a bird would, looking at me almost upside down, and makes a garbled noise in its throat. Then it skitters up and across a branch, closer to me.

I could run, but it would just follow me—or head back to Boss Demon with intel. If I could trap it somehow . . .

"Connor," I say stiffly, my eyes never leaving the demon. "You don't, by any chance, have a hex box in one of these packs, do you?"

I hear footsteps behind me. "Is something wrong?" Connor asks.

Jax skids up beside me on my left, and the demon's eyes jerk to him. He's giddy, his grin as big as his head. "Seriously? The newb's seeing something? Awesome!"

I wish I could share that sentiment.

My fingers find the salt in my pocket. Not enough to make a circle. I'll just piss it off if I toss this at it. "I need something. More salt or chalk to make a circle. Now."

Sid's voice comes from behind me. "Aidan, remain calm and tell us what you see."

"It's a demon," I say, trying to slow my breathing, "and if I don't trap it, we'll have very moody company in a few minutes. Large, moody company."

"I can feel it," Kara says from somewhere on my right. Her voice shakes. "I've felt this before, Aidan. At the party."

"I just need to trap it," I say. "I need chalk, or salt, or sacred dirt or something. You guys had to have brought something. You're fucking demon hunters."

"We deal in ghosts, newb," Jax says. "Big difference."

Someone is moving, clearing the needles from a spot on the ground to my right. I glance over to see Kara drawing a circle in the cleared dirt. "If you can keep it from running, we can do a banishing spell."

"That isn't going to work without the Enochian runes," Connor says, "and I still don't have them all memorized. Do you?"

"No," Kara says, sounding defeated.

Jax raises his hands. "Don't look at me unless you want some-one to recite Hamlet."

Sid comes forward and hands Connor a small bag he pulled from his pack. "Here's the sacred dirt." Then he looks at me, no trace of worry or concern in his voice, as if we're just standing in the woods chatting. "You only have to open yourself up to your abilities, Aidan. You shouldn't need anything but your will once you've mastered them. These tropes of protection will only matter as much as you want or need them to."

Is he insane? I'm a human. This is a demon. Yes, a small one, but it has really big claws and teeth. I take the sacred dirt from Connor, turn to the creature, and move to the side. The thing doesn't seem to understand what's coming—probably because lower demons have fairly low IQs.

The dirt isn't foolproof for an eternal prison, but with any luck this demon isn't strong enough or clever enough to know its way around the stuff.

I need to get it onto the ground, into that circle Kara drew, so I can sprinkle this stuff around it. I move closer, slowly. This isn't the first time I've done this—that's what I tell myself. I've trapped dozens of these bastards. But there's no getting out of my head the revelation that they can bite me now—they can fight back. God knows what else they could do to me.

But then something dawns on me: if it can get a grip on me, I should be able to get a grip on *it*.

I set the bag of sacred dirt down and slip my fingers inside, coating my palms with its sharp protection. I point to the sack. "Put the rest of this around the circle."

Kara takes it and moves to obey.

The demon scuttles to another branch on the other side of me in a sudden burst, like a crab. And its form begins to change, getting clearer, as the creature readies to flicker away, likely heading back to its boss with an update on my whereabouts.

Shit.

Before I can second-guess myself, I leap, grabbing it by a bony limb.

It clings to the branch, screeching and flailing in shock and pain from my touch, from the sizzle of the sacred dirt on my hands. The surprise jolts through me too, but I recover faster than the creature does, grabbing it with a second hand and yanking. It springs free of the tree, and I've got it. I find my balance and sprint to the circle with it tucked like a football under my arm. But before I reach the circle, the demon digs its claws into my bicep an inch deep, sending me to my knees.

I cry out in pain, fire filling me, making me lose my mind for a second.

"He's bleeding!" Kara yells, dropping the bag of dirt to run at me.

Connor starts to run over too, but I wave them off with my free hand. Panic overwhelms me, and fight or flight kicks in like a jolt of electricity as words begin to flow from my mouth, words I've never heard before, words even I don't understand.

But the demon does. It screams even louder and unlatches its claws from my arm to lunge for my mouth, nearly slicing off my bottom lip.

Somehow I get to my feet and make it the last three paces to the circle of sacred dirt. I slam the creature into it; its body hits the ground with a loud crack. The words keep coming from my mouth, so fast I can barely feel my tongue anymore as the demon convulses, black foam bubbling through its teeth.

I can feel everyone gaping at me now, fear rolling off them in thick, billowy waves.

"Holy shit," Jax says. "He's lit up like ET."

All I can do is grip a stick in my fist and write in Hebrew, Greek, and Latin in the blood-coated dirt, Palm 91, Zachariah 3:2, then Deuteronomy 9:3: . . . *it is the Lord Your God who passes over before you, as a consuming fire He will destroy them . . .*

The demon goes perfectly still at that, as if frozen, and my movements slow. The last letter of scripture trails off in the dirt as my hand goes limp, all my energy gone.

My mouth stops muttering the strange words, my vision turns dull, and my head starts pounding like I'm being whacked by a hammer. Repeatedly.

"Holy shit," Jax says again, sounding breathless. "What the hell *was* that?"

Connor shakes his head, obviously stumped—and freaked.

Sid says in an awed voice, "Excellent, Aidan. Just stunning."

Kara hesitates for a second, but then she takes me by the arm, trying to help me to my feet. "Are you okay? My God, Aidan."

I grip my head, glancing back to make sure the demon's still trapped. I'm not sure how, but it's frozen in the same contorted pose of terror, its white eyes now a dull grey. It won't be any trouble anymore. I don't think.

———

"We need to get these cuts cleaned," Kara says as we head back to the car.

Sid pats me on the shoulder, making me flinch. "Amazing, just amazing."

"Holy mother of all shit!" Jax is shouting. "Did you *see* that? He was a damn Christmas tree back there."

"Calm the hell down," Connor says. "You're giving me a migraine."

"What the fuck was that?" Jax continues. "Toward the end his damn eyes were fucking glowing! That was some alien shit, man! Frackin' Cylon alien shit!" He laughs at the sky.

Sid must really be happy, because he's not saying anything to Jax about his language.

"You're not helping," Kara growls at Jax. She turns back to me. "You're going to be fine. It's just a few scrapes."

I study the gashes on my arm. They're still bleeding thick red streaks. "I don't know. That was . . ." Insane. Terrifying. Fucking nuts.

Kara looks like she wants to say something, but she just swallows hard and looks into my eyes. Fear leaks out of her. Fear of me or for me, I can't tell.

"It felt like a freight train rolling through my body," I say. It wasn't like it normally is when I trap a demon—not even a little bit. Something happened. Something took over. Inside me.

Sid stops ahead of us on the trail and turns to face us. "That was your power manifesting itself, Aidan. A stunning and glorifying sight. And we were all very privileged to see it."

"He was fucking glowing," Jax says again. The guy has a one-track mind.

"Was I really?" What does that even *mean*? How does someone glow?

"It was awesome, man!" Jax says. "Your skin at that tattoo thing on your arm went marbly and lit-up, and whatever you were writing burned into the ground as soon as you wrote it in the dirt. Then your eyes did this smolder thing for a second." He looks at me all tense, like he's mimicking my smolder. "Right after that you went limp." He smiles as if I should be thrilled at what he's describing.

I didn't feel anything hot, didn't see the words burn in. I didn't feel anything but pain and the urgency to act. I said words I don't know. That's never happened before. I always know—that's part of my weird thing. I always know. And now, suddenly, I acted without a clue. Like I was being guided.

I wipe my forehead with my hand, and my palm comes away wet with blood.

"I have a feeling that this is just the beginning," Sid says. "We're all in for quite a ride."

TWENTY-SEVEN

Once we're back at the house, Kara gets the first aid kit. Sid takes it from her, saying he wants to talk with me alone, and leads me into the office.

"Don't be afraid of your gifts," he says, rolling a second chair next to the one I've plopped myself into. "You'll learn to use them. And once they're finished awakening, you'll be in full control."

"What do you mean *awakening*?" That doesn't sound as cool as it should. Not after what happened today.

"That will be a discussion for another day. For right now I want to let you know that I may have found a lead on your family. Your mother's family, that is." He studies my wounds.

My pulse picks up at the idea. "What did you find?"

"Are you positive that you want to know these people, Aidan?"

"Why're you asking that?" Maybe he found something he knows I won't like.

"Just merely making sure that you want the whole truth. Sometimes it isn't what we think it will be."

I pause, looking at the lines and marks working their way up my arm. "Yes, I want to know everything. I need to know." Because, if anything, today showed me that this thing inside me is a hell of a lot more powerful than I thought. Maybe this is what will save us.

Sid starts cleaning my wounds delicately with a Q-tip, like I'm six. It's weird. And comforting. He knocks me off balance, but he's genuine, I think.

Have I finally found someone I can lean on? As he gingerly bandages my wounds, I find myself wanting him to really know me. Like a dad knows his son.

The idea makes my chest ache, as does thinking of my real father, so I just ask, "What have you found?"

"I'm not sure of it all yet, but I have found an address where your mother may have grown up. It's on the beach, in Malibu."

"She told me stories about growing up on the ocean. She loved the sea."

"Well, I'm hoping to get the names of the residents from my contact tonight or tomorrow. I just wanted you to know that I hadn't forgotten."

"Thanks."

"You'll know the truth soon, son. I promise."

———

When I get up to my room, I open the door, and Ava and Holly are sitting on the floor, huddled together near the bed, talking. Ava's head snaps up, and her hand moves behind her back, hiding whatever she was showing Holly.

"Hasn't anyone ever told you to knock?" she asks with a frown.

"Nope," I say.

Holly's eyes grow. "Whoa, what happened to you?"

Ava's frown deepens. "Did you get in another fight?"

"Demons don't like being trapped for all eternity," I say, tossing off my shoes and lying on the bed. "They tend to fight back."

Ava stands and slips whatever she's hiding into her bag and shoves it under the bed. "Demons? Really, Aidan, you need to be more careful."

"No, what I need to do is sleep," I say, rolling over, too exhausted to find out what secrets Ava is sharing behind my back.

"It's only six o'clock," Holly says. "Not much of a party animal, are we? And you left your girlfriend here all day. You need to go hang out with the poor thing."

"She's *not* my girlfriend," I say.

"Well," Holly says, "she won't be for long if you keep up that 'tude."

I growl into my pillow.

They gather their things and leave the room, Ava taking her secret with her. I wonder if I should warn Holly to be careful. Ava isn't in the best place right now. And what if her powers manifest? Holly would freak.

My head hurts from all the worry and demon fighting. I'll think about it after some sleep.

———

I wake in a rush in the middle of the night and sit up in bed, feet finding the floor before I can tell what jolted me. My cuts burn, but I push the sting away. I have to sit for a second, blinking at the darkness, listening, before I feel it again, a quake in the air. Slight, but there.

And then a muffled cry comes from the wall—from Kara's room. She's having a nightmare. The conversation with Holly about Kara's night terrors comes to mind. But why would that affect the air?

I take a deep breath and make myself lie down again, even though I want to go check on her. I've done enough already to mess shit up with her. And after today we might finally be in a better place. So I squeeze my eyes shut and hope it'll pass. I can't let myself think about how she felt in my arms, the peace that settled around us, the small hum of her pulse in her skin. The night we were together . . . I haven't slept that good in forever.

"Aidan?" Ava says, her voice thick with sleep.

"Yeah."

"I know what you're doing. I can hear your brain arguing with itself all the way over here. Why do you like her so much?"

"Go back to sleep, Ava."

"I wanna know."

"Are you gonna do a spell to dig it up if I don't tell you?"

"Probably." I hear a smile in her voice.

I think for a second, and then I just say it. "She's different than other girls. She's tough, but not in a mean way. She does have this crust around her, but it's all a facade. It's how she protects herself. And I want to see deeper into her, to know her. Because she's strong and complicated and . . . I don't know. It's lame."

"What about Rebecca?" she asks. "Is that how you feel about her?"

I close my eyes, not wanting to think about any of it anymore. I need to go back to sleep. "I don't feel anything you need to worry about, Ava. Let it go."

"It's not the same, I know. But Rebecca is pure and soft. Why would you pick Kara over her? Kara's so . . . well, Kara."

I roll over and cover my head with my pillow, groaning. Between the burning of my cuts, the sounds of Kara's nightmare, and Ava's pecking, I'm about to jump out the window.

"I think she's done something to you."

"Ava! Stop. Kara hasn't done anything."

There's silence for a few beats, and then she says quietly, "You're not going to kiss her tonight. You may as well just go back to sleep."

"Thanks for the heads-up."

"It's what I'm here for."

"Aidan," Mom says, "look." She points with a charcoal-stained finger at the pen mark on the doorframe where she measures my height. "You're a giant already." There's charcoal smudged on her face too, from her frantic drawing session last night. She must've had another vision. She always stays up scribbling strange images of ocean caves and cliffs when she's had one of those.

I turn and study the ink mark she made over my head. "Was my dad tall?" I ask. I know she carries a sore in her heart that he left behind. But I want to know about him. Is he real?

Maybe he's not. Maybe I'm not. Sometimes Mom looks at me like I'll disappear any second.

Now she's staring at me with a faraway look. I ask so many times about him, and she usually gives me a sad look or an angry look, but she never gave me a look like this one before.

"He felt tall," she says, her voice hollow. It sends a chill over me. Like the voice she makes when she's in the circle. "Like a king or an emperor."

"Was he a king, Mom?" I ask, suddenly afraid of the answer. Would he come and take me away from Mom and Ava someday? Take me to some faraway land?

Her brow creases in focus, as if she's trying to see him again through the fog of time. Her white-blond hair glows with light from the candle behind her, and the smell of sage drifts from her skin.

"No, not a king," she says with a sad smile. "Or an emperor."

She turns and walks away, forgetting about the measuring, forgetting about me. "He was just a man."

TWENTY-EIGHT

The next morning, the moment I step out of my room, I run into Rebecca.

Her hand flies to her mouth as she notices my scratches. "Oh my God. What . . . ?"

I shake my head. "I'm fine. It's nothing. Just a . . . cat." I back away a little. I don't want her caring about me. Not like that. Not now. "Listen, now that you're here, Sid says he can help you. If you want. He has a special, um, blessing he can do to help your sadness and stuff."

God, what am I doing? I suck at lying. But then again, how can I explain that he is going to use magic to bind a protective amulet to her aura that will make her invisible to demons? I don't think she'll stick around for that.

"Oh, Sid can help," Rebecca says. "Well, that's good." She doesn't know what to think; I can see it in her eyes.

"Yeah, so I just have to talk to my sister, and then we'll go find Sid, and he can fix this so you can go home."

"Leave? Today?" She glances down the stairs, a worried look on her face.

"Um, sure. Or tomorrow. It's gonna be okay." I pat her on the shoulder like a lame-ass, then hurry past her, toward the bathroom, away from the conversation.

Ava's coming out, her hair all braided with ribbons and twisted on top of her head. Her eyelids are covered in blue shadow; her lips are pink with gloss. "Holly said I could use her makeup," she says like she's worried I'm going to be mad at her.

"I need to talk to you." I nod to our bedroom. I've decided something in the last twelve hours. I'll give one of the amulets to Rebecca, but I'm not going to take the other one for myself. Ava needs it more than I do, the way things are going. I can fight my own battles. She can't.

After we shut ourselves in our room, I sit with her on my bed. "I have something for you." I take her hand and press one of the amulets into her palm. "Sid gave it to me and said it'll keep you safe from *them*. It could mean no more demon attacks on your birthday. No more running."

She looks down at the amulet. "What? But how?"

"We're going to do a spell, lock it to your aura. It'll hide you from them."

Her eyes snap to mine. "Aidan . . . casting magic? But you—"

I wave her shock away. "I know, I hate it. It terrifies me. But I love you more than I hate it. And right now, losing you scares me more than anything in this whole wide world. You need to be safe. This is the best way. The only way I can see, really. We're running out of time and options. I don't trust the wards on this house. It's too much property to keep hidden entirely. And I have a feeling whatever's been chasing us all this time is fairly powerful."

She rolls the amulet in her palm. "A bonding spell. That's it?"

"That's what Sid says. We'll do it today. As soon as we can."

"And he just gave it to you?" She bites her lip, looking troubled.

"Yeah, why?"

"Well, I've seen this before. And I wasn't wearing it."

"When?"

"That spell I did when I saw Rebecca. She was wearing it around her neck in the vision I had."

I fold my arms across my chest. "Well, there are two of them. She'll take the other one."

"Two?" Her mouth opens in realization. "But what about you?" She starts to panic when she sees I'm not budging. Her eyes search mine. "Aidan . . . it's not right."

"It is right. You said so yourself; you saw it in a vision. Rebecca's wearing one. And I'm with her, right?" She just keeps staring at me with those ancient-looking eyes until I can't stand the silence. "It's right," I say again. "So get dressed and then come down to the backyard so we can do this thing." I turn away before I change my mind and take back everything. I've made a choice. And it's the right one.

———

I've gained a level of respect from Jax, it seems. He's still buzzing about what happened yesterday, blathering to Lester about it when I walk into the office looking for Sid.

"Hey, there he is," Jax says, holding out his arm like he wants to side-hug me. "The man of the hour."

"Did you really glow?" Lester asks, looking my skin over.

"I didn't see anything glowing," I say as Jax catches hold of me.

"Oh, he was glowing." Jax squeezes my shoulder to his. "This badass actually held on to a demon with his bare hands, like he was wrangling a beast."

I was.

I pull out of Jax's arms. "Have you guys seen Sid? Is he up yet?"

"Him and Connor and your goth girlfriend are in the shed *together*." Then he winks.

I scowl at him, and Lester whacks him on the bicep. "Seriously?" Then he turns to me. "I think Sid wants you to meet them out there. He said something about you going with them to some church thing."

"Yeah, to repent," Jax says. "You big sinner."

Before I head out to meet them, I stop in to say hi to Finger and sit beside him on the couch for a second. It's more for me than a charity chat. The kid settles my nerves, and all this talk of my glowing marks and the demons is making my insides frantic.

Things are all right, though, when I think about it. They definitely could be worse. Sure, Ava is keeping secrets from me— sharing stuff with Holly she obviously doesn't want me to know about—but she's almost twelve. Aren't preteens supposed to rebel? I know I did. And it's probably good for her to have an older girl as a confidant. She still hasn't used her powers yet—that I know of. We only have to get through a few more days before D-Day, and we have a place where we're safe until then.

Plus, Sid is helping me find out more about my parents, and he's making sure Rebecca and Ava will be protected. I have help. I'm not alone in this anymore.

Really, things are looking up when you think about it.

After a few more minutes of watching Finger kill zombies, I feel better and ready to figure out what's next.

"Thanks, man," I say, patting him on the back before I rise.

He makes a sound of approval and kills two zombies with one swing of his bat.

TWENTY-NINE

"They already did the protection thing on Rebecca," Holly says as I come into the kitchen. "You totes missed the boring chanting." She's sitting at the kitchen table flipping through a magazine.

"Where are they?"

"Still outside, I think." But before I can walk out the back door she asks, "When you're kissing a girl, what are you thinking about?"

My hand freezes on the door handle and I turn. "Excuse me?"

"It's for the quiz." She points at the page with the tip of her pen. "What do you think about when you're kissing?"

"I don't."

"You don't, like, *think*?"

"I don't talk to you about it, that's for sure."

"Whoa, bad boy on the loose." She leans back in her chair, looking me over more closely. "It's just a question. Like, what did you think about when you kissed Kara?"

How much I never wanted to stop. "This is not a conversation I'm having with you."

"Suit yourself." She grins wide and leans back over the page, circling a number. Then she waves without looking up. "Ta-ta, grumpy."

I walk out of the house with the sound of Ava's violin beginning a sad tune upstairs. It follows me into the yard, making my nerves wake back up again. Or maybe my nerves were poked by Holly. It doesn't matter; they're at attention either way.

As I walk to the shed, the muted energy of the property lifts a little, letting me feel a tug coming from the white shack where a strange man sleeps every night.

The door is cracked open.

It's empty when I peek inside. Wherever the others are, they aren't here. The dank smell swirls around me, drawing me in. But I pull back, fear rising at the same time. As I move my head the door shuts, the latch clicking tight. The red circle painted on the door seems to blur and shift and then solidify again as I look at it.

I touch one of the crimson lines on the edge.

A flash of pain sears through me. The marking on my arm sparks with red lights, and electrical current hits me even as I step back, gasping.

All I hear is the sound of Ava's violin and my racing heartbeat.

And I suddenly know without a doubt, with everything in me, that I need to get in that shed. I need to see what's inside it. I pull on the handle, but the door doesn't budge in spite of the fact that I can see all the metal locks hanging unlatched. Desperate, I search the ground and grab the first thing I see, an old rusty pipe, and I whack the door with it. It takes three hits, but on the third the silver handle falls to the side.

The door creaks open again.

I fix my inner walls tightly in place, take a deep breath, and slip inside.

The space is very small—the size of a closet. The air feels heavy, like I'm underwater. All I see at first is the darkness, with the shapes of Sid's bed and the altar at one side. As my eyes adjust, I realize my foot is touching the chest Sid was digging in the other day when he gave me the amulets.

I search the space for a light and find a small gas lamp beside the bed. There's matches sitting on a stack of books right beside it. I pull a stick from the box and strike it, lighting the lamp.

As I lift it, my surroundings are revealed.

I nearly drop the lantern.

Over every surface of the walls are more of those same circle spells like the one painted on the door. And I'm very sure now that they're painted with blood. The symbol repeats over and over, *grounding, grounding, grounding*. And in the gravity of their energy, I weigh a thousand pounds. The feeling makes me want to run, but I stand firm and lift the lamp higher to study the altar.

I'm not sure what I'm looking for, but I know I'm looking for *something*.

Or maybe something's looking for me.

The altar was once a wine cabinet. Through the glass doors below, I can see rolls of paper instead of bottles in the circular spaces. The surface is coated in melted wax, dried blood, and burned paper. My mouth becomes a desert looking at it all. The skull of what looks like a cat sits to the side, with a symbol for slyness on the forehead. A bowl rests in the other corner filled with tiny bones that I'm hoping are from a bird. There are vials of various liquids and dried things. I don't want to know what.

My walls are up tight as they can get, but I still feel the death, the loss. Something horrible happened to make this place. But what?

Urgency fills me as I kneel down and open the chest, the desire to run growing stronger. My fear tells me this is where the answers are. I move several scarves, pants, shirts out of the way, and my hand finds vials, a stack of thick books, what I think might be rolls of money, and a larger, hard, square object that I can't get a good look at.

I lift the light closer and move a shirt out of the way. And uncover a stone that must be more than a thousand years old. Assyrian lines the top.

Bringer of Fire.

A chill works over me as the knowledge sinks in. It doesn't say *Aidan*, but I know these words are my name. It's about me. Just like my mom told Ava: *The father's place is another time, the son is becoming; Fire Bringer.*

Everything around me goes still for a second.

I can't stop looking at the words. I touch the stone with a shaking finger.

An image of robed men, commotion, arguing, flashes in my mind.

I pull my hand back, not wanting to see more.

But I can't stop myself from reading across the surface: *The end follows behind him, a fire of cleansing sight. Broken from the vine. Unspoken of, he is hidden. The eyes that seek him lose their soul. Awakened through Love's key. All hail, the one who brings Death to that which was Everlasting.*

My mind hears the word *death* over and over and over, and I can't stop seeing the robed men, feeling the anger and turmoil. All because of the words on this stone.

Voices come from outside the shed, bringing me back to reality with a jolt. I panic. Tossing the clothes back into the trunk over the stone, I quickly shut the lid, ready to bolt. But before I can, the door to the shed shuts with a click.

I try to lift the latch, but it won't budge. I press on the wood, but my arm sparks with red again, sending me back in pain.

I shake the zap from my arm and stare at the door, horrified. Then I hear Kara say, "We need to tell Aidan, Sid. It's way past time. After that mess yesterday with the demon."

All my attention focuses on listening.

"You need to finish your part first, Kara." That's Sid.

"It's not going to work. He doesn't want me." Her voice moves closer to the shed.

"That is a lie," Sid says. "The boy would follow you off a cliff. He's smitten. And so are you."

"No, I'm not," she answers, sounding very sure. I suddenly wish that I could see her eyes. "I don't like him, not like that."

My gut turns hollow. She doesn't like me—I knew that. I think I knew that. But hearing a denial, after the feelings I had when I kissed her . . . And I'd kiss her again, in a heartbeat.

"You've done well making the rest of us believe the opposite," Sid says, sounding almost sad. "Including him."

"I did what you wanted me to do. I kept him here so you could figure stuff out."

My brain ticks back to all the moments Kara and I had together . . . She's been manipulating me this whole time? She sure seemed to like me when I kissed her.

Kara's voice grows more quiet. I have to strain to hear. "If Aidan's really this kid you've been looking for, he should be having a lot tougher time keeping his hands off me."

"The spell wasn't meant to work on its own," Sid says. "Your job is to bring him to me fully awakened so that I can finish this."

There's another voice coming closer: "He's not in the house." It's Connor. "What's the big deal? We did the spell to protect his redhead. Now she can go home, and we can get back to work."

"It's not that simple, Connor," Sid says, sounding tired.

"Aidan's the one," Kara says. "The one Sid's been looking for."

There's silence for a second before Connor says in a disbelieving tone, "The *one*? As in the golden goose? You're actually serious about this, Sid? I thought you were just . . . high."

"No, Connor," Kara says. "Aidan's really the one Sid's been looking for."

My heart speeds up.

"Shit. But that means . . ." Connor's voice fades.

"Yes," Kara says.

"Are you sure?" Connor asks. "How can you be sure?"

What do they mean—Sid's been looking for *me*?

"You saw it with your own eyes, Connor," Kara says. "The way the mark on his hand and arm glowed? And it changed before that; it grew after I kissed him the other night—he said it did the first time, too. When I met him at Eric's club."

"Wait . . ." Connor sounds confused. I'm right there with him. "You met this guy before he got here? That's why you came home all weird that night that you and Sid went to pick up those coins?"

My head spins with a million confused thoughts. *The one*? What the hell? Are these people nuts? Have they spent too much time watching *The Matrix* or something? God, if they start calling me Neo I'm going to flip out.

"Yes," Kara continues, "I didn't know who he was, but I saw him in Eric's club, and I was drawn to him."

"I can't believe it," Connor says. "Sid's a bastard to do this to you."

"Now, now," Sid says. "Everyone has a choice—"

But Kara cuts him off. "No, I asked for this. It's not Sid's fault. He helped me, saved me. He saved you too, Connor."

"So you're going through with it?" Connor asks with a bite in his voice.

"I don't know," Kara bites back.

Silence answers, and my heart speeds up. Something about the whole exchange is wrong. I'm missing a vitally important piece. What does Connor mean *going through with it*? With what?

They've been expecting this kid—The One—who they think is me. But Kara hasn't been trying to keep me here or draw me in like she said; she's been pushing me away. She's actually been acting a little terrified of me. And she said earlier that she felt something with me that frightened her. Like I was affecting her.

She definitely affects me.

God, by the sound of it, she's made some psycho deal with Sid to keep me here, to keep me *happy*.

"But you really think it's him?" Connor asks, breaking into my thoughts.

"There's no doubt anymore," Sid says.

"It's just like Sid said it would feel, Connor," Kara says. "Like I'm standing on a precipice, facing a pit of hungry beasts. But when I touch him, it all fades away." She pauses and then says more quietly, "I had the nightmare again. You know, the one I started having after Sid did the spell on me to hold back the curse, about the lions."

So she's been having horrible nightmares like the one I heard through the wall ever since the spell. Sid did that to her, too.

"The men were dragging me to the mouth of the pit like always," she continues. "But this time when they tossed me in, the lions surrounding me were quiet. They had blood on their claws and flesh in their teeth, and they were close enough to touch me, but this time they didn't attack me. They just stood there, staring at something behind me, and when I turned around *he* was standing there, in the shadows."

"Aidan was?" Connor asks.

"Yes," Kara says. "He was holding them back. The lions—like Daniel in the lions' den."

Connor scoffs, "I'm supposed to believe a Bible story now?"

"You should," Sid says.

"I believe it, Connor," Kara says, sounding awed. "I've dreamed it—felt it on him. It's Aidan. He's the one we've been looking for. He's the Son of Daniel."

The name echoes in my head: *Daniel. The Son of Daniel . . .*

Then the door in front of me unlatches, swinging open with a loud squeak.

THIRTY

"Aidan?" Kara's voice comes closer.

"How did you get in here?" Sid asks, angry.

But I barely hear them or see them. My face is buried in my hands. What in the name of God is going on?

There's got to be some explanation. Sid's been looking for someone he thinks is me—someone who Kara thinks is me. She even had a dream about me, a dream about lions.

A dream that echoes what my mom said that day she painted my wall: *"The lions won't touch you, Aidan. They can't hurt you. God's closed their mouths."*

No. No, this doesn't make sense. This can't actually be happening. I've been duped. I've gotten mixed up with a bunch of crazy people.

They called me the Son of Daniel.

"He looks like he's in shock," Connor says.

"Aidan, come out of the shed," Sid says, sounding concerned. "Being in there is affecting you, son."

Daniel.

Daniel who? They were talking about the Bible. A lions' den. A Sunday school story: Daniel in the lions' den? The prophet Daniel lived a million years ago—okay, about twenty-six hundred years ago. But in any case, the guy can't be my father.

No way.

It's literally impossible. Maybe they're thinking of it symbolically.

Someone takes me by the arm. "Wake up, Aidan."

"He can't hear you, Kara. He's freaking right now."

"He needs to get out of that shed."

I knew this place was off. I knew something was up with Sid. I should've listened to my instincts. You'd think by now I'd know better. But . . . my instincts also told me to come inside, to look in that trunk.

Nothing makes sense. I have to get Ava out of here.

Now.

I push through the bodies in front of me and stumble from the shed, nearly diving headfirst into a pile of old paint cans.

"Take it easy," Sid says.

"Go get some water, Connor," Kara says, and then she's standing in front of me, holding my chin in her small hand. "Are you here, Aidan? Can you hear me?"

I blink at her and feel the weight that was coating me lift from my chest. But so many questions stay behind.

Connor comes up beside me, and a glass of water is shoved in my face.

I push it back and jerk from Kara's touch. "I need to get out of here," I say.

As they watch me, fear obvious on their faces, I turn and head for the house. Inside, I take the stairs two at a time and burst into my bedroom.

"Ava, you need to pack your—" But she's not there. The room's empty. My eyes catch a piece of paper resting on my pillow. A note.

The amulet is on top of it. And written in the bubbly script of an eleven-year-old are the words: *Protect yourself. I can fix everything so we'll both be free.*

It's signed off with a heart and the letter *A*.

My shaking body goes cold. Her words sound just like my mom's did the day she told me she was pregnant, right after she started calling up the darkness.

Ava.

I pick up the amulet and clench it in my fist. I stare at the empty hook on the wall where she's been hanging her bag—the one she keeps hiding things in. I fumble with my mind, looking for her, saying her name through the din of my frantic thoughts. But she's not answering.

I race downstairs. The house is empty. I check the office, and even Lester's not in his usual spot. I ask Finger if he's seen Ava, but he just chews on his lip.

Kara, Connor, and Sid all come back into the house, watching me like I'm about to lose it completely. Which I am.

I focus my energy on Sid. "Did you do something that'll hurt her, you evil shit?"

He flinches a little, but his eyes remain on mine. "Who, Aidan?"

"My sister!"

He shakes his head. Then he looks over at Kara. "Do you know where the others went?"

I can tell from the way she's breathing that she's debating what to say. I can also see that she's afraid of me.

I'm afraid of myself right now. "Tell me what you did to my sister, or I swear to God—" But I can't finish. I swear *what*? I swear I'll kill you? I'll do something else horrifying? What the hell am I prepared to do?

Connor steps forward, holding out a calming hand. "Look, Aidan, you're freaked out. I get it. I assume you just got a fairly huge dose of dark casting magic standing in that shed. And you may have heard some things. Just take a deep breath and—"

A toilet flushes, and everyone turns to see Jax emerge from the downstairs bathroom holding a Victoria's Secret catalogue and chewing on a Red Vine. "Yo, what up," he says, oblivious. As he looks from one face to the next he stops chewing. He swallows hard. "Everything okay?"

"No," I say.

He points at me like he just thought of something. "You're looking for your sister."

I nod slowly.

"They all went to some beach."

"The *beach*?" I say, incredulous.

"Yep." He points at the living room behind us. "I'm gonna hang with F-Boy and kill me some Nazis, is that cool?" He's asking as if I have a gun to all their heads. They all have that look in their eyes. Like they're worried I'll pull the trigger if they make the wrong move.

"See, the others are just at the beach," Sid says in his calming voice. "It's nothing nefarious, Aidan."

"And if they're all together we can call them," Connor says, pulling out his phone and queuing up a number. He hands it to me. "I'm sure she's okay, man. I get it. Family's vital. But if she's gone, it's not us."

I take the phone from him and listen to it ring.

Holly's voice comes on the line. "Hey-loo," she says in a sing-song voice.

"Where's my sister?" I growl into the phone.

She hesitates for a second and then says, "Calm down, *Dad*. She's in the shop with Lester."

I breathe in slow. "What shop?"

"The ice cream shop, duh. You said she could come with us. We're doing a beach run with Rebecca now that she's all invisible and all that skitch. But first an ice cream run for me. PMS, ya know."

"I never said she could go anywhere."

"What are you, her jailer? It's ice cream and sand, not a night on the town."

I take a few more breaths. Everything sounds normal. It's just ice cream. Maybe the others are right. I'm overreacting. "Is she okay?"

"No, we're selling her on the black market. Of course she's okay. Jeez."

I'm tense because of Sid. Holly isn't some snake in the grass. She's just a homeless girl like Ava. And Kara.

"I want her back here."

"Wow. Controlling much?"

"She needs to come home, Holly," I say as calmly as I can manage. "Please. As soon as you can."

"Fine. God. We were gonna go to Malibu, but whatever. I'll let her know that the freedom from the tyranny of her older brother is over. Give us a while; we're off Wilshire, and it's almost lunch rush."

I hang up. Ava's okay. She'll be home soon.

And then what?

All the fire seems to have drained from my bones. I walk past Connor, handing him his phone, and lower myself to the steps.

"What the hell is going on?" I ask, exhaustion overtaking me. "Who are you people?"

"Let me talk to him," Sid says, sounding resigned. He motions for the others to leave and comes to stand in front of me. "Can we go for a drive, Aidan? I promise to explain everything. Look at me and see that I'm telling the truth."

I look up at him, and he says it again: "I promise to explain everything that I can."

No spark lights his eyes. So I lift my tired body from the stairs and follow him back outside to the car, feeling as if I'm following him to my end.

THIRTY-ONE

It's a ways to our destination, and neither of us speaks the whole time.

We end up in Pasadena. The answers are in *Pasadena*?

Sid leaves the car in a dirt parking lot, and I follow him down a trail. It looks like we're heading toward a large bridge. Or maybe it's a dam. Are there dams in California? Almost immediately I start to feel strange. Dizzy. And there's a very familiar tug. Like the gravity in the shed, but a thousand times stronger.

"What is this place?" I ask, my legs becoming weak.

Sid walks farther down the path before answering. "This is how I would go home if I could."

That answer makes no sense, so I stay quiet, studying the surroundings and the brush and taking in the dank smell of settled water far off. And that intense pull of something just ahead.

We go through a tunnel and find ourselves on the other side of the road, and then we're walking in what I think is a dried riverbed. Trails have been cut through the brush over the years, but some areas look like they recently carried water. The path stays flat for a while, but then we're almost climbing as we make our way up a runoff crevice in the hill that's coated with dark stones. When we're at the top, the pull nearly makes me run forward. I have to clench my fists the last few paces.

Until I see it, and my feet no longer want to go any closer.

A large rock juts up from the trees, carved out by wind and water into what appears to be a poor rendering of a demon's profile. A cave mouth opens up at its base, blocked by iron gates. The surrounding stone edifice is painted in massive amounts of graffiti, making it all look like the perfect rave hangout. That's where the pull is coming from. Right there in that dark cave.

"This is it," Sid says. He's visibly shaking, and his fist is gripping his walking stick like it's a lifeline.

"This is *what*?" I ask. "Where you kill me and bury my body?" I'm only half joking. The feel of this place is full of murder and casting and darkness.

He breathes out. "No, son. This is where I come from." He points at a sign that says *Los Angeles County Flood Control District,* and in large bold letters underneath: *Devil's Gate Dam.*

"You're from . . . hell?"

His shoulders slump like he's tired, and he moves farther from the mammoth rocks, facing away from me. "You can see into other worlds, and you know when a person lies. You speak several languages long dead and have countless amounts of knowledge locked in that skull, but you're as dumb as a post, boy." When I don't comment, he asks, "Can you see into a man's soul?"

I hesitate, but then I realize that the time for hiding is over. "Yes."

He faces me again. "Have you managed to see mine?"

"I tried, but I couldn't."

He nods. "I take precautions. Apparently they work." He breathes in deep and lets it out slow. "If I show you my soul you'll understand, I believe."

"I sure hope so."

"I can explain. I can *show* you why it's vital you stay here with us." Under his breath he adds, "So much depends on it." The fear and intense focus in his eyes make my heart speed up a little. There's tension in every muscle, like he's about to let something loose that he's been holding for a long time. "I was sent here to find you by men who want you dead. They want you extinguished before you can harness your potential, before that mark on your arm begins to grow. Of course, it's too late for that now."

My skin tingles as his words sink in. "Sent. To kill me. Are you high?" I want to scoff at him, but I can see in his eyes that he believes every word. In his heart what he's saying is the truth. His job was to find me and kill me.

I take a step back.

"I won't kill you, Aidan. Not now. Maybe I never would have. I see now how vital you are, how this may be what was meant all along—no matter what my fellow prophets say."

"Prophets? What are you talking about?"

"Where I come from there are still prophets. Or seers, as some call them."

"Where the hell are you from?" My heart thunders as I imagine him saying, *I'm from Krypton*, or even that he's from some hidden monastery in the Holy Land. But instead he looks at me with a heightened sense of unease, like he knows what he's going to tell me is even more insane than that.

And then he motions to the cave and the *Devil's Gate* sign, again gripping his cane tight, and says, "That cave over there is a doorway. Part of the name is true, it is a *gate*. But not to a *devil*. I came through that doorway from another time, Aidan. Ancient Babylon. The sixth century BC."

I laugh out loud. It's absurd.

But then all the breath is sucked from my lungs as I remember my mom's words: *his father's place is another time . . .* And I watch Sid begin to change before my eyes, his face growing more etched, skin darkening as if he's been in the dust and sun for days. I watch the air around him blur, see his pin-striped vest and pants turn into a sort of tunic made of coarse tan fabric, and the tattoos on his arms and chest morph into a language, symbols lost to history long ago. His markings clearly say that he's a slave, and I suddenly have knowledge about him as I see his soul: he's a servant of the king, a maker of potions and keeper of knowledge. His rank is low, but his teacher was the highest ranked in the palace. The head prophet.

His teacher's name was Belteshazzar: the prince and protector of Bel. Once named Daniel of the Israelites, of the tribe of Judah.

"I know this is difficult to comprehend," he says, studying me, "but it's true. I came through a tear in the fabric of Creation, much like your father did. It's how we prophets tell the future. We peek through the keyhole of time."

"No." I back up a step and nearly fall over a rock.

He keeps speaking, lost in his need to spill out all his secrets. "When King Darius's council sent me here to kill you, they assumed you were merely a mistake, easily gotten rid of, that if you had any power at all you'd just be another magician, another prophet like them. But then I saw you, and I knew they were wrong. You're a whole other creation. You can straddle the lines between spirit and flesh without any effort at all. I've never heard of such a thing. It's why you can't be put down as if you were only a mistake of nature, why you must see this through and finish awakening your powers."

I put my hand up. "Hold on. What do you mean King Darius's council?"

I know Darius was the name of the second king when the prophet Daniel was held captive and that Daniel was a servant in the palace—beloved by the king. Darius was the king who sentenced him to the lions' den and then embraced Daniel as a brother when God saved him. Daniel was head of his *council of magicians*. But that would mean . . .

"Is Daniel one of the men who want me dead?"

Sid seems thrown by my question. "Your father? No, no. He was sentenced to execution because of his crime."

"He was *killed*?"

"No, the story in the annals would have changed soon after my arrival here if that was true, and it didn't. The story still says that Daniel remained in the palace of Babylon well into his life, even after his people, the Israelites, were set free of their captivity. So I can only assume God saved him from death a second time, as he saved him in the lions' den."

I swallow, too overwhelmed to know how to feel about it all. "What crime was he being punished for?"

"He broke a very important law by forging a relationship with your mother. That bond never should have happened. But that alone wasn't the problem. He crossed a line that must never be crossed: he left something behind in his wake." He gives me a pained look. "You."

I blink at him, eyes stinging.

"When your parents conceived you, all the elements and threads of the future changed. All past futures became irrelevant. If you'd been a normal child, or even a boy like I was, with small gifts, it might not have been so catastrophic. But because of what you are, because of the potential locked inside you, it changed everything. The spiritual world has been affected. Your father should've taken care of it before leaving here and made sure your mother didn't give birth to you, but he must not have known. He seemed pained beyond anything I've ever seen when he was brought to the temple and charged. He was the best of us all."

I try to imagine him. My father. Not some alien, not an angel— or a demon, like I'd always seen in my nightmares. Flesh and bone. But not just any man. A prophet, a magician, who could travel through time, who lived thousands of years ago. And made the mistake of creating me.

"Your father asked that I be the one sent to find you," Sid continues. "And because King Darius loved him, his request was granted. Before I left, he told me the story of how he met your mother, how he'd only just been taken from his father's people and brought into slavery. A boy of twelve, Daniel was powerful even then, truly close to God, and he found a way through a doorway one night while he prayed. He stumbled into shadow and collided with your mother, a girl who felt as lost as he did. He said he only stayed a day, but it was as if his spirit had been lit on fire after that. He went back every year, soon discovering that the day he was slipping through the tear was your mother's birthday. The last time he went they were both sixteen—that was the night before your father was going to be brought into the fold of the magicians' council."

Sid pauses for a moment before saying, "His manhood was going to be severed. He must have felt the fear of it."

"Wait, what?"

"I believe you call men like your father and myself eunuchs."

I look down at his crotch. "They cut off your . . . ?"

He smiles at my shock. "It's quite common for men who live in the palace as servants of the king to be castrated. It keeps us focused on our tasks. Less . . . distracted, if you will. Plus, it keeps the king's bloodline unsullied."

My stomach rises. I shake my head as I try to wrap my mind around something like that. My own balls ache with the thought.

"I think your father knew I wouldn't be able to kill you once I found you," he continues. "In fact, I made my decision soon after Eric told me about you three years ago. He said there was a young man who could see demons and read the energy of ancient objects. Hearing him talk about you, I knew he'd found the child I was looking for.

"It was more than a relief; I could finish my task and return home. Of course, first I had to kill you." He gives me an odd smile, and my insides squirm. "But then I saw you. A scraggly whelp of a boy sitting in Hanna's office. You were eating a sandwich, so focused on your meal you didn't even seem to notice I'd walked in the room."

My pulse speeds up, thinking how stupid I was back then. Must've been around the time Ava's foster parents were murdered. I was so hell-bent on blocking out everything and pretending I was normal.

"You had this glow about you—I can't describe it, but I couldn't stop staring at you. You look so much like your father, even the way you carry yourself." He pauses. "I had a job to do, but in that moment I knew I couldn't go through with it. I knew you were meant to be here in this place, in this time. So I found a way to remain here, to help you fulfill your destiny. And now that you're here, now that I see what you're capable of, I know I made the right choice."

He leans forward on his walking stick like he's exhausted himself. "Please don't throw away everything I've sacrificed to find you and keep you alive—everything your father sacrificed. You have to see this through, follow the path that your destiny asks. You have to remain where you can stay safe."

"Safe?" I say in disbelief. "How can things ever be *safe*? I have demons that may soon be after me, I have men in some other time plotting to come kill me and drag my body back to the stone age, and my sister is—" I stop, realizing what slipped out. Ava has to stay out of this. If her troubles collide with mine, my brain might implode.

"You don't understand, Aidan."

"I understand survival. That's all I need to understand. I've been doing things on my own for eight years now—longer, really. I can do it on my own again."

Sid reaches out but then lowers his hand. "You can't leave before you've finished your awakening. You don't understand everything that's happening to you."

I glance at the mark on my hand. "Is that why this thing on my arm is growing?"

"Yes. As it reaches your heart, it will near completion."

"And it's Kara that's making this happen?" I still don't understand how Kara's connected to all this, why Sid is using her. I'm having enough trouble digesting all the bits about my father being some eunuch Bible character. Plus, the idea that Sid is from a time even archaeology can't totally figure out.

"I chose her because of her curse: her power to attract would bring you to her, then to us. The counterspell I put on her could act as a sort of key to unlock your potential. And when you were finally . . . linked . . . you would find a sort of balance. Or at least that was the thinking."

My teeth clench listening to him talk about her like that, like she's a means to an end. I consider socking him in the balls and then remember he doesn't have any. "Do you know how sick that sounds?" I ask.

"Kara understands what's at stake. She chose this path as much as I did. I never lied to her."

"No, you're a saint. You just used her vulnerability to manipulate her."

"Ask her yourself. I saved her, Aidan."

"You've lied to yourself so much you believe your own bullshit now."

The air around him flickers again. His clothes go back to the pin-striped suit, and his tattoos become more circus variety than ancient. It makes me wonder which version of him is real.

"How do you do that?" I ask. "Change what you look like?"

"I only allowed you to see a past version of me in my soul, to see through the veneer of flesh a little deeper than you normally go. Nothing about me actually changed as we stood here in this place."

"But the tattoos on your arms . . . ?"

He lifts his hands, showing me his colorful forearms. "I had these images of dragons and vines and bones inked over the ones I carried with me from the past. What you saw a second ago was my state of being as I came through the tear in time."

"Can you see souls like I can?" I've been wondering this since the moment I met him.

He gives me a sad smile. "Once I could. But the longer I've been here, the more my sight has failed me. What little connection I had to the spirits is now waning. It's a consequence of my having stayed longer than I was meant to. There are many rules to this time game."

I shake my head. "I have no idea how to absorb all this."

"Ask me anything. I can help."

"I don't know." I don't know anything for sure anymore.

"I can help you and your sister," he says, like he's bargaining. "Think of your sister, Aidan. She won't fare well on the streets."

He has no idea how true that statement is, but not for the reasons he's thinking.

"I have a warm bed for her at the house," he says. "Food and shelter. I can keep you both safe." He comes closer. "I won't harm you, I swear. Look in my eyes and see I'm telling the truth. I won't do anything to harm you as long as you remain here."

There's no red spark of a lie in his eyes, but something in me can't quite give in until I'm sure. Maybe it's the dark gravity of the doorway behind me. Maybe it's because I'm totally exhausted, but I pull my knife out of my pocket. "Hold out your hand."

He steps back and blinks at me for a second. But then he holds out his hand to me.

Before he can figure out what I'm doing, I take it in mine and slide the edge of the blade hard against his palm, opening up the skin.

He hisses in pain and pulls away, cradling his fist against his chest. Blood seeps through his clenched fingers, running along his knuckles in shiny red lines.

I grip the sharp blade in my left hand and slice my own palm open. It stings like a fire, but I grit my teeth and hold the wound out to him in offering. "An oath in this place of power. You will never raise a finger to work against me or mine. If you do, everything you've worked for will be turned to ash."

He only hesitates for a second before reaching out to grip my bleeding hand with his own. "I swear it. I'll never raise a finger to work against you."

"Or mine," I say.

"Or yours."

I release his hand and back away a little. My body tingles from exertion, and my lungs burn, like I finished sprinting up a hill.

"So you'll stay with us," he says like he's checking.

I don't answer. I pull the amulet from my pocket and toss it at his feet, not wanting anything from him now. Then I turn and walk back toward the car.

THIRTY-TWO

I knew the truth of where I came from would be . . . unusual. But how do you prepare yourself to find out you're a cosmic error in the space-time continuum, the son of some long-dead biblical prophet, and marked for death?

As unreal as it all sounds, though, the pieces fit: my different gifts; the robed men in my vision when I touched that strange tablet in the shed; the way Sid acts around me; the demon's claim that I have no father here . . .

I don't, because he's been dead for more than two thousand years.

God, that's just . . .

Fuck.

The ache in me grows. I cover my face with my hands, fighting the emotions threatening to consume me.

Someone knocks on the door, but I can't move.

"Aidan," whispers Rebecca's voice through the wood. "Are you okay?"

I should probably answer her, open the door or something, make sure she's okay, but I can't bring myself to face anyone right now. To face anything.

After a minute of my silence she walks away, and I breathe a little easier.

Darkness falls eventually. Ava comes into the room, plops her bag down, and crawls into her bed.

"Rebecca's worried about you," she says. "Everybody knows you're in freak-out mode, and they want to know why."

I stare at the ceiling, seeing the house of cards that is my life ready to fall. I make myself breathe deep.

"I didn't think you'd want them knowing it's my fault," she says. "But I know it is. I'm sorry about taking off."

The beach . . . God, that seems so long ago. I should still be angry—furious, really—but I'm too tired.

"I thought you'd left," I say. "For good."

She's quiet, like she didn't expect that. "I really am sorry, Aidan. I just . . . I'd been inside for way too long."

But that's not the whole reason. Why is she lying?

I look across the room at her. "What was the note about, Ava?"

"I told you, I freaked out."

"You said you knew how to fix things."

She rolls over and faces the wall. "I had an idea, but it didn't work."

"What idea?"

"It doesn't matter anymore, Aidan." She sounds disappointed.

"Why won't you tell me what you did?"

She doesn't answer.

"I wish you knew how much this is killing me," I say. But I don't want to argue with her anymore. And I feel like I have something new in my arsenal, something I didn't have before, with this knowledge about my origin. If I really am as big a deal as Sid says, then maybe that can help me protect Ava. Somehow.

"I love you, Aidan." But I can hear tears in her voice. "Everything's gonna be fine."

I want to shake the answers out of her, to force her to tell me everything she's been hiding. But I just listen to her breathe and pray that this new revelation will give me a way to save her. A way to be free from this life. A way to be free from the lies and the pain.

I turn to the window and stare out at the night sky. It's a dark midnight-blue dome shimmering with the glow of city lights on the horizon. Only a handful of stars are visible; the rest hide behind the shroud of modern progress. You have to leave the city, go into the mountains, to see the actual sky. Here, in this glow of humanity, all that's discernible are remnants of the truth.

———

I watch Mom from the doorway across the room. She rocks back and forth in the rocking chair, eyes gazing off into another world. The sun comes in from the window beside her, shining on her pale skin and making her golden hair look like she's bathing in liquid light.

She rubs her rounded belly and turns, spotting me.

"Come here, Aidan." She waves me closer.

I cross the room, feeling odd, like I'm not quite walking on solid ground. "Does it hurt?" I ask, amazed at her swollen belly.

She smiles and shakes her head. "Of course not. It's the loveliest feeling on earth." She takes my hand in hers and brings it to her side. "Feel."

My palm lies flat while she presses it tight to her skin.

A few seconds pass, and something moves under my fingers, making Mom giggle. "See? She's saying hello." Tears fill her eyes, and she presses my hand closer.

"She?" I ask.

"Your little sister."

A shiver of excitement works over me. "Really?"

Mom nods, and tears spill out. They're happy tears that sparkle and shimmer on her cheeks like glass. She's happy—I'm not sure she's ever been happy before. I want to hug her and hug her until we both disappear into the warmth. Until my heart bursts into a million pieces.

"You're a big brother, Aidan."

I nod, my throat starting to hurt.

"Soon she'll belong to you, and you'll get to care for her and watch over her. You'll keep her warm, and you'll keep her safe from all the darkness, won't you?"

I nod again. "I'll always watch over her."

"Yes," she says, sounding tired. She kisses my head, wetting my brow with her tears. "You'll keep her hidden from all the lions."

THIRTY-THREE

I open my eyes, a weight instantly settling on me.

I turn to Ava's bed.

She's not there. Her bag's gone, too.

I sit up and rub the sleep from my eyes.

Something cold slides against my chest.

I look down, blinking at a gold medallion on my sternum. The other amulet Sid gave me—the one I threw at his feet yesterday afternoon. It's on a chain. Around my neck. I can't stop staring at it. I sit there for a long minute, my mind totally blank.

Then I notice a square of paper on my lap. I pick it up, unfold it, and read in Ava's handwriting: *Don't be mad*. I know immediately what it means: she did a spell to bind the amulet to me.

I don't bother getting pants on. I jump up, open the door, and yell over the banister, "Ava!"

Lester peeks into the entry from the kitchen. "Oh, shit, did she not tell you again?"

"Where did she go?"

He looks back into the kitchen like he's considering his escape route, then says, "She went to the grocery store with Rebecca and Holly to get dinner supplies. I can call them."

I curse under my breath and go back into my room. Ava's a missing person, technically kidnapped. What's Holly thinking? The ice cream shop and the grocery store?

If that's even what they're doing . . .

I look down at the amulet now dangling from my neck. It's so small. Looks like a useless trinket you might find in a Cracker Jack box. Did Ava really bind it to me? Could I actually be invisible to demons now?

I touch it with my finger. There's only one way to find out.

Someone knocks. I put my jeans on and grab a shirt and my phone before I open the door. It's Lester, a worried look on his face. I walk past him into the hall, shoving my phone into my pocket.

"Do you need anything?" he asks.

"Yeah, a tracking device for my sister," I say, starting down the stairs.

He follows me. "Where you going?"

"To find her."

"But . . ."

Jax comes out from the kitchen as I open the front door. "Sid wants to download with you, man."

"Where's the grocery store? The one Holly goes to?"

Connor comes into the entry behind Jax. "Gelson's, off Franklin. But that's quite a walk from here. I can give you a lift."

"I can handle it." A walk will help me clear my head so I won't strangle Ava when I find her. I can always grab a bus if I need to.

As I make my way to Franklin, I watch the shadows for creepers, looking for the Boss Demon that's been following Rebecca, but I see nothing—not one single otherworldly thing. No ghosts. No time slips. No demons. Just dilapidated yards and miles of cracked sidewalk.

Of course, now that I'm looking, I won't find anything.

I'm out of the neighborhood and in the shadow of some taller apartment buildings when Kara's Camaro pulls up beside me. "Get in," she says. When I ignore her and keep walking, she speeds up, turning in to a parking garage. I consider crossing the street and going down an alleyway to try and lose her, but before I get a chance, she comes running out of the garage. "Aidan, wait. Please."

I walk for half a block as she follows me before I turn, and she nearly collides with my chest.

"*Now* you want to talk?" I bark, sending her stumbling back. "It's a little late."

She blinks up at me and opens her mouth, then shuts it again.

"What?" I ask. "No biting comeback this time? No snark left?"

"Don't just run off," she says, her voice a little shaky. "It's not safe."

"Didn't you hear? I'm The One—the Bringer of Fire, in the flesh. Whatever the hell that means!"

"Aidan, please."

"Please, what? Don't you want to make fun of the insanity that has become my life?"

"I just need to talk to you."

I turn to yell at the passing cars. "At last! She wishes to speak, folks! It'll all be cleared up now!"

A homeless man cheers from the alley across the street.

Kara points behind her, growling, "Just get in the freaking car and stop being a bitch about everything!"

I bite back a laugh and study her for a second: her squinting eyes, her tense neck muscles, and the smell of exasperation spilling off her skin. She's caught up in this as much as I am. And as infuriating as my life is right now, she's living her own drama.

"Answer me one question," I say. "Just one explanation, and then I'll get in your car and go wherever you want."

She frowns at me. "What?"

"What is it you're supposed to do to me, Kara?"

She shakes her head. "You're an ass."

"Don't I have a right to know?"

Her keys suddenly seem very interesting to her. "I was going to explain everything to you."

"Well, here I am. I'm all ears. Talk to me."

She glances around. "The car's double-parked."

"Kara, stop avoiding."

"It's one of my many talents."

"I've seen your talents at work."

Her nostrils flare.

"I'm not under any illusions anymore that you like me," I say. "Obviously you were playing a part: make the sucker think I'm attracted to him. Make him think I want him. Like a game. I just don't understand fully why you went along with it."

Her chest rises and falls, like she's running out of breath. "This isn't a game."

"Not a game? Okay, a con, then. Sounds like the apple doesn't fall—"

She socks me in the stomach, sending every ounce of oxygen whooshing from my lungs.

I hunch over, holding my palm up before she uses her knee on a second target. "Okay, okay." I cough, trying to find air again. I may have deserved that.

"I wish I'd never met you in that club."

"I'm sorry. I shouldn't have said that about . . ." I look at her, not wanting to say the words. I can't seem to stop hurting her. "I shouldn't open my fat-ass mouth when I'm pissed."

"Can we just go?"

I shake my head. "I came out here to find my sister, and on the way I planned to check something."

She gives me a doubtful look.

"This." I pull the amulet from the neck of my shirt.

She squints at it. "You let Sid bind it to you?"

"It wasn't Sid," I say. "I'm not letting it go to waste, though. If there's some chance I'm finally hidden from the demons, it may solve a myriad of problems."

"Fine, I'll help you. First we check on your sister and then we test it," she says.

I glance back at the parking garage. "I thought you were double-parked."

"I lied." She smirks at me. "But it's gonna cost me twenty bucks to park in there, so you owe me."

"I think you trying to control my brain with your sex powers should keep me in the up column of our relationship for a while."

Her teeth clench. "I told you, I never used my abilities on you."

"Of course not. And you never lie to me."

"I thought you could tell when people lie. Are you getting rusty with me, freshman?"

I look her over, wondering, and mumble, "Maybe."

She seems to consider this for a second and then says, "I can prove it. Right here. Now."

"Prove what?"

She moves a little closer. "That I wasn't lying; I never used my powers on you."

My heart speeds up. "And how do you plan on doing that?"

"Like this," she whispers, moving closer, her breath warm against my lips.

The air around me shifts, her energy suddenly filling every atom, her eyes sparking to life like the sun reflecting off the ice. I reach out my hand as if it could ward her off and try to step back, but as I blink, my body goes suddenly still, mind blank . . .

Where am I?

She's pulling away, her hand sliding down my arm, back to the steering wheel.

Steering wheel?

I'm in the passenger seat of her car, The Carpenters spilling from the speakers as we drive down what looks like Franklin Avenue.

"You back?" she asks, giving me a tired look.

My head spins as I try to grab hold of a memory of how I got in the car and what she might have said, done, to me. I study my mark, trying to see if it's grown, looking for some sign of what happened.

"Don't worry," she says. "I didn't rape you or make you rob a bank or anything. I just suggested we take a drive. Oh, and you may cluck like a chicken for no apparent reason at some random moment in the near future." Her lips curl into a smirk.

"You . . ." I try to gather my thoughts. "That was your hypnotic thing? Like you did to the teacher at the school."

"Do you believe me now? My 'sex power,' as you call it, isn't something I enjoy using. Ever."

My pulse slows a little as I study her. She looks worn down and sad, and the usual sweetness of her energy's turned dull, now smelling more like the city after the rain. "I believe you."

She clears her throat like my eyes on her are making her uncomfortable. "So now that we have that settled, let's go get your sister and find a way to test that amulet."

THIRTY-FOUR

We get a call from Connor as we're pulling into the Gelson's parking lot. Ava's back at the house. He promises to lecture her as if he were channeling me. I'm too pissed off to talk to her right now anyway. I need to cool down.

Since Ava is safe, I ask Kara to take me somewhere to test the amulet. "Anywhere you're sure there'll be some demon action," I say. It's not until we pull onto a long drive and through a wrought iron gate that I realize we're in a graveyard. A graveyard. *Seriously, Kara?* Graveyards are a sure bet for activity, but it's not always *safe* activity.

We head up an incline, passing rows and rows of headstones in all shapes and sizes. Old trees speckle the grassy hills surrounding us, with clusters of flowers dotting the grass, but other than that it's green as far as the normal eye can see. My eyes, however, spot hundreds of small lights hovering over the ground. The dead.

"We're bound to find something here," Kara says, pulling along the curb to park.

"No shit."

She puts the emergency brake on and gets out. I follow her into a section farther back to the east, where the headstones are older. The orbs in this section seem stronger, brighter. They float around us, just off the ground.

The lights aren't ghosts. They're spirits. There's a difference between the two. A person is made up of three parts: body, soul, and spirit. A ghost is a small fracture of a person's soul, a mark left behind from a horrifying event or something left undone. The spirit is what waits to be merged with the soul—the mind, will, and emotions—and the body again, someday. A spirit is the truth of the person. The core of who they are. As far as I can tell, after death the spirit exists in a place beyond the reach of anyone or anything. Safe, in a sort of limbo.

"This place gives me the creeps," Kara says, walking along a row of graves, "so can we hurry it up?"

"I don't see any ghosts or demons to hide from," I say, looking around.

"Not here. A little farther." She points past a small family crypt.

"You know where they are?"

"I'm fairly sure."

We walk for another few minutes in silence and soon come to a fenced-in section. Withered morning glories climb the chain link that's hedged by dandelions and thistles. Patches of the weeds are dead, but they seem to be fighting to hold on. Several white sticks marked with numbers protrude from the ground on the other side of the fence. The orbs here hover in large clusters, with one or two small ones off to the side that flicker, like they've grown tired.

"What is this place?" I ask.

"Haven't you ever heard of a mass grave?"

I shake my head. The last time I was in a graveyard was the day they buried my mother. Since then, I avoid them like the plague.

"It's where they bury the forgotten," she says. "People whose bodies were never claimed. There's a demon here, I think."

"Where?" I don't see or sense anything.

She waves for me to follow her, and we walk along the over-grown fence. We go through a gate, entering the area set aside for the forgotten.

The smell hits me almost immediately. A sharp, pungent shot of sulfur that cuts the air.

Kara doesn't say anything; she just walks over to one of the numbered markers and turns to look at me. As my eyes follow her movement, they catch on a creature on the other side of the grave. Medium size for a demon, hunched over, with gnarly tumorlike protrusions on its shoulder blades—where wings used to be, maybe? It digs at the ground with its claws, growling under its breath, something that sounds like a repeated phrase. Green pus oozes from its piglike nose. It seems like it's almost in a trance, focused on something at its feet.

Then I realize I know what it's saying. Something like, *Inside shell, back to shell.*

Shell? Body.

It's a body-hopper.

It doesn't look like the other body-hoppers I've seen, though. Usually they're more snakelike. This one is obviously missing its host.

Fear inches up my spine like a slow crack in the ice.

This is no weakling demon.

"I can feel it," Kara whispers, even though it's not paying any attention to her. "It's usually right here."

"You should step away," I say. It's only a foot from her. "Come back to me." I hold out my hand to her, urgency tightening my muscles.

She seems a little surprised by my obvious concern, hesitating before she steps toward me, her foot treading on the grave.

The demon looks up at that. Its chant fades as it spots Kara, and it stares at her like it's found lunch after a long famine. My worry morphs to terror.

A long black tongue emerges, licking its lips as the demon rises up from its hunched position, garbling under its breath, "Mine."

It reaches full height, more than six feet, and I grab Kara by the arm, yelling, "Run!" even though in the back of my head I know it won't do any good. It has her scent now—all that sweet sadness and pain, just waiting to be capitalized on.

We sprint back through the gate and down a small hill, but as I look up, the demon is waiting in our path, only three yards away.

I react without thinking, skidding to a stop and yanking Kara behind me. I begin yelling the first thing that pops in my head: a prayer a priest taught me at the Catholic hospital one night when I was in the ER, the prayer to the archangel Michael. I yell it at the top of my lungs in English, telling Kara to say it with me. *"Saint Michael the Archangel, defend us in battle, be our protection against the malice and snares of the devil . . ."*

The demon flinches and looks around. It swats at the air like it's shooing a fly, but then it keys back on Kara with a growl.

It's obvious that the thing doesn't see me. And also that the prayer's useless.

"Tell it to leave you alone, Kara!"

She gasps for air and whimpers, "Leave me alone."

"Like you mean it!"

"Leave me alone," she says more forcefully.

But the demon only hesitates.

"You have to believe, Kara. Tell it to leave you alone in the name of El Yeshuati!"

She shivers against my back. I know she feels my terror. She yells at the top of her lungs, "Leave me the fuck alone in the name of El Yeshu-whatever, you goddamned bastard!"

The demon pauses, looking irritated.

"Tell it to go back," I say, a small amount of relief trickling through me. "That it has no right to you."

She pauses as if unsure, but then she yells, "Go back to my father! You have—" She nearly chokes on her words, a small sob escaping. "You have no right to me."

Her dad. I turn from the demon to look at her. "Kara, what is it?"

She shakes her head, tears filling her eyes. And I realize she's not strong enough to push it back.

So does the demon.

It huffs out a snarl, steam and saliva dribbling from its mouth. It bares its teeth at her and stomps its clawed foot on the ground. Then it lowers onto all fours, like it's about to charge. It's going to shove itself into her skin. Use her like a puppet as it torments her and feeds off her weakness until she does something to silence the pain.

Like take another razor to her wrists.

I reach down and pull the chain and amulet over my head, tossing the thing to the grass.

The demon blinks, doing a double take.

I step closer, still holding Kara behind me. "Pick on someone your own size, asshole."

"No, Aidan," she breathes, gripping my shoulder. "Put it back on!"

I put every ounce of determination I have into my words. "She. Is. Mine." I growl. "You want her; you'll have to come through me."

It looks me over, bulbous eyes lingering on the marks on my arm. Then it returns its gaze to Kara, studying her as if seeing her for the first time, searching for weakness. It snarls and gurgles, then moves forward and back.

"Just try it," I say. The thing could tear me to shreds with those teeth, but I remember what happened at Griffith Park, and something tells me I'd give this beast a run for its money. I feel it, a vibration in my hands, behind my eyes: there's something in me wanting this bastard to lunge.

But after a few thundering heartbeats, it lifts its crooked chin and releases a low keen of annoyance.

It's cowed. Somehow.

More strange noises continue to emerge from its chest, and I feel genuine disappointment as the demon crawls away, back to the spot on the small rise where the cluster of orbs are. Then it hunches back over and starts clawing at the ground again. Like we were never there.

I snatch my amulet up off the grass. Kara slips her shivering hand in mine, and we put more and more space between us and the demon, first walking quickly along the graves and then running.

We jump into the Camaro. It takes several tries for Kara to get the keys in the ignition because her hands are shaking so hard. The engine is the most beautiful sound in the world as it roars to life, and we speed off, heading back into the city.

———

We're near Griffith Park when she pulls off the road. The gravel crunches under the tires as we park beneath a pine tree at a deserted vista point.

Kara sits for a second, taking in large breaths. Then suddenly she swings the car door open and runs to the brush at the edge of the cliff.

She heaves, her body convulsing.

I slip out of the car and walk over to her. I want to touch her, to reassure her, but I'm not sure how.

After a few minutes, she stands up straight again and wipes her forehead with her hand. "You shouldn't have taken the amulet off. What were you thinking?"

I move a little closer. "Kara, we're okay."

She shakes her head violently. "You don't try to save me, Aidan. You just don't. Not you."

I nod, not sure I understand, but not willing to argue with her right now. "We're okay," I say again.

She just breathes and stares at the ground.

I wait, letting her take her time. We are okay. The amulet worked. And for some reason, claiming her stopped the demon.

She must be thinking the same thing, because she says, "You said I belonged to you."

I nod again.

"And it stopped, didn't it?"

"Somehow."

She says under her breath, "I may know how."

I give her a questioning look.

She nods at my arm. "It's your mark." Then she motions to her side. "And mine."

My hand flexes almost involuntarily. "What is it?"

She swallows. The smell of her fear shifts to a childlike sense of fright. "It's why it had to be me. To do that, make it grow." She points at my mark. "It's waking up your power—your core energy."

"Sid says that once it reaches my heart, it's complete."

"I'm sorry. I should've told you. Every time we . . . connect . . . that's what makes it grow stronger."

"But why would that change how the demon saw us?"

"Because." She turns slightly away. "I do belong to you."

"What do you mean?"

"When Sid marked me, when he turned my curse upside down, there was only one way to lock it in. It had to become a key to something—someone—else. To reverse the curse, the spell had to have a purpose. You."

My pulse speeds up. "How does that mean you belong to me?"

"The spell made me into the second half of a whole. The other half of you. Like the legend of Adam and Eve: they were one person, but God separated them so they wouldn't be alone anymore."

"*The woman came out of a man's rib*," I recite. "*Not from his feet to be walked on. Not from his head to be superior, but from the side to be equal. Under the arm to be protected and next to the heart to be loved.*"

She looks at me, wide-eyed. "What's that from?"

"The Talmud." Things begin clicking into place in my mind. "So that's why our markings match."

"They do?"

"You can't see it because it's on your soul, not your skin, but your tattoo is overlaid with three symbols. The first one means *Intimacy,* or *Knowing,* and the second means *Awaken Power.* It makes sense now. Awaken my power—with, you know, intimacy. My mark seems to have only one symbol that I see, and it's also on yours. It says: *Demon. Seer. Complete Death.*" I kneel down and draw it in the dirt with my finger to show her. "Like this."

"That's the symbol of your power," she says, kneeling beside me. "Sid showed it to me when he was explaining what I might see when we touched."

"What else did he tell you would happen?"

She glances at me, her body close. "He told me that your energy might feel warm, like sunlight on my insides. And that I'd be drawn to you. And when we kissed in the club, I felt a piece of it." She pauses and says more softly, "I was so sure it was you."

I stand, and she stands up with me. "So once I came to the house, you were supposed to keep me *busy*? I still don't see how that makes you my other half."

"Finding you was only part of it—the next step was waking up your power."

"By kissing me."

"No." She chews on her lip for a second. "*You* had to kiss *me*. Then the spell would start to work. And eventually we'd . . ." She makes a motion with her head that tells me I should be able to complete the puzzle on my own.

"I'm supposed to have sex with you."

Instead of looking away, her eyes burn into mine. "Yeah."

I nod, my mind ticking through it all. And I remember—

"But you stopped me." I know I wouldn't have stopped on my own that night after the party. "Why?"

She comes forward a little, like she wants to touch me. But she doesn't. "It felt wrong, Aidan. I know you now—I saw into you when we kissed. I realized I couldn't trap you like that. You have a right to choose this power if you want it, but it's not right for someone to force it on you—to force anything on you."

I know she's not just talking about me. Having sex with me because she was *supposed* to would have been like what happened with those men her father handed her to. How could Sid trap her like that?

"You're not going to follow through with this now, Kara. It's okay. Sid can forget about using you as his pawn."

She studies me. Her hair wisps across her mouth; a strand brushes my sleeve. "It's not that I didn't want to. Whatever this is— this link when we connect—it makes me nuts inside. Like all I am is hunger, and you're—" She swallows, but then finishes. "You're the only thing that'll satisfy me."

"It's just the curse." I feel my insides stir as she holds my gaze. "We're not slaves to anything. Even our own desire." But in the same breath, I reach out to brush her hair from her eyes, and my thumb grazes her jaw.

A buzz races up my arm.

I'm suddenly mesmerized by the way her eyelashes brush at her cheeks as she blinks. Her lips part, just a little, and something hooks me in, pulling me closer. My head clouds with all the memories of kissing her, the feel of her in my arms, in my hands. I want that feeling again. The sense of urgency and rightness. The sensation of a million sparks bursting under my skin.

I graze her neck with my fingers, and she leans into the touch.

I need this connection with someone. We don't have to follow it to its end. Just one . . . small . . .

. . . kiss.

Our lips touch, delicate and effortless.

Like we're merging clouds.

Folding over each other.

Becoming one.

Two halves of one whole.

At the thought, the sensation in my hand goes from a slight buzz to engulfing flames, searing and sharp.

I hiss in pain, stepping back as it travels up my arm, past the elbow, arching over my shoulder, pushing me to my knees.

Kara collapses with me. "Oh, God. Aidan!"

I suck air in and out of my lungs, trying to see past the raging energy that's suddenly made it impossible to think. The fire dims a little as I focus. And after another few seconds it's down to a dull throb.

"I'm so sorry," Kara says, sounding tormented.

"I'm okay," I manage to get out.

"We barely touched that time."

"Must be getting stronger." Everything is.

"Wonderful." She sighs and helps me to my feet. "We should go back to the house."

I release an exhausted laugh. "Where we can't accidentally have sex, you mean?"

"Exactly."

As we're walking to the car, something dawns on me. The thing she said to the demon, telling it to go back to her dad.

"Where the demon was in the graveyard—that's where your dad's buried, isn't it?"

She doesn't respond, but I know the answer.

"I'm sorry, Kara."

She shrugs and says, "The man doesn't deserve any better. Wish I'd thought to put the bastard there myself."

THIRTY-FIVE

Ava's on the couch snuggled next to Finger when Kara and I come through the door.

I walk to the archway and give her a pointed look. "You said you were sorry before. Are you sorry again?" I hold up the amulet to make a point.

She hugs Finger's arm tighter. "It was just the grocery store, Aidan."

"Nothing is *just* anything right now, Ava," I say quietly. "You know that." I can't say more with other people in earshot. And I shouldn't have to. Ava knows what's at stake.

Jax yells from the upstairs landing, "The lovers are back. Guess I lost the bet, Holly. Chick flick night is on, people. Dammit."

Rebecca emerges from Holly's room and gazes down at me and Kara. Her expression is confused. And maybe a little hurt.

Holly's behind her. "Oh, good. We won't have to watch *Die Hard* again."

"I like *Die Hard*," Ava pipes in.

"It's *Pitch Perfect*, bitches!" Holly yells, looking giddy as she skips back into her room, hair ribbons and ponytail swaying. "Aca-mazing!"

Connor watches us from the kitchen. Kara gives him a nod, as if she's trying to tell him everything's okay, but he still shoots me a look full of brotherly warning. I give him a thumbs-up just to mess with him.

I trail behind Kara as we walk up the stairs. Jax punches me in the arm as I pass. "Bitches are in heat."

I lean closer to him and say casually under my breath, "You talk to me like that about them again and I'll break that crooked nose on your smug face."

Rebecca's gaze feels glued to my back as I walk away. I need to talk to her, but at this point I have no idea what I'd say. All I know is I'm tired as hell. And hungry.

Movie night and junk food might be all I can handle right now.

———

Sid finds me in my room after I take a shower. I tell him I'm not ready to talk to him again. Not until I digest what he already told me.

"I just want you to know I didn't bind the amulet to you," he says. "I wouldn't do something like that against your will."

I walk past him into the hall and hang my damp towel over the banister. "I know it wasn't you."

"I gave it to your sister, hoping you'd change your mind."

He appears to be waiting for a response, so I say, "That's so helpful."

"She obviously did the spell to bind it to you." He pauses. "I didn't know she had that ability, Aidan."

I glare at him and move in closer, hoping he feels what I'm about to say in his bones. "You talk to me about her or try to get in her business, you're not going to like how I react."

He studies my face. "I merely wonder why you've kept her talents a secret."

"Because she's none of your goddamn business."

"Very well." He starts to leave and then turns back to say, "I know you're angry with the secrets we've kept from you, but you have to see it was for a good reason."

My jaw tightens. "All I see right now is a liar."

———

The whole house smells like burnt popcorn, and there's a bunch of chicks singing pop music in blue blazers on the TV. We're piled in the living room—even Finger; he's still got his Xbox controller in his hand even though the others took over his domain. Jax keeps sticking Jujubes up his nose and snorting them at Holly. She's snuggled on the love seat with Rebecca and Ava. Jax and Lester are on the floor with me. Kara, Finger, and Connor are on the couch behind us. Apparently it's required that everyone take part in family night.

But thankfully "Uncle Sid" isn't joining us, or I wouldn't be sitting here at all.

There are a million unsaid things in the air. Rebecca keeps glancing across the room at me, and I wonder what the hell I'm planning on telling her. She deserves an answer. It's not helping that I'm leaning against the couch with Kara's leg an inch from my shoulder. She brushes up against me once, and I nearly jump across the room.

"You okay, dude?" Jax asks, holding out a Jujube.

I take it and pop it in my mouth. "Peachy."

Nothing about the movie really registers, even as it wraps up in a big dance number and the boy gets the girl. If only reality could be like a musical.

The last few days are swirling around in my head like a tornado. I'm going back and forth from the conversation at the Devil's Gate with Sid, to the kiss with Kara after her revelation, and back to what Ava's been doing when I'm not looking. What is she hiding? Why can't my sister just let me protect her?

I'm so wrapped up in my thoughts, I don't notice Sid come in.

He leans on the archway. "Let's have a meeting in the morning before everyone starts their daily tasks, folks. There's a job in Anaheim we're working on that we need to make a plan of attack for, so to speak. And a decision about our biannual YouTube special needs to be made: Griffith or the mental hospital. But for now, it's clean up and off to bed." He looks so normal—well, not normal, but definitely not some ancient Babylonian magician. I can't begin to imagine how freaked the others would be if they knew. Because who assumes there are people who travel through time? Or that they hang out in LA and become ghost-busting con artists?

Lester turns off the TV, and everybody gets up, cleaning candy and popcorn off the floor. Sid disappears out the back door—heading to his dark shed, no doubt. Just the thought of that place makes me nauseous.

Trying not to think about it, I pick up and arrange pillows and then stand on the arm of the couch to pull a gummy bear from the ceiling.

"Hey, that's from two weeks ago when we watched *Footloose*," Jax says, pointing at the red bear pinched between my fingers.

"Sick," Lester says.

"I double-dog-dare you to eat it," Holly says to me with a wicked grin.

Everyone says *oooohhhhh* in unison like we're ten years old and she just dared me to kiss someone.

So I play along, jumping down from the couch and popping it in my mouth.

The whole room bursts into surprised laughter.

I wait a second, letting them all relax. Then I spit the juicy red glob at Jax.

It hits him in the cheek, sticking for a beat before plopping to the carpet.

Silence fills the room until Jax reacts, flinging his whole box of Jujubes, pelting me with a dozen hard jellies.

Then chaos erupts. Kara throws a fistful of popcorn at Finger, Holly smashes the remnants of a Ho Ho into Lester's nose, Jax shakes a soda and sprays it onto the girls, yelling, "Wet T-shirt contest!"

Everyone's throwing candy and pillows and Xbox remotes. Finger panics at that point and gathers all these into his arms and runs from the room. Ava's even caught up in it all, giggling harder than I've ever heard. I let myself fall into the fray, whacking Rebecca with a pillow as she lunges for Lester with a blanket, trying to throw it over his head. She swats back at me and bursts out with a squeal, and then I'm laughing, falling to the floor with Ava, trying to wrestle the remote from her hand as she yells, "Make them watch it again! Turn it to the kissing scene!"

Movie night is officially my favorite idea ever.

———

We're still recovering an hour later as Rebecca, Ava, and I make our way upstairs. The others have already gone to bed, except for Connor and Kara, who're finishing cleaning up in the kitchen. I would've offered to help, but it was clear that Kara wanted some time alone with him. And it gives me a second to talk to Rebecca.

Ava heads to our room, giving me a thumbs-up as I walk Rebecca to her door.

"Thanks for convincing me to come here, Aidan," she says, leaning on the frame and hugging a notebook to her chest—a sketchbook, I think. "Being here's really helped. You know, with everything."

"How did things go today?" I ask. "Is the protection working?" I haven't seen the Boss Demon around at all, but I'm not taking anything on faith with that guy.

She holds up the amulet around her neck. "Seems to be working great, I think, keeping all the bad energy back, or whatever, like Sid said it would." She touches my chest where my amulet rests with her fingers. "How about you?"

I back up a little, and she pulls her hand away.

"Sorry," she says, studying the floor now. Her copper hair falls like a curtain over her face. "I can't help it."

God, this is going to kill me. "Rebecca. Don't be sorry. You and me . . . it's just not good timing."

"Because of Kara. I know you like her."

I sigh. "There's a lot going on. It's not just Kara. My life's a shit storm right now. The last thing you need is to get tangled up in it."

She tilts her head a little. "It's a bit late for that."

"You need to go home as soon as you can and forget about me."

"I won't ever be able to forget you." Tears glisten on her pale lashes. "And I know it's you, Aidan—you're the one I need. It doesn't matter if you want that to be true or not. From the second I saw you sleeping beside my bed, I knew."

She sounds so completely sure of this.

"I used to draw this angel," she continues, her voice soft, "before Charlie died. Sunsets and crashing waves and fierce battles, and this angel was always in my work, golden and magical. Powerful." She lowers her head, running a finger along the top of her sketchbook. "But after Charlie left me, I had nothing inside. I couldn't see my angel anymore, you know?" She sniffs and wipes a tear from her face and smiles this odd smile at me. "Then you appeared in my life, and you talked to me, you gave a crap—it was almost like you were sent to me. And suddenly he was back, my angel, amazing and full of light. So I drew him again. But it wasn't until the party that I realized . . ." She reaches into her sketchbook and pulls out a folded piece of paper and hands it to me. "It wasn't an angel I was drawing. It was you."

I unfold it and see the image of a young man surrounded by gold and silver lightning. He's standing firm in a lake of fire, like he's ready for battle, a dagger in his hand.

His marked hand.

"I drew this after I saw you at the school," she says. "And look." She points at the warrior's chest where a small gold amulet rests.

My pulse speeds up.

"That's the amulet you're wearing right now," she continues. "This is you. And it's the same figure I've been drawing since I was thirteen."

There are gashes on his arm like the ones healing on my arm right now from the demon's claws. "Wow" is all I'm able to come up with.

She takes the image and folds it again before slipping it back into the pages of her sketchbook. She hugs it to her chest protectively. "We're connected, Aidan. Somehow. I don't know how. But it was true before I met you, and it'll be true after I leave this place."

Her words feel so much like Kara's. How can this be happening to me with two girls at once? And it's not like they're just feeling it and I'm numb. It's in me too, this urge. But I *can't* be drawn to both of them. How the hell do you make a choice like that?

I blink at her, stuck.

Then she's leaning in, pressing her lips to my cheek, before slipping into her room and shutting the door behind her, leaving me to my confusion.

———

Mom sits beside me on my bed, tucking me in. She brushes the hair from my forehead and touches her finger to the tip of my nose. There's something different in her eyes tonight, something clearer. Like maybe she's seeing me. Really seeing me.

"You're such a strong boy," she says, smiling down at me.

I grin, letting her glow warm me. "Like the Incredible Hulk?"

"Well, if you turned green, I'd probably have to take you to the doctor."

I giggle and slip my hand into hers, squeezing tight. Her pulse is quick, the familiar ache in her skin still there. But there's a determination in her that wasn't there before. I see it, suddenly clicking into place.

"Can we have pizza tomorrow night?" I ask. Whenever we have pizza nights, Mom sits with me and we watch movies. I like the way she curls us up in the blanket together and then props the pizza box on our laps.

"Tomorrow night you'll be putting Ava to bed early and having reading time."

I frown at her, not liking that idea. Early reading time in bed means she'll be in her circle. The glow I felt a second ago darkens.

She studies me, tears now glistening in her eyes. "I need you to be even stronger after tomorrow, Aidan." A tear spills out and trails down her cheek. "Can you do that?"

"I can try," I whisper.

"Don't forget all the things I've shown you," she says. She leans down and kisses my forehead. "God has you held tight."

THIRTY-SIX

Something's pecking. The sound lifts me from my dream into early morning light.

Tap tap tap on the window.

I open my eyes. There's an object moving above my head.

I squint at it, wondering if I'm still dreaming. Because it looks like a book. Hovering over me.

What?

A pencil flies past, and its sharp point hits the window repeatedly. *Tap tap tap.*

I sit up in a rush, whacking the book and the pencil away and sending them clattering to the floor. "Ava!" She's lying in bed, and there are several tiny red, blue, and green orbs hovering over her. Then I see a wrapper still in her hand—Peanut M&M's—like she fell asleep eating them.

I scramble over to her and shake her shoulder. "Ava, wake up."

She grumbles for me to go away, and the M&M's keep hovering a foot over her chest. Something slides against the outside of the door, and I imagine more objects floating all over the house. And someone seeing them.

I close my eyes, trying to feel for her energy. There's a slight whirring and a sort of silver smoke just over her chest.

I shake her shoulder again. "Control it, Ava. Lock it down." *Please don't do this now.*

She jolts straight up, gasping, like she's coming up for air after a long dive. The M&M's *tink* to the floor, and in the distance I hear the sound of falling objects all over the house: *Thunk. Crash. Thud.*

Shit.

I wait for the sound of bedroom doors opening or the creak of feet on the landing, but nothing comes. After counting to ten I can almost breathe again.

"That was weird," Ava says.

"No kidding. It's never happened before?"

"How would I know? I'm asleep."

"You can do that when you're awake, though."

"Only when I mean to. I've been focusing on controlling it. I thought I was doing better."

"You are," I say. The last thing I need is for her to start getting scared or upset—that'll only make control harder. "It takes time, though. And things are getting closer."

She looks at me. "I wonder if it's the spell. Could that make it harder, you think?"

"The spell?" My pulse quickens. Did she do others that I don't know about?

"Yeah. You know, the looking spell, or the one I did to bind the amulet." She reaches out and touches my hand. "I know you're still angry about it."

So she's only done the two. Good. "Mostly because I wanted you to have it, not me."

"You need it more. Rebecca told me about her brother. Something evil is after her, and it's probably going to try and hurt you for helping her."

She has no idea.

"We only have three days till your birthday, Ava," I say. "This amulet could've solved everything for you this year—maybe forever."

She shakes her head, looking suddenly weighed down. "Hiding who I am won't solve anything. There's so much more to this than we know."

Her words strike me as odd: *who I am*. Who does she think she is?

"You're my sister. And I want you safe. With me." I lean over and kiss her forehead, trying to get a sense of what's going on in that mysterious mind of hers. "So quit running off. No more adventures until after your birthday passes. You *have* to stay on the property."

She pecks me on the cheek before she pulls a book from her sheets and leans against the wall. Looks like a typical tween read: *The Baby-Sitters Club*. "Well, I won't be sleeping any more tonight," she says.

I go back to my bed and check my phone. "It's six fifteen anyway—pretty much morning."

She looks out the window, eyes distant. "It was fun last night, wasn't it?"

I can't help smiling at the memory of Holly shoving the Ho Ho up Lester's nose. "Yeah."

"You should stay here, Aidan. After my birthday. This could be your family."

The air around me prickles. Even in the darkness of early morning her ratty hair seems to glow like a white halo, and with her tiny frame she looks like a glass doll washed ashore after a storm.

"Don't think like that, Ava."

She gives me a sad smile. "You're right. Sorry." But her words are empty. She doesn't believe them.

I lie down again, wide awake. After a few seconds of staring, I sit back up.

"I'm going for a run," I say and start to get dressed for the occasion.

Ava blinks at me from across the room. "You're gonna *run*? When cops aren't chasing you?"

"Very funny," I say. "That was only once."

She giggles, and my heart lightens a little.

"Okay, maybe twice," I add, sticking my tongue out at her as I tie my new shoes.

THIRTY-SEVEN

I stand in the front yard stretching my legs post-run. The sun's just over the horizon behind me, casting a warm glow onto crooked trees and weedy yards. Even the cracks in the sidewalk seem to add character to the neighborhood in this light. The cold morning air still stings in my lungs, but it's a good sting. It feels like I ran several miles, but it was more like three times around the block. I obviously need to work out more.

Just as I'm about to walk up the pathway and into the house, something prickles at the back of my neck. My feet freeze. I glance slowly around me.

Then I spot it. Rebecca's demon is across the street, about twenty yards away, under a tree, staring intently at the house.

It can't see me, I tell myself. *Or Rebecca.*

The thing has to be seriously pissed that I've not followed instructions. It must know that Rebecca and I are together. I wonder what it's thinking about its missing minion. Everyone knows a cornered beast is at its most dangerous.

I watch for several seconds, studying the curve of its broad shoulders, the way it huffs at the air like a bull. It shapes itself into the shadow of the tall bush behind it, keeping out of the light. It won't be at full strength now, with the sunrise breaking over the horizon. But even at half strength, this thing could squish me like a bug if I tried anything.

Trapping it comes to mind—but even if it can't see me, it will likely feel anything I try to do to lock it in place.

I breathe in deep and take a step toward it. I'm not sure exactly what I'm doing. I'm supposedly this amazing son of a prophet. Men have been sent through time to kill me. You'd think I'd have one power that could help me with this. But I'm coming up blank.

When I'm halfway across the street, someone calls from the house, "Aidan! Where you going?"

The beast's head snaps to attention; its dark eyes scan the yard.

I freeze for a moment and then turn around.

It's Jax—of course. "The meeting's started. We've gotta get this thing talked through before Connor has to meet the gay guys at eleven."

I wave my arms, trying to motion for him to shut up, but he just squints at me like an idiot.

"Are you having a seizure?" he asks. "What the hell is wrong with you?"

I give up and walk back toward the house. "Seriously, dude. You suck."

"What'd I do?"

I stop at the porch steps. "Go inside. Give me a second, for crap's sake."

"Whatever, Touchy." He walks into the house, leaving the door open.

I turn back to look for the demon, but it's not there anymore. I scan the street, the shadows of neighboring yards. Nothing.

It's gone. For now.

———

I shut the door behind me, and someone—Jax, I think—calls from the office, "Meeting's in here!"

I don't answer, just head for the stairs. But then Sid comes from the kitchen, stopping me.

"You're back for the meeting," he says, looking pleased.

"Just finished a run. Shower."

"I got something for you." He pulls out a roll of papers from his back pocket and hands them to me. He beams like he's waiting for me to unwrap a gift.

I take the roll without opening it.

"It's papers," he says before I can read it over. "A birth certificate, adoption papers, and a Social Security number. A driver's license will be forthcoming once you take the test. And you now have a brand-new last name."

Jax comes up behind me. "What name'd ya get?"

I open the papers, feeling a twinge of amazement. "What's all this for?"

"Well, I'm your legal adopted guardian now," Sid says.

I look up at him.

"If you would like me to be, that is." He points at the top page. "These papers will allow you to have a clean slate and for me to protect you under the law."

Jax snatches the papers from my hand. "What's your name, dude?"

After skimming the papers a moment, he smiles. "Aidan O'Fallan. Okay, Irish boy." He shoves the papers at me and walks back to the office, saying, "We've got an Irish Jew with demon-snatching powers. Did anyone have money on Ireland?"

Sid smiles. "I tried to keep it as close to O'Linn as I could."

"Thanks."

"I got some for your sister as well." He holds out a second roll. "I wasn't sure how old she was, so I guessed that she was twelve. Is that all right?"

I take them and have to swallow the panic that rises at the sudden reminder of what's coming in three days. Those floating objects this morning were a clear sign of her powers coming alive. A warning of what's to come. "Where is she?" I ask.

"In the office. She wanted to join the meeting."

I can't seem to move. A part of me wants to tell him what's happening. But something stronger in me holds the words in.

"I may have more for you, Aidan. If you want it."

Is it a bomb shelter to hide my sister in for the next few days so she doesn't accidentally bring the house down around us? Or perhaps a parallel universe that demons can't get to?

"What is it?" I ask.

"Your mother's family. But I don't want to tell you unless you're sure."

I glance toward the office—no sign of listening ears. I sit on a step and ready myself. "What did you find?"

He sits beside me and shows me a scrap of paper with an address on it. "Her name is Laura O'Linn, and she's your great-grandmother."

"My great-grandmother," I echo. "What about my grandma?"

"She died when your mother was about three. Suicide. Your mother was raised by her grandparents. Your great-grandma is the only one left alive."

I have a great-grandmother. I have family.

"I hope you don't mind, but I had my connection mention LA Paranormal to her. Apparently she's been having some trouble lately with a ghost in her TV or something—she could just be very old and not fully there. But I thought it would be a good way for you to connect with her. We could offer her our services, and you could meet her, if you wanted. I'd give her a discount, of course."

I rise to my feet, the idea of meeting this woman making me want to run away for some reason.

"She doesn't have to be aware of the tie," he adds, standing with me. "You can visit her as Aidan O'Fallan. It may be interesting to see her."

My mom said very little about her family. Nothing about who they were or how they treated her, or if she loved them or not. On the rare times she talked about her childhood, she talked about the beach. She took me to the ocean for picnics all the time as a kid. Usually we'd just sit and watch the waves in silence, like it was a holy place and we needed to be careful not to awaken the ghosts. But very rarely she'd tell me stories about learning to sail with her grandpa or how she used to love to chase the foam.

A warm hand touches mine. "Is everything all right?" Kara asks from beside me.

"We're going to go see Aidan's great-grandmother."

The declaration startles me. "No, we're not."

Sid starts to argue. "But, Aidan, you need to—"

Kara cuts in. "No, he's had enough for now, Sid."

Sid turns to her. "Until he's finished his awakening it won't be enough, Kara. This needs to be completed. Now."

"You're pushing him away," she bites back.

"He needs to know every part of this." He points at me emphatically. "Then he can accept his fate with open arms. If this woman is a part of that, her truth needs to be heard. Isn't it odd that she'd be having paranormal trouble at the same time her great-grandson is awakening to his power?"

And at the same time her great-granddaughter is set to turn twelve and be taken by demons.

"I'm not awakening anything," I say, "if it means Kara has to have sex with me."

I feel Kara start.

"You don't understand, Aidan." Panic surfaces in the pitch of Sid's voice.

"You're right—I don't understand why I have to bone some girl for power! So explain it to me, for fuck's sake."

"You have to finish this. Your power *must* be awakened. It's the most important thing—more important than even my life." He rests a hand on my chest as if trying to calm me down. I smack it away, but he keeps talking. "You won't be able to save them if you don't follow this through. Everything will be lost—all the bright sparks in this world, the love, the thin connection humanity feels to the Creator. It'll all slip away. So much depends on that link. Without it, life will disappear from this earth forever."

"What the hell are you talking about?" I'm so tired of all the riddles.

"You know now that you're important, but you don't know why." He points behind us, to the office where the others are gathered, and whispers, "*They* are why, Aidan. There aren't many of them left, souls that *see*. There are barely a hundred born in a generation. They're Lights—beacons that shine the truth of things to the souls that are blind to it. And there are more out there, in the streets, huddled in dark corners, lost, young people who have spiritual talents—like Jax and Connor and Holly. These gifted souls allow humanity to peek into the worlds outside their own, keeping them linked to Life and Love in more ways, deeper ways, than what they can see and touch and taste alone. All the people in this house, all the ones out there that we haven't found yet, they play a vital role. Their loss will be the destruction of humanity. Your birth changed the balance and put them in greater danger, but you also have the power to save them all."

"Save them from *what*?" Humanity is going to be destroyed if I don't play his game?

"Save them from the demons looking to destroy them. There's a reason these young people's lives were hell on earth before they got to me—they've been chased down like dogs by darkness their whole lives because the demon kings know they need to kill the Light if they want to win."

He studies my face like he's searching for some spark of understanding in me. He's not going to find it.

"Aidan, the future has changed. The demons have seen the same thing Darius's council saw in the prophecies. They know that you'll cut their rule short and that the power center has shifted strongly against them. They will do everything they can to remedy that, even if it means killing every last young person in the city—in every city. Just in case they have the ability to *see*."

"And I'm supposed to save them. Suddenly it's all up to me?"

"It's always been up to you! Why do you think I didn't kill you when I found you? I realized there was more at stake than my fellow council members wanted to see. They only saw their own power waning with your arrival, but they didn't see the cost that would have to be paid to regain it. I see that cost. I look it in the eye every time I take one of these young people under my wing, these Lights. And there are so few of them left."

I shake my head. It's all too much to take in right now. "I'm not sure what I'm supposed to do. I have other things I'm responsible for." This can't be about saving anyone but Ava.

"You must believe me. They need you. We all do." He pauses and says in a quiet voice, "Rebecca is one of the Lights as well."

My skin prickles.

. . . *The Light he found will lead him; its wings sit beneath the heart* . . .

"Rebecca?" She's the one my mom told Ava about? But Kara is a Light too by Sid's definition—kids who can feel things beyond the physical world. And she has the violets and lilies; she's the one I'm feeling led to. Rebecca is only a distraction, she—

But then I realize . . . wings beneath the heart. Rebecca has wings. She has a butterfly tattoo on her ribs. I saw it the morning I brought her home, after my shower.

How could I have missed the connection? Kara and her violets and lilies, Rebecca and her butterfly wings. Two girls, not one. *The Light he found will lead him; its wings sit beneath the heart. But he must touch the violets and lilies to find surrender, to find his hidden blood.*

Sid is oblivious to my revelation as he rambles on. "Yes, Rebecca is one of the strongest of the Lights that Fate brought before you. Then you came here and began bonding with these new Lights as well, although most of the kids in the house don't have the strength of her gift. I didn't believe it until I saw it. What she'll soon be able to do is unique."

I'm not sure what he means. I glance at Kara, who's studying her shoes intently, wondering why Sid has left her out of the discussion.

Sid notices me looking at her and adds, "Kara is also a part of this. But she wasn't born with her talents. Her gift was created with magic. It makes no real difference in the scheme of things; they will all eventually help you, each one completing you in one way or another. They are very important, Aidan, and it's your job to protect them, to lead them. They have to be close to you if they're going to stay safe."

I frown at him. "But you acted like you didn't want Rebecca to get mixed up in our lives. You said she was supposed to go home today. And now you're telling me it's vital that I stay close to her?"

"I was wrong when I said that. I wasn't aware that she was a Light until I did the spell on her. I was going to tell you, but things became . . . unhinged. In any case, you could never have left her. Once you're linked with a Light, they'll likely remain with you out of innate loyalty. A handful of them may have dreamed of you for years."

My world tilts again. The drawing Rebecca showed me, the way she talked about her angel . . .

Holly pokes her head out of the office door and interrupts. "Hey, what's the sitch? Is this meeting the haps or what?"

"In a moment, Holly, please," Sid says, sounding distraught.

Holly seems to get the message. She disappears back into the office, shutting the door.

Sid continues. "The kids in this house, they're your army, Aidan, your main weapon against the demons. They're how you'll open humanity's eyes to the truth."

"I don't understand," I say. "How am I supposed to lead a bunch of kids when I barely know what I'm doing myself?"

"For now, your powers enable you to find the Beacons, or Lights, and draw them to you." He swallows. "Eventually your powers, harnessed with theirs, will enable you to kill the demons."

I bark out a laugh. *"Kill?"* Now I know he's completely off his meds.

"Demons."

I shake my head. "No. You're crazy. Demons can't be killed." This I know. This I wished a million times wasn't true. But you can't kill something that's not flesh and blood. You can't kill a spirit.

"In Griffith Park, Aidan. Remember what happened? I saw it with my own eyes. You were full of light, like it was coming from your eyes, your skin. It's your power starting to spill out. It's growing in you as your mark grows. Why else would you be able to touch them?"

"This is insane."

"You have to see he's telling the truth, Aidan," Kara says.

I look at her, trying to find something in her eyes I can grab hold of. It's all too much. A father from another time. My ability to touch demons. A group of kids that will be my army. My *army*?

"You don't belong here, Aidan," Sid says. "You never should have been born. You cross all boundaries of nature and spirit. Yet here you are. Something—*someone*—watching over all of Creation doesn't want it all to end in blood and torment. Maybe that someone made sure the mistake of your birth happened in a way that most wouldn't notice until all the prophecies had changed. If you hadn't been born, maybe the end of the world would've been very different. But it's too late for that now. You have to follow this through. Everything depends on it. Everything."

"So Rebecca *is* linked to me, then." It's a statement, a confirmation of what she said in the hall last night, of what my mom said in the dream to Ava.

"She was meant to meet you," Sid says. "And she's very important—the first of the Lights to find you. Why do you think the demon was working so hard on her? But until you have full use of your power, you're very vulnerable—which means they are, too. If the demons discover that they can physically harm you without being on this plane, you'll be sliced to bits in seconds."

"But . . . what does it all mean?" I ask.

"She and the others have to stay near you, under your protection," Sid says. "It's why I started this house. A place had to be made ready for you and your soldiers."

I don't know whether to laugh or cry. "You couldn't have told me all this yesterday when you spilled the beans about my dad being some time-traveling biblical character?"

"You don't have to like the truth," he says, "but you do need to find a way to believe it. It's vital that you complete your journey, that you finish this with Kara, that you open yourself up and awaken your powers fully. You won't be safe—no one you care about will be safe—until you do."

I glance at Kara. "It's not happening." Even though just looking at her makes me want to touch her again. It doesn't matter—I can't hurt her like that.

Sid releases a long sigh. "Once you have time to consider what I've said, I think you'll see I'm right. You'll see there's no other way."

———

Mom's standing on the outside rim of the circle, studying what she's drawn on the floor, checking her work, the names of angels written in symbols that only I seem to understand. There's white dust on her shirt, on her nose. The chalk stick that she used to draw the summoning circle is in her right hand; her grimoire is opened in the other. She looks back and forth between the floor and the book.

I need to go into the room to put Ava into her playpen, but I don't want to interrupt. I'm afraid of the panic I see in Mom's eyes when her concentration is cracked, like whatever connection she's making is drifting away like smoke. But I feed Ava, feed myself. I wash her tiny cheeks and hands. Put her in her bear jammies. Now she stands beside me on her tiny three-year-old legs, gripping two of my fingers.

I dare a whisper. "Mom?"

The chalk in her hand cracks as she breaks focus.

I taste dust on my tongue, dry and bitter. "Can I put her in her playpen now?"

Mom looks up, eyes far off. "It's not time yet. Not time!" She nearly screams when she says it. Tears spill down her cheeks. "They tricked me. How could I let this happen?"

My chest clenches at the panic pouring out of her in frantic waves. Ava grips my fingers tighter, and a tiny whimper escapes her.

"It's okay, Mom," I say, even though I'm not sure it's true. But I want it to be.

She sees me finally, eyes clearing of fog. "Don't forget, Aidan. Never trust your heart."

And then she kneels and draws a new symbol in the four corners of the circle. She's mumbling Latin, something about "one for another" and "binding light." She's slipped away again, gone back to her magic, her need to make something right, searching for something I know she'll never find.

I look again at the circle and see a flash of blood, of pale skin, eyes wide to another world. Mom's eyes. Mom's blood. Inside the chalk circle.

I walk past her into the room to tuck Ava in for her birthday night.

The last night.

THIRTY-EIGHT

Rebecca giggles and slaps another ace down in the middle of my bed. "You lose!" She high-fives Ava, who's sitting beside her, and they both laugh.

I feign frustration, but I'm actually floored to have spent the last day doing totally normal and mundane things. Rebecca and Ava and I have happily spent the last three hours playing a game of rummy. It's been good to have time with my sister. Without even one discussion of demons or magic or destiny coming up. I can almost feel my feet finding earth again.

I haven't slept since Sid unloaded on me yesterday about my Great and Terrible Duty. Nothing in me is still enough to sleep.

I need to get my head straight or it's going to explode. I need to decide what to do about my great-grandmother. There are a lot of reasons in front of me now to confront that part of my life. And only one reason not to.

Fear.

I'm terrified of what I'll find. And I have no idea why.

I need to get over it, though. One of the top reasons for me to meet this woman is for Ava. To find out anything I can that might help me protect her. I can worry about saving Earth after she turns twelve tomorrow.

Ava gathers the cards off the bed and starts shuffling them again. "Five card draw this time."

"No, let's play war," I say.

Ava rolls her eyes. "You always wanna play that. Anyway, we don't have enough cards."

Rebecca tosses me a look that says, *Little sisters are such a pain, aren't they?*

She has no idea.

"How about go fish?" Rebecca asks.

"Your wish is my command, my sweet." I wink at her.

She blushes, and I instantly regret being flirty. I didn't mean it in any way other than being playful, but I can tell Rebecca's caught off guard—she's biting her bottom lip and turning girly all of a sudden.

I look away, but study her out of the corner of my eye as she watches Ava shuffle the cards. Her hair is pulled back into a knot on top of her head, her skin is pale and soft, and the freckles across her cheeks stand out from her lack of makeup. Her eyes have seemed less sad the last day or two, especially since Sid told her she could stay a little longer. I wish I could say I wasn't attracted to her, that I didn't want to touch her jaw and kiss her neck—

I clear my throat, trying to distract myself from my train of thought. She's a girl, she's beautiful. Of course I'm attracted to her. I'd have to be blind not to be. But there's something else. Maybe connected to what Sid was talking about—that she's one of these Lights and I'm linked to her. Because I don't just feel attracted to her, I feel protective, responsible. And I barely know her. What am I supposed to do with that?

I pick up the hand Ava dealt me, and there's a knock on the door.

"Aidan," Kara says through the wood. "I need to talk to you."

"Hold on," I say.

"Just meet me in my room when you're done," she says.

"Yeah, sure." I can't look at Rebecca.

Ava glances over at Rebecca and then at me. "Kara's going to have to wait her turn."

I give her a look over the top of my cards, and she gives me an eye roll back.

We play one round of go fish, but none of us are feeling it anymore.

One more day keeps rattling through my head. *Ava will turn twelve tomorrow.*

One more day.

———

"What now?" I ask as Kara opens her door.

"Hello to you too, oh chipper one."

I walk past her and fall back onto the bed. "Where are my manners? I forgot, I should be thrilled my world is spinning off its axis."

She comes over to lean on the wall next to me. The *Gone With The Wind* poster we yanked off the wall in our frenzy to get at each other the night of the party is fixed and pinned back up.

She fiddles with the taped edge next to her hip. "Sid thought we should go meet your great-grandma today. With or without you. I just wanted to give you a heads-up. We're leaving in an hour to tell the old lady that we can maybe help her with her TV thing."

"Seriously? He's just going to butt into this now?"

"It's Sid," she says with a shrug, like I'll understand. And I do. It's silent for a long moment as she fiddles with the corner of the movie poster some more, like she's not sure what to say. Then she adds, "I just think . . . if it was me, I'd be excited to meet someone connected to me. Think how many questions she could answer for you. Don't you have questions about your mom? Sid said she died when you were young, a robbery gone bad or something." Her voice turns quiet at the last bit, fading off.

I grip the mattress. The air goes cold around us as the vision of my mother rises . . . *body sprawled in her casting circle, thin white gown twisted around her middle, a gaping hole in her chest. Her eyes stare off into nothing, her mouth open in a frozen gasp of terror . . .*

"I'm sorry," Kara whispers, bringing me back.

I shiver and blink away the memory. I wish I could turn my heart to stone to keep from feeling it all—the endless ache from seeing her like that throbs in me like a gaping wound.

"I don't know why I said that," she says.

I shake my head. "Don't worry about it." I stand and begin pacing, and then I confess, "I'm just afraid. I've always been afraid to know about my family."

"Why?"

"You know what I am, the things I can do, how scary it all is."

She nods slowly.

"That's the good part of my past. That's where it actually makes sense."

I have no idea why I'm telling her this—the words I never spoke aloud before, the door I've never opened for anyone: "She was a witch, my mom. A mess. I watched her all the time doing spells, talking to demons, calling them to her. I don't want to understand that—I don't want to dig deeper. The idea is actually terrifying me right now." I look into her eyes, and the mark on my arm begins to pulse with a dull ache. "My mom only brought pain to my life, Kara. Her weakness took away everything I cared about. What'll happen if I follow her down that rabbit hole?"

Her hand moves to mine, and she takes it with her delicate fingers. I sense the strange connection, that yearning where my skin seeks her out. All of it. And I suddenly feel myself balance inside.

"You deserve the truth, Aidan. You deserve a family. Love. And isn't there a chance that maybe you'll find salvation? Something good in it all?"

I won't find salvation. That much I'm sure about.

———

Ava lowers her violin from her chin and gapes at me. "What do you mean you're going to meet our great-grandma?"

"I told you, she might have answers."

"Well, I'm not going." She actually looks a little nervous.

I study her. "It shouldn't be more than an hour or so."

"Whatever."

"No spells while I'm gone," I say. "And stay *inside*."

She gives me an annoyed look. "Don't worry."

"And if you feel like you might manifest, just play your music."

"I know. I'm not an idiot."

I give her a peck on the forehead and grab my hoodie. "I mean it, Ava."

She growls.

"Love you, Peep."

"Right back at you, demon dork." She touches her violin back to her chin and lifts her bow. "Tell the grams I said hi."

THIRTY-NINE

Kara, Sid, and I walk down a pathway through some overgrown tropical plants and past a small greenhouse to the front door. The house is old, the pink paint weathered, the wood trim rotted from the salty air. Waves crash in the distance. I know we're high above the water, but from here you can't tell how far away the edge is. All I see in the direction of the sea are neglected tropical plants.

Sid knocks on the door. He's acting like we're really here to see a client.

Seconds tick by before someone comes to greet us. It's a large Samoan woman with a very bright, flowered dress on—it looks like the garden behind me threw up all over her. "Hello. How can I help you?"

Sid gives a wide grin and a slight bow. "I'm here to talk to Mrs. O'Linn. She's expecting me."

"The missus is resting now—"

"I am not!" comes an affronted voice from the shadows of the house.

The woman turns and addresses a small figure in a wavy pink robe. "Laura, you should be lying down. Your blood pressure."

"Stop fussing, Fa'auma." The older woman waves her tiny hands in the air, shooing the larger woman off. "You go back to your knitting and soap operas and hush now. Let me take care of these things. You don't know how to speak properly when people come calling."

"Whatever you say." Fa'auma gives us a wry grin and heads into the darkness of the house, saying over her shoulder as she goes, "I'm here if you need me."

The pink woman grumbles something under her breath about being able to do things for herself and then turns her attention to us. Her delicate frame looks even smaller in the tall doorway. Wispy white hair floats around her head. A pink barrette dangles to the side, hanging on by only a few strands. There's a stubborn set to her birdlike shoulders, and I can see something in her that's so familiar, as if my mom is standing in front of me in older skin.

"What's your business here?" the woman asks. Her focus is on Sid. She barely seems to notice that Kara and I are there.

"I'm Mr. Siddhapati, Mrs. O'Linn. From LA Paranormal. We spoke on the phone about—"

"The ghost man! Yes!" She nods and barrels past us, heading toward the garden. "Follow me." She waves us on before she slips through a bush.

She's fast for a frail old thing.

The bushes are thick and smell like unripe bananas. Stiff branches and monster-sized leaves block the path, but I walk forward anyway, praying I don't end up falling off a cliff because I can't see where I'm going. I fully comprehend right now why those explorers on TV walk through the jungle dramatically whacking at leaves with three-foot-long machetes. I never thought I'd need one in LA.

"Over here, Aidan," comes Sid's voice.

A hand reaches out. Kara's on the other end, her hair mussed.

"Quite the yard you have here, Mrs. O'Linn," Sid says.

Mrs. O'Linn is digging around in a bin beside the greenhouse door. "Yes, my husband was a botanist. He traveled . . . all over." She waves her hand at the sky and digs some more. "I don't have the head for it."

"What was it you did before you retired?" Sid asks.

"This and that. Mostly I was an actress, I suppose. But a woman needs to be practical." She pulls something from the bin with a triumphant grunt. It looks like a rock. "Plus, there were children to raise." She flashes a grin at Sid, and her eyes find me. She goes still, blinks, holding the rock loosely in her hand. "I had a daughter," she says, pensive as she stares at me. "Her name was Deirdre. She was reckless. Died very young. So reckless." Her voice cracks a little.

"I'm terribly sorry," Sid says.

Mrs. O'Linn shivers and then draws herself up. "Yes, well, it runs in the family, it seems. I'm not sure how I escaped it, really. But here I am, old as Moses. The only one left."

"You mentioned a granddaughter on the phone," Sid prompts.

My throat tightens.

Mrs. O'Linn frowns. "Did I mention her? Fiona. Crazy child. I tried my best to raise her, but she had her mother's ways. All that talking to walls and hiding in caves—oh yes! That's why I called, wasn't it? The ghost!"

"In your TV?"

"What? No! Not the TV, the *thimbleweed*."

Sid looks at her, genuinely confused. "Thimbleweed? Like, a plant?"

Mrs. O'Linn hugs the rock to her chest. "Oh my, what a thing! You thought I was worried about my television speaking to me? What an old biddy you must think I am." She seems pleased with the mix-up. "Here, let me show you."

She waves us through another bush behind the greenhouse. I give Sid a questioning look, but he just shrugs and follows.

"He really thought it was the TV," Kara whispers to me. "He's actually a little deaf."

"Seriously?"

She nods. "It's a prophet thing. He's losing his senses the longer he's out of his own time." She leans in closer. "When I met him he could tell things about people, like secrets. Or read objects. Now he depends on Connor for that. He could also sense spirits and energy like me, but now he can't as much. And he could read old writings in weird languages. Now he has to take them to Eric—who I heard was having you read them."

Those scrolls Eric called me about last May. Was it Sid I was reading them for? "So he was like me. Sort of."

"I think he used to be."

That's why he has that look in his eyes, like he's always digging into you, looking deeper than a normal person. "So he really *is* getting weaker the longer he's here?" I think part of me wondered if he exaggerated that a little. Apparently not.

She nods and starts walking into the bushes. "Yeah. He's never going back now, probably. He told me he'd never make it; he's too weak—he'd end up floating in the middle of nothing. That's why he has to sleep in the shed. He's put a spell on the walls to keep himself held here mentally and spiritually. And that cane is spelled for when he's out of the shed. That's why he keeps it with him all the time."

"That's nuts."

"Well, he believes in what he's trying to do."

I follow her, feeling disjointed, wondering what it all means. The plants tangle around my arms and legs as I walk, and I struggle for another few yards before the jungle ends and I stumble into open air.

We found the cliff.

Four feet in front of us the ground cuts off with what must be a fifty-foot drop to the ocean. I walk to the edge and peek over. The water churns in white curls, crashing violently against the rocks below. I feel a sudden déjà vu, as if the urge to walk over the cliff playing at the edge of my mind is a memory.

"This way," Kara says, motioning to a pathway carved into the side of the cliff. "Looks like they're down there already."

We work our way along, descending to a small beach. Kara slips every few feet, grabbing at the rocks to steady herself.

"Careful," I say. The air is making me dizzy. Maybe she feels it, too. Could there be a demon nearby trying to make her fall? I glance around but don't see anything. Just the wild of it all, the turmoil of the sea below and its desperate pull. And then I realize it's not a demon or a spell. This off-kilter feeling is the same as the shed, the same as the Devil's Gate, where Sid came through. A place where time is carved out. And it's coming from the rock wall ahead of us.

We make it to the bottom, and Sid and Mrs. O'Linn (it's too odd to think of her as my great-grandmother) are standing across a stretch of sand near the mouth of a cave.

A very familiar cave.

And the gravity of it is strong.

It's just like my mom's paintings. The golden color of the cliff wall, the dark opening, earth and stone shaping the doorway into a teardrop. The déjà vu comes back like something tapping me on the shoulder—and then I realize that it is a memory. I've actually been here. With my mom. If I walk closer, I know that I'll find a circular stone formation at the entrance to the cave and the carving of a heart in the sandstone wall.

I move toward it in a sort of trance.

"Oh, I see," Kara says, disrupting my focus. "Mrs. O'Linn must mean those flowers. I think they're called thimbleweed."

I look over to where she's pointing. There's a green-and-white trail sprouting from the sand leading to the mouth of the cave. It starts at the shore, even growing in a few spots around the tide pools, on dark lava rock, trailing its way into the cave opening. It looks unreal, impossible; things that green don't grow in salt and brine.

"Wow, weird," Kara says as we come up beside Sid and Mrs. O'Linn.

"Yes," Mrs. O'Linn says. "My thoughts exactly. Very odd."

"When did this start?" Sid asks. He's gripping his cane, totally fixated on the cave. He's feeling the pull, too.

Mrs. O'Linn bends over and plucks one of the white flowers from the ground. "They sprang up about a week and a half ago, the night of the full moon. I know because I was out here for the meteor shower that night with Fa'auma, and instead of watching stars, we watched these little things sprout up like magic."

The full moon. The same night I got bitten and met Rebecca. And Kara. That same night these flowers grew in the place where my mother lived as a child. The place she'd drawn over and over again since I could remember.

"Thimbleweed?" Sid mutters. Like he's trying to recall something. "And it leads to that cave?"

"They grow up the walls in there, too. I didn't go very far into that dank place, though. Far too adventurous for my taste."

Sid shifts his feet, looking away from the cave, like he purposefully wants his back to it. "You mentioned there was trouble with a ghost. Do you think these flowers are connected with that?"

Her mouth becomes a small *o*. "Yes, I keep forgetting. The ghost! That came after the flowers."

"So the flowers grew and then—"

"I watched them!" she says like she's trying to convince us. "Before my eyes, they just popped right up! I called in a young man who knows about green things—a student of my late husband's—because I was sure it was some sort of rogue weed. I didn't want it taking over my husband's garden. But the young man didn't believe me. He said I must be mistaken about how they grew.

He looked at the plants in the tide pools and sand and told me I must've put them there and forgotten. Just because I'm old doesn't mean I'm senile. Or magical!"

My skin prickles.

"When did the ghost come into the picture?" Sid asks again.

Mrs. O'Linn points a crooked finger at the opening in the cliff. "The ghost stands there, at the mouth of the cave. A wisp of a thing, so pale. I've seen it twice. I swear it looked exactly like my granddaughter, Fiona—nearly told her to get something warmer on and get back in the house, it felt so real. I forgot for a second that she'd run off on me all those years back, after she had that baby." She shakes her head, looking more annoyed than sad. "I raised my granddaughter, you know, after her mother killed herself. No father in sight, so it was left to me to fix the mess. Foolish girl, my daughter, Deirdre. And she'd left me with another foolish girl, Fiona." She humphs and then continues. "My granddaughter was a fanciful one growing up; always talking about faeries and boys coming out of walls. I tried getting her help—I'd failed her mother, after all—but the child was too wrapped up in it all. She insisted she could do magic. Can you imagine?"

My heart aches listening to the words, the tone . . . as if my mom was a pest. No wonder she always had that look of sadness and longing in her eyes. If this was the woman who was supposed to be loving and nurturing to her, she must've been miserable.

"It sounds like Fiona was a troubled girl," Sid says.

"Yes," Mrs. O'Linn says with a sigh. "My granddaughter was obsessed with symbols and books about magic. She would collect plants and tie them into odd shapes, setting them on the ground or hanging them on the walls. At first I thought she was eccentric—my husband thought she was a botanist in the making." She laughs. "But then the child started talking to someone in her room. I'd hear her from down the hall, chattering away, but when I went in to check on her, she'd be alone. Well, that's when I knew she was going to end up just like her mother."

"You said your daughter killed herself, though," Sid says, a weight in his voice. "Did Fiona kill herself, too?"

Mrs. O'Linn shakes her head, her shoulders sagging a little. "I'm sure she did, eventually. It's in the blood. My own mother did. And my daughter, Deirdre, of course. You see, she was always talking about invisible creatures too, saying something was in her room, something in her closet. She said things whispered to her, told her to do bad things. She was far into her insanity by age ten. I'm sure that's why she eventually jumped off the cliff that night. Those voices . . ." She points to the rise up by the house, to the spot where I felt the odd gravity begin. "It was three years after my granddaughter, Fiona, was born—on the child's birthday, actually. Unconscionable."

I'm shivering now. I clench my fists tight at my sides to stop the shaking.

"Truly a sad tale," Sid says.

"Yes . . ." She sighs. "Fiona was such a sad, pretty little thing, too."

"I'm sorry for your loss, Mrs. O'Linn." He moves closer and touches her on the shoulder in a consoling way.

I feel like taking her in my hands and shaking her, asking her why, why she couldn't have been loving and kind and understood all the horrors that come with being able to see those things? Why did she have to be heartless and cruel? Maybe it would've changed things, kept the darkness back a little.

Instead I choke out, "Why did Fiona leave?"

Mrs. O'Linn looks at me like she forgot I was there. "It was a few months after her baby was born, the week after her seventeenth birthday. She'd been coming down to the beach, to that cave, for days." She nods at the opening of the dark teardrop. "Even sleeping here, baby and all."

My heart speeds up, realizing she's talking about me. I'm the baby.

"We got into a fight," she continues. "Fiona was yelling and crying, asking why *he* hadn't come, over and over, like I would know the answer. She was distraught about some boy. She'd started talking about him after her twelfth birthday, said he was her best friend, her only real friend, and that he came from the cave.

"I thought she was making him up, like she made up everything else—until the day I saw the two of them down there, walking in the surf, throwing stones into the waves. It was her fourteenth birthday." She points to a spot down the beach. "And every year on her birthday, she came here to this spot. Even after she ran off with her baby, she'd come back for the day of her birthday, and I'd see her down here, staring into that cave like she could will the thing to give her what she wanted. I don't believe for a second that boy came from the cave. I think some young man was tricking her and eventually took her innocence, leaving her pregnant. Then he ran off—as men tend to do." She shrugs. "But Fiona believed. That's why I think her ghost came back here. She's still looking for him." For the first time she sounds like she might care.

"That's possible," Sid says.

I'm stuck on the vision of my mom and the boy who must have been my father. Every year on her birthday, he came through that crack in the cliff, through the doorway in time. She would scramble down here before sunrise and wait for him, her heart anxious until she saw him in the shadows. And then she'd run to him, hug him close, and it would be like they'd never been apart, the year of space between their visits completely forgotten. They would walk for miles up and down the beach, play in the surf, collect sea glass, and talk about each other's worlds.

Until the year they created me inside those cave walls. Then he disappeared into the void and never came back.

But my mom didn't understand. She waited, she wanted to show him—share what their love had created: me.

Years later, she made a deal with a demon . . .

All the personal, intimate details of Fiona's story flood my mind, even though they aren't part of what Mrs. O'Linn has shared.

I see my mother's tragedy just like I saw what happened in that apartment where the ghost was protecting the boy, Marcus.

It always happens this way when I'm near a ghost.

I look around, past Sid and Mrs. O'Linn, to the mouth of the cave.

And I see her.

My mom. Fiona.

The world around me blurs. My breath falters.

She's there, standing at the entrance to the cave. The white thimbleweed flowers brush at her bare legs with the breeze. A blue summer dress covers her thin form, her bare toes curl in the green at her feet, her white-blond hair whips across her neck and face. She's so young, so vibrant.

She gives me a tired smile.

"Aidan?" Kara says, putting her hand on my arm. "Are you okay?"

"Is he having a fit?" Mrs. O'Linn asks, sounding annoyed.

"She's here," I breathe. "My mom—" I cover my mouth, holding in a sudden cry of pain, seeing her there. Her essence was captured as she was then, existing in that moment when she lost her love.

I collapse to my knees, gasping for air.

Someone says, "Oh my!"

Fiona's pain, sadness, loss—it's all there between us, and I know she's sorry, so, so sorry, wishing she could go back and change things, if only she'd understood. If only she hadn't left me like her own mother left her.

I start to sink into the ache of her soul, into her eyes, as she pleads with me to forgive her. And I want to go to her, tell her I love her, to feel her arms around me, smell her warmth, just like it was before the Darkness came.

But her sorrow is so strong, too strong, as if it's gripping me by the throat, trying to drown me . . .

Then Kara's there, kneeling at my side, her arms holding me, her fingers sending vibrations through my skin, bringing me back a little.

"I forgot . . ." I choke out, "how beautiful she was."

"Oh, God, Aidan," she whispers.

"What's happening?" Mrs. O'Linn barks. "Who is this boy?"

"Please, Mrs. O'Linn," Sid says, sounding calm as ever, "can we perhaps get some water? He may be coming down with something. He hasn't been well."

"Oh! Of course," she says and scuttles off, heading for the house.

Sid's beside me in a flash. "What do you see, Aidan?"

"It's her . . . my mom . . ." I whisper.

"Amazing! Is she alone? Is there another spirit?"

I shake my head.

Kara grips me harder. "Not now, Sid. Leave him."

"This is the place, Kara, the spot where it all comes together." He sounds almost elated. He doesn't feel the pain here, the loss.

As I find myself again, my mother's ghost fades. But the presence remains, sorrow pulsing in the air. I squeeze my eyes shut, but I still see my mom's wispy form in the darkness of my mind. I have to focus on something else: the sound of the waves, the cry of a gull . . .

"What're you talking about, Sid?" Kara hisses. "This is his mother's ghost. Not just some job. You can't make him hurt her."

"No, no!" He waves off her accusation. "This is a doorway, similar to the one I came through. A pivot point, so to speak, in time.

I had a hunch that there would be one near the mother's childhood home, but this"—he motions at the swath of green across the beach—"this is beyond anything. Even with my failing ability I sense the vortex here, don't you? That open feeling, as if you're being pulled toward something."

Kara says, hesitant, "Yes . . . I feel something odd, but I wasn't sure—"

"It's the opening, the doorway. Two things happening at once: time and spirit crossing in a confluence. It has a sort of gravity to it. The two don't usually coincide on this—"

"You're babbling, Sid," Kara says. "I think we should just get Aidan out of here."

"Wait! Listen. The way Mrs. O'Linn's daughter and granddaughter kept hearing voices, seeing things, that's the spirit side of it. Whoever resides here in this place experiences it, but only if they already have the talent for it—the bloodline of a medium, or a talent for prophecy, like Aidan. This family is obviously brimming with it—Aidan's grandmother, his mother, and even his sister seem to have a very strong bloodline! They would most certainly—"

"Wait, Aidan's sister can see stuff, too?" Kara asks.

"No, I don't believe she has Aidan's gifts. It's more like she's just pulled toward things of the spirit. She would have the ability to call up spirits and sometimes control them, though. Obviously Aidan's mother was a medium. But Aidan sees things because of his father, not because of his mother. Of this I'm sure—a prophet is a creature of knowledge and vision, not a conduit. But having someone living here who's strong in abilities of *any* kind would definitely draw things to this place. Add the gravity of the time rip in the same location—and bam! A Crux. Aidan's mother and father were bound to find each other in such a place."

Kara shakes her head. "I'm lost."

Sid kneels beside me. "Aidan, I need you to focus, focus on your mother."

I look at him, panic filling me. "No. I can't feel any more of her pain."

"Yes, you can." He sounds so sure. Like he wants me to dive in and drown.

"Sid," Kara says, a warning in her voice.

"Just hold him, Kara, keep him centered—use the connection you have with him to keep him safe."

"I can't," she says.

"Aidan, listen to me—"

"Stop!" I yell.

"Here's the water!" Mrs. O'Linn says over the sound of the tide. "Is the boy all right? Should we call a doctor?" She bustles to my side, and Fa'auma comes up behind her, looking wide-eyed at me.

"Oh my!" Fa'auma says. "Let's get him inside!"

"He's fine," Sid says, as if everything is perfectly normal. "Just a little dizzy is all."

"No, he's not fine," Kara says.

Fa'auma and Mrs. O'Linn look back and forth between them and then turn to me.

"I'll be all right," I say, sounding more sure than I feel. I try to stand, but my bones are throbbing too much. Can heartache kill you?

"You don't look all right," Mrs. O'Linn says. "You look like you've seen death!"

I bite my lip to hold back the tears. "I need to eat something, maybe."

"Poor boy!" Fa'auma says with a *tsk* in her voice. "We will fix you something. You'll feel better in no time, you'll see."

I shake my head. I just need to go home.

Sid frowns and grumbles about needing to be sure of things and how we're not done with the interview yet, until Kara gives him a look that could boil concrete and he shuts up.

We begin walking back toward the path, me trailing behind with Kara. She pauses, picking up a yellow ribbon blowing past her feet, then turns and takes my hand.

I can only watch in numb half awareness as she ties it around my wrist. It reminds me of the ribbons Ava had in her hair the other day.

"It's going to be okay, Aidan," Kara says, kissing the knot.

She moves to release my wrist, but I take her hand and walk beside her.

Mrs. O'Linn stops suddenly, waving her arms. "Oh my! I almost forgot!" She pulls something from her pocket—the stone she dug out of the bucket earlier—and hands it to Sid. "I'm supposed to give this to you."

When Kara and I move closer, I see it's a simple stone, nothing important. Light color, silver grey, smooth and oval—the perfect skipping rock.

Sid rolls it in his hand, looking it over, and his eyes suddenly widen. He drops it like it burned his palm.

It falls to the sand with a plop.

My pulse quickens, seeing his reaction. "What is it?" I look down at the stone.

"Don't touch it," Sid says in a dark voice.

"Well, my word!" huffs Mrs. O'Linn.

"What is it, Sid?" Kara asks.

"It's a message."

"What in heaven's name!" Mrs. O'Linn yells. "It's just a rock!"

"Where did you get it?" Sid asks, his cool slipping. He's close to irate.

Mrs. O'Linn opens her mouth to answer and then snaps it shut with an odd confusion on her face. She hums and looks to the side. "Well, now. I don't recall."

"Did someone give it to you?" Sid asks.

She nods. "Yes. I believe someone did." Something seems to occur to her, because her face lights up. "Oh! I remember! They said I should give it to the marked young man." She waves to Sid's tattooed forearms as if that explains why she handed it to him.

Sid looks over at me, and I realize what she just said—the message was meant for me. I stare down at the rock in the damp sand. Then I release Kara's hand and bend over to pick it up.

"Aidan," Sid says, like a warning. But he doesn't try to stop me.

It's cold in my palm from the sea air. I turn it over, thinking it looks like any other rock you'd find in the surf, rolled by the sea. There's no odd energy to it, nothing—but then I freeze as something forms on the surface of the stone. A symbol. Then another. And another.

Three words: *Sister*, *Brother*, and *Severed*.

My mouth goes dry.

I rub the ribbon now tied to my wrist, one just like Holly wears in her hair, one just like Ava had tied in her white braids the other day. And as I touch the yellow silk I see her, my sister, as if she's walking past us, up the shore, toward the cave. I stare in wonder as the image fades. Could Mom draw Ava here, show her in the grimoire where to go? Ava hasn't heeded my warnings. She keeps digging into what Mom was, and why. If Mom's ghost is here now, and Ava's been chasing her . . .

"What could've left a message like this?" I ask Sid. A message only Sid and I can see. To everyone else this would just be a rock.

He looks a little pale. But he doesn't know anything about my sister, not really. Why would he be reacting to this rock so strongly?

"A demon," he answers after a second. "It's the only thing that could take away her memory." He nods toward Mrs. O'Linn.

Fa'auma's jaw drops open in shock. "Demons?"

"Folderol!" Mrs. O'Linn barks.

"Has anyone been down here on the beach recently?" I ask the two women. "Maybe some kids?"

Mrs. O'Linn shakes her head, looking indignant, but Fa'auma frowns, like she's thinking.

"There were those kids the other day, Laura," Fa'auma says. "Remember, you chased them off, nearly lost your shoe."

Mrs. O'Linn scrunches up her face, looking annoyed. "No, no!"

"What did they look like?" I ask.

"Didn't get a good look," Fa'auma says. "They were runnin' off before I could see clear. But it appeared to be two girls and a boy."

"What'd the two girls look like?"

She shakes her head. "Sorry, sweetie. I only know it was two girls and a boy." But then she adds, quickly, "Though I did think the one girl was smaller than the others. Younger. And her hair was light, while the other two had darker hair."

"Ava," I say under my breath.

"You think your sister came here?" Kara asks.

"She's been running off with Holly. Plus, she's been looking like mad for answers about my mom; my guess is something led my sister here." That *something* being my mom.

"This isn't good," Sid says.

"No shit, Sherlock."

"Why?" Kara asks. "What am I missing?"

"The message," I say. "It says my sister and I will be separated."

Sid looks at me funny. "That's all you saw?"

"What do you mean *all*?"

Sid shifts uncomfortably.

I study the stone again, seeing the same message. "You see something else?"

"Kara," Sid says, sounding distracted, "we need to go see Eric about some scrolls."

"Sid," I say, "tell me."

"Aidan, if you don't see it, perhaps—"

I get in his face. "Stop hiding shit from me. What the fuck did you see?"

Mrs. O'Linn gasps, and a hand flies to her mouth. "Such language!"

Sid gives me a nervous look but says, "It's the symbol of Dark Opening."

"What the hell does that mean?"

"Someone's going to open *the* doorway."

I shake my head. "That's not an answer. What does it *mean*?"

He swallows hard. "A force is working to open a permanent passageway between the spirit world and this one, to cut down the Veil completely. If it succeeds, it will be the end of everything. The beasts of Sheol, demons and monsters chained there for longer than memory, they'll come to this plane, and nothing, not even you, will be able to stop them."

FORTY

Traffic on the 10 freeway is brutal as we make our way to the club, and no matter how many times I ask for an explanation, Sid's answers aren't clear. His head is obviously a mess, and most of his rambles make no sense to me—something about a rendering and the weaving of circles. He does explain about demon messages, though, and how they're hidden until one is ready to be read. But the subject of the big doorway opening is really bothering him. He won't even look at me when I prod him about that. He just says he has to check a scroll and to leave it be for now. Since I don't have room in my head for any more looming tragedy, I comply.

"I need to go back to that beach," I say to Kara, "soon." The thought of seeing my mom's ghost again fills me with horror, but Ava went there for a reason.

Sid shakes his head. "No, Aidan, not now, not after—"

"It's not your call," I say. "You can either help me or get the hell out of my life. I won't let my sister sneak around and get herself killed."

Sid folds his arms across his chest, looking irritated. "For someone who is so black and white, you sure do keep a lot of secrets, boy."

"I'm not your *boy*! And my family is none of your business."

"It's my business when it's got the potential to bring down my house."

I shake my head. "You have no idea what you're talking about."

"Oh, don't I? There's a reason that message mentions your sister. There's a reason the demons want you two severed. What does she have to do with this? Why are you protecting her?"

Exasperation fills me. "I have no idea, okay!" I toss my hands in the air, feeling useless, done with holding it all in. "My mom did something—she must have. I don't know what, but the demons have been after Ava since she was three. They killed her foster parents to get to her. They want her." I nearly choke on the words as years of secrets, fear, and loss threaten to overwhelm me.

But then the air goes cold; Kara and Sid's fear stings my skin.

"Demons?" Kara says.

Sid's rage boils out of every molecule. "This is what you've been hiding?" he asks. "Your sister is . . . what? A Nephilim? Demon spawn? What have you done, Aidan? What sort of horror have you brought under my roof?" His volume rises with each question.

"I . . . No! No, of course not. What do you even mean?" I choke out, both defensive and confused.

"Well, she's obviously not just a *girl*. Demons don't want humans for any reason other than to kill them or have them kill on their behalf. If they want Ava that badly, it's because she's useful to them—she's a piece on a chessboard, like you. Not just a simple eleven-year-old. Not even a Beacon or a Light, but something *more*. And anything trying to keep the demons away from her will be destroyed." He leans forward and says, "That's *you*, Aidan. That's me and Kara. All of us!"

He's wrong. He has to be. My sister's just a girl. An innocent girl.

But I know that Ava's not innocent. She never has been. I've known that forever, but I've never questioned why. I just assumed it was because of what she'd been through. But there's always been something more, something I chose to deny.

"I've only tried to keep her safe," I say.

Sid's anger fades a little at my tone. He asks more gently, "When they came for her the first time, how were they stopped?"

My head fills with the memory, threatening to drag me under. "My mom. My mom stopped it."

Kara takes my hand. I feel it, like an anchor in the storm, holding me fast. I look out the window and realize she's pulled off the road. We're parked at an overlook, facing the ocean.

"Sid," she says, sounding as breathless as I feel. "Leave it. Please. Can't you see it's too much for him right now?"

I want to agree, to ask him to stop, to pretend like the last few hours, the last few days, were just a nightmare that I can wake up from. But I know I can't run from this. Not anymore. So I ask the thing I never wanted to know: "What could she be?"

Sid releases a heavy sigh. "If she was born from a heavenly encounter, she would be a Nephilim, but if somehow a demon found its way into a fleshly form and mated, then the child would be doomed to Darkness. The truth is, only she can answer who— or *what*—she is." There's a pause, and he adds, "She'll have known for a while now."

"But a *Nephilim*?" My sister is the child of some angel? Or demon. Would my mom have really gone into something like that willingly?

"A Nephilim is actually very unlikely," Sid says. "The woman would most surely die during childbirth, and your mother didn't die when your sister was born."

"Well then, w-what exactly is a demon . . . spawn?" My mouth doesn't want to form the words. My body is numb.

Kara's voice shakes. "Aidan, don't."

But Sid answers, "It's the child of a corporeal demon and a human. A female medium is usually the mate, since a demon can only be called up by and controlled by a medium."

"Like my mom."

"Yes, like your mom," he says quietly. Then he adds, "I didn't sense anything in your sister to cause alarm, Aidan. But my talents are so depleted. Normally I would have seen something like demon blood or angel blood in her."

"How?" I ask.

"She would have a soul mark on her hip or on her back. And she would be able to move things with her mind."

My chest constricts.

"But beyond that it would be a feeling," he continues, "something when you're near her, like looking down from a high perch—almost disorienting. As her sibling you wouldn't feel it, though, since you grew up together."

Kara releases a quick breath. "Oh, God. That's what it was. I felt it when we picked her up that day. I just didn't understand what it was. But it totally freaked me out."

"But what does all this even mean?" I ask.

Sid shakes his head. "If she's a Nephilim, she's the child of an angel and a human woman. She wouldn't necessarily be a creature of Darkness, but her allegiance would be questionable due to the unstable nature of their kind. But if she's the child of a corporeal demon and a human, it would mean she's marked as a tool of Darkness. She won't be able to escape it. Eventually they will find her and take her from you, as is their right."

My body goes tense at the thought, and my sorrow and fear morph into rage. "No way." There's no way in hell I'm letting that happen. They'll have to slice me to bits to get to her.

Sid frowns. "Aidan, you have to understand—"

"No."

No.

This doesn't change anything. It doesn't.

My mom thought I could protect Ava; she felt it. She saw this thing in me, whatever it is—this piece of me that's connected to my father. It'll save us. It has to.

———

Eric's club is an empty shell during the day. The only signs of life are several delivery trucks with men unloading crates. Kara drives around them and parks in the back lot.

"This will only take a minute," Sid says as he slides out of the car.

"Wait!" I say, scrambling out of the backseat. "I'm coming."

"Aidan, it isn't necessary." He waves me off as he walks away. "I'll get the scroll and bring it to you." And then he disappears between the trucks.

I want to chase after him, but I'm also unsure I can take any more surprises . . . any more *knowledge*. All the emotion and urgency of what happened on the beach, the possibilities of who— and *what*—Ava might be, have filled my mind since we left there. And my mom . . . I saw my mom.

I hear the car door, and Kara's beside me. "You okay?" she asks.

I stare at a flock of birds gathering on a wire above.

After a few minutes of watching them in silence, we spot Sid and Eric walking quickly across the parking lot to the larger warehouse in the back. Sid's arms are waving frantically, like he's reenacting the last five days.

I want to go over there, to hear what Sid's saying, know how much he's lying, but Eric's head turns and he catches my eye, sending a jolt of dread through me. The look on his face is pained, worried. And I know they're talking about me.

Then the two men go through the warehouse door, disappearing from view again.

"We'll figure this out, Aidan," Kara says. She stands in front of me and reaches out.

My skin pulses as her fingers graze my arm, but I barely feel myself respond through the panic in my head.

"I know this is hard," she says.

"No. You don't know."

She stares at me for a few seconds and then says, "I want to understand, Aidan. What can I do?"

"Her birthday's tomorrow," I say. "There's no more time to do anything."

"Her birthday?"

"Every three years they come for Ava on her birthday. Year three, six, and nine, they came. She'll be twelve tomorrow." I look up at the bright blue sky. "That's why I asked Sid for help. I was hoping to find a place where I could hide her, protect her until her birthday. But I feel like they'll find us tomorrow anyway. It won't matter how many wards I put around her. It's inevitable." The weight becomes almost unbearable as the words leave my mouth. The hope I had when this all started is slipping away like smoke through my fingers. Truthfully, it was never a *real* hope to begin with.

Kara moves closer, her energy heating my skin. She pulls me to her, rising onto her toes and wrapping her arms around me in a tight squeeze as she buries her face in the crook of my neck. "It's going to be okay, Aidan."

My hands respond, sliding up her back to her shoulders. The connection between us is a pulse, a steady urgency, warm and comforting. We stay like that for a long time, locked in, as if we're both trying to hide. Seconds pass, minutes, and I'm so settled in the moment that when she moves I barely notice. Until her lips brush my neck, my jaw, turning comfort into something else, the pulse in my skin becoming a hum.

My hands run down her back to her hips, and I press her closer as her palms slip under my shirt, her breath coming faster now. My head fills with a million thoughts I shouldn't be thinking.

I turn to find her lips with my own, and a voice breaks in, shattering the moment.

"Well, well," Sid says, sounding more pleased than when he left us.

Kara and I pull apart, and the lack of her in my arms lets the ache back into my skin. She's shaking a little, so I squeeze her hand before letting go. She gives me a tiny smile, but Eric and Sid are too close, and I don't get a chance to say anything.

Eric studies us as he approaches, his eyes moving first to my mark and then to Kara. How much has Sid told him?

Sid pats Eric on the arm. "This man was kind enough to allow me a quick peek at the collection of scrolls I needed to see. I believe I found what I need." He has a wooden box tucked under his arm.

"No problem," Eric says. "Just remember, if you break it, you buy it, my friend."

Sid smiles. "Yes, yes. We should be going then, so I can return them to you quickly."

He gets back into the Camaro, and Kara walks around to the driver's side. I move to open the passenger door. Eric comes closer, like he wants to say something to me, so I pause. But all he does is look at me—at my mark. His gaze slides up my arm to my chest, and then he looks me straight in the eye. It unnerves me, his intensity. But I feel no emotion from him at all. I see it on his face: fierce concern.

"Don't forget your prayers, Aidan," he whispers. And then he turns and walks toward the club, leaving me with the feeling I've just been handed some sort of warning.

"Spit it out, Sid," I say once Kara's pulled the Camaro onto the main road. "What's the deal?"

"Yes, yes, I know," Sid says, opening the box on his lap. "Answers, answers. You are very impatient."

Kara looks at Sid in the rearview mirror. "I'd appreciate knowing if the world's coming to an end tomorrow myself."

"Perhaps I should've taken a few more minutes to get what I needed." Sid tilts his head. "The two of you looked very comfortable together."

Kara's cheeks turn pink.

"You do realize that I could kick your ass and just take the damn scrolls, right?"

He laughs and pulls out one of the rolls of paper, only about four or five inches wide. It looks like it's made of papyrus, the surface striped with tiny ridges, hinting at a weave. His eyes scan the faded writing, and he begins to read aloud. "*The six corners of Death's realm*—that would be Sheol—*opened by any other means than blood is not passable.* I believe that means blood is the way to open the doorway." He scans down the page a little farther. "*The gate is carved of bone and ash, stitched together with the sinew of* . . . hmm . . . I'm not sure of this word here." He frowns at the script and then looks up at me. "This is a grouping of scrolls from Chaldea that I read during my studies under your father, but it was never fully clear to me, this theology of the afterlife, soul chambers, and whatnot. Seems all very speculative. Still, it's difficult for me to recall the language—some isn't even in a human tongue, I don't think."

"Can I see it?" I ask, holding out a hand.

He hesitates but then passes it to me. "Be very careful. The paper is easily corrupted by oils."

I take the scroll and scan the script—looks like Chaldean and Assyrian mingled together. I find the section he was reading from:

"the gate is carved of bone . . . It's talking about the formation of the doorway, what it's made of. Bone, ash, tendon, and the word you couldn't read translates as *wing*. The bone is from a human, the ash is from a demon heart, and the sinew is from a seraph's wing." I begin reading aloud. *"In all of these resides the key, of blood and dirt molded in earth and womb*—this word is *combining*, or *mixed*, I think—*combining into one form."* I look up from the page. "So the key is made of all these things: angel, demon, and human."

Sid takes another scroll out of the box and begins reading. Then he places it back in and takes out another. "This can't be right."

"That's what it says," I say.

"No, I mean why would this be happening now? The end of things isn't meant to begin until much later. Hundreds of years from now. Even with your birth, the end of it all wasn't until the next generation—" He stops speaking, and all the color washes out of his face.

"Sid, what's wrong?" Kara asks.

"My gods . . . Aidan, I'm so sorry. My gods. It's me."

"*You?* You're the key?"

"No, no, not the key. I'm the reason they're using the key so soon."

"What? Why?"

"I wasn't supposed to stay!" He takes the scroll from me and puts it back into the box, shutting the lid. "I was meant to *kill* you and go back. But I stayed! Everything has a ripple effect. You being born, then your sister, then me staying. Even Kara. Now it's all changing again. The prophecies, the predictions, none of the things I knew before I came here will be right." He gives me a frantic look. "The demons have moved up their timetable. They're a step ahead somehow. And they've gotten their hands on a key to the doorway of Sheol."

My pulse speeds up. "Someone who's angel, demon, and human."

"Or someone they can make that way," he whispers. "My gods . . . your sister."

I go still. "Ava. But she's not all three."

"And you know this *how*? You know she's possibly something other than human and that the demons have been after her since you can remember. But do you know what runs in her bloodstream? Your mother could be of mixed spirit herself! Most mediums have descended from the time when demons and angels walked the earth—she could likely have one or the other in her blood already. All the demons had to do was allow for her offspring to contain the missing piece."

My lungs feel like they're full of cement.

"We have to know if it's really her," Sid says. "A test or something. Somehow we have to find out."

But I can't hear anymore. I see the pieces of the puzzle finally falling into place, the years of wondering why they want Ava, why they didn't care about me. And why my mother made the deal to give her blood over in the first place. And I'm the only thing that can mess up the storyline. The only hope I have left to save her is what's possible because of my father's blood; the hope of this Fire Bringer. Whatever that means.

And there's only one way to awaken it.

FORTY-ONE

We pull up to the front of the house, and Sid gets out of the car, the box of scrolls tucked under his arm. He's talking to himself as he shuts the door and heads for the side yard, muttering how mindless he's been, not thinking of the ripples he's made, not thinking of everything he's set in motion. His cane taps the ground harder than normal as he opens the side gate and goes through the backyard to his shed. Maybe to read more of the scrolls, find more answers. It doesn't matter.

I take my seat belt off and start to open the passenger door, but Kara stops me with a hand on my arm. "Don't give up, Aidan."

I look down at her fingers gripping my bicep and try to feel her energy, but for once I'm so numb I can only sense the wounds inside of me.

She unbuckles her seat belt and slides across the bench, pressing herself into me. She touches my face and cradles my cheek in her palm. "You're important, you have to believe that. There's a way to save her, a way to save yourself. Just let it happen." She kisses the corner of my mouth.

My body goes tight, feeling the vibration of our connection as it sparks inside me, running over my skin in a surge. I know what she means, and I know she's right, but . . . "Kara it's not—"

"Please." Her thumb strokes my jaw, sending the charge down my neck. "Let me do this for you. For your sister. I want this."

My throat goes dry, and my body wars between desperation for her and the throbbing sorrow inside me. I don't have the strength to lie. "I want it, too. But—"

She slides her fingers over my lips, stopping my words. "No. Let me do this. It's my choice." And then she leans in, kissing me again, longer, sweeter. She pulls away before I can respond. "Tonight," she whispers. "Come to me."

And then she slides across the seat and out the driver's door.

Tonight.

If I go to her, it's because I'm a selfish bastard. I want her to help me fix this, to awaken my power fully so I can stop everything, all of it, but I'd also be burying this pain in a night of pleasure. A night I've wanted since the moment I kissed her in that club. And I don't care if it's right or wrong.

I slide from the car and walk toward the house, feeling defeated. I open the front door and walk into the entryway, stepping right into a puddle.

Disoriented, I look down. The light from the setting sun behind me reflects across the puddle's surface.

Glittering red.

My stomach rises. I follow the shape of the puddle, to where it smears into footprints—

"Kara!" I yell, looking around, feet frozen. No one answers.

Where is she?

I step past the entryway and study the shadows. No one's in the family room. No one's in the kitchen.

Bang!

Something upstairs crashes against a wall. Shattering glass. A muffled scream.

I move toward the noise and then freeze at the base of the staircase. Lester comes out from the bathroom at the top of the stairs, dragging a limp Kara across the wood floor, even though he shouldn't be that strong. He lays her at the top of the landing. Beside a second form. There's another body up there where Lester is arranging Kara. Red hair spills over the top step; an ivory hand is folded over a pale chest. Rebecca.

"What happened?" I choke out, starting up the stairs. "What's going on?"

Lester arranges the two girls side by side. "I'm getting them ready for you." And then he raises his head to look at me. And smiles.

I stumble back, nearly losing my footing.

His lips are thin, inhuman. The odd turn of his mouth twists his features, making them almost unrecognizable. This isn't the same Lester I saw this morning. His eyes . . . even from here I can see that they're hollow black holes.

My God. That's not Lester anymore. He's possessed by a demon. A demon that can see me—apparently the amulet doesn't work if the demon is looking through human eyes.

"I've got everything arranged," he says. "I think you'll be very pleased."

I don't have any breath to ask what he means. I look along the rest of the landing for Ava's body, but I only see Kara and Rebecca.

"Don't worry, they're still alive," he continues. "I figured you'd want to say good-bye."

"Whose blood is that?" I ask, surprised my voice works at all. I point to the pool in the doorway.

"I had to break the house's seal somehow. You should know, Seer. Blood is the only way."

"Who?" I demand, not sure I want to know. There's no trail of blood up the stairs, which gives me hope that it's not from Kara or Rebecca. But where's Ava?

"I wouldn't waste a human on these measly spells. Especially since all the disposable characters of this play are conveniently on an errand that my current pubescent host sent them on"— he pats his chest—"foolishly trying to save them from me. But things being what they are, I couldn't wait for them to return. So I used what I had on hand: a mediocre-grade cat. I'm doing the neighborhood a favor, really."

Cat blood. I'm relieved and horrified at the same time.

I almost don't ask the question in my head because of how much I dread the answer. "Where's my sister?"

Demon Lester's features shift, like he's hiding a fun secret. "Oh, that will all come clear soon. First I have to invite someone in so I can pay off my end of the deal. And you're here just in time for the show." He bows his head, takes in a deep breath, and then mumbles something in a demon tongue: *Let Hunger enter here to claim your prize.*

Instantly the smell of sulfur billows into the air, strong enough to make me gag.

"He's anxious to finish his task," Demon Lester says to me, pleased. "He was very helpful finding the child—your sister. And now I'll repay him."

Ice stings at the back of my neck, and I turn.

Rebecca's demon appears, emerging from the puddle of blood behind me, its sigil forming on the surface of the pool as its large shape becomes clear.

My whole body reacts. I want to run away, to attack, but I force myself to stand still. It can't see me. Yet.

Demon Lester continues, as if we're just chatting, "This allows me to kill two birds with one stone, so to speak." I turn back in time to see him pull a small kitchen knife from his waist and hold it over Rebecca's chest. "Pun intended." He laughs. It's woven with other sounds: the snarling of a dog and the creaking of tree limbs.

My eyes flick between the knife in Demon Lester's fist and the demon in the doorway. My insides are warring, begging me to act. The daunting seven-foot-tall, leather-skinned creature moves forward. It passes me as it starts up the stairs. Walking toward Rebecca. Totally unaware of my presence.

My fingers fly to my amulet, ready to tear it off. To do . . . something, anything.

A small hand touches my arm, stopping me. "No, Aidan. Don't."

My breath catches as I turn to her, my heart cracking in my chest as realization filters in. "Ava," I whisper, not sure where she came from. "What's happening?"

Her pale eyes glitter with unshed tears. "I did what needed to be done."

I shake my head, all hope leaving me. "No." I turn back to Rebecca and Kara, to the demon nearing the landing and the dagger in Lester's fist poised to kill. "You called a demon here . . . Why?"

"I needed to know what happened to our mother," she says. "And I needed help. So I made a deal."

"My God, Ava. You've killed them."

"No, I've saved *you*." It's like she's pleading with me to understand. She touches my hand, and I hear her whisper under her breath, "Remember what I told you about what I've seen. Remember." I don't know what she means, but she pushes an image into my head of the note she left me the other day with the amulet: *Protect yourself. I can fix everything so we'll both be free.*

She bound the amulet to me when I wouldn't do it myself. She's protecting me, but at the same time, she's going to be the death of me.

Demon Lester's voice breaks through the storm inside me as he greets the larger demon. "Hunger, you've come!" He sounds like a boy who's glad his friend showed up at the party. "I'd like to repay you for your help in finding my charge by doing away with yours."

But the demon inside Lester didn't need help finding Ava. She had already found *him*; she called him here. What game are they playing?

The beast, Hunger, growls in pleasure and bows its head, looking grateful.

My mind spins as I look for answers, a way out, a way to save Ava—to save all of us from what's about to happen. A million scenarios flash in my head, none of them ending in anything but death.

"Good!" Demon Lester says. He smiles at me. "People really shouldn't leave sharp things lying around when someone's clearly suicidal." And then he takes Rebecca's wrist, lifting it up and putting the knife blade to her skin.

I gasp "No!" and jolt forward, shaking off Ava's hold on me and scrambling up the steps.

The blade sinks in, flesh parting in a thin line down the inside of her arm. And her life begins to flow in a gush of red. *Oh, God, oh, God* . . . I reach out for her, grabbing her shoulder, trying to pull her to me.

Demon Lester drops her hand, and her arm flops to the side, the blood spilling onto the stairs.

I take Rebecca's wrist, grip it in both hands, trying to hold the wound closed, red running between my fingers, panic filling me as I pray the rhythmic current will slow. "Oh, God. No."

"God's not interested in helping you," Demon Lester says, sounding oddly jealous. "Time to give up, Seer. Time to let go of your sister and everyone else you care about." He picks up Kara's scarred wrist and raises the knife. "No one will be surprised at this one. She's already made me an outline." He presses the blade to her scar.

Something inside me snaps.

I drop Rebecca's arm and lunge before Demon Lester can dig the sharp edge into Kara's skin.

I fall onto him with a scream, pounding with bloody fists. His smile turns crimson as I feel his cheek crack against my knuckles. He takes me by the throat in an iron grip as I go for his knife, as if I'm nothing to him, a fly buzzing around his head. I fumble for a hold on his neck, hit him, scratch him, press my weight down, trying to be free, but it does no good. He's too strong.

Even as the world blurs, rage consumes me like fire. I see my mother's heart ripped from her chest, Ava staring into nothing as she sits in a circle of death to protect herself, the demon whispering to those boys to hurt Rebecca, Kara's bruised face from being beaten. And me, alone, as this *thing* drags my sister from me for good.

My fist closes over his knife, trying to yank it from his grip, cutting my hand as I fail to get it from him. And then I remember my own knife. I fumble in my back pocket, taking hold of the hilt with slick fingers. I raise the blade as the world goes dark. And stab him in the neck. Without a thought. Without blinking.

I kill Lester.

As I come back to earth, I watch in a daze as Lester's eyes clear. All the black fades away in a hiss of breath as he returns to normal, the shadow of the demonic gone. He gasps and chokes, his muscles beginning to jerk.

"Aidan!" Ava screams, yanking me off Lester's gurgling form.

I killed him.

I've killed.

Rage is washed away by a tide of horror as Lester's body convulses. His now human eyes stare at the ceiling in confusion and shock as his mouth fills with foamy red fluid.

Guilt falls on me like thick tar as I look down at my bloody hands.

"Stop it!" Ava screams at the top of her lungs. Like Lester can hear her and stop dying.

But his form goes still. As if a switch just flipped.

Then his head turns, and he smiles, the blood that pooled in his mouth leaking over his cheek. The shadow fills his eyes once more, turning them to pitch. "I couldn't help myself," he says as he swallows, the cut on his neck moving unnaturally. "Your reaction, Aidan, was beauty itself." Then he says to Ava, "Did you see his face?" And he laughs, all beast and evil.

"Don't worry," he says to me. "This Lester kid is definitely dead as soon as I head out. But I still need his meat suit for a while, so we'll fake it."

Confusion and rage fill me, making me want to attack him again.

But a growl vibrates the air, and we freeze, remembering our guest.

The demon stands over the three of us, its claws open to strike.

Looking at me.

It bares its teeth. "Seer."

Ava scrambles over to the wall, her shoulder bag bumping against her hip. "Aidan! Your amulet!" She snatches up the golden chain that must've come off in the violence.

Demon Lester holds up a hand. "Whoa, down, boy."

"This Seer is my enemy," it growls. "He must be destroyed. Word is spreading he can touch us through the Veil."

"Yeah, yeah," Demon Lester says. "He's a pain in the ass, I agree. But I have this deal, see. He can't get hurt right now. It's a witch thing. You know how it is."

The bigger demon huffs. "I made no deal with a witch."

Demon Lester stands, moving between me and the large beast. "You see that girl over there?" He points to Ava. "She's the descendant of a very powerful force. I wouldn't get on her bad side."

The demon looks at Ava as if seeing her for the first time. "She is small."

"She's not reborn yet," Demon Lester says, as if that explains everything. "And the Master wants her. So if you're clever, you'll do as I say."

The demon seems to consider this, but then sneers at Lester. "You are below me, snake. I will do nothing you say."

Demon Lester glances sideways at Ava as if signaling something. And then she moves. Quick.

I scramble away from the demon's reach as Ava pulls Mom's grimoire from her bag, opens it to a marked page, and begins to chant in Latin while kneeling beside Rebecca's head. Then she takes a handful of something from her pocket and sprinkles it along Rebecca's body—dried violet flakes that catch in her amber hair, rest on her eyelids, float in the blood on the steps.

Lavender.

Ava's chanting: "*Expediam vincientes, fregerit hoc signaculum, dimittere nocte . . .*" *Unfolding protection, binding light, break this seal, cast out the night.*

The demon seems oblivious, coming for me, until the word "*nocte*"—*night*—sounds for the third time.

It stumbles back as if something struck it. A fiery breath puffs from its nose. Little fissures grow over its black, leathery skin. White and blue lights fill the cracks, a glow of power creating a halo around its body. The creature snarls and throws its head back as the air vibrates, turning to shivering ice. It disappears with a pop.

Gone.

I stare at the space where it was, amazement and relief filling me.

"Ava," I say, looking over to her. She did that.

"He's gone. Hopefully for a long while," she says, short of breath, like she's run a long way. "And its hold on Rebecca will be severed now. It won't be able to find her again."

Demon Lester pulls out a phone and dials. "Yeah, 911," he says loudly. Panic fills his voice. "My friend tried to kill herself. Please! I need help! Please!"

I can hear someone on the other end say to remain calm.

"No, please! Help!" he fake cries, gives me a wink. "There's blood all over!" And then he rattles off the address and hangs up. "Okay, so that's done. Let's go before that horned Hunger guy comes back."

I stumble to Rebecca's side. "What the hell is going on?" I ask, looking back and forth between the demon and Ava. Who exactly is in control here?

"Well," Demon Lester says, "your sister called me up and made a deal with me: she'd come with me quietly if I answered a few questions and helped fix this mess you got yourself into. We were going to trap that creature—a more permanent solution than what just happened—so it wouldn't tie you up with your own entrails. Even though I'd have kind of liked to see that . . ." He seems to consider for a second, and then, sounding disappointed, he says, "You, however, ruined everything by jumping me and killing this shell I'm inhabiting. So I guess 'safe for a while' will have to do."

Bile fills my throat.

"You must really like this girl." He motions to Kara's still form beside Rebecca.

I pull my shirt off and wrap it around Rebecca's arm. She looks so pale. Her lips are turning violet. I need to stop the flow of blood. It's already slower, though, and her pulse is beating like butterfly wings against my fingers.

"Don't worry, Aidan," Ava says, sounding tired. "Lester didn't cut deep enough to kill her quickly. He just had to make it look real." She turns to Demon Lester. "Right?"

He shrugs, and I want to kill him again.

"How could you do this, Ava?" I ask. "What if she dies?"

"I had to," she says, sounding small. "It was the only way to save you."

"No. You could have talked to me. We could've done things together, figured it out."

She laughs weakly. "As if you ever listen to me. I'm your *little* sister. And you don't trust me." She looks down at her hands. "I see it in your eyes."

"Blah, blah, blah," Demon Lester says. "Cops are coming any second. Say your good-byes. We need to go."

"No one's going anywhere," I say. I need to wrap my head around what just happened. And I need to make sure Rebecca's all right.

"Aidan, you're staying," Ava says. "I'm going. With him."

"No."

"It's where I belong," she says, sounding defeated.

"Ava." My voice cracks. She can't be saying what I think she's saying. She can't have just given up. "This is insane. We're going to figure this out, we're going to keep you away from them. I have powers now. You don't understand."

She shakes her head, closing the grimoire and putting it back in her bag of secrets. "I love you for thinking we can fix this together. But it's *you* who doesn't understand."

"I do, Ava. Please—"

Our gazes lock, and the pain in her eyes makes my throat clench shut, stopping my words.

"I made a deal," she says. "It's for the best. I'm not a part of this world, Aidan. I never was. Our mom made sure of that."

"You're a part of me."

She gives me a shadow of a smile. "This is all going to work out. You'll see. It's how it was always supposed to happen."

"I don't understand."

"You will." She leans over and kisses my cheek. "Remember what I said. I saw it, Aidan. And I'm never wrong."

The sound of sirens fills the air.

Demon Lester stands with her, points at the slice in his neck, and says, "Catch you on the flip side," before heading down the stairs and slipping out the back door.

Ava follows him.

"Please," I say. "Don't do this." I can't let her go. What if Sid is right? What if she's some key to Death's gateway? More than that, I need my sister to be safe.

She pauses when she's halfway down the stairs. "You belong here, Aidan. With her." I start to rise, but she holds up a hand. "If you let go of her right now, she'll die."

Confusion and disbelief keep me captive. I'm unable to move. And then Ava's at the bottom of the staircase, slipping into the shadows of the kitchen as the banging on the door begins.

FORTY-TWO

Chaos. That's the only word for what happens next.

The cops come through the open door when I don't answer their warning shouts. The paramedics slip in and surround Rebecca and Kara, pushing me to the side as they ask a million questions I can't answer.

They lose Rebecca's heartbeat for a second, and there are shouts and needles and people pressing at her chest, her head lolling to the side. They try to wake Kara as a cop pulls me down the stairs, grilling me about the blood in the entryway, the bodies on the landing.

I say nothing. I'm still seeing it all in my head: the two girls limp and lifeless, the blade cutting into Rebecca's skin, my own knife killing Lester, Ava disappearing into the shadows.

She made a deal.

I stare at Rebecca as they wrap her arm in white gauze, knowing my sister brought the darkness that nearly killed two innocent girls.

But I'm no better. I killed Lester. Poor, kind Lester.

I killed.

"Yo!" yells one of the cops. "I've got another one outside."

I wonder if Lester's body is out there, lying in the grass, abandoned by the demon. But after a few seconds, two paramedics walk in, Sid limping between them. He has blood running down his face. Lester must've gotten to him, too.

Someone leads him to a kitchen chair. And then the questions begin all over again.

———

It's a good thing Sid got me that new identity. And that he's got a really good lawyer. The cops release me on the scene when Kara vouches for me, fingering Lester for the mess. We can't leave the area, and I'm still a person of interest, but they seem to believe that I was an innocent witness to it all. But Lester's a teen fugitive. And I'm free. Even though I killed him.

I killed Lester.

Rebecca's in stable condition, they say, but they won't let me see her. She's a runaway. A troubled girl in need of help. They believe she tried to kill herself. While we wait in the ER, one of the nurses takes pity on me and says she'll tell Rebecca that I wanted to talk to her but wasn't allowed. She also says she'll give me phone updates, let me know which room Rebecca's transferred to, if I ask for the nurse by name when I call.

Kara is released after a check by the doctor. She's only a little bruised up. Apparently Demon Lester drugged both the girls so they would stay under, but there aren't any lasting effects. When Kara follows us out of the ER several hours later, she's quiet and heavyhearted. It's obvious whatever Lester did or said to her before I came into the house wounded her more than just physically.

Sid is bandaged up and looks like he got an anvil dropped on his head. While he's waiting for his clean bill of health, he calls Eric at the club for help. Well into the night the three of us finally leave the hospital in a state of exhaustion. We don't talk about what happened; we don't talk about what's next. Because it's obvious we lost before we even started fighting.

Eric sends his car to pick us up. He's having the house "cleaned" and the protections strengthened again, but it'll be a few days before we can go back since it's now a crime scene. Apparently Sid called Connor and told him to bring the other kids to SubZero.

When everyone has arrived, we convene at the bar. Kara explains in a shaky voice what happened. She sounds like someone else, not the Kara who threatened to kick my ass a million times. Hearing her describe how Lester grabbed her, how he drugged her, makes me ill. And she doesn't even know everything. She only knows up to the point in the tale where she blacked out—before I came in. She does know that Lester was possessed, though. She said she could tell that when he first attacked her.

Holly is curiously silent. I don't have to ask if she had an inkling that something was up before today, with all the adventures she and my sister went on. I'll be asking her very soon why she did nothing, said nothing, and allowed this all to happen as the result. But now's not the time. I'm too raw, too angry.

The others look to me to fill in the blanks after Kara's done, but I can only shake my head and tell them I don't know anything. Because I don't. Not really. I'm not about to tell them that my sister's chosen to embrace darkness, something she believes will save me, something she thinks is inevitable. I won't say that Lester is now a walking corpse because of me. When they ask about Ava, I can't speak. Sid seems to understand, but I know he'll be grilling me later. It won't matter. There's no way out of this mess now.

My head spins. I failed. I didn't protect her. She made her choice. Just like our mom.

The meeting ends when they realize I'm useless and Sid seems disinclined to push me, which I'm thankful for.

Eric says he'll pay for a few hotel rooms for us, and we end up heading over to stay at a five-star place off Avenue of the Stars, next to Nakatomi Plaza—from *Die Hard* (exclamation point), as Jax won't stop reminding me. I'm stuck in a room with Finger and Jax—who I'm now sharing a bed with, apparently.

As we settle in the room, Jax can't seem to shut up or stop asking questions that I don't want to answer. I finally make my escape and go downstairs to the patio to sit by the pool. It's quiet now. Still. Only the lingering smell of sunscreen and chlorine fills the air. The sun sets a bright orange fire along the horizon as night swiftly approaches.

I'm not surprised when Sid finds me after an hour or so. He grips his cane as he walks toward me. The bandage on his head is stark against his now sallow complexion.

He sits beside me and releases a long breath. "I need you to tell me what happened, Aidan."

"I'd rather not talk right now." I'd rather pretend it never happened at all.

"Your sister's birthday is tomorrow."

"That doesn't matter anymore." I can't help the bitterness in my voice. "It's done."

"So this *was* about her."

I rest my head in my hands with a groan. "This was about a million things I can't understand. Like why I was born in the first place, or why my mother made some mystery deal with a demon that's now being paid off by my little sister who didn't do anything to deserve her fate except to be born."

"I know this is difficult—"

"No. You really don't."

"Aidan, I want to help. We have to figure this out."

I lean back, looking up at the sky. "I'm done trying."

"But the scrolls said—"

"I don't give a shit what some ancient scroll says. She is my *sister*. I love her. And she made a choice." Just like my mom.

"If the door is opened, Aidan, it will be more than your sister's soul at stake."

"*If the door is opened?*" My frustration turns to rage. "I've spent my whole life trying to save people that didn't want to be saved! I've done *everything* to stop something that was inevitable. And I failed. Every. Time." I take in a shaky breath. "If it's the end of the world, there's nothing I can do anymore. I'll watch it burn."

I expect him to argue, to fight and say I'm wrong, but instead he leans back, looking a hundred years old. After a few minutes of silence he says, "I'm so sorry. I've been a fool. A prideful fool. The way I've gone about this was all wrong. Please believe I never wanted anyone to be hurt. I wish I could've helped you save your sister, stopped what happened today. If I'd only gone through the front door instead of the yard, maybe . . ."

The smell of his guilt filters into the air like a muggy fog. My anger dissipates a little. "You wouldn't have been able to stop it," I say.

He shakes his head. "I should've told you right away, told you everything. Maybe then you would've trusted me more, and maybe I could've helped your sister."

"No. She made her choice."

"I truly am sorry, Aidan," he mumbles again.

We sit there together, both of us lost in what might have been, if only . . .

I don't dare think about what *will be*. If those scrolls really were referring to Ava, it seems fitting for the end to begin now. I can't even fathom my life if she's truly lost to me. And she knew it was coming. She'd known since that day in the trees, when I went to her after I'd saved Rebecca—she knew everything had changed.

I wanted to save her. To protect her like Mom told me to. Instead, all I did was watch her fall.

An hour or so later Sid stands up, telling me he has to go sleep in his shed, but that if I need anything I should call him. He says he'll be back at the hotel in the morning, and we'll talk more then and make a plan, but I have no idea how that'll help. He hands me his key card.

"I may return in the morning to use the room," he explains, "but there'll be an extra bed in there if you want it." And then he walks away.

I decide to call Rebecca's ER nurse at the hospital and take her up on her offer for information. It's only been a few hours, but my nerves won't let me relax. When the woman gets on the phone she says she remembers me and that she told Rebecca's dad that I called 911 and saved her life. Not true, but whatever.

"Her father will be here in the morning from Paris," she says, sounding motherly. "If you'd like, I can give him your number, in case he'd like to thank you personally."

I'm not sure what to say. "Um . . . sure. Yeah, I guess that's fine." Probably not, but I don't want my connection with Rebecca to be severed. Thinking about that now makes me panic.

"She was asking for you," the nurse says.

"When can I see her?"

"I'm not sure, sweetie. That's up to her father."

"Then tell her I'll come to her as soon as I can." I wish I knew when. It suddenly seems important to keep her close.

I thank the nurse, hang up, and walk through the lobby, heading for the front of the hotel. I leave through the tall glass sliding doors, walking past the valet staff and up the street toward what looks like an outdoor mall. Maybe the crowds will help me hide from everything in my head.

The sounds of a concert filter out from across the street where there's an outdoor stage. Hundreds of partygoers in expensive clothes crowd the sidewalks. The city is full of color and light, as if nightfall actually brings it to life. Excitement has a savory zing to it, like a warm summer night. Joy, an earthy urgency that catches you by the heart and makes you feel like dancing. And lust . . . lust is a rich spice that fills the head, making you drunk on the aroma. It all swirls in the air, coating me, and I welcome it.

There's a demon hunched in a shadow across the street, but I can ignore it this time. I'll be just another body, another face in the masses. I can pretend I'm not the boy who can see a lie in your eyes or smell your emotions. I'm not an experiment of fate—the boy who can touch demons. Or the boy who may have a half-demon sister.

I am No One.

"Aidan," comes a male voice in the crowd. I turn and see Connor and Kara walking toward me through the mass of people.

They look like a couple. He has his arm on her shoulders.

It's hard to look at them.

Kara doesn't seem to want to catch my eye; she gazes off into the crowd as they approach.

"Hey, you okay?" Connor asks, sliding his hand to hers.

I pause, studying Kara. "Sure."

"We're heading back. Do you want to walk with us?" he asks.

I shake my head. "I just left. Getting air."

Why won't Kara look at me? She keeps her eyes down or on the people passing by.

Connor nods. "We'll see you back at the hotel, then."

"Kara." I say her name so she'll have to acknowledge me.

She blinks up at me. And that's when I smell it, even over the mass of sensory input from the people around us—her fear. It's in her eyes, too.

"Are you okay?" I ask.

She swallows. Gives a shaky nod.

"She's fine," Connor says.

I act like he didn't say anything and move closer to her, ready to ask again, to hear her say it herself, but she steps back a little, and my gut sinks.

"Why don't you walk back with Aidan," Connor says to her. "Then you guys can talk."

Kara looks like she's going to protest, but instead she says, "Sure," through clenched teeth.

Connor leans over and gives her a kiss on the cheek. It feels like he's trying to make a point. When he glances at me I know I'm right—he smells like a protective brother as he walks by and disappears into the crowds.

I start walking, and she falls in beside me. "So how are you feeling?" I ask, even though I already know.

She shrugs.

There's an ocean of unsaid things between us suddenly, and I have no idea why.

I stop walking and turn to her. "Kara, please."

She bites her lip.

This afternoon she was offering to have sex with me, and now she's not talking to me. "What's going on?"

Her eyes turn glassy. I can't help touching her, running my fingers over her arm, trying to draw her out.

Warmth tingles at my fingertips, and her body sways toward me, almost involuntarily. She's so lovely. Her dark hair framing her face, the colorful lights of the city casting a soft glow on her skin.

I move closer and whisper, "I'm sorry." Because I feel it needs to be said. My being in her life nearly got her killed. And it makes me crazy thinking of her lying there so vulnerable, with Demon Lester ready to cut her open.

I felt crazy with fear when he sliced into Rebecca's arm, but Kara . . .

I killed for Kara.

The realization comes in a rush, washing over me. "I can't lose you," I say, feeling breathless. Just the thought of her slipping away too makes me frantic.

Her eyes lock with mine.

"I need you." I reach up and touch her face, running my thumb over her cheek.

Her brows draw together, like she's confused. Or in pain.

A tear slips down, wetting my palm.

But then she's moving in, curling her light-blue energy around me. Her lips meet mine, her breath hot in my mouth. Her fingers twist in my shirt, pulling me closer.

I grip her face, her hair, drinking her in, so familiar, so real it hurts.

Kara releases a small sigh, like she's relieved, and pulls away, but I don't let her go. I keep my arm around her, holding her to me, and kiss her nose, gently.

"I thought you wouldn't want me now," she says, her voice shaky.

I lean back to see her face clearly. "What? Why?"

She hesitates like she doesn't want to say it. "I was going to help you save your sister." Pain fills her features again. "But now that might not be possible. And you don't care about your powers or your destiny. So you don't need me."

"I didn't kiss you because I wanted some mystical power, Kara. I did it because I wanted to kiss you."

"But the curse is what makes you want to kiss me."

As true as that is, it doesn't represent everything I feel about her. "It's not that simple, and you know it."

"I'm not playing games anymore, Aidan."

"Is that why you were afraid of me when you saw me walk up?"

She bows her head, embarrassment filtering between us. "I was afraid you'd leave. That you'd want to forget all this ever happened."

I can see how she'd think that. I haven't been Mr. Congenial over the last few hours. And I'm not even sure what comes next for me. My sister just ran off with a demon and might be ending the world. Oh, and I killed someone. "I'm just processing, Kara. It has nothing to do with you—or how I feel about you. That hasn't changed." If anything, it's only intensified how I feel about her. I don't want to let her go.

"How do you think I felt when Connor kissed your cheek?" I ask. "I wanted to break his face."

Her lips tip in a half smile. "Connor just wants to protect me."

"From me."

"From what you're doing to me." She says it so quietly I wonder if I heard her right.

"What am I doing to you?"

She leans into me and rests her forehead on my chest. "You're making me fall for you."

I wrap my arms around her and pull her closer, feeling her fear, her vulnerability. I have it in me too: the awareness of being dragged into the current, taken against all sense into this place I've never been. "I know," I say, pressing my lips against her hair.

It's terrifying.

FORTY-THREE

We walk for a few more minutes in silence, but soon end up turning back and heading for the hotel again. I follow Kara to her room, across from Sid's room and three down from the one I'm supposed to be sharing with Jax. We pause. She doesn't reach for the door. She leans against the wall instead, looking exhausted.

I shift my feet, wondering if I should just say goodnight and keep walking. I'm standing on another ledge, deciding if I want to leap. God, I want to kiss this girl. But mostly I just don't want to hurt her. And part of me knows that I will if I'm not careful.

I can't see the next step, that's part of the problem. Where will I live, how will I survive, how should I—how *can* I—go on now that Ava's gone? She was my purpose. She was everything. Now I'm cut loose. But then that could be a reason not to care about the consequences and just leap for once.

"Holly's in the room," Kara says, glancing up at me. "She's probably not asleep yet."

"I should go back to my room."

She nods.

We both agree, apparently. Now's not the time.

But I don't leave.

Her finger brushes against my hand. A current runs up my arm, and I hear her breath catch, like she felt it, too.

"I should go," I say, thinking of the key in my pocket and wondering if I should mention it.

She licks her lips. "Yeah." She moves closer, her heat filling the small space between us, but she shoves her hands in her jean pockets, like she's having trouble keeping them to herself.

I reach out and brush my fingertips over her knuckles, and the feel of her skin is like heaven. I decide to claim it. "I have Sid's key."

She looks at me with wide eyes, realizing what I mean.

My touch runs along her arm to her elbow, strengthening the current between us even more. She sways into the energy with a small sound in the back of her throat, and I lean closer, every muscle in my body tight, every molecule screaming at me to grab her and drag her across the hall to the empty room.

The door opens with a loud click, and Holly pokes her head out. "What're you two up to?"

We blink at her, both of us a little dazed.

"Should I vacate so you two can DIY?" She pushes her reading glasses up her nose. "I can study in the hall."

Kara rolls her eyes and then slips past Holly into the room. Disappearing.

Shit.

I squint at Holly in annoyance. "Seriously?"

"What? I'm just trying to help." She snorts, obviously aware of the help she's *not* giving.

I recall all the other things she's been "helping" with lately, and I push the door open and invite myself in.

"Hey," she says as I walk past her, "this isn't going to be a three-some, buddy, NFW."

"I'm heartbroken." I pull a chair from the desk and sit down, making myself at home.

"What the hell?" She gives me an annoyed frown.

"Oh, I just thought you could tell me what happened between you and my sister and Lester."

Her eyes bug out of her head. "Excuse me?"

"You heard me, Holly. Come on. There's no point in hiding it now. I mean you've done such an awesome job of sneaking around and screwing me over that there's no way for me to fix any of it, so your wicked plan is safe."

"Hey! That wasn't *my* wicked plan. It was your sister's." She points at the window like Ava's out there beyond the dark glass. "I never would've helped her if I knew it meant Lester was gonna be . . . ya know."

"She's just a kid," I add, even though I'm aware that's not true anymore. "You should've talked to me."

"She said you'd freak."

"For good reason!"

Kara sits on the bed looking like a child who's watching her parents fight.

"Sure. Like I'm psychic." She shakes her head, obviously not seeing the full picture. "That first night when you all went on the job and you told me to babysit her, we girl bonded about how she wanted to find her mom. I felt bad for her. She's really sweet when she wants to be."

My heart sinks, thinking of Ava talking to a perfect stranger about our mom. How lonely and desperate she must've been.

"And then," Holly continues, "the real shit happened the next night or so. Your mom came to me in a dream."

"What?"

"It's my thing, ya know. Ghost dreams." She motions like I should get it. "So anyway, your mom's ghost came to me and said to get a message to Ava. So I gave her the message, and—"

"What was the message?" I ask, interrupting.

"To come find her at this cave."

Kara and I share a look. The ocean cave. I was right: Ava had been there, looking for my mom.

"In Malibu?" I ask. "Is that when you said you were going to the beach?"

"No, when I said we were at the ice cream store-slash-beach, that was the second time—can I just tell the damn story, please?"

I lean back in the chair and groan.

"So," she continues, "I gave your sister the message about the cave, and she pleaded with me to take her to this place that she said was a bookstore, and it had to be a secret. *But* it turned out to be some sort of creepy witch den with potion stuff and animals. She bought a bird and a bunch of tiny bags of herbs and candles, and then we went to the cave her mom talked about in the message, and she did some ritual that was supposed to tell Ava *more* stuff about her mom—at least, that's what she said, but then it ended up being completely insane. She pulled the tiny bird from the box and held it all sweet, chanting, then stabbed it in the heart with a needle." She gives me a confounded look. "Stabbed! She, like, *killed* the bird! Bleck!" She visibly shivers. "Then she did some sort of magic thing that had her trying to talk to a spirit, but she couldn't hear what it said, so that's why she needed Lester."

"To channel the spirit." Kara looks at me as the pieces start to click into place.

I suddenly feel like vomiting.

Holly nods in agreement. "Yeah, she kept saying she was feeling muddled energy in the cave." Holly starts pacing. "So she asked Lester to help her—that was the ice cream day. Your sister told him she'd help him practice his ability if he'd help her talk to her mom. But the cave was way creepier the second time. The smell of these flowers growing around the cave was making me gag."

"You saw my sister call up our mom's spirit?" I ask.

She scoffs. "Oh, man, I wish that's what I'd seen. She tried to raise your mom's spirit, but she raised this demon instead. She seemed surprised, but she also seemed to recognize it. She kept talking to it about something or someone called Heart-Keeper, and it must've been one badass spell 'cause stuff was flying around your sister in circles, sand and bits of rock and wax and stuff, spinning around the pentagram. Her voice turned deep and strange and then this gross smell came, like, really strong.

"Lester was sitting on the other side of her circle, and she'd killed some other poor creature and painted his palms in its blood. According to your mom's witchy book, the blood acted like an open door. Of course, Lester started talking in this freaky voice. Ava asked the spirit about her mom—your mom—and the thing told her there'd been a deal his boss made with your mom. Ava seemed really pissed off when it was all done telling the story."

The deal. Ava knows now what it was. From what Holly's saying, it doesn't seem like she was able to accept it very well. "What did he say?"

"About the deal?" Holly looks to the side like she's trying to remember. "It was something about your mom wanting to see her lost love one more time and how she bargained her body for it, or something. Like, she became some demon's whore is what it sounded like—and all these demons and angels paid this Heart-Keeper so they could have sex with her—"

"Angels?" My stomach churns. "What do you mean? Did she—"

"I don't know!" Holly barks. "God. I was too busy being freaked out by Lester being a puppet and how everything was floating around."

Oh, God. One of those bastards my mother slept with is Ava's father, and they were both angels *and* demons. But which one created my sister?

Kara must be thinking along the same line, because she says, "Like Sid was talking about: Nephilim or . . ."

Or demon spawn.

I still have no idea which is worse; it seems like being the daughter of an angel instead of a demon would be better, but any angel that would sink to having sex with a woman who's been slaved out to some demon can't be very pure of soul. I try to recall something about the men who would come to her—their faces, their smells—but my stomach clenches just thinking about it. How could I not have seen what they were? I should've seen through their illusions. Could my mom have done something to me to keep me from seeing right?

"But Lester didn't just channel the demon," Kara says. "It's inside of him now."

Holly shrugs. "I totally would've said something if I'd thought that could happen. I had no idea that something was up. I thought it was weird that he'd buy us all movie tickets, but I think that was Lester trying to keep us safe from what he knew might be hanging out inside him."

The demon must've been hunkered down, waiting for the right moment. "Do you remember Ava talking to the demon about a deal that *she* wanted to make?"

Holly sits down on the bed and falls back. "So all I know for sure now is that this Heart-Keeper demon definitely wants your sister—because of the deal it made with your mom—and that the thing's minion inside Lester then made a deal with Ava for you to be safe as long as she came back to the cave on the dark moon. Then Ava could do some kind of rebirthing thing. It was all very cousin's brother's uncle to me, so I don't know."

Be reborn. Just like Demon Lester said to the Boss Demon when he was warning it about Ava's potential: that she wasn't reborn yet. That's going to happen tomorrow night at the dark of the moon, on Ava's birthday.

"He said they would do the rebirth at the cave?" Hope filters into me, a thin thread.

"Uh-oh," Holly says. "Not a fan of that look."

"What is it, Aidan?" Kara asks, scooting to the edge of the bed.

"I think I can save her." As the words emerge, they feel true. I can still save her.

"Excuse me?" Holly asks, looking suddenly worried.

"But, Aidan—" Kara starts.

I won't let her finish. "I can't let them take her if I have the power to stop it—if I still have time."

"She chose that path, Aidan," Kara says, a frantic tone growing in her voice. "We all make choices."

I shake my head. "If she did this to save me, it's my choice, too."

"She did it to find her mom," Holly says. "Saving you was just part of the deal."

"I don't care," I say, rising to my feet. "I can't just stand by and let this happen."

"Not smart," Holly says. "But it's your funeral."

FORTY-FOUR

Kara chases after me as I leave the room. "Aidan, please, think about this."

"If there's still a chance to save her, I have to take it."

She catches up to me as I stop in front of Sid's door. There's no way I'm sleeping in a room with any of the other boys. I need to be alone.

"They'll kill you!"

I slip the key card in, and the latch clicks. I open the door. "That doesn't matter anymore." I walk into the dark room and toss the key on the TV table.

She comes at me, letting the door slam behind her. "Doesn't matter? Are you kidding me?"

"I promised my mom that I would protect her!" It turns out that I was supposed to protect Ava from what was *inside* her heart more than what was chasing after her, but that doesn't change my commitment to my promise.

"And how about what you said out there in the street, huh?" she says. "*I need you, Kara*—what the hell was that?" Her voice cracks, but her expression is all fire and indignation.

I move closer. "Kara—"

She glares at me and steps back. "Don't you dare act like you can have it both ways. I'm a part of this now too, you know. Whatever happened between us, it's *done* something to me. And you're ready to just die—to rip my heart from my chest on a hope!" She chokes on her words and then releases a bitter laugh.

"God," she says, "I wish I'd never met you—do you know how many times I've thought that? And you know why? Because I know how this will end. This *thing*"—she motions to the air between us—"will disappear once we've had sex and gotten it over with. Everything you felt for me will evaporate."

My throat goes tight. "That's not fair." I do want her. And I know it's not just because of the spell, but she obviously won't believe me no matter what I say.

"Life isn't fair," she says, tears in her eyes now. "Believe me, I'm an expert at how unfair life is." Her chest rises and falls, her sadness, her defeat, leaking from her like weighty mist.

And then she reaches down and pulls her shirt over her head.

I blink at her bare skin, her bra, confused.

She unbuttons and unzips her jeans, starts to peel them down her legs—

"Whoa, what're you doing?" My confusion turns to panic, even as my body reacts to her standing there in her underwear: pink cotton panties and a green lace bra.

"I'm getting this over with," she says.

"Kara, holy shit," I say, stepping away as she moves forward, determination on her face.

She takes me by the waist of my jeans. "Come on, Aidan. Soldier up." Then she tries to pull my shirt over my head, but I won't raise my arms, so she moves down to my jeans again.

I whack her hand away. "Stop! What's wrong with you?" The girl's lost it entirely.

"It'll be over quick, I promise." She gives me a tight smile as she tries to unbutton my fly.

"Kara, please, this isn't right."

"I know. That's what makes it so much fun."

She reaches into my pants.

I jump back with a hiss of breath. "Stop it!" That was really not fair.

She releases a nervous giggle, then moves closer again. "Well, that part of you seems happy with the idea."

I'm trying to back away, but I hit the wall. She presses herself against me and kisses me full on the mouth. Hot and unholy.

My breath catches, and my body reacts before I can stop it; my hands grab her, pulling her into me, fingers sliding down to her waist to grip her as she moans into my mouth.

The feel of her hits me strong, and I know I'm tumbling down, giving in, but suddenly I don't care. I kiss her harder, trying to pour out my urgency, to rid myself of this rabid need, as her limbs cling to me, hands under my shirt, against my skin. I grab her hips and lift her up as I move to the bed and set her on it, pulling my shirt over my head, crawling over her, kissing her deeper, pressing her into the mattress. I touch her everywhere, trying to get more of her skin on mine.

My fingers find her bra, tug at it, needing to feel her, all of her. But I can't break the connection, I can't let go. I might stop breathing.

She slips the bra strap off for me and shivers, a tinge of fear leaking into my skin giving her away. But she doesn't release me or pause, so I press closer and let my stomach touch hers. I wrap my hand around the back of her head, caressing her neck, and she melts again as we kiss and gasp and fall back into the oblivion of it all, the white fire of the connection, the blinding need we have for each other.

She tries to push my pants down, but I don't want to go there yet. I shift out of reach, kissing her neck, her chest, her shoulders; I don't want this to be over quick. And I know that as soon as her body and mine meet, it'll be finished. I kiss my way down her body, her breasts, her belly. But as I go lower, she pulls me up, back to her lips.

Then she reaches down my pants again.

I pull back.

And that's when I see her eyes. Glistening with tears.

"Please, Aidan," she says, her voice full of emotion.

"What's wrong?" I ask, hearing the impatience in my voice and wishing I didn't.

"I just need you to take me. We can't draw this out."

Is she talking about sex or ripping off a Band-Aid?

"You're really into this, I see." Now my irritation is impossible to hide. How did I not notice her emotions? I wish I could shut my hormones off for ten minutes so I could *not* be an ass about this, but it's like I have no control over any of it.

A tear slips down her cheek, and my stomach clenches.

"It's fine." She touches my bicep, but I feel her fingers shiver.

I roll onto the bed beside her. I stare at the ceiling, wishing it had a map on it that explained the female psyche. "You started it, you know."

"I know, because I want this. I do."

"You sure have a weird way of showing it."

She rolls toward me, laying her head on my chest, curling against my side. "I want you so bad, Aidan. But it's like the scars inside me won't let me just take what I want."

Cold awareness falls over me. How could I forget, even for a second? Now I definitely feel like an ass. I bring her closer, her skin warm against mine. The hum from our connection is like a bee in my head, distracting me.

"I'm sorry," I say.

She kisses my chest. "I know. I thought if we just dove into the pool . . ."

"You mean the frozen lake?"

She laughs softly. "Something like that."

I turn my head and put my lips to her hair. "I think we both knew this is how it would be."

"I want so badly to be someone else for you," she says. "Someone less broken."

"Kara, you're the one I want."

"But you need someone strong. You need power to save your sister."

"I wish that you could see what I see inside of you. You *are* strong. But it should've never been your job to fix this. That was put on you for all the wrong reasons." I close my eyes, trying to wrap my head around what comes next and decide if I'm willing to drag her in even further. "I would be trying to save Ava either way. You know that." I need to be there at the end of it all. I need to see the final moment when our hope dies, or I'll never be able to rest.

"But you'll be so vulnerable." She runs her fingers along my torso.

I lean closer and take her lips with mine, but I pull away when the fire sparks for a second, not wanting it to control me again. Then I fold her hand in mine and kiss her fingertips. "Let's just lie here. I want to enjoy this." I squeeze her into my chest. "You fit so perfectly against me."

"I'm sorry," she whispers.

I run my palm over her soft hair. "I'm not."

It's quiet for a second, until she says, "You're a pretty good kisser, you know that? You gave me Jell-O legs."

I can't help but grin. "Really?"

"You must practice a lot. It was like Olympic-training good."

"Well, since it's all I've ever done . . ."

She goes still for a second, then rises up to look at me. "What?"

"I'm a virgin, Kara."

She covers her grin with her hand. "Ohmygod."

"Howl it up, Chuckles. I had you fooled. You thought I was a player."

She laughs again and rests her head back on my chest. "Amazing. You're like a rare fossil."

"That's me. The last of my kind."

"And to think I could've been the first." She kisses my chest again. "I would've felt so special."

"You are. You're mine." I kiss her temple, and we lie in silence, melting into each other, and then somehow we begin telling stories of what we wish our lives could've been until we're kissing again, touching each other gently, resting in the space we've created, just the two of us. And when we feel the urgency grow, we both stop and pull the covers around us, snuggling.

She lets me touch the scars on her arms, telling me about the night she put them there. I hold her wrists, running my thumbs across the old wounds, and tell her how glad I am that she failed, how alive she made me feel that night when she kissed me after the party, and how I wish she could look inside me and feel it, too.

I decide to peel back more of my own wounds, the pieces of me I never show to anyone. Ever. But somehow I know that it's her I'm supposed to tell. I let the whole story come, about my mom, about the things Fiona did and how they terrified me, how her sadness was like an infection. About the night when everything turned to blood as the spell was worked and the wolflike demon marked Ava and grabbed my mom by the throat before it ripped her heart from her chest. That was the moment my life became night, the moment death's shadow became my constant companion, the moment I became a man.

Kara grips me tight, shivering.

Then silence falls. Both of us are lost in our own thoughts. I lose track of time and place as I think about the last few years and the next few. My life and my possible death.

Kara's energy clings to me like a guard against the darkness. It's protective and full of warmth. And as it sinks into my skin, I feel myself open up to it, as if she's diving into me and me into her. And I'm at peace after everything; finally I'm in the right place, in the right moment, the home I've been searching for all this time. Love.

And I know, from this moment, I'll never be the same again.

FORTY-FIVE

I wake up on fire.

I try to scream, but nothing comes. No air fills my lungs. Just heat and torment. I'm empty. I'm becoming ash.

"Aidan," says a calm voice. I want to be calm; I want to escape these flames.

"Aidan, open your eyes."

Through the pain, I hear that it's a man's voice. Familiar.

I manage to create a sound through the heat in my throat. "Help." But I can't open my eyes. I'm scared I'll see flesh melting from my bones and that my eyes will burn up.

"Yes, you can," the voice says, reading my thoughts. "You only have to try. Just for a moment. The pain is only in your mind, Aidan. Breathe. Just breathe."

I struggle, wondering if the voice is right, if the fire isn't real. But how can this torment that's tearing me to pieces only be in my imagination?

"It's the purification," the voice says, "but it's passing through you now that you're not a part of the process any longer. You can breathe. I promise you."

I try to push the flames away. I try to take a breath. In and out and in. I breathe.

I find air for my lungs that doesn't singe or taste like ash. A few more breaths and the pain fades, settling to a dull ache. My eyes squint open. No fire. No ice. I'm in a hotel room. The air still.

And the memory comes back to me in a rush: Kara taking her clothes off, kissing me . . .

"You've been awakened," the voice says.

I turn toward it—

"Eric," I say.

What the hell is Eric doing in my room?

"I'm here to lead you through the awakening," he says, reading my thoughts again. His usual expensive suit is now a plain shirt made of rough, off-white material and a pair of brown pants. His hair is several shades lighter, almost gold, and a little longer. His skin is white, and his face is scruffy from several days without a shave. There's a scar on his jaw, running down his neck, and what appear to be burn marks on his chest at the opening of his shirt. He looks like someone from a long time ago.

I just saw him a few hours ago when we checked into the hotel, and he didn't look at all like this. "But . . ."

"You've allowed the key to connect. You are returning to Origin, becoming the Bringer of Fire."

The way Mom described me. The Assyrian tablet.

"I don't understand," I say, feeling like it's suddenly hard to breathe again. "How do you know all this? What's happening?"

"I've been watching over you." He bows his head a little, like he's trying to look submissive. "My name is Azri'el. I'm one of The Brethren." I open my mouth, but he quickly answers the first question that pops in my head. "The Brethren are within the order of angels. We watch over earth and Creation. At times we're charged with watching over a soul's life here."

"You're an angel."

"Not as you're thinking of them right now. I'm a type of angel. My kind don't fight against the demons, we only exist on this plane within humanity. In the past, you've called us many things: the faire folk, Sleagh Maith, or sometimes elves."

I release a nervous laugh. "You're a little tall to be an elf."

"The legends have changed much over the passing of time, until my Brethren were all but forgotten. Now demons fill the tales of old. Most humans don't realize The Brethren exist at all, choosing only to recognize the messengers of the Lord, or the archangels."

I've only seen regular angels before, when I've seen the side of good. And now I barely see them at all.

"You have seen us," he says, again hearing my thoughts, "but you don't recognize us, because we live as you do, on the physical plane, and we have ways of hiding ourselves from certain kinds of humans, like you. Those angels you've seen exist on the same plane as the demons, warring and keeping the balance, and at times carrying the Spirit of God."

"But they don't keep a balance," I say. "I've only seen a handful of them in my entire life. And I see demons almost every day."

"Because angels are much more powerful than demons, and recently the soldiers have begun slipping away, going to the higher realms to prepare for the next Cycle. In this hour, in this world, it is only me and my Brethren left here to hold the front lines. And we are only keepers of Creation, not warriors."

I shake my head, amazed and frustrated by what he's saying. "But why? We need them!" Now more than ever.

"You were born, and it changed the balance. Demons rule here in this Cycle, so the angels had to leave as you grew and became more powerful. Now that you've come into your true self, they will have gone almost entirely."

"What?" The angels are gone. How is that possible? It's true I never see them. I always thought they were keeping a low profile. Apparently they were keeping no profile at all.

"It is the agreement. For now. You've been born, and the scales have shifted. Still, your birth was as HaShem willed it. You represent a formidable force on this plane with your strong connection to the Ruach Elohim. Only human, yet full of more power than the highest angel—if you can allow yourself to tap into it. This is why He sent me to you, among others."

"*God* sent you?" Why would God choose me?

"He chooses the willing," Eric says.

"What've you done with Kara?"

Eric moves to the side and motions to the bed behind him.

Kara is there, twisted in the sheet, sleeping. With her arms around me.

Me.

I stare at myself, at Kara, her arm draped over my chest, my chin resting on her head. I look at my bare skin, so pale against hers, violet in spots, like I've lost oxygen. There are dark circles around my eyes. It looks like . . .

"Am I dead?" I ask, nearly choking on the question.

"Yes," Eric says. "In a way."

I stare at my body and see that it's only my shell.

I've heard people tell stories about after they die, how it's like they're outside of their bodies, looking down at themselves—

"No." This can't be happening. This isn't how it was supposed to be.

"It is. You must die before you can come back again. Your body must be re-created. That was the fire you felt—your soul and your spirit and your flesh being made new."

"What the hell does that even mean? None of this is possible."

Eric, or Azriel, or whoever, steps over to stand at the window and gazes out at the city lights. "Your soul and spirit are with me, outside of time, while your body is being healed and brought back."

"But Kara and I didn't have sex!"

"Kara merely needed to touch your soul. She didn't need to physically connect—you were all thinking too much like humans. Not all things are flesh. More is spirit than you know. Your intimacy grew over days and became fully recognized in a moment of connection."

We connected. Intimacy didn't mean what I assumed it meant—what we all assumed it meant.

"So I can save Ava now," I say.

Eric tilts his head, looking sympathetic. "It is possible you can destroy the demons sent to collect her, but there is more to it than that. They desire her for a purpose. And she is not a child of Adam."

"I know." At least I think I do.

"You know a piece of the story."

A bitter taste fills my mouth. "My mom was some other-worldly whore."

"She was in pain," he says, his brow furrowing, like he's not happy with how I said that. "It led her to make a deal with a very powerful demon."

"But why?"

"She wanted to see your father again, desperately. And the demon took advantage of that. It needed something from her and knew a desperate witch was a useful witch. So it told her that it would grant her wish if she would allow five men into her bed whenever they asked, until she became pregnant—this is very common."

Common? It's disgusting.

"Witches will often trade sex with the demons they call up for favors. Most often the demon takes on a benign form when it becomes corporeal so the witch doesn't realize she's having sex with a hideous beast from her worst nightmare. Instead he or she looks like the loveliest form in the human imagination—whoever the witch wishes to see."

"So the demons trick them." Just the idea of what these witches were falling into bed with sends shivers through me. I'd seen hundreds of demons. None of them were remotely human looking.

"Just as your mother was tricked. And even after she agreed to what they wished, she was never able to see your father in the flesh as she wanted. The demons manipulated her and only gave her a dream of him. But she still owed her end of the deal." He comes closer, a pleading look on his face, like he needs me to understand what my mother was going through. Why he cares about her, I have no idea. He's an angel—aren't they supposed to despise evil things like witches?

"But then she became pregnant," he continues. "She knew the child wasn't normal, and she realized what she'd agreed to—she just didn't know how to stop it. But there was a light in her life that she hoped would prove her growing child's salvation." He nods toward me. "You.

"She made a plan to meet the demon who would come on the third year for her daughter—to meet it and sacrifice herself, creating a blood protection spell over her two children. What she didn't realize was that it would only work to hide one of her children. For you, as a human, the sacrifice has kept your power invisible to the other side for the most part. It held the demons back from seeing what you truly were. It wasn't until the night of the full moon when the demon bit you that I realized your power was about to be awakened—it had shown itself to the other side of the Veil. That was also the night your mother's ghost returned to the beach, perhaps as a counterweight to the darkness beginning to surround her children."

"You were the one who protected my sister on her sixth birthday, weren't you?"

He nods. "Yes. I was the one sent to guard you. Both of you. You were both put under the same covenant when your mother sacrificed herself."

"But isn't Ava evil?" Saying it aloud makes me ill.

"Evil surrounds her, and she chooses to delve into its power, but no, she is not herself evil. It is what she does, not who she is."

"I don't understand the difference."

"The difference is her choice."

Hope sparks again. "So I can still save her."

"It isn't that simple, Aidan. She has free will."

I squint at him, wondering if he knows more than he's saying. "Has she already chosen darkness?"

"Not yet. That comes at the time of rebirth."

"Tomorrow."

"For your sister, yes." He motions to me. "And soon you will choose as well."

My head jerks back in surprise. "Me?"

"Yes, we all must choose. Soon you will come to your time of choice."

"But . . . how?"

He turns to face the bed, looking down at my body. "You will awaken in a moment, a new creature, still human, but with a resurrection form—the form of Origin that was meant for all humans before The Fall. An Adam, if you will. But you will not be finished with your transformation until your power seal is broken and you make your choice. You won't have to do anything. You'll know when it's time. The demon's energy will be what flips the switch. You'll feel the breaking, and then you merely let it do what it wants to do. Your heart will grab hold of the path that will decide which side you will finish on in the end."

"What do you mean *the end*?"

"The end of all things."

"I don't understand."

He moves closer. "You will. But it's time to go now." He reaches out like he's about to place a finger on my head, but then he pauses. "My spirit will remain with you until you have awakened fully. Remember, you'll know when it's time."

He gives me a sad smile and then touches his finger to my temple, sending white across my vision.

And I catch fire once more.

FORTY-SIX

I rise from the lake of flames retching and gasping for oxygen.

Someone screams, and another voice says, "Holy shit!"

My eyes try to focus as arms grab me, cling to me. Someone is weeping against my shoulder. "Oh, God . . . oh, God, Aidan." Kara's clutching me so tight it hurts, kissing my cheek, my neck.

I gulp at the air, confusion twisting inside me.

Shit. I was dead.

I look at the stunned faces around me—all of them. Kara, her body clinging to mine, Connor standing at the foot of the bed looking like he's seen a ghost, Jax gaping, Holly leaning on the wall beside the window, palm to her forehead. And Sid frowning from the shadows. Even Finger's here. But how did they all get here so quickly?

"What's going on?" I ask. My voice sounds like it hasn't been used for a decade.

Jax plops down, rocking the bed. "We've been sitting here staring at your corpse for the last three hours, wondering what to do if you didn't wake up like Sid said you would. I voted for tossing you off the balcony, but Holly thought you'd prefer drowning in the pool. We were gonna make the story exciting, like you'd been running from the mob and—"

Sid grabs Jax by the arm, stopping his yammering, and yanks him to his feet. "Enough. Give him space." He pulls Jax to the desk and settles him in the chair.

"I was dead," I manage to get out of my dry throat. Even saying it aloud doesn't make it feel any more real.

Kara shivers beside me, not releasing me, like she's desperate to keep me there. "I woke up and . . . oh, God, Aidan." Then she moves back and socks me in the arm, sudden rage billowing out to mingle with the sorrow between us. "What the hell were you thinking?"

I shake my head. I wish I knew.

Sid moves forward. "Let me talk to Aidan alone." He begins shooing the others out. Kara starts to pull herself away from me. She's wearing her clothes again, and I wonder what she's been feeling over the last few hours. While I laid here, a corpse.

I grab her wrist and won't let go. "Kara stays."

The others file out of the room, but Connor straggles behind. "You scared me, man," he says, touching a hand to my shoulder. "No breaking Kara's heart, right?"

"Right," I say, finding Kara's hand.

Her fingers slide through mine.

"Good. Stay alive then."

Once Connor is gone, Sid sits on the bed and sighs with obvious relief. "I knew you'd be in a deep sleep during the awakening, but you seemed very dead, son. It was difficult to convince myself not to call the ambulance and request some sort of medical miracle. You nearly gave me a heart attack being out for so long."

I try to form a coherent thought. "I was dead, so I didn't have a whole lot of say in the matter. But next time I decide to keel over I'll be sure to get it approved by the committee first." My voice cracks. My throat is a desert. "Is there any water here?"

Sid gets a water bottle from the minifridge and hands it to me. "In the scrolls it implied a sort of coma state. Not *death*."

"I guess a death of sorts was supposed to happen. The angel said—"

"An angel!" His eyes grow even wider.

So apparently he doesn't know everything. He doesn't appear to know that Eric's an angel. He's not even aware there's an angel involved at all. Somehow the idea of him being somewhat in the dark makes me feel a little better.

"When I was . . . dead, I saw an angel," I say, deciding not to tell Eric's secret. "Then, after he talked to me, I woke up here, and all of you were gawking at me." I take a swig of the water, and my insides soak it in like parched earth.

"Amazing," Sid mumbles. "And do you feel it? The power?"

I pause, taking stock of how I feel, to see if anything seems different. But I have to say that if it is, I can't tell. I look over at Kara. At her hands fiddling nervously with her shirt. "Do I seem different?" I ask.

She considers, and then she says, "Maybe a little."

Sid moves closer, examining me. "What?"

Kara hesitates. "You feel . . . I don't know. More *other*. Less real."

I blink at her, not sure what to make of that—is that good or bad?

Sid frowns at me. "Hmm, yes. I see what you mean," he agrees. "As if his skin is . . . shiny, maybe—oh!" He points at my chest.

I look down.

Across my chest is the continuation of the marking on my arm. It runs from my hand up to my elbow, curling over my bicep and shoulder muscles and spreading out like thick brown veins over my pecs. And where my heart is there's a sort of brand: a circle with a symbol inside. A sigil burned into my skin. The flesh around it is puffed red, but it doesn't hurt. I don't feel it at all. "What is that?"

Sid squints at it. "It appears to be a sort of seal—perhaps on your powers?"

"I thought you were supposed to know all this," I say, concerned by how unsure he sounds. "You're the one who pushed this to happen."

"I wanted your powers to be awakened because it was what was best. Now they are," he says. "I only know what the scrolls tell me, son."

"Well, can you at least tell what it means? I can't read it upside down."

Sid shakes his head. "It's not anything I recognize."

Wonderful. "Well, it doesn't matter now." But I realize as I look around for my shirt that it's not night anymore. The sun is full in the sky. "What time is it?"

"It's four thirty."

"Four in the afternoon?" Shit. I'm running out of time.

"Aidan, what difference does it make?" Sid asks. "This is just the beginning."

I jump out of the bed, reaching for my shirt on the floor. "There's too much to do." My legs scream in protest as I stand. I wobble, but manage to stay on my feet.

Sid frowns. "Do?"

"He's going to try and save her," Kara says, sounding defeated.

"You mean your sister? Aidan—"

"No use telling me what a horrible idea it is. I already know." I pull my shirt over my head. "And I'm going anyway."

"But you barely received your powers," Sid says. "You don't know what you can do! And the demons . . . Aidan, this is suicide."

"I'm really not interested in your thoughts." I know I'm not *less* powerful, and I was determined to act before this event, so I'm certainly not letting whatever this is change my mind. "You can either help me or I'll figure it out on my own. Your call."

"I'll help," Kara says quietly.

Sid opens his mouth to say something to me, but then he closes it and finally says, "Try to see reason!"

I ignore him and turn to Kara. "I need to find some things."

I'll need salt to keep them back, cinnamon to throw them off my scent . . . Eric will have a hex box or spirit bowl. I can get him to give them to me—now that he's my guardian angel and all.

"I'll drive," she says. She smells like defeat, but her shoulders are set in determination. "Just let me get my keys. I'll meet you in the lobby in ten minutes." She heads out the door, leaving Sid and me alone in the room.

"You need to stop and think about this," he pleads. "There's no reason to rush into anything—"

"Yes, there is. Her awakening is tonight."

Sid's eyes grow.

"And I think that's when the darkness will really take root. Unless I stop it. And we still aren't sure if she's the key or not."

"You could die. For sure this time." He sounds crushed. "After all that I've sacrificed to save you."

"You're a crazy bastard, but I'm grateful for everything you did for me." He did try to help me, even if his methods were a bit faulty at times. "Just let it go now, Sid. My future isn't in your hands anymore. And this was always about saving Ava."

I turn and leave him standing by the bed that was my grave ten minutes ago, and I realize I'm not doing this for just Ava anymore, or for my mom. I'm doing this to prove something to myself, to show that little boy who watched from the doorway as his mom was torn to shreds and tossed to the floor like a rag doll that it's okay he didn't save her. Because I can save Ava.

Today I'll do what I should've done that night so long ago—I'll redeem what I love.

Or die trying.

FORTY-SEVEN

Kara parks the Camaro in the back lot of SubZero, and we head to the club's service entrance. She lifts her fist to knock on the door, but I stop her.

"What's wrong?" she asks.

I pull her closer, leaning down to take her lips with mine. She's hesitant, but she doesn't resist. When I move away, she stares at me for a second and then asks, "What was that for?"

"I want you to know how I feel about you." I'm full of anxiety. Death is a strong possibility.

"You're freaking me out, Aidan."

"I know. I'm sorry. It's just, this thing between us is never going to be something we can keep neat and tidy—I'm not that guy, you know."

She gives me a look that says she doesn't understand why I'm telling her this.

I continue anyway. "Before I jump into this thing tonight, I want you to know why the spell worked and my powers were awakened, even though we never . . ."

She rolls her eyes. "Had sex. You're allowed to say it."

I don't let her snark keep me from telling her what I need to say—I know she's putting up a front. "Something happened last night," I say, "when I told you those things, when we were lying there together and talking."

"You told me about your mom," she whispers.

"I've never told anyone those things. Not even Ava knows. You know more about me, about my heart, than anyone I've ever known, Kara. Whatever happens I need you to know that."

I feel her tremble as I hold her arm. "Please don't do this," she says, desperation threading her words. "You can't leave."

"I have to." I have to try.

She jerks her arm from my hand. "You don't *have* to. This is your choice." She steps back, and tears glisten in her eyes. "Do you know what I thought when I woke up beside you this morning? I felt how cold you were, empty. It wasn't you—I knew that the minute my eyes opened. I was lying beside a corpse."

I don't know what to say. "Kara . . ."

"And now you're going to run toward death again. Is that what love looks like? Because if it is, then it sucks."

I feel beaten, robbed. In a way, she's right, but there's so much more to it. I won't be able to make her understand. I barely understand it myself.

"But two can play this game, Aidan." She wipes the tears from her chin. "You won't be going into this without me. If this is death, then I'm following you into it."

She opens the back door to the club and escapes me, heading into the dark hall before I can argue with her. Kara coming with me? That can't happen . . .

Hanna's talking to a delivery guy in the hall when she glances up. "Aidan." She doesn't look terribly surprised to see us. "Is everything all right?" Her eyes move to Kara and back to me.

"I need to talk to Eric," I say.

"He's not here. He left last night on a business trip. Maybe I can help?"

I study her as if this is the first time we've met. Knowing now that Eric isn't what he seems makes me wonder if Hanna is one of them. An angel in disguise. Or is he deceiving her, too?

"Where is he?" I ask, voice hard.

She seems taken aback at my push, but she's not going to budge. "Just tell me what you need, Aidan."

"Supplies."

She finishes up with the delivery guy and waits for him to leave through the back door before she motions for us to follow her as she walks in the same direction, heading to the warehouse. After the delivery guy is out of earshot, she asks, "Demons?"

I nod.

She glances sideways at Kara, but Kara's lost in her own thoughts, following along without a word.

We walk across the parking lot and enter the warehouse through an open bay door. After going through the garage, we walk down a hall, passing several offices before stopping at the end in front of a large door. There's a keypad and a fingerprint lock on the wall beside it. Hanna blocks our line of sight and types the code in and presses her thumb to the screen. Something in the wall clicks, and a seal breaks with a hiss. The five-inch-thick metal door opens, revealing a large, dark room.

We walk in, and Hanna seals the opening behind us. She turns to another keypad on the inside wall, typing in a new code that results in a loud thunk as the latches fall back into place behind us.

The lights flicker on, one by one, immersing the entire space in a fluorescent glow and revealing rows of shelves.

I've never been in here. Eric always brings things into the office if he needs me to check them out. I can see why he'd guard this room so fiercely. It's a treasure trove. I see a standing globe that can't be less than six hundred years old, with several wrapped paintings leaning against it. To the left there's a full wall of scrolls, sectioned off in cubbies and tagged with colors to catalog them. There are countless statues lined up in the far corner: Greek and Egyptian and Persian gods and goddesses. Artifacts cover every surface, in gold and silver and tarnished copper. Jewels glitter from a few items. There's a huge glass case that's full of weapons: daggers, broadswords, and bows of all shapes and sizes. And along the wall to our right are crates stacked to the ceiling filled with more stuff. The place is like something out of an Indiana Jones movie. I wonder suddenly if the Ark of the Covenant is in here somewhere, too.

I find myself drawn to a sword that's more than four feet long leaning against the desk in the center of the room. The desk is covered in scrolls and old books. The sword's energy seems to hum against the air, tickling the back of my throat.

"What sort of things are you looking for?" Hanna asks.

"Not sure," I say. "Do you have any hex boxes?"

"I have a Persian spirit bowl," she says, "but it depends what you want to catch. What kind of demon is this?"

Kara looks curious about my answer to that question, too.

I consider how much I should tell Hanna, but then decide there's no use hiding it from her. I'm done with secrets. "It's a possession. I need to get a demon out of a body and into something that can lock it down. Plus, there may be another demon or two hanging around as guards." Better to be safe than sorry.

She doesn't seem fazed at all. "So more than one kind. All right. How do you plan on doing the exorcising?"

"I was going to do it the old-fashioned way, immersion in water." I'll have the ocean right there—and some herbs and oils.

She shakes her head. "No, no. You'll have no time for that—not if there's more than one." She goes to a shelf and pulls a small box down. After digging around in it she pulls out a necklace. There's a large amulet on the chain with a Star of David etched in the gold, circled to harness power, and in the center is the word *yatsa*, the Hebrew for "go out," in its hiphil form, meaning the demon is made to vacate.

I take it from her. The medallion is about the size of a silver dollar and cold to the touch. It's lightweight, but it's powerful. I can sense the tentacles of energy just below the surface.

"You have to press it against the sternum of the possessed body," she says, motioning dead center at my chest where it should be placed. "It'll force the creature out of the human host. Just remember to say the name of the power source aloud. The demon can sense the energy coming for it, so be careful to time it right, or the thing may harm the body it's in."

I consider mentioning that the body is dead already, but I don't want to see the look on Kara's face. I don't want to think about what I did. I killed him. Me.

The medallion singes my palm for a second, and I hiss in pain, grabbing it by the chain instead.

Hanna gives me an odd look.

I slip the necklace in my pocket and walk over to the weapons case, pretending to study the daggers inside.

"Do you have any rowan ash?" That's always good to keep the darker spirits back—something about the smell, I think. It can also work as a disguise if I smear my face with it. For some reason it confuses lower-ranking demons.

Hanna walks over to a cupboard, looks inside, and pulls out a small jar.

Kara takes it from her and asks, "And maybe some sacred dirt?"

Hanna points to a medium-sized sack next to the door. "You can take the whole thing."

I walk over and pick it up, tossing it in my backpack. "Thanks."

Hanna seems to think for a moment, looking at the weapons case, but then she turns back to me. "Be careful." She moves to the door and types on the keypad lock again, pressing her thumb to the screen.

"I will," I say.

"*We* will," Kara corrects.

I don't acknowledge her comment because I'm not about to get into a debate with her about the fact that there's no way in hell I'm letting her put herself in harm's way. I may be willing to run headlong into certain death, but I won't let her follow me.

Hanna hesitates. She looks back at the weapon case again, and then she seems to decide something. She walks over to the desk, opens a drawer next to the sword handle, and pulls something out. A stone box. As she walks back to us, I realize it wasn't the sword's energy that was reaching out to me. It was this. The box is ten inches long and four inches wide, made of alabaster. There's a winged circle carved in the lid—a "winged sun." It was a symbol of power in many ancient cultures.

My skin tingles as Hanna holds it out to me.

"Take this with you," she says, her lips set in a determined line, "but don't look inside. Not yet. You'll know when it's time."

I stare at her, trying to sense if she knows about me, my abilities. It comes to me in a rush, as if she decided right at this moment to let me in: she knows. Everything.

She looks me straight in the eye. "Do you understand what I'm saying?"

I nod and take the offering.

My skin hums with the box's energy. I know what she's saying: *You'll know when it's time*—the words Eric used in my death vision.

When it's time to make the choice.

FORTY-EIGHT

We pull up to Mrs. O'Linn's house as the sun disappears below the horizon. I'm seriously considering tying Kara to the steering wheel, since she's not listening to me at all.

"You're being ridiculous." I shove the box and a few other things in a backpack.

"Me? That's rich."

"I should've just left you at the hotel."

"Maybe I should just use my 'sex powers' on you to make you shut the hell up about it." She smirks.

It's obvious I'm not going to be able to stop her from following me into this fight—she's made it clear the whole way here she'd be happy to force me to let her. "You're impossible," I grumble. I toss the pack over my shoulder and look for the path.

We make our way through the jungle of a yard, quick and quiet, and come to the pathway that leads down the cliff. I wish we'd brought a flashlight—it's getting darker by the second. With no moon in the sky tonight it'll be almost impossible to see.

As we start down, Kara slips in the same spot she did yesterday and grabs my arm for balance.

I steady her, feeling her tough shell crack a little as my fingers skim her arm. "I told you, this is a bad idea, Kara."

She shoves me off. "Seriously? Shut up. Once this is over, you'll be rid of me all right."

"I don't want to be rid of you," I snap back. "I just don't want you to die!"

"Well, ditto, asshole!"

I grunt in frustration and start moving more quickly down the path.

The horizon is a pink and orange swath above the calm grey water. It feels wrong—the beauty and stillness don't match my mood at all. The tide should be crashing and beating at the rocks, echoing the emotions in my gut, reflecting the knowledge that everything I care about is about to be crushed.

Even as we make our way to the sand, I begin to feel the force of the doorway and the tug of the power around us.

The swath of green that trails from the cave is even larger now; the white flowers are stark against the gathering night. I sense my mom's spirit from here. She fills the beach with her urgency. *Run, run!* she seems to call. And my feet itch to obey her.

The opening of the cave is like the mouth of some horrible beast waiting to swallow us whole. The ghostly figure of Fiona flickers. She can't hold on much longer. She knows her daughter is almost lost.

"My God, Aidan," Kara whispers. "Do you feel that?"

"It's my mom." My throat goes tight. The anguish of her spirit overwhelms me.

"That can't just be your mom," she says. "There's something else, something not good."

I close my eyes and focus. Yes, there, under the urgency and desperation, is a presence that's clinging to the shadows.

"I think it's a demon, but I can't tell," she says.

I'm not sure either. "We need to hurry." My mother's energy is turning my already raw nerves frantic. I kneel down and slip the backpack off my shoulder, pulling the jar of rowan ash from the bag and handing it to Kara. "Rub this on your face." Then I pull out the sack of sacred dirt and set it at her feet. "And this on your hands."

She smears the ash onto her cheeks and forehead and drops the bottle back to the sand. I do the same. Then we both knead our hands and arms in the sacred dirt.

"Here." I reach in my pocket and pass her the exorcism medallion. "This will be your job." I have my amulet, and I need her to have some sort of weapon to defend herself or I'll be too distracted worrying about her.

She takes it, hesitating. "I just press it against Lester's chest?"

"Yes. Then say *Immanu'El*. It means 'God is with us.'"

"That's it. The demon will just obey?"

"According to Hanna, it won't have a choice. The command is on the amulet, so your pronouncement of power should seal the deal."

Kara bites her lip. "What about Ava?"

"What about her?"

"Well, you heard what Holly said. Your sister may not want to be saved."

"I know."

"She might fight us, Aidan."

I look over to the cave opening. "She won't hurt me."

"Not you, maybe."

"Let me handle Ava." But I can't fight my own sister. If she's too far gone, what'll I do?

"I'll take care of Lester," Kara says, like she's making it clear she's not here to help Ava, only to help me.

"Listen," I say, realizing I can't go into this with anything hidden. "There's something I have to tell you." I take in a breath and try to say it. "When that demon comes out of Lester, he won't . . . well, he's not ever going to be Lester again." I swallow. The taint of what I've done seems to peel back my skin to reveal itself. "He's dead. I killed him."

Her mouth opens with a small gasp.

"It happened yesterday when he was going to cut you. I couldn't see straight. I went crazy and slit his throat." I choke on the words.

She's still for a second as she lets it sink in, but then something seems to dawn on her. "He said something before he knocked me out . . ." She leans forward a little, looking desperate. "Aidan, I think the demon *wanted* you to kill Lester."

"What? Why?"

"He told me if I lived, it was because you'd made the wrong choice—I wasn't sure what that meant. But then I lived. Maybe he wanted you to kill him—to weaken your purity. You've killed, Aidan—you have blood on your hands. Didn't Hanna say something about a choice?"

"What Hanna was talking about hasn't happened yet." I'm pretty clear on that. "I'm not sure what the demon meant, or what this will mean for my soul, but you need to know so you won't think that exorcising the demon is what kills Lester—that his death was your fault."

She's studying me intently, like she's seeing me again for the first time. "I know what those stains feel like, Aidan."

Her energy reaches out to mine, tentative, as if she's wanting to console me but doesn't know how. I'm struck by the way her soul looks in the moonlight. My eyes follow the lines of scars and handprints that I've gotten to know so well on her arms and throat. The mark on her nape shimmers light blue. My own mark casts a light golden color—I can see it reflecting a warm glow onto her face as I move to touch her. A heartbeat passes and then another, and it's as if an opening unfolds between us and there's an understanding,

like we're finally seeing the truth of how we fit together. It's so sub-
tle. I would have missed it if I'd blinked.

I run my fingers over her hair and whisper, "I know."

Our souls carry scars. Hers are handprints. And now I have
my own—those little cracks along the skin at my eye that speak of
what I've done—the blood on my hands.

Innocent blood.

Because it wasn't Lester who hurt Rebecca and Kara. It was the
demon.

Kara slides a switchblade from her pocket; I hadn't even realized she had it. She flips it open like a pro, and I suddenly want to
grab her and kiss her. She wraps the chain of the possession necklace tight around her knuckles and grips the amulet in her palm.
Then she holds out the bag of sacred dirt to me. "Let's kick some
demon ass."

I take it and fill the pockets of my hoodie until they overflow
with dirt and shove the remainder of the sack into the backpack.
I hold the stone box under my arm and take a deep breath before
making my feet move forward. We walk toward the gaping mouth
of the void.

FORTY-NINE

We skim our backs along the cliff wall, me in front of Kara, as we try to keep out of sight. I only hope the Darkness won't sense us like we can sense it. I grip the stone box with one hand and take a fistful of dirt out of my pocket with the other as we approach the edge of the opening.

A voice comes from the cave.

The demon inside Lester.

He's speaking to someone—or some*thing*. He's saying it's nearly time.

Fiona's spirit is a blur against the black, so close I can almost touch her. She's outlined in a swirling green light, her hands reaching out, fingers grasping like she's trying to pull me in, urging me to hurry. I try to breathe slow and attempt a glance into the mouth of the tunnel. I can't see anything except pitch-black nothing, but the force I felt earlier hits me hard, nearly knocking me backward. I cling to the rock and press against the energy, trying to block it out as much as I can. I have to keep my head straight.

But just as I tense my leg muscles and get ready to face what's around those rocks, the crunch of approaching footsteps comes from behind us, breaking through the thunder of my heartbeat.

Kara screams.

I spin around. She's kicking and fighting against the hold of a guy—twentysomething, light skin, muscular—as he drags her by the hair, yelling into the cave, "We have visitors!"

He socks her in the face as she comes at him with her blade, the amulet still gripped tight in her fist. She goes limp from the blow, and he pulls her to her feet, twisting her arm behind her back, trying to hold her still.

I move to act, but he slips Kara's switchblade against her throat, his arm tight across her middle.

I freeze.

The guy's eyes are blacked out with possession and rimmed with red. He licks his cracked lips and takes a whiff of Kara's hair. And that's when I recognize him.

It's the guy who attacked Rebecca in the alley. The ringleader.

Kara jerks in his arms, and the blade digs into her skin.

"Kara, don't move!" I scream as a thin line of blood trails down her chest from her neck. "Don't hurt her," I say desperately to the demon boy, as if he'd listen to me. He wouldn't hesitate to slice her open.

Demon Lester comes from the darkness of the cave, the wound I gave him on his neck now puffy and red. A bit of skin is peeling beneath his eye, like he's already begun to rot. "Dinner's here," he yells into the void behind him.

Ringleader hugs Kara closer, his eyes hungry. "And it brought dessert."

"Screw you," Kara growls.

Ringleader's mouth twists into a horrifying grin. His eyes turn to me. "This body I'm in remembers you, boy, and it wants to rip your head off. Right after it makes you watch as I rape and kill this delicious girl."

My horror is swallowed by rage. I clench every muscle in my body to keep from tearing into him. Not yet.

Demon Lester steps closer. He's only a few feet away from me now. "You're not going to save your sister. You're too late," he says, but there's a spark of doubt in his voice.

It's enough to give me a window of hope.

I don't think. I just drop the stone box and lunge, tossing a handful of sacred dirt in Demon Lester's eyes and shoving into him with my shoulder. The dirt doesn't singe him like it would a demon, but it blinds him for a second so I can pull out my pocket-knife. He snarls in rage and grabs for my neck.

I duck and sock him in the kidney; it doesn't even faze him. He grabs my head and slams it into the cliff wall.

Color flashes across my vision and pain sears through my skull.

Ringleader hesitates, loosening his grip on Kara as he tries to back away from the fight.

She shifts in his arms, coming up with her fist and striking his jaw with the chain still wrapped around her knuckles. He stumbles back, and the switchblade slips from his hand.

She lunges at him, screaming "*Immanu'El!*" as she shoves the medallion against his chest. Both of them fall to the sand. "Get out, dammit!" she yells again, her face strained as she straddles him, smoke coming from where her fist grips the medallion.

Demon Lester scuttles back at the sight of the talisman. Ringleader starts to shriek and squeal.

I use the distraction to ram Lester in the gut as I lift him up off his feet and take us both down with a thud against the ground. I pound his face as he bites and scratches. We roll, closer to the water, sand flying around us.

He spits blood in my face and hisses at me in demon tongue. The thunder of the waves drowns him out, but I hear his meaning: what he'll do to my sister once I'm dead and then what he'll do to Kara. My mind goes blank as fury takes over. I drag him to the water, hitting him again and again when he tries to stand, my rage making me stronger. I'm tugging him closer and closer to the tide, the wet sand sticking to my clothes.

"I'm already dead!" he yells at me. "You killed me. You killed me! I can't drown! I can't!"

"Let's try it anyway," I say, gasping for air as I fight against him, splashing into the shallows. I have to get where I can immerse him so I can yank the demon out—a little incantation, determination, and water is all I need.

He flails and slips from my grip.

Then he punches out, hitting me in the chest, a sudden impact against the seal over my heart, knocking the air from my lungs with a rush of breath.

I stumble back, hearing a crack as something knocks free inside, and I lose my balance, falling with a splash into the waves. The cold bites at me. Lester takes the opening, falling on me, pressing my back into the sand as the sea water comes at us, washing over my head. I spit and gasp, twisting to get free, but something has stopped working. It's like I have no control. My body won't listen to my brain, leaving me helpless as another wave rolls over my face, the salt water choking me.

The tide pulls back, and I gulp in a mouthful of air, trying to get out from under my attacker. Lester releases a maniacal laugh and grabs me by the arm, pulling me farther into the waves.

"You reap what you sow," he says in a singsong voice. Then he drops my limp body into an approaching wave with a splash, and the freezing, brine-thickened water swallows me. My head strikes a rock. I try to fight the tide, but I can't. Something happened when Lester hit my seal; he broke something—

Sand and salt fill my throat, my nose. Black splotches flash across my vision. And just as I'm being pulled under, the pressure too much, not able to fight against my body taking the water into my lungs, it comes to me in a flash of awareness. I'm standing in the hotel room again, and Eric's reminding me: *The demon's energy will be what flips the switch. You'll feel the breaking, and then you merely have to relax and let it do what it wants to do.*

Everything in me goes still as realization courses through me. But I can't hold my breath any longer.

I take in a gulp of the sea even as my mind screams *no!* The water rushes in, filling my lungs like hungry fire. Everything in me turns to stone. The painful weight in my chest sinks me deeper. The tide drags my body farther into the ocean as my muscles twitch.

I blow out the sea. Then take a second gulp into my lungs. As if I'm breathing underwater. I blink as I resurface and find myself on my feet, the waves now wrapping themselves around my waist. I cough out a lungful of ocean. One spasm and then another.

Lester is walking out of the water. He's almost at the dry sand. He turns, hearing me, and his facial expression changes from satisfaction to shock.

I stumble my way through the waves toward him.

He can't seem to move; his feet are stuck to the sand. I glance up the beach, but I can't see Kara or the possessed ringleader through the darkness.

"What are you?" Lester asks, black eyes wide.

"The guy who's going to send your ass back to hell."

"It won't matter," he says. "I'll just come back and find a new game to play."

Standing there, it's all suddenly clear. I can see both human and demon. Lester's soul is weakened, nearly flickering out, and the demon is woven into the human spark, wrapped around it like a python strangling its prey.

"Let go of him and leave," I say, the tide wrapping around my ankles. "Now."

Demon Lester hisses at me and steps back.

I know what I have to do. I see it like a blur of movement around us, as if I'm sensing the future. I lunge and grip him by the throat as the same burst of energy that came to me at Griffith Park surges in my bones. I begin muttering the same strange words that I didn't understand before.

But now I do.

My strength and my shield is Elyon.
Hear what the servant says, dever.
Your spark is weak.
Your life is mine.
Into stone and ash I cast you.

Over and over it comes from my lips until it takes on a life of its own, burning in my gut so intensely it nearly doubles me over. Every ounce of my will pushes into the shell of Lester. "Let. Him. Go."

Light bursts to life inside me. I see it this time, the glowing molten colors on my skin, running along my marks like a river of lava, radiating golden shards of light over Lester's terrified face. And the demon obeys; the snake uncurls from the soul of its host, rising up. Its black form emerges from Lester's forehead, bursting its energy from the body in a surge of power.

The demon flops to the sand, writhing and convulsing on the shore for a second before it stops. Going perfectly still. Like stone. The same way the cat-demon did.

I release my hold on Lester. His lifeless body sinks to the wet sand like a rag doll. His mouth gapes, his eyes stare up at the stars, clear of corruption. His weakened soul flickers out, and his spirit rises, hovering above his chest—a small white orb.

And Lester, the boy, is gone.

When I look up, Kara's standing a few feet away, blood staining her face, her neck. She steps into the water, breath coming hard like she ran to help.

I reach for her, taking her in my arms and clutching her to my chest, relief and sorrow like the rush of the tide washing over me.

"I did it," she says, gasping. "It's gone."

"My God, Kara," I say, not sure words can express what I'm feeling.

We hold each other, catching our breath for a minute. But we have no time. As I pull away, she slips her hand in mine. We stumble from the water, both weak from the surge of adrenaline. The dark cave rises up to meet us, almost as if it's opening wider to swallow us whole. After a second of walking toward it I realize we're not on sand anymore; we're treading on the swath of thimbleweed, following the path that my mother laid out for me.

I pick up the alabaster box from the sand, somehow sure I can open it now. I pull on the lid, and it unseals with a chink, revealing a white feather inside.

Confusion fills me. And anger. *This* is what I have to work with? A feather.

I almost toss it away in frustration, but then I see something written on the quill. A line of Hebrew: *He shall cover you in His feathers; and under His wings you will find refuge.* Psalm 91.

I pick the feather up, trying to see the writing more clearly.

"I don't get it," Kara says.

I shake my head.

Suddenly my arm jolts with a spasm, and my skin stings like I've been stung by a hundred bees at once. Then the pain is gone, and I'm not holding a feather anymore.

It's a dagger: polished iron blade, curved a little at the tip, with a hilt of etched gold.

"Oh, wow." Kara steps back.

I drop the empty stone box onto the sand and take her hand again, readying the dagger at my side.

FIFTY

The cave is deeper than it appears, the ceiling higher—twelve feet or more above our heads. The damp walls glisten as if reflecting starlight.

The dark presence inside is a force, a live thing, sadistic and hungry, pressing at our skin. It is mutilation, agony, a rending of flesh, and it overpowers any sense of my mother's pain as we move farther inside.

After about fifty feet, the tunnel opens up into a large circular room with dark rock walls. The sound of the far-off tide echoes around us, and when I look up, I notice an opening in the roof of the cave, framing the stars. On the wall opposite us there's a white stone archway, inset in the black rock like a doorway. I sense the pull of it and I know: that's where my father, Daniel, came through.

Kara grips my hand, keeping me grounded.

The shadows around us lift as my eyes adjust to the darkness, and my worst nightmare is revealed in the center of the room: an altar carved from the same stone as the floor and walls, and laid out on it like a waiting sacrifice, my sister.

Her thin form is small and white on the dark slab, her delicate hands folded over her chest, her white hair almost giving off a light of its own. A delicate sleeping beauty.

The air rumbles around us, and a thin red mist appears. Everything surrounding us twists and writhes. The darkness divides itself, and two separate entities grow from the shadow: a wolflike demon and a man.

They stand on the other side of the altar. The demon is in front, a hunched thing, familiar. I nearly fall to my knees as I recognize it, and the past comes up to meet me once more: Mom in her circle; Mom rocking and crying as she pleads with a creature in the shadows; Mom's chest clawed open.

It's not corporeal, not like when it came that last night to my mother. Now its form shimmers like a reflection, but it's still more terrifying than anything I've ever seen before or since. Its body is hunched and lanky, a hairless creature, thin muscles visible through pink and violet flesh, ears pointed, snout long, and canines sharp over its gums.

My fist tightens around the hilt of the dagger. I'm so focused on the creature that I barely notice the man until he speaks.

"She said you would come." The voice is not human. It's the sound of scratching wood and cracking bone. "She's lovely, isn't she?"

He's dressed in a pair of jeans and a black wool coat. The normality of him, his model-like features and dark brown hair, is such a sharp contrast to his energy and voice that it's unsettling—a predator in sheep's clothing. But it's his eyes that give him away as something . . . more. They're a glowing midnight blue. A demon in corporeal form. And somehow I know: this is the Heart-Keeper.

"She's mine," I say, trying to put all my will into the words.

The man gives me a sad smile. "No, son of Adam. She cannot be claimed by you now. It's too late. I have already done so. She is a daughter of angels and Eve and can only be claimed as a child."

My skin shivers. "She's Nephilim."

"She's the key," he says. "And I've brought her here with my will. She is mine by right." He moves closer and sets something at Ava's side: an open wooden box.

I glance inside it. And my knees turn liquid.

A human heart.

My mother's heart.

I grip the wall of rock beside me.

The demon man motions to the wolf creature. "Because he is under my rule, everything my servant touches I have power over. He marked your sister as his, and so she is now mine."

The memory of the demon scratching my sister on her tiny shoulder that night flashes across my vision.

"She isn't yours," I say through clenched teeth.

"Saying it again won't make it so. She was a necessity after the imbalance your existence created. It seemed only fitting that both master of Light and master of Darkness would come from the same womb. And soon this child will rise up against you. And kill you." He smiles in satisfaction.

"No," I say, shaking my head, unable to even fathom his words. They have to be lies. "That's not going to happen."

He laughs. "Perhaps you should ask the sorcerer what the prophecies are—why he was sent to kill you. Then you'll see the necessity. She is the key to your destruction and my triumph." He sighs. "Your sorcerer was weak. He did not do what should have been done. If he had, the Marshalls wouldn't have needed to die. But something had to spark the seed of inhumanity within your sister. Senseless, really. Merely because your sorcerer couldn't commit his duty and dispose of his mentor's mistake. You."

He reaches into his coat pocket and slides a shiny object from it. A small, four-inch blade. "When your sister's loved ones were torn to pieces in front of her, everything was set in motion. The remainder of the process is simple. I take her heart. And from that moment she'll live forever without remorse or concern. The perfect counterbalance to you."

My own heart thunders in my chest.

"Oh, she will not die as a normal human—not like your mother," he says. "Her blood provides her with the ability to continue on. She's a true immortal."

She'll live forever. Without a heart.

She lies on the altar, unaware, the vision of innocence, bathed in starlight. She made this choice for me, thinking she'd save me. But I'm supposed to save *her*. I made a promise. A promise to give my heart, my life, to keep her safe.

I lunge.

The Heart-Keeper's blade rises over Ava's chest as I leap onto the altar and go for his neck with my own dagger.

Right before I reach him, he jerks back in a flash, swatting the weapon from my hand.

It flies to the side, hitting the wall with a chink. His thin silver blade comes at my head.

I grip his arm, stopping it.

Smoke rises from his coat; something sizzles under my palm. The wolf demon raises its snout in the air like it can smell it.

The Heart-Keeper smiles. "You know what I am, Seer. And yet you touch me?" He reaches out before I can react, snatching the amulet from my neck and tossing it in the same direction that my dagger went. Then he shoves all his energy at me.

I'm hit by an invisible blow. I soar backward through the air, slamming into the jagged rock behind me before collapsing to the floor with a rush of breath from my lungs.

Everything blurs.

"Aidan!" Kara screams. She's at my side, tugging on my arm as if to drag me up.

I cough, and blood splatters from my mouth.

Kara is yanked away. She flies back, landing in a crumpled mass by the archway at the feet of the Heart-Keeper.

He moves to stand over me, holding his hand out, like he's ordering the wolf demon not to strike. "I won't let my servant kill you," he says to me, "since it doesn't serve my purpose. Yet I feel it's only fair that he is able to taste your blood since he's seen what you will do to his race in the future."

He steps aside, and the wolf demon is there, red-lit eyes on me.

I scramble along the wall toward the cave opening. Those hunched shoulders, those familiar claws that held my mother's life in their grip . . . They tore into my world, killing my childhood, marking Ava, taking everything I cared about in a moment.

Before I can twist out of the way it has me, claws like thorns digging into my shoulder, sliding me across the sandy floor. A snarl of satisfaction comes from the creature's snout. It huffs its misty-red breath in my face and then swings wide, raking me across the cheek.

The smell of ash fills my head. The smell of blood.

I struggle, trying to get to my feet. The beast moves in for another blow. I duck, and my head spins, the ground tipping, my stomach rising. It grips me from behind, encircling my neck with a large claw, talons sinking into my skin, drawing more blood. It drags me to the middle of the room, yanking my arms behind my back. Then it shoves me to my knees, forcing me to face the altar once more, this time as its captive.

I watch the blurred shape of the Heart-Keeper as he paces back and forth along the other side of my sister's body. I try to breathe, to think clearly past the pain and the terror. I won't let it swallow me.

The Heart-Keeper taps the dagger against his chin in consideration. "Since I cannot kill you right now, I've decided we'll play a game."

The wolf demon releases a low, rumbling laugh. Its large bone fingers crush my trachea as it raises my chin so I'm forced to see what's about to happen. The Heart-Keeper lifts Kara's limp body from the ground.

Sand peppers her hair and one side of her face. Her eyes are listless. He holds her against him like a lover. Caressing her neck, her arms. Her head lolls to the side, resting on his chest.

I jerk against my captor with all my strength, but the talons only clench harder at my throat. The demon pulls my arms back until they're close to breaking, forcing me to cry out in pain and rage.

Kara's eyes crack open; a moan escapes her lips.

The Heart-Keeper smiles again. Then he brings the dagger up, resting the tip against her cheek. He touches his nose to the top of her head and takes in a long breath. A rumble sounds deep in his chest. "If I had more time, I'd take her flesh. I see you haven't claimed her." He looks over at me. "Weak boy. You missed your chance."

I close my eyes, unable to watch the horror. Helplessness overwhelms me. I have nothing, nothing to fight with. Without even realizing it, I begin to mumble under my breath, if only to block out the Heart-Keeper's chain of sickening words about what he'll do to Kara, how he'll torment her. I whisper, "*Baruch atah Adonai elohaynu melech ha'olam asher*" over and over again: *Praised are You, Adonai our God, Sovereign of the Universe who* . . . but I have nothing to ask for, nothing to connect the blessing to. I recite it again and again, hoping that something will come to me, until it feels like a song and everything else slips away.

The wolf demon whines like a nervous dog. The Heart-Keeper goes silent.

I open my eyes, the words going still on my tongue. The Heart-Keeper's human facade flickers for a second, revealing a hint of twisted demon features.

"Quiet!" he snarls, his skin looking like it wants to crawl off his bones, like his whole body wants to escape the simple words.

I begin again, speaking louder, more sure of myself.

The Heart-Keeper hisses, "Rip out his tongue!"

The wolf demon obeys instantly, loosening its grip on my wrists to grab my jaw.

I take the opportunity to slip a hand free, reach into my pocket, dig out what's left of my sacred dirt, and then twist, shoving my fist into its doglike face.

Its skin sizzles. It screeches and swings a fist, striking my temple.

The world spins again, but I manage to roll away before the beast can lunge a second time.

I land in the corner where my dagger was tossed, my amulet beside it. I snatch up the dagger, coming around in an arc of movement, slashing at the apparition from hell as its claws swing, digging shallow cuts across my chest.

I barely feel them as my blade catches its target.

Leather skin and muscle give way. The beast freezes for a second, its jaws opening in a growl of pain, red eyes wide with shock. Even I'm not sure what to do as I look at the molten crack across its arm muscle made by my dagger.

"Foolish creature," the Heart-Keeper growls, "get hold of him!"

The wolf demon snaps back to attention, keying in on me again. I glance down at the blade in my fist and then up at my attacker, and I see in its face that it's considering the same thing I am: demons can be killed.

I rise in a surge of power and charge. It twists out of the way, but my next dagger strike is ready. In a flash, I spin in the opposite direction, bring the blade up, and slam it to the hilt into the taut belly. A cry of rage comes from us both. I yank up, tearing the creature wide open.

I'm frozen for a second, trying to register the contact. The demon's black blood is spilling over my hands and pooling at my feet. I pull the blade out and step away, taking in the sight of what I've done.

The wound begins to spark, turning molten orange, like the dying embers of a fire. Fissures open along the demon's torso, bright and crackling, until they're sizzling with a hiss. Then the figure crumples in on itself, skin drifting up like floating ash, revealing twisted bone before the remains fly up in a surge of wind, disappearing into the air with a burst of cinder and dust.

I turn to the Heart-Keeper. Kara's still held against him, his blade at her pink throat.

He looks at the floating ash of his minion and snarls. "That wasn't wise."

I try to catch my breath. But just as I'm getting ready to move closer, test his resolve, something shifts in the air, and I pause.

The Heart-Keeper looks up.

I follow his line of sight to the opening in the ceiling over the altar. A shadow falls over the hole, casting itself on Ava's form.

Ice crawls over my skin.

It's time.

The Heart-Keeper goes for Ava in a blur of movement.

But the second he lets Kara go, she spins, slipping a knife from her pocket and ramming it into his neck.

He hisses angrily and shoves Kara with his powers, slamming her into the altar. Her head strikes the edge with a loud crack.

She collapses to the floor as the demon raises the needle-thin dagger over Ava's chest.

I cry out, surging forward.

But it's too late.

The blade slides into my sister's heart. The hilt hits her ribs hard enough to crack bone. And all the air leaves my lungs.

"Mine," the demon growls, his voice echoing against the stone walls like a curse.

Ava's small chest moves once, then again, until it goes perfectly still. A shadow of blood blossoms on her shirt.

I choke and cry out as I stumble to the altar. The weight crashes in on me; too much, too much to carry.

I failed. God, what have I done?

Then suddenly her body jerks as the Heart-Keeper slices into bone, trying to dig out what's inside.

The pain fills me in a rush, propelling me to my feet. I leap onto the altar and shove him back. His hand slips off the dagger as he falls.

I land on him and raise my own blade, bringing it down again and again, into his neck, his chest, his shoulders, screams of rage and horror filling the cave, until I'm spent and he's not fighting back anymore.

I blink, looking down at my new creation. There's no blood. He's just lying there, staring up. Grinning.

I stand and back away, putting myself between him and Ava.

He rises to his feet. His face is a strange mask of bloodless cuts and misshapen features. His skin hangs in flaps at his neck. "This will only end one way," he says through his sliced lips.

"I'm going to kill you," I say.

He sneers. "No." He glances at the white stone archway. An escape?

"Don't even think about it," I say.

He shakes his head and raises his dagger hand, showing it to me. It's smeared with blood. Ava's blood. "Now it will be much worse for you." He grins, his features like a badly fitted mask as he places his bloody palm flat against the wall behind him.

Cracks instantly emerge in the stone, growing from the smudges of Ava's blood. The ground shudders. The air hisses. And the wall within the archway indents with a thud. The fissures multiply, more and more of them, until the sound of snapping granite vibrates in my skull.

And then, in a suck of air, the cave wall disappears, revealing a torrent, a vortex of wind and gasses, angry and alive with sparks of silver and flashes of red energy. Its will is fierce, a raging storm, pulling me closer, urging every molecule in me to fly into its arms.

I stumble back, tearing my gaze from the eye of the torrent. My hip bumps into the altar. I reach for Ava—she's so cold and so stiff.

She can't be gone from me.

"I have a deal for you, young man," the Heart-Keeper says as the world thunders and swirls behind him. "Sheol is on its way. I can mitigate the approaching war. I merely need to come back with your sister."

I look down at Ava, at her violet-tinted lips. Her humanity is fading. "You can't have her."

"You would sacrifice the world's fate for her?"

"She's mine."

He clenches his teeth. "This is my game, Seer, not yours. Her heart belongs to me."

A spark lights in me, an idea. "Not if I allow you to have me."

That's the answer. It always was. My life for Ava's.

"If I take her place," I continue, "you have to release your hold on her. You have to balance the scale back to the way it should be."

His eyes widen in surprise. He licks his misshaped lips. "It is not what I want."

"I claim her. You can only have me." The demon that put the mark on my sister to claim her is dead. Shouldn't that mean she doesn't belong to anyone now?

He stares through me, and I wonder if I'm wrong—if he won't have to take the deal just because I claimed my sister like I claimed Kara. But then he motions for me to come closer.

I force myself to move toward him. This is the only way. Me for her.

The Heart-Keeper reaches out and places his hand over my heart, slinking his dark energy over my skin. He closes his eyes, and his visage flickers again, revealing for a flash the twisted demon beneath the mask.

"Surprising," he whispers. His eyes fly open, and he grins wide and horrifying. "You bear murder on your soul. It's delicious." His fingers slide down my chest, and something like elation fills his sapphire eyes. "My brothers will enjoy ripping the flesh from your bones. You are not Other as your sister is, but perhaps we can make your soul into something even more wonderful." He takes my hand in his, like a lover would, and nudges me toward the swirling black of the doorway.

It's impossible to move. But I step forward, following his lead, unable to stop the shaking, the overwhelming fear that wraps around me as we face the darkness. Cries filter out of the vortex, soulless screams of anguish that I suddenly know with stark clarity will soon be mine. I prepare to step into it, resigning myself—

Something green moves out of the corner of my eye. A leaf uncurls over the stone near my head. Then a budding stem emerges, bursting open into a white flower. Another follows beside that, and another, and another, until they're growing everywhere, covering the archway and the sandy ground beneath my feet like a blanket.

Fiona.

A burst of energy heavy with emotion unfurls in the air, swirling around me. The spirit takes shape, a warm caress against my skin, just a breath, and I'm wrapped in her arms, wrapped in a love so strong it hurts.

Just as quickly as the warmth comes, it ends. The spirit becomes a force. Fury and wind. A golden mist shimmering in the air. It pushes through me, into the Heart-Keeper, catching him off guard and knocking him off his feet.

I jerk back, slipping from his grasp as he tips into the void.

He reaches out, trying to catch hold of something, but the golden mist moves faster, sending him reeling. Fiona's shape appears, falling with him, her spirit curled around his body, holding him captive, as they fade further and further into the dark storm. I watch in horror as they descend, until they're gone from view.

And I'm alone, staring at the torrent.

Suddenly a claw emerges, gripping the arch from the other side. Then another, larger one—talons digging into the stone rim. Something's trying to climb through, into the cave.

Out of instinct, I run to Ava and swipe my hand across the blood that's pooled beneath her on the altar. Hand dripping, I race back and hold my palm where I think the wall might be.

The stone wall reappears with a quake in the air and a loud *thud*. The void is gone, the air still, the arch wall solid once more. All that remains to tell me that the last few minutes of horror weren't just a dream is the ringing in my ears—and the three severed talons in the sand. It was real. And yet I'm still here.

And Ava . . .

I turn back to her. I touch her porcelain cheek, her soft hair, saying her name, trying to call her back. My vision blurs. I put a shaking hand to the silver hilt of the dagger in her chest and pull. It slides out with a hiss of breath. I toss the blade across the room.

I try to close the wound with my hands. Her blood smears on my arms, on my face, as I fold the tear in her shirt and try to wipe the dirt from her cheek and arrange her hair. But I can't put her back together. "Ava, please," I say, feeling it all well up inside me. "Please, wake up."

Her features are unnaturally smooth, like a wax figure frozen for all time. I reach out with my spirit looking for her, trying to hear her, to see her. Like I always do, I call out to her with my mind, with my heart. But there's nothing.

I've lost her. Everything I am, everything I've done, was for her. And now she's gone.

I hear a groan, and it breaks through my sorrow. Ava?

Not Ava. No. It's Kara.

I pull myself away from Ava and kneel at Kara's side. She tries to lift her head and gasps in pain, bringing her hand to her temple. Her fingers come away red. "Wha . . . what happened?" And then she moans and covers her mouth with her hand, like she might throw up.

"Don't move," I say, gripping her arm. "You probably have a concussion. You hit your head really hard."

I sit on the ground, shivering from shock, and hold her against me. I try to decide what to do. Kara needs medical attention, and I don't know if I can still help Ava. The Heart-Keeper said Ava would survive if he cut out her heart—because of her blood. But he never completed the ceremony. Was there something he was going to do to bring her back?

I don't know any of the answers. All I know is that I need to get help for both of them. I pull out my cell phone, but it's smashed to hell and waterlogged. I feel around in Kara's pocket and find hers. I punch in Eric's number and pray for reception.

It rings. Faint, but there. Hanna answers, "You're all right!"

"I need help," I say, my voice hollow. "Kara hit her head really hard and Ava—"

I can't say anything else.

"It's okay, Aidan," she says. Her soft tone only makes the ache in my chest grow. "Where are you?"

"Sid knows," I mumble and hang up. I rest my head against the altar, drawing Kara closer, needing to feel her. She curls into my chest, and the smell of her pain filters into the air around me. I touch her shoulder, her face. My fingers graze her bruised cheek and brush the hair from her eyes. I cradle her, wishing I could go back in time and tell her that I love her. Tell Ava that I love her, no matter what she is or what she does.

I settle in to wait for a future I don't recognize.

FIFTY-ONE

Sid takes Kara from me. I can barely move. I want to follow him to the hospital, to watch after her. But I can't leave Ava in this dark place. Alone.

I sit for what feels like days, staring at the stone archway, the bloody dagger lying in my lap. But the sun never comes up; the stars just keep shining like silver pinpricks in the piece of the sky that I can see through the hole in the ceiling. I wonder if time ended. I still feel like I'm on the edge of a precipice. I'm tempted to cast myself over it, like my grandmother. To put another bloody palm to that doorway, take Ava's hand, and pull us both into the void, following our mother.

But when Fiona's spirit wrapped herself around me in that last moment, it was like an order to not let go, to not lose hope. She threw herself into Sheol to save me once more. I can't give up. Not now. Ava's still here with me. I have to hope.

———

Sid is sitting across from me. I didn't even notice him come back. He's holding the alabaster box in his lap.

He motions for me to set the dagger back inside. I hesitate for a second and then rest the blade in its casket.

As soon as I remove my fingers, it shifts, becoming a feather again. There are specks of blood on it from where my hand gripped the hilt.

"It's meant to become whatever you need at the time that you need it." He holds out the lid to me. "You have to be the one to replace the cover. And once you do, you won't be able to remove it again until you require the object's help."

I can't take the lid from him. I can't think about anything he's saying. His words gather like fog in my head.

I look back at Ava. "I didn't save her."

He drops his hand. "But the demon didn't get her, Aidan. It didn't finish its task."

"To awaken her."

"She's safe where she is."

I shake my head. "You can't know that."

"Her soul is safe. She hasn't chosen darkness yet. There's still a chance you can save her."

"How?"

He rests his hand on my shoulder. "We'll find a way. I promise." He holds out the alabaster lid again. "I'm here for you. Whatever you need from me, I'll give it. I swear to serve you as I did your father."

I take the lid from him this time. "How do you know all this stuff about the box?"

"Hanna explained."

"This dagger helped me kill a demon in spirit form," I say.

"No, it was your mark that allowed that. You could've used any blade—well, almost any blade. It should be gold or iron to do the job effectively."

"The dagger isn't special?"

"No, Aidan," he says. "You are."

"I can breathe underwater," I blurt out, the memory flashing back.

He nods. "Yes, that makes sense."

"How exactly does it make *sense*? How does any of this make sense?"

"Well, you've been given your resurrection form. It's going to be more . . . resilient."

"What, I'm immortal now or something?"

"No, no. Merely more in tune with nature—like Adam was before death was born."

"I thought you didn't know everything about this after-the-awakening stuff."

He pulls a book from the folds of his coat and sets it between us, beside the open alabaster box. "Hanna found me and told me what I needed to do to help you. Eric left you his journal until he could return. He told Hanna she was meant to give it to you once you were able to face your choice. I assume that's occurred."

Yes. My choice. I chose to take Ava's place, but my mother's spirit did it instead. Once again she sacrificed herself for us.

I set the lid on the box. It settles with a sharp chink, locking into place.

We sit there like that for a while, just staring at the ground. At the stone box. The book left behind by Eric. And I silently swear to follow this calling. This thing that I am now. I will open myself up to it and accept it. Because what else do I have now?

Except hope.

FIFTY-TWO

I stand on the cliff and watch the waves below as they crash against the rocks and chase their way up the distant beach, toward the cave. The swath of green is gone now, sunk back into the sand as if it never was, and the mysterious tug from before is more distant, like it's satisfied for now.

The damp air sticks to my skin in a coating of salt and sea. I fold my arms across my chest for warmth. A gull cries in the distance. Or maybe that's Mrs. O'Linn hollering from the house behind me that I need to come in for coffee or tea or stale cookies. I think the woman is trying to drown me in Irish hospitality.

She still doesn't know who I am. At least I don't think she does. But by letting her think I'm here to help her with the yard and other things as penance for my odd behavior, she lets me hang out here. This way I can be close to Ava—who Mrs. O'Linn knows nothing about.

Ava sleeps in the cave. Exactly the same as she was two weeks ago. Not decomposing or waking up. Just . . . still.

I set her violin beside her, hoping the strings might call to her, a sort of familiarity. I hid her bag with Mr. Ribbons and Fiona's grimoire in a crevice in the stone wall. Sid did a spell over the spot to make it invisible to human or demon eyes until we can figure things out. It wasn't an easy spell, and I know it wasn't natural or right, but I felt no hesitation in letting him do it. I'm ready to do what I have to now in order to protect her. I've killed; there's not much worse than that. And even though Lester's body is gone now, cremated before the authorities could find him, I can't just forget. I still have that weight on me, the heavy stain of murder.

I've been reading through Eric's journal to try and find answers, to find a way to be free, to wake Ava; half of it is a jumbled mess of things I barely understand. The other half of the thing is unintelligible.

My phone vibrates in my pocket, interrupting my thoughts. I check to see who it is, and my heart lightens at the picture on the screen: Rebecca crossing her eyes and sticking her tongue out at the camera. I tap the answer button. "Hey, you," I say. "How was France?"

"Ireland, silly," she says. Her father never left her side while she was in the hospital. After agreeing to put her in counseling, he decided they needed a vacation together, so he took ten days off and whisked her away to wherever she wanted to go. She sent me postcards of castles and texted lots of pictures of sheep and of old men smoking pipes with captions like "Acting the maggot," and "On a pig's back?"

"Ireland, France, it's all Greek to me," I say.

"Don't let the folk of Erin hear you say that. Them's fightin' words."

"Glad you're home safe." I smile. I am glad—it feels like I can finally set down one of these bags of rocks I've been carrying around.

"Well, Dad says I get to see friends now, and I pick you!"

"I'm weeding a garden at the moment. You're free to come join in the fun."

"Uh, no thanks. Just got my nails done, and I'm back to school tomorrow. Have to keep up appearances." She giggles, but I wonder how that'll go. Her friends aren't the most sensitive humans. "But I have the car today. Maybe coffee later?"

"Sounds good."

"And, um," she pauses, like she's not sure how to say something. "Maybe it could just be you."

She means no Kara. "Sure." I still haven't told Rebecca about my feelings for Kara or about my powers waking up. It's not the first thing you tell someone when they come out of the hospital: *Oh, by the way, I sort of bonded permanently with someone else.* But then maybe she's over it. It's not like there are no guys in Ireland. And they have those accents that girls melt over. "You can tell me all about the bangers and mash."

She laughs again, and we talk for another few seconds, bantering back and forth about nothing. I know Sid was right. She's connected to me—she's a part of everything, a Light, like my mom said. It's becoming clearer whenever we talk. I feel our link now, like a string tied to both of our wrists. The others are linked to me as well. They don't know it—they sure don't act like it—but the thing that urges me to walk the halls at night, to double-check the wards on the entrances, and to keep track of where everyone is in the house, all this makes it clear to me that I'm settling into something. Something larger than myself.

"Boy!" Mrs. O'Linn barks from the house, interrupting the story I'm telling Rebecca about the potato bug I found and put in Jax's backpack.

"I gotta go," I say. "Duty calls."

I hang up and yell, "Yeah?" toward the house where I know my great-grandmother is waiting.

"The unwashed masses have descended!" she yells, sounding perturbed. "Please tell these foolish children to leave! I told you they were not welcome."

I bite back a smile and move to save her from the "uncultured vultures," as she calls them.

When I come around a large hydrangea bush, I'm tackled by a small form. "Hey, sexy," Kara says with a giggle at the surprised look on my face.

She pushes me back into the bushes.

"Kara," I say, trying to put a warning in my voice. But secretly I'm glad when she ignores it.

She leans into me, attacking me with a kiss. Her hands grip my shirt, holding me close. It's the only thing keeping me upright as my body responds to hers.

She pulls away and smiles at me wickedly. "I just had to get some love in before we were surrounded by morons again."

She's so different than she was when I ran into her at the club, all sorrow and desperation. Now she's full of light. There's no more heaviness between us. No more fear. It floated away when I sat beside her hospital bed for three days and nights, holding her hand and reading to her from *Great Expectations*. Over those hours and days her spirit seemed to open up: a flower bud finally seeing the sun. Even now, as I look at her, I realize the things I felt for her have only grown more complex—the urge to study her, be near her.

She grins at me. "You look so cute when you're frowning at me like that." She tugs on me to follow her through the garden toward the house. "Sid found us a good spec. This one's got a sexy divorcée and a murder and everything—like an episode of *Dallas*."

"Lovely."

"You can be Cagney, and I'll be Lacey."

I laugh. "Were we teleported to the eighties when I wasn't looking?"

"If you prefer, I can be Laverne, and you can be Shirley."

"Please stop making me a girl. You're going to have me questioning my manhood."

She leans in, pecks me on the cheek, and whispers, "Maybe it's time we looked into that more," which makes my face turn hot. Then she pulls me toward the car where the others are waiting, not giving me a chance to make her clarify that statement.

There's a loud bang, and Jax bursts through the front door of the house, Mrs. O'Linn squawking after him, whacking his arm with what looks like a *TV Guide*, saying, "Put that down, you cretin!"

Jax's holding a golden statue out to us, like he just found the cup of Christ. "Holy shit! The old bat won an Oscar!"

Sid shoos him into the car and hands the statue back to Mrs. O'Linn with an apology. We all pile into the Camaro, Connor driving, Kara, Jax, and me in the backseat, Sid sitting shotgun.

As we pull out onto PCH, I watch the waves rolling up the golden sand of the shoreline. I imagine that I see two figures down there near the rocks, laughing and searching for sea glass. A vision from the past, of my mother and father, maybe?

Whoever they are, they look happy. I hold tight to the idea, believing I can find a way back to that innocent joy. I settle into the seat, letting this new road take me to my next destination. I feel the future in front of me. And for once I'm not afraid.

"Because we are not wrestling against *basar vadahm* (flesh and blood), but against the rulers, against the authorities, against the powers of the *choshech* (darkness) of the *Olam Hazeh* (physical world), against the *kokhot ruchaniyim ra'im* (evil spiritual forces) in *Shomayim* (The Heavens)."
~ Ephesus 6:12 ~

ACKNOWLEDGMENTS

A book is never created by just one soul, and there is never enough room (or memory) for all the names. But I'll try my best.

In the birth of this story, to the souls that were there at the start: Merrie Destefano, Rebecca LuElla Miller, Mike Duran, and Paul Regnier, thank you for not falling out of your chairs at Panera from hysterical laughter on that fateful day when I brought this story idea to you, because it made no sense at all. To my ever-encouraging and talented bitches at LB who kept me going when I wanted to throw in the towel, and to my inspirers at CODEX, for challenging me to reach higher in my craft. To Cheri Williams and Catherine Felt, the most perfect conference roomies and encouragers a gal could ask for. To my bestest friend, and first editor, Cayse Day (you too, Dave!), who read with great enthusiasm when I was ready to give up on this publishing game altogether; you are amaze-ballz! A huge hug to the great Orson Scott Card, who made me see through the words to find the true heart of a story. And to James Scott Bell, who took his personal time to encourage this unknown gal; you are a saint among men.

I have the best agent in the whole wide world in Rena Rossner. And you wouldn't be reading this book without her die-hard spirit and her kick-ass battle strategies (not to mention her serious skillz with the red pen). And to the amazing Courtney Miller, who caught the vision of Aidan and his ragtag crew. I am so grateful she's made this book a reality—an even more shiny one than I imagined—with the awesome team at Amazon Skyscape. And to Marianna Baer, a stunning and thoughtful editor, who challenged me gently and helped make the truth of this tale shine. I am epically grateful for her wisdom and insight.

To my mom, who put up with me talking endlessly about this tale, and listened even when it made no sense. I can't thank you enough for all the support, both spiritual and practical, for being patient with my weird brain, and for all the carpool and dinner help—you are Super Grammy!

And to my kids: you rock #AllTheThings, you fabulous munchkins of mine. You were my first creations, and you will always be my most favorite. Thanks for putting up with Mommy's crazy all these years. You've earned a bazillion trips to Disneyland and ten gagillion Xbox games for your patience.

But most of all, in this human world where I reside for now, my Joseph will always be the one who holds me together and keeps me sane. Thank you a million times over for twenty years of adventures, and love, and a lifetime more to come.

And all glory to Him, who holds us, even when we don't see the hands of grace.

ABOUT THE AUTHOR

Rachel A. Marks is an award-winning writer, a professional artist, and a cancer survivor. She is the author of the novella *Winter Rose*, and her art can be found on the covers of several *New York Times* and *USA Today* bestselling novels. She lives in Southern California with her husband, four kids, and six rabbits.

For more information, please visit www.RachelAnneMarks.com.